This Mat  n

Andrew Richardson is an author, teacher ... first novel.

This Matter of Faith is the first book in the series *These Matters of Faith*. The second book, *Heaven's Avenging Angels*, will be released in the summer.

For more information on the author and forthcoming titles in the series, see
www.thismatteroffaith.net

For the chops, without whom this would have been a great deal easier, and her mum, without whom this wouldn't have happened at all.

This Matter of Faith

1: A Duel

On Saint Stephen's day of 1544, on the road between the hamlet of Abbeydale and the rising city of Sheffield, two young men ride at walking pace, deep in conversation, their horses following the road without intervention. The mid-winter air around them is cold, the horses' breath billowing clouds of white.

The one who is speaking is of above average height, and wears his dirty-blond beard cropped close. He is perhaps eighteen years old, wrapped in a riding cloak that doesn't disguise his fine physique. "And what did they say?" he asks.

The second youth is a few inches shorter. He is clean shaven, softly spoken. His dark hair hangs about his forehead. "They said that I was a schismatic, a heretic, an atheist even." Each of the epithets rolls around in his mouth. He smiles thinly, and adjusts his gloves.

"Heretic? You are... different, certainly, but not a heretic." This bigger man nods with enthusiasm. Then he stops, adding, "you aren't, are you?"

The other thinks for a moment before replying. The smile flickers on his face as he speaks. "Heretic or not, I wasn't welcome. In the end, I had to leave before they sent me down." Whatever has passed, whatever it was that was said amuses him even now as he recalls it. He looks younger by a year or two than his companion. He leans forward and strokes his horse's mane.

"So, no degree and no comfortable parish to live off? Shame, Edward! Your father must have been livid. I wish I'd been there to see it." The tall man laughs as he speaks, his strong jaw and light blue eyes apparent under his broad hat as he throws his head back.

"I think Sir Nicholas may have had designs on an archbishopric for me. He did control his temper, though. I still have all four limbs." A shudder ripples his back, visible through his riding cloak. This memory is not a pleasant one.

"Did you tell him why they were accusing you of heresy?"

"No. My father would not be able to understand how such a good Christian as I could read those heretical pamphlets, those Moslem books and pagan tracts, and yet not be a heretic. But then, he never could make much of reasoned argument. Blunt assertion and flat denial... I do not think he was ever much of a scholar, my father." Edward turns to his friend. "I am no heretic, James. I am as much a

Christian as you."

James replies, "so not much of a Christian at all, then?" At this, they laugh together. Their humour is broken, though, as from somewhere nearby, they hear a man's voice call out. Both turn their heads in the direction of the voice. As it calls again, it is closer. Two more riders are visible through the undergrowth. They have cut across from another path, straight through the woods. One wears a black cloak, with a doublet of fine black velvet visible underneath. The other is modestly dressed in brown and green, a woodsman or gamekeeper.

"Longshawe?" the man in black calls out, his horse half-turned so he looks out over his left shoulder. "Longshawe!" he calls again. This time, there is no question in his cry, it is determined, threatening. His hand, covered by an elegant black leather riding glove, drops to the hilt of the sword he wears at his hip. "James Longshawe. I would speak with you, though it pains me to do so."

James Longshawe does not respond. His hand searches for something at his waist, but he realises he has come out unarmed. A moment passes. He looks at the man who has called his name, gathering thoughts, assessing possibilities. The newcomer is not a stranger to him.

"George! What great pleasure it gives me to meet you here," he says with a sigh. There is no pleasure for him in this meeting, and yet he smiles, displaying fine, white, even teeth.

"You have paid my family a great insult!" George hisses, the words rasping through his lips. Longshawe's smile fades, briefly. Again there is the slightest pause before he replies.

"On the contrary, my dear de Winter. In fact, I paid one member of your family a great compliment," Longshawe says in a bantering tone. He is smiling again, pleased with the joke. He watches, alert, waiting for what comes next, as de Winter's eyes narrow. Longshawe sits forward in the saddle.

"I shall address you no further, blackguard. Pike!" He signals his companion to come forward. This movement is matched by Longshawe's companion Edward, who likewise moves forward from Longshawe's side, meeting Pike halfway between de Winter and Longshawe.

Pike begins to speak. "In the clearing up the hill towards Norton from the Bishops' House. Master de Winter's blade is thirty-four inches. I trust you will find one close to the same," Pike says slowly, gesturing with his hand in the direction of the location he specifies. It is clear enough what he means, though he does not say it.

"Tomorrow at dawn?" Edward asks, without aggression.

"Tomorrow at dawn," Pike confirms. He too is friendly rather than challenging, the tone contrasting sharply with the exchange between de Winter and Longshawe moments before. "I did not know you had come back, Master Strelley." He speaks as one who is greeting a returned acquaintance, a friend even, offering a polite nod of his head.

"I only came back to Beauchief yesterday, Will. Are you well?" Strelley asks. William Pike nods, smiles, and turns away, rejoining de Winter. He nods again, this time to his companion, and they spur their mounts to a gallop, and within moments are gone, lost in the depths of the wood.

Strelley turns to Longshawe. "Well then, James, a morning duel? What *possible* cause could there be for such ill feeling?" He is no longer smiling, but his mordant tone doesn't disguise his amusement.

Longshawe replies, "I met his sister's carriage while she was on her way from Sheffield to Baslow. I was riding home and I stopped to talk to her." He grins as he finishes speaking.

"So what was the insult to his family, then? Not even George de Winter would take enough offence at you talking to his sister to come and challenge you to duel. But I suppose you've always had the power to make people angry." Strelley does not look Longshawe in the eye as he says this, but there is affection in his voice.

"I, um... I demanded a kiss." Longshawe is embarrassed, regretful of his foolishness, but even so he cannot suppress a laugh as he says it. Strelley remains impassive, saying nothing, waiting for further explanation. It comes quickly, without pause for breath. "I told her that a young woman as beautiful as she is should not deny a gallant gentleman such as me the opportunity to speak with her, tete-a-tete. She didn't refuse, exactly." Strelley is shaking his head, joining in the laughter that punctuates Longshawe's sentences. Longshawe continues, "her father didn't give her the chance. And the coachman had his hack-butt..."

Strelley lets the reins drop, brings his horse to a halt. He stares at Longshawe. "You demanded a kiss from the baron's daughter while he was there in the carriage? I admire your courage, but not your reason! You were lucky not to be shot there and then as a highwayman." He shakes his head, repeating the scene in his mind. He pauses, the image has faded. The coming duel has risen to the fore again. "Will you beat him? He is a good swordsman, is he not?"

"Neither of us has anything to gain by killing the other. I'll strike to wound, and he will too. If I lose, it'll be no more than my pride." Longshawe is unworried, almost dismissive. Strelley is less calm, not as certain of his friend's swordsmanship, nor that de Winter will want only to wound. His frown disappears as he resolves to settle with Pike before the duel begins tomorrow, to clarify, indeed to ensure that there is no more at stake than a few drops of blood.

They move off again, without speaking. Longshawe's eyes are fixed ahead, unfocused. Strelley turns to him, looks away, and then turns to him again. He does not speak. They ride on, silent, for some minutes. Eventually, Longshawe turns in his saddle.

"I've missed you, Edward," he says.

"So, tell me about Cambridge, then." Longshawe taps the table with his cup. "What were they all like?" They sit in the main room of a coaching inn, midway between Longshawe Hall and the village of Beauchief. There are a couple of other drinkers, travellers or merchants perhaps, who sit quietly, each alone with his thoughts.

"They argue about God, and God's blood, and the Mass. They dispute for hours: whether Jesus and God are one, or they are of different substances. They discuss whether he and the disciples kept their own possessions, and why it matters. What the stories are supposed to mean. Whether faith or acts are key to salvation." Longshawe begins to appear bored by Strelley's list of ecclesiastical disputes. Strelley changes tack. "Some of them are wise, some kind, a few foolish and one or two are dangerous, most are just boring." He swills his beer in his cup, looking down into it. "None of them *know*, and I'm not sure it matters, whether Luther is right, or the Pope, or the king. If God is kind, and forgives our sins…" He stops, and takes a long draught.

"My father has adopted new ways of worshipping. He didn't crawl to the cross at Easter." Longshawe smiles at the memory of his father kneeling to approach the crucifix. "He says that Catholic doctrine is old-fashioned. That since he has never tasted blood at the mass, the wine must be just wine… I never was so happy myself with that whole drinking blood part."

"*That* the Lutherans may well be right about. Though I've never drunk blood to compare. But then, the Lollards were saying that nearly

8

two hundred years ago. Wycliffe was dug up, and then they burned him, didn't they? No 'requiescat in pace' for him."

"Who is Wycliffe?" Longshawe's bottom lip pouts. "Anyway, the king doesn't seem to know what he thinks either. My father said that the reformers will have the upper hand in time. Didn't all those books you've read have an answer somewhere?"

"I told you. They each have their own answer. The schoolmen have read a lot of old philosophy and lots of them confused learning with piety, for good as well as ill. Some of them seem barely to have read the Bible at all. And then there are books in those libraries which would lead you straight to the devil." Strelley speaks with definite mischief, and Longshawe flinches ever-so-slightly at the last word. "The Moslems know things, James, they know about the sun and the stars, about human bodies. Things which our doctors don't even imagine. And yet we call them heathen."

"Don't, Edward." Longshawe raises his hand in a gesture to halt his friend. He thinks, before continuing. "Perhaps you are a heretic."

"God doesn't strike me down." Strelley smiles.

"And a blasphemer!" Longshawe laughs, but there is a nervous strain in it. "You should be careful who you share these ideas with."

"*You* should be careful who hears you talking about your father and his Protestant ways. They'll burn Protestants, when the king is in the mood."

They both drink, contemplating what has been said. It is Longshawe who speaks next.

"I've been so bored, Edward. Hunting and hawking don't give the same pleasure when done alone. Not that you ever brought much enthusiasm to the hunt. Anyway, my father says that we will be off to war with Scotland again soon. I heard him say that the king is resolved to make that child Mary Stuart his son's wife. *We* should go and fight." Longshawe points dramatically, imagining glory and riches or perhaps simply the chance to see a different part of the world.

"Have you seen a man die, James?" Longshawe shakes his head. "Well, one thing I did learn at Cambridge is that I don't want to see that again. I saw a surgeon operate on a man whose legs had been crushed beneath a horse, and... Well, there is nothing glorious about dying." Strelley's eyes are unfocused, his mind occupied by the memory. Longshawe watches his friend shiver slightly. "Besides," Strelley carries on, "Mary Stuart is not much more than a baby."

Longshawe's voice and expression show that he is not persuaded. "The prince isn't that much older, though, is he?" Strelley nods in agreement. "So what do you plan to do next, then? A heretic priest isn't something that many parishes will tolerate."

"I don't know yet. I never felt the call, in any case. Someone must need a clerk who can read and write. I might even be able to work as a tutor. I could teach children not to fight about the finer points of religious doctrine."

Longshawe shakes his head, then drains his cup. "A tutor? Who's going to take you on after you've been sent down? And you were educated by Lutherans. What manner of father engages you as tutor to his precious son? Anyway, don't you want to get out of this place? You barely left Beauchief before you went away to Cambridge. You must want to see some of this world that you're always reading about."

"Yes. I want to understand men better, to see the greatest of what mankind has achieved. I want to see Rome, Constantinople, Jerusalem. Perhaps I'll find God there."

"You don't find him here? You practically live in that Abbey." Strelley grunts a snigger in response. "So... learn to fight. Soldiers will always be able to find work anywhere." Longshawe's enthusiasm builds, his tone fervent. "It'll be like one of those poems you were always reading."

"It won't. I don't *want* to fight, James. I've no interest in killing men to keep kings happy." Strelley pushes his hand through his dark hair, which covers his temples. "You would have thought our king would be reasonably happy with his lot for now."

"You mean Prince Edward? I heard Francis Talbot talking about him when I was at the Ponds Hall a few weeks ago. Very clever, but the king doesn't let him do much. Scared of him getting killed." Longshawe seems relieved by the change in subject.

"Henry's torn England apart to father his son. He's not going to let him get gored by a stag, is he?"

"You can't say that your family didn't benefit from the dissolution, though."

"Well, yes... The Abbey has proved to be something of a boon to the Strelley family."

"And its library something of a boon to its third son."

"Indeed," Strelley says. He smiles.

"How is it that your eyes don't fail you?" Longshawe laughs. "All that strange writing. Some of it doesn't even look like Latin or Greek."

"Some of it isn't Latin or Greek," Strelley replies quickly. There is a pause, neither quite sure what to say.

"Best not to ask, then," Longhsawe picks up. "Did you hear in your tower that Henry put his daughters back into the line of succession? I'd prefer the younger one."

"You'd prefer the younger one for what?" Strelley asks, head tilted. "I did hear, yes. He hasn't acknowledged their legitimacy, though, which seems strange. They're *his* children, aren't they? Now that he's Supreme Ultimate Pontiff of the Church in England, or whatever he calls himself, he can pick and choose as he wishes. I don't understand how he can *legally* allow the children of those women – women whom he divorced and killed – into the succession, but then not acknowledge them as legitimate daughters. Perhaps he can't..." Strelley says. Longshawe sighs, blowing out his cheeks, confirming his ignorance.

"My father met Anna Bolena, did I ever tell you?"

"Once or twice, yes," Strelley groans, but lets Longshawe continue.

"Said she wasn't *so very* beautiful, and she stared at you when you were talking. Quite unnerving, he said. He always thought that Henry had her killed because of that stare. He could see it in his dreams." Longshawe frowns at the thought.

"Your father does hold some elaborate theories, James. Still, if that prince dies young we'll have civil war again. Even if he doesn't, the king can't have long left." Longshawe meets this treasonable statement with a sharp intake of breath. "And a child king is nearly as bad as a woman on the throne would be," Strelley says. "One thing I never did find in any of the histories was a truly great queen. Great women, perhaps. Livia Drusilla –"

"Who? Look, I really don't care about these ancient dead people," Longshawe interrupts. "Anyhow, the prince will be king, the Privy Council will rule until he's older. That's simple. But Henry lives."

"I wish I could be so confident. The councillors could well start a civil war amongst themselves for control."

"You've got no trust in the nobility."

"That's right. They're all out for themselves. Henry married that

Parr woman, didn't he? She's a reformer, I think. I'm sure I heard one of the dons say that she was a Lutheran. If she has seen to it that the child is as well…" They smile, aware that an answer to this question of the future king's religious beliefs will not be forthcoming just yet. Longshawe rises.

"Stay at Beauchief, James. It's a long ride to Longshawe Hall."

"No. I must see my father tonight." Longshawe pushes open the door and leaves, letting in the watery daylight and the bitterly cold air. The innkeeper mutters some words from his position behind a wooden bar. Strelley walks out, following Longshawe, and pointedly pulls the door closed. Outside, Longshawe has already mounted his horse. "I'll be at Beauchief an hour before dawn. Be ready." He calls the last words as he spurs his horse, riding off at a gallop.

Longshawe and Strelley arrive half an hour before dawn at the clearing up the hill from the Bishops' House. Longshawe has slept soundly, unworried, confident in his own swordsmanship, and perhaps his own luck. Strelley in contrast wears the look of a man who has not slept at all, his eyes slow and heavy, his arms and hands moving sluggishly. They have tethered their horses, and stand at one edge of the clearing.

Longshawe tests the sword that Strelley has handed him, a few swings and thrusts whirring through the cold air before dawn. "This blade is too short," he mutters, his face grim. Strelley stands opposite him, draws his own sword. They wordlessly exchange feints, attacks and parries. Both are practised swordsmen, but it is immediately clear that Longshawe has the superior reach. He would win were they to fight in earnest.

"I don't remember de Winter's sister. What is she like?" Strelley smiles. "If he does kill you, will it have been worth it?" They test each other, neither attacking with vigour. As they break apart, Longshawe replies to the question.

"Beautiful. Dark eyes, white skin, coral lips." Longshawe's guard drops momentarily at the recollection, and Strelley touches him on the shoulder with the flat of his blade.

"James…" Strelley begins, then hesitates. "Just be careful."

They look at each other, swords still. Strelley struggles for words. Whatever he wants to express will not come easily. A moment passes as he thinks. Before he formulates his piece, their heads turn as they hear the sound of horses approaching. De Winter rides ahead, Pike is behind. They stop, de Winter dismounts expertly, then he walks calmly over to where Longshawe and Strelley are standing.

"I will grant you this one opportunity to atone for your insult," de Winter says. "You will apologise to my father and sister for your insolence. If not, I will have to kill you." He speaks without looking at Longshawe, adjusting his gloves and removing his cloak, handing it to Pike, who has tied the horses and followed.

Longshawe starts at the last sentence. "I was not aware that we would be fighting to the death, George." His tone is firm but forced, his assumed sangfroid betrayed as false.

"Apologise, then," de Winter replies. "A letter to my father, appear in person to my sister in my presence. These are not difficult tasks, James. Nor are they degrading for *you*." De Winter raises his eyes to meet Longshawe's, which have not moved, focused on his adversary throughout the exchange.

Longshawe lowers his gaze to the blade in his hand. "No." He says it quietly, but de Winter hears, and he frowns. He does not reply, but positions himself en garde. Longshawe matches his movement, the swords ringing as the tips meet. Each man is cautious, guarded, moving only slightly, looking for an opportunity to strike. Longshawe tries to manoeuvre de Winter so the early morning sun will shine in his eyes, but de Winter is wise, maintaining his position.

Strelley stands by Pike, behind de Winter's left shoulder. They watch wordlessly as the two duellers probe each other's defences. After a moment, the blades clash, sparks fly, and Longshawe issues a grunt of frustration. He is not wounded, but de Winter's speed and agility have surprised him. The blades clash again, this time Longshawe's defence is sound, and he turns the attack away confidently.

"You base lout!" de Winter growls, "how dare you approach my sister?" Longshawe ignores the words and watches his opponent's blade.

The two men thrust and parry, but neither touches the other. Longshawe's brow glistens with sweat in the dawn light. De Winter is calm, barely moving, watching his opponent carefully, gauging him after his insult to find a mistake to exploit. They are not aware of the group of riders approaching through the woods, but Strelley and Pike have heard them.

Pike calls out. "Stop, George." He points to the riders. "Talbot's men." De Winter curses audibly. Longshawe relaxes his guard, the tip of the blade falling to the grass. Both turn to face these new arrivals. There are six men, mounted on sturdy horses, armed and armoured. They wear a black-and-red liveried uniform, with a simple design of a lion rampant.

The man at the head of the mounted party speaks, his tone authoritative. His breath is visible in the cold morning air. "Gentlemen, you know, do you not, that My Lord Shrewsbury has forbidden duelling?"

They do not respond other than to cast glances at each other. The mounted man continues. "You will come with me to my master's Manor." Longshawe sheathes his sword and turns to Strelley.

"You do not have to come," Longshawe says to Strelley, but so that the armed men can hear.

"Begging your pardon, Sir," the leader of Shrewsbury's men replies with a sneer, "but the edict is quite clear. Duellers and their seconds..." He breaks off. De Winter takes his riding cloak back off Pike and fixes it around his shoulders, before mounting his horse. His manner suggests that an encounter with the Earl of Shrewsbury holds no fear for him. Pike follows, as Strelley and Longshawe exchange a look. Reluctantly, they mount. Longshawe brushes his forehead with his sleeve as they ride off towards the Manor house.

2: Francis Talbot, 5th Earl of Shrewsbury

Francis Talbot, by now in his mid forties, sits by a fire that is burning fiercely. His own portrait hangs above the fireplace, flanked on either side by the four previous Earls of Shrewsbury. Even in the heat of the fire, he wears furs outside his doublet, with more furs arranged over his legs and feet. The footman who enters the room is familiar to him, but the announcement is unusual.

"My Lord Shrewsbury, we arrested four men this morning duelling behind the Bishops' House. One of them is the son of Baron de Winter, My Lord." Talbot looks up at the mention of the baron. He thinks for moment.

"Which of his sons?" There are several, and the earl's face suggests that he knows what is coming next.

"George, My Lord. The second son. It was George that made the challenge over an insult to his sister." The footman continues to look forwards, never dropping his eyes to the earl. He is bolt-straight, drilled well and accustomed to the scrutiny of My Lord Shrewsbury.

"Who are the others, then?" the earl asks.

"De Winter's second was a footman of his father's, called Pike. He was fighting a young man called James Longshawe, from the Longshawe Hall on the way out to Hathersage. Longshawe's second was one of Nicholas Strelley's sons." The names Longshawe and Strelley trigger some recognition in the earl, and he thinks again for a few moments.

"Bring them in." The footman disappears into the anteroom. Francis Talbot shifts himself in his chair so he is able to look at the young men as they come in.

De Winter enters first, still clad in his black cloak with doublet and finest linen shirt beneath. He smoothes his moustache with his left hand, now ungloved. It is pale, almost white. His eyes fall on Talbot, and remain there. He is not intimidated by the grandness of the room or the man, indeed it seems he has been here before. Pike, behind him, is less comfortable. He shifts his weight from foot to foot as he moves to stand beside de Winter.

Longshawe enters, talking as he does with his head turned behind. As he crosses the threshold, he falters and falls into silence. He positions himself as far away from de Winter as he can. Strelley stands beside him. Longshawe's eyes flick from the man to the portrait, then back again.

Talbot studies the four young men, eventually focusing on de Winter, who returns his look, unflustered. "Gentlemen," Talbot begins, "as I'm sure you've been told, duelling is forbidden in lands under my jurisdiction. I cannot allow this breach to go unpunished-" de Winter shifts, making clear he wishes to speak, but the earl continues, "which suits my purpose perfectly. Now that he has finished with France, the king has asked me to provide him with men for his campaign in the North. You four will pay your penance in the king's name."

Longshawe cannot hide a half smile, which draws Talbot's gaze. Talbot strokes his beard. "Longshawe, isn't it? I know your father. You may not yet have experienced war, but I shall ensure that you have that... *opportunity*. George," he says, turning to de Winter, "we shall find you a company to command. That is the least I could do for your father. Perhaps you will make your name there."

Talbot leans back in his chair, folding his arms. He considers the four young men in front of him. He is familiar with the Longshawe Hall and its estate, and the de Winter family is well known to him. The satisfaction shows on his face as he allows himself a smile at this apposite solution to the request for men.

De Winter gestures, raising an eyebrow. He still wishes to speak. Francis Talbot raises a hand palm-upwards to allow him his say. "My Lord Shrewsbury, I thank you for your consideration. My father will be grateful that you have found a way to turn my... indiscretion... to my own advantage. I hope that it – that I – will reflect well upon you." As he speaks, Strelley and Longshawe exchange a look, which Talbot notices. Talbot stretches, arching his back and lifting his chin, and thinks for several moments before he asks his next question.

"Which of you instigated this?" Talbot directs the question to Longshawe, expecting him to answer. No one says anything in reply. Talbot raises an eyebrow, before continuing, "it does not signify. All four of you were involved in the duel, and all four of you will represent me in the king's war. I understand, Master Longshawe," he rolls both title and name around in his mouth as he speaks, then leaves a substantial pause before continuing, "that it was your insult to Miss de Winter that caused this ill feeling?"

"I did not mean to offend Miss de Winter," Longshawe replies, without his customary bravado, "I... I acknowledged her beauty, Sir." George de Winter coughs hard, and both Longshawe and Strelley turn to him. Longshawe's face is cold, aggressive. Strelley arranges his face as neutrally as he can manage, but his eyes remain slightly wide, in spite of the light from the fire and windows. Pike hides his half-smile by inspecting his bootlaces.

"Enough!" There is an edge to Talbot's voice. "I will not have this contretemps leaving this room. Master Longshawe, you *will* apologise for your transgression."

James Longshawe colours, and stares into the fire, mustering himself for the humiliation of apologising to de Winter. "George, I am sorry for the insult to Miss de Winter. I apologise for the shame I may have caused her." His voice is steady. He is surprised to see George de Winter offer his hand in conciliation, and it is only after a second's consideration that he takes it. De Winter smiles at him.

"I would have been sad to have killed you, James." Longshawe does not reply, but the colour has left him now, and he has recovered his composure. He does not react to de Winter's comment. Francis Talbot watches both of them carefully. They break apart, and face him.

"You will need to acquire your campaign equipment, gentlemen. I suggest that you ensure that you have your swords, guns and mounts made ready. You will leave for Doncaster in four days. Masters Strelley, Longshawe, leave us."

The two young men do as they are bid, Strelley leaving first. Longshawe's voice is briefly audible inside Talbot's room as the door closes, where, may it please the reader, we shall remain.

"George," Talbot begins, "I do not wish you to expose yourself to any unnecessary dangers. Your father thinks very highly of you, and I should not like to be responsible for taking you from him. Pike," He turns to the young man, and pauses briefly in appraisal, "you shall be responsible for the safety of Master de Winter."

Pike murmurs, "it was ever thus." But it is too quiet for either Talbot or de Winter to hear.

Talbot carries on, addressing George de Winter again, "I shall ensure that you find yourself in command of a company, and you, George, you shall ensure that you show your quality. Do not fail, my lad." Talbot rises from his chair, and puts his arm around de Winter. "Perhaps, George, you would be willing to do something else for me. My own son is ready to taste the glory of battle, but I should like to know that he is safe as he does so. I will attach him to your company, as he is yet too young to command it himself. Instruct him, harden him if you can. He is too much accustomed to the hunt, and to the fine things that I provide."

"I would be honoured, My Lord," de Winter says, smiling.

"I will send a message to your father. Doubtless he will provide you with your trappings. Master Pike, do you have your accoutrements?"

"I have a fowling piece, My Lord, but no mount of my own nor a cavalry sword." William Pike is deferential, unused to the scrutiny of someone as lordly as the earl, directing his short speech at his own feet.

"Well, then, I shall see to it that you are well provided for. I am sure the armourer at the castle will find you something suitable." He scribbles several lines on a piece of vellum, tears off the section he has written on, then signs the reverse. He hands the paper to Pike. "Take this to the castle," he instructs Pike, "and they will see that you are given what you need. George, would you take Master Pike to my armourer at the castle?"

"I shall see to it, My Lord," George replies. Talbot holds out his hand, which de Winter takes warmly. De Winter and Pike leave the chamber, and head outside to the stable where their mounts are tethered. Those belonging to Longshawe and Strelley are already gone.

Half a mile or so down the road towards Beauchief from Sheffield Manor, Longshawe and Strelley ride at a trot. Longshawe is talking, loudly, Strelley is listening, straining to hear what he says over the noise of the horses' hooves.

"It's this or disgrace, in any case," Longshawe says, his hand moving to the hilt of his sword in indication of his meaning. "Though I'd rather not serve under George. Perhaps Shrewsbury won't put us in his company." Strelley is thinking as his friend speaks. Longshawe looks at him, seeing he is about to comment, and waits expectantly. Strelley chews his lip.

"For all his faults, James, de Winter is not a bad man. You and he are not so different, in any case. If he had insulted your sister…" Longshawe holds up his hand.

"I didn't insult her, remember!" Longshawe laughs.

"If he had insulted Grace," Strelley persists, "you would have done the same. And you would not have accepted any apology he offered."

"I would have challenged him, you're right about that."

Longshawe considers for a moment, before continuing, "Indeed I would not have accepted his apology. But Grace wouldn't listen to a word from dear George."

"And George would never have accosted your sister in her carriage. And who is to say that Caroline de Winter took any notice of you?" There is a sharp edge to Strelley's voice, enough to shame Longshawe into saying nothing, waiting for Strelley to continue. After almost half a minute of silent accusation, he does so. "When we go to war, I do not want to die for your rashness. We aren't children any more, and the things we do have consequences."

Longshawe looks back at him, eyes narrow. Colour flushes his cheeks. "*You're* reminding *me* that my actions have consequences! After you've just been sent down for possessing heretical texts!" He hovers between anger and incredulity, but both dissipate quickly. He settles in the end for laughter again.

"I'm sorry," says Strelley. "But I don't want to go to Scotland."

"I'll look after you!" Longshawe cries, clapping his friend across the back. "It won't be too dangerous, anyway. I've heard rumours that this war doesn't quite live up to the name. My father had a dispatch from one of his men who is serving there. It's more a campaign of looting and fear than actual battles. The bulk of the soldiers are mercenaries, and they wouldn't risk their necks for the sake of a few coins. Shame, really. No danger, no glory."

"So to what use does our noble Lord of Shrewsbury intend to put us, I wonder...?" Strelley looks relieved at the suggestion that there will be no hard fighting.

"It's no more than keeping the king happy. He wants to know that *his* Englishmen serve his ends."

Strelley nods. "And I think what Talbot wants more than anything else is to keep Henry happy, because when Henry is gone and the child is king, old Francis Talbot will want to exert his influence over the boy." Longshawe winces when Strelley mentions Henry being gone.

"Imagine! If we're the ones who bring home this baby queen, we'll be rewarded!" Longshawe follows this with a wry smile. "You shouldn't talk about the king dying, you know."

"So, having descended into heresy I've now moved on to treason this very morning. If I don't burn at the stake for reading books by men who each know more about the world than all the Doctors at Cambridge together, they'll gut me and feed me my balls for suggesting that old Henricus Rex is not long for this world. Only, like I said yesterday, God Himself doesn't strike me down..."

"Edward!" Longshawe cries, exasperated. "You of all people ought to understand! You will have to make your account for every sin! God may not strike you down now, but when you stand before him at the judgement..." He is lost for words, casting around for a way to express what he hopes his friend will be able to understand without further explanation. "*He* misses nothing, Edward."

"I'm sure God will be gratified at your concern for my soul, James. But you said yourself, your family no longer celebrates the Mass! Some would say your father is a heretic. And do to him, and you and your sister, what they do to heretics."

"I'll thank you to keep that to yourself, Edward." Longshawe is bitten by the comment. "For all my father's ideas, I am not yet sure that I can abandon the Mass. But then I cannot fathom this idea that the wine and bread actually become blood and flesh."

"Indeed not. Have you a Bible – an English Bible – in the house?"

"My father acquired the Bible from the church in Hathersage. The priest there did not want – what did he call it? - *Tyndale's heretical work* in God's house."

"Heretical? Henry declared it sound. And he's as high up as we can go for guidance now."

"The priest is an old man and not much for change. I don't think he liked his flock knowing what he was talking about. In any case, he let my father take the Bible and keep it at Longshawe Hall."

"Have you read much of it?" Strelley's voice is earnest, signifying that he is pleasantly surprised by this unanticipated chance to discuss the Bible with his friend.

"I have read a few of the stories, but not a great deal. It seems that it's full of lists of Jewish names." Longshawe pulls a face to show his distaste. "To be a man of God, one has to have an unhealthy interest in genealogy." He smiles at this.

"There are some long lists. Perhaps those are the parts that God would be happy for you to leave to the men of the cloth... But the passages where Jesus instructs the disciples, they are not so clear as the scholars make out. To have the Bible in English, good English, is a great boon for the people. They can make their own minds up about what it says. If they could be taught to read, of course." Strelley speaks the last sentence with a sigh.

"Not all of us want to spend our time with a book. Some of us prefer entertainments more... immediately gratifying," Longshawe laughs.

"I wonder what Miss de Winter would say if she heard you saying so!" Strelley says. "One can read and still enjoy life's pleasures, James."

"Caroline de Winter is rather fond of her books, actually. I'm surprised you haven't had some sort of gymnasium-" Strelley frowns and interjects, correcting him, "symposium." It cuts Longshawe short in his thought.

There is a pause, and then: "so what were the women like at this university of yours, then?" Longshawe asks with relish, then less excitedly, "I don't suppose you saw many."

"It is not a town blessed with a large female population. The academics think it distracts the students." Strelley tries to hide the smile that forces itself onto his face by looking down at the back of his mount's neck.

"But you managed to find the best of them?"

"I was there to study, James."

"And what did you study!" Longshawe laughs loudly. "Heretical books and the female anatomy!" Strelley's face remains impassive for a moment, before he too joins in Longshawe's laugh.

The following day, George de Winter and William Pike ride to Sheffield Castle. A footman stationed on lookout calls out that the baron's son approaches, at which a stout man in a wide ruff and beautiful scarlet doublet enters the courtyard from a door in the base of a tower. The gate is opened, and de Winter and Pike enter and dismount, handing their reins to a stable boy.

"Father!" de Winter calls, as he strides quickly over to the stout man, whom he embraces for a brief moment.

"George," the baron begins, "My Lord Shrewsbury informed me of your meeting yesterday. You go with my blessing, and your mother's. She bids you take great care of yourself, and sent you this." He presses a small sealed pot into his son's hand, then turns to Pike. "Dear William, do look after my son." Pike nods, but says nothing. The baron holds his son's shoulders at arms' length for a moment, before turning and going back into the tower from which he entered the courtyard.

"Mercifully brief," George whispers to Pike, who shows his amusement by the rush of air from his nostrils. "Let us get your gear from this armourer."

They make their way in a different direction through the castle, down steps into the base of one of the heavy walls. Ten minutes later, they return, Pike carrying a long harquebus and a curved cavalry sword over his shoulder. De Winter has a pair of long spears with broad, heavy, vicious-looking heads.

"We must practise riding with these before we see battle," de Winter says. "I haven't handled a long spear like this one before."

Pike looks at the weapons de Winter holds. "Why is Shrewsbury sending us to join this war?" he asks.

"Henry wishes to secure the infant queen as bride for Edward, you see." Pike nods in agreement, but isn't satisfied.

"Why *us*, though? Surely they can pay mercenaries to fight these battles. I can't see how our presence is necessary, even given your-" he corrects himself quickly, "-Longshawe's lapse."

"Perhaps the king has need of good Englishmen to prosecute his war. Would you fight as well for coin as you would for your country? Our presence may be to ensure the loyalty of the rest." He considers a moment. "Henry has always relished war, has he not? For him, there is great honour and pride in arms. And now that he cannot fight himself, he sends the young noblemen of England to fight in his stead." Pike nods. They walk out of the castle, heading up the hill towards the Far Gate.

"Longshawe will make this difficult for us," de Winter says, shaking his head.

"Why?" Pike asks, "Strelley is the one who never wanted to fight. Longshawe wants this, doesn't he?"

"Yes. But he won't want to serve under me. And he will be piqued after our conversation with Talbot yesterday. Still, he won't want to face the humiliation of a flogging for insubordination!" De Winter strokes his moustache. "I'm sure he will find it in himself to be pliant."

"Have you really forgiven the insult to your sister?"

"Longshawe is a braggart, very high in his own estimation, but he is harmless. His apology cost him more than accepting it cost me. I wouldn't really have killed him, you know? I just wanted to scare him."

Pike nods, and starts to inspect his newly-acquired harquebus. As he runs his hands over the barrel and stock, he starts to speak. "I'm not sure I'm ready to be a soldier," he says, quietly. De Winter looks at him carefully. "All these weapons don't make me capable of killing."

De Winter's eyebrows rise. "You kill every day, Will."

"Not people, though."

"Not people, that's true. But people die just as rabbits do."

"Not by my hand, George." He finishes his check of his new gun. "Not by my hand," he repeats. De Winter sighs gently. They look at each other for a moment, then without speaking further, they mount, and ride away.

3: George Talbot

Our four young men ride out to the north-east of Sheffield, following the Dearne Valley past the castle at Conisbrough on their way to Doncaster. They pass under the long winter shadow of the castle in tense silence. At their head, George de Winter is again richly dressed in a black riding cloak trimmed with velvet in the hood. His man William Pike rides next to him, well-mounted on a trim-looking three-year bay. Behind them James Longshawe and Edward Strelley ride side-by-side. Longshawe looks out uninterestedly at the countryside as they ride, occasionally turning briefly to Strelley but not speaking. Strelley stares straight ahead, eyes unfocused, his thoughts occupying him fully.

As they emerge from the lee of the castle, Pike turns to de Winter. "I don't remember meeting George Talbot."

"His father has always kept him close. Perhaps the boy has asked for this opportunity." De Winter spends a moment thinking before carrying on. "He's young for his age, but we'll look after him. Shrewsbury was right, though, the boy has grown up accustomed to the best things."

"My Lord Shrewsbury asked you to look after his son, but he asked *me* to look after you..." Pike trails off, and makes a face at de Winter, who responds with a raised eyebrow. Pike breathes in sharply, but does not continue to speak. A few minutes silence follow, de Winter stroking his moustache and Pike staring at the mane of his horse. There is a tension between them that neither of them knows how to break.

Behind them, Strelley is speaking to Longshawe. "Talbot's son is sixteen years old. We shall be making a soldier out of a child." Strelley almost spits the word 'soldier', his distaste evident.

"For heaven's sake, Edward, it will be good for him. Besides, you aren't any older."

"No. But he's a spoilt rich brat who has never had to do anything for himself. It won't be good for us." Strelley's anger swells then subsides. He sighs. "But then, he's Talbot's only son, and he's been sent under our ludicrously inexpert guard. That must say something about how dangerous this war really is."

"He's George's responsibility, anyway. We only have to look after ourselves." Longshawe shrugs his shoulders. "You might even learn something from this that your books can't tell you!" Both of them smile, as Longshawe looks at the back of de Winter in front of them.

Strelley rubs his chin. "I've never been able to understand all this glorying in war... What do we stand to gain? Even if Henry secures this girl-queen for Prince Edward, what does it signify? I suppose Scotland is the prize. But Henry barely rules up here, never mind further north. Men will die, and not much will change."

"Perhaps you'll find that you can win renown in war. Or if not, then another reward." Longshawe rubs his fingers together in a gesture suggestive of money.

"Have you ever met a rich, retired mercenary?" Strelley asks, and Longshawe returns a mordant look. Strelley continues the thought. "Kings might benefit from war, but I doubt it this time. That girl is more French than Scottish and Henry can't stand the French, so it'll all be called off the minute she gets to London."

"I think he has *always* wanted Scotland. Maybe he will find it in himself to ignore her breeding."

"But James, Henry will be long dead by the time Scotland and England could be united. There was a treaty, and the Scots aren't fulfilling their side of the bargain. That's what this signifies. I don't see the Scots accepting a Tudor king, anyway. They hate us nearly as much as Henry hates the French." Strelley looks in front to see if de Winter and Pike are listening, but they are some way distant. "Why should it be treasonous to foretell the death of the king? It's one thing common to kings and us ordinary men, dying."

His question does not want an answer, but Longshawe gives one. "I suppose that the law is to prevent people starting rebellions by declaring the king dead. Someone could cause no end of trouble by -" He speaks slowly, testing his idea as he goes, until Strelley interrupts.

"Ah! I have it. The law says it is treasonous to *imagine* the death of the king, not to foretell it! Imagining his death is plotting it!" he whispers in a low hiss, pleased with his reasoning.

"Your trickery will not save your manhood nor keep your guts in your belly. If Henry, or one of his men, accuses you, that's it. Avoid testing the law on this. It won't be much of a comfort knowing that you were right in the eyes of the law when they mutilate you." Longshawe's mime to accompany his description of the punishment for treason is graphic, but not without humour.

"Will we reach Doncaster today?" Strelley asks loudly, pushing the conversation elsewhere. Pike hears and turns in his saddle to answer.

25

"By nightfall. Talbot's son is there already. There are some more men who are joining our company. Talbot told us that we can pick up a lackey there." Pike seems to be relieved by the prospect. He has acted the lackey to de Winter for longer than he would have cared to.

Longshawe nods his approval. "At least we can get someone to cook for us," he says, smiling.

"To cook?" Pike asks, before continuing, "to look after your weapons and tackle, perhaps." He turns forward to whisper something to de Winter, who smiles in amusement. De Winter then turns and addresses himself to Strelley.

"Edward, might I suggest you return to Sheffield to fetch Longshawe's mother? She is perhaps the only person able to keep him happy!" He laughs, as does Pike. Strelley turns to his companion, who bristles at the insult. "I'm sorry, James. You must not take my raillery as insulting your family. Who knows where that might lead?" In response, Longshawe's hand drops to the hilt of his sword. Strelley reaches across to him, laying his own hand on his friend's.

"No, James. Not here, not now." Longshawe takes his hand from his sword, and flexes his knuckles. His face colours, he mutters a curse, but eventually he composes himself.

"I'll kill him," Longshawe says, quietly. "One day, I'll kill him. Do you think he knows?"

Strelley shakes his head as they ride on.

Later the same day, our four ride into Doncaster. A few questions are asked and answered, and they come to an inn with a sign of Our Lady of the Bridge. They dismount, hand their mounts to the stable boy, along with their gear, and enter, to find George Talbot seated between a pair of retainers, dining luxuriously. The retainers wear the same design of lion rampant as the men who arrested the duellers a few days previously. De Winter is the first to speak.

"My Lord Talbot!" he announces, bowing deeply. Then, more informally, he continues, "young Master Talbot. I am George de Winter, and I am sent by your father to escort you on campaign in Scotland."

George Talbot chews thoughtfully on the leg of some game-bird. "Well met, Master de Winter. I seem to remember having seen you previously. My father has sent to me already informing me of your coming. I look forward to serving in your company, if so it shall be."

De Winter nods his approval. "May I also introduce William Pike?" he says, indicating him. Talbot lowers his head slightly. "And *Messieurs* Edward Strelley and James Longshawe." He flourishes dramatically on the French word. Again, Talbot drops his chin in a gesture of acquaintance as Strelley and Longshawe make their own obeisances.

"Good evening Sirs, and welcome to Doncaster. I understand we are to ride north at dawn the day after tomorrow. I trust this gives you time to organise what you must." Talbot is small for his sixteen years, but there is authority in his movements, and his words.

"Thank you, Sir," de Winter replies. "We must speak with Mine Host." He bows, and turns to seek out the innkeeper. Little time is wasted in finding him, and de Winter inquires of him on the subjects of accommodation and where they might find men to employ as lackeys. The rooms are secured, and they are told to go early to the market, where they might find such men as want employment at first light.

"Be there early, mind, as the merchants tend to pick up the best men for protection on the road." The innkeeper is pleasant, eager to please his new customers, no doubt because at least one of them appears rich. De Winter asks him to bring out food and wine. Longshawe catches him by the arm and asks that he brings beer as well. They sit around a table, stretching limbs wearied by the long day's ride.

As Longshawe's beer arrives, de Winter grimaces. "Beer, James? It can't be any great wonder that your family fails to advance itself out of provincial obscurity! Whilst ever its scions drink *beer,* it will remain base." Longshawe, in a better humour than earlier in the day, contemplates how to return the banter. He smiles and shakes his head.

"George... It's a brave man that drinks wine here in Doncaster. They have a word for people like you." He doesn't lift his eyes from the tankard containing his beer, and utters a curse, abrupt and grossly indelicate. Strelley, sitting next to him, becomes alert, agitated. Pike throws a look across to him, anticipating another heated exchange. But de Winter laughs heartily, accepting the rebuff.

"You will have to change your tone when you are serving in my company, James." Despite the words, he isn't threatening. "It would not do to have you fighting for a man who you can call such names."

"Ah," Longshawe replies, "*I* didn't call *you* that. I was just saying that the locals may find your choice of drink a little... refined?

Like your clothes."

De Winter inspects his exceptional purple damask doublet. "Then perhaps the locals do not appreciate the finest things." He considers briefly, before turning to Pike. "Will, I should like to hear the Mass in the morning. We must ensure that we have found our man by the lauds." The innkeeper has returned with food, and overhears him.

"You may wish to attend St Mary Magdalene, Sirs. It is a rather beautiful church. And our priest is very well regarded. He preaches a fine sermon."

"Do you understand the Latin, Sir?" Strelley asks, with surprise.

"I do not, Sir. It is not right for men such as me to understand the language of God." The publican smiles, showing a mouthful of wooden teeth.

Strelley's face contorts as he tries to find words to reply. The innkeeper does not notice, and disappears into a back room. Longshawe waits until he has gone, before laughing loudly.

"Your face, Edward!" he cries. "You looked as though you were about to suffer an apoplexy!" Pike and de Winter join the laugh.

Strelley sits back in his chair, links his fingers behind his head and says to no one in particular that "Latin is hardly the language of God."

They drink and eat, exchanging nothing but requests for some dish or other as they do. Eventually, de Winter asks Longshawe, "will you join us at the mass? Or has your father adopted these new Lutheran practices?" De Winter's smile suggests that he already knows the answer. Longshawe is taken unaware by the question and gropes for an answer for a few moments.

"My father is a good Christian, George. He does not crawl to the cross, but he still respects the authority of the Church." Longshawe chooses the words carefully, speaking unusually slowly.

"And which church is that, James? That of the Holy Father in Rome, or Henry's bastard, the *Church of England*?"

"My father follows the word of God, George. He waits to see how God reveals himself."

"So, he refuses to pick a side?" de Winter laughs. "When the Church of Rome reasserts itself after this heresy, will he claim never to have abandoned the Mass?"

Pike puts his arm across de Winter, who turns to him. There is a moment of silence, which Pike breaks. "We are all good Christians,

George. Even if James's father worships God in a different way. Do not jest about religion. Men have died for less than this."

Strelley watches the exchange, eyes flicking from one to another as they speak, but does not say anything. The relief is clear on his face as Pike stops the argument. He considers, briefly, before asking, "have any of you actually *read* the Bible?" His question is met with a trio of more or less blank stares.

They eat, drink and talk of other matters, comparing their weapons and their mounts, anticipating the campaign ahead. An hour or two passes as they discuss the war in Scotland, and the likelihood of hostilities with France being renewed. Eventually, they retire to bed, knowing they must be up early to find the best men at the market place.

De Winter and Pike arrive to breakfast an hour before dawn, to find Strelley already up and active. Longshawe himself does not come down from his bed for twenty minutes more, after Pike and de Winter have eaten and left. He looks dishevelled, as if he has woken only moments before. Strelley shakes his head at him, frustrated by the lack of urgency he shows.

They leave a few minutes later, after Longshawe has forced down some mouthfuls of bread and watered beer, mounting and riding to the market-place that lies in the centre of the old town of Doncaster. It is just growing light, but even at this early hour and in the middle of winter, there is a bustle about the place, suggestive of its importance as a market-town on the route North from London.

A few men stand around, advertising their services by the clear display of weapons. Most are rough men, young but weathered. One or two are younger-looking, perhaps those who are not yet experienced as muscle-for-hire. It is to these that Strelley leads Longshawe. He begins by asking one, a nervous, chafing teenager, a simple question of addition. He is met by a blank stare.

This same exchange takes place with a couple more of these younger men, before a fourth, with a pale face and wide, light eyes answers almost immediately, and correctly. The boy, who is perhaps thirteen years old, asks, "why... um.... Why have you asked me to reckon, Sir?"

Strelley replies that "if we are to take a footman, we must be sure that it is one we can rely on. One who can think. At least you would return with the right change from a transaction." Longshawe looks from Strelley to the boy in front of him.

"What's your name?" Longshawe asks as he takes the boy's arm in his hand, feeling for evidence of muscle. He is disappointed by the result.

"Guy, Sirs. Guy Fletcher, for my father." Strelley gestures for him to carry on telling them about himself. "I've come to seek my fortune with the mercenaries, Sirs, though I know I am not yet of much use as a fighter. I thought I might be able to fetch and carry, and learn how to fight from the older men." His voice is a gravelly rasp, just broken.

"I'm Edward, and this is James. We're on our way to fight in Scotland. Clean our kit, look after our horses, pitch our tent and strike it in the morning, and we shall show you how to fight." Strelley turns to Longshawe as he speaks, knowing that it will be his friend who teaches fighting. Longshawe nods slowly, as he weighs the advantages of this boy as their lackey.

"Edward, he's…" Longshawe's left eye narrows, as he looks uncomfortably at Guy Fletcher, unwilling to insult the youngster directly but clearly unimpressed with him. Strelley presses on, ignoring his friend's reservations.

"We'll pay you," he says, but isn't sure how much to offer, "see to your meals and such." Guy Fletcher looks frightened at Strelley's eagerness, but he is starting to think more carefully about this idea of serving with the king's army in Scotland.

"I should like my own weapon," he says, "and to be shown how to handle it."

"Good. It shall be so. We leave tomorrow at dawn from the inn of Our Lady of the Bridge. Be there with whatever you need for yourself, an hour before dawn." Strelley offers his hand, and Guy Fletcher takes it.

"Go on then!" Longshawe says, as Fletcher stands around waiting. Strelley, reading the look on Fletcher's face, stops him.

"You may join us to dine at the inn today if you wish." Fletcher smiles happily, before turning and walking away. Longshawe watches him disappear across the marketplace, before shoving Strelley roughly about the shoulder.

"Ned! He can't be more than twelve years old and there isn't an ounce of flesh on him! And why've you asked him to share our dinner?" There is more edge in Longshawe's voice when he asks about the dining arrangements than when he is complaining about their new servant's strength.

Strelley smiles. "That boy has barely eaten in days. He's probably been turned out by his father as a useless mouth, eating all that's put in front of him but not contributing." He changes tack. "In any case, he's sharp. If he comes with us tomorrow morning, we've got ourselves a good lad." Longshawe snorts and looks about the market. A stall holder selling cakes and fancies catches his attention, and he fairly marches over, followed a few paces behind by Strelley, who wears a look of satisfied contentment.

Across the town, de Winter and Pike leave the church of St Mary Magdalene. Outside, chewing a grass stalk under a wide-brimmed hat, a broad man nods to them in a gesture of acknowledgement. De Winter looks back at him, wondering why he has been greeted by a stranger.

"Lorenzo Calonna," the man says, with the bouncy accent of a southern Italian. "You're the Earl of Shrewsbury's men, aren't you? I saw you arrive at the inn yesterday."

De Winter and Pike stop, shuffling out of the way of the other churchgoers who pass along the stone path. "What of it?" de Winter asks, sharply.

"I am lieutenant in your company, Sir." He raises two fingers of his left hand to point at de Winter. "I am sent to bring you safe to your men." De Winter looks at the Italian, noting his worn clothes and leathery face, covered by a luxuriant black beard that doesn't quite hide two scars that run down from his left ear across his cheek.

"Calonna, you say?" he asks. The Italian confirms with a nod. "Well met. Join us at the inn of St Mary of the Bridge tonight. I would speak with you about an important matter."

"The earl's son?" the Italian asks. De Winter's nostrils flare briefly.

"Yes, the earl's son. He is my charge on this campaign and he must not come to harm."

"He will not, Sir. Tonight, then?" Calonna asks, and de Winter nods. Calonna turns and walks away across the churchyard, between the gravestones, towards a black horse tethered outside the wall surrounding it. He mounts almost without breaking his stride, and rides away.

At the inn of Our Lady of the Bridge, Guy Fletcher arrives shortly before lunchtime. He wanders back and forth outside for a minute or two, his nerves apparent by the look on his face and the way he hooks his thumbs in the top of his breeches. Eventually, he opens the door and looks through. He sees Strelley, who waves him over to the table where he and Longshawe are seated. Strelley does his best to make the young man comfortable, whilst Longshawe maintains what he considers to be a dignified silence.

"Have you told your family that you are leaving with us tomorrow?" Strelley asks, leaning over to Guy Fletcher.

"I have, Sir," he replies quietly, with a nod. "My father is glad to be rid of me." Longshawe struggles to hide the contortions of his face.

"Well, we're glad to have you, Master Fletcher!" Strelley narrows his eyes at Longshawe. "We'll keep you safe, well-fed and watered, and you can keep our blades sharp and our guns clean. Is this acceptable?"

Fletcher murmurs a "yes." The afternoon is spent with the two young men showing the boy his duties. As Longshawe begins to realise that Guy Fletcher is a quick learner with a bright mind, he warms to him, gradually accepting Strelley's assertion that he will be a good lad. They eat together again in the early evening, but there is a brief period during which Fletcher is unsure whether he should leave. Longshawe, realising the boy's dilemma, offers him the opportunity to sleep at the inn. Perhaps he has already been cast out by his father, and has nowhere better to sleep than a barn or outhouse.

Across the inn, Calonna speaks with de Winter. After a brief conversation Calonna leaves, and de Winter sits with Pike. They do not dine with George Talbot, who does not make an appearance in the communal room during the evening, prompting Longshawe to comment to Strelley that he must have dined in his own room. It is not much later that these two, with Fletcher behind, retire to their rooms.

Dawn comes, her rosy fingers finding Strelley and Fletcher up, with horses ready and gear packed. Strelley has found Fletcher an old cob, their equipment slung across its crupper. De Winter and Pike are equally ready, as is Talbot with his retainers, and Calonna, watching without commenting. De Winter is followed by a boy of about thirteen, tall and firm-looking, who is mounted on a pony. The boy introduces himself to Guy Fletcher as "Andrew Shepherd". A few minutes later, Longshawe steps out of the inn, stretching his arms emphatically. De Winter shakes his head.

"I thought you wanted to be a soldier," he sighs. "You'll be late for the battle!" Longshawe smiles, and for a moment the others around him join in. Then he frowns, and the feeling is passed. They mount and ride away, the frozen earth of the early January morning clacking with hoofbeats.

4: The Camp at Jedburgh

The small company of men rides north. George Talbot, with several of his retainers, rides in front with George de Winter. Behind, towards the back of the short column of men recruited from Shrewsbury's estates, Edward Strelley and James Longshawe talk with William Pike, and the two lackeys, Guy Fletcher and Andrew Shepherd. It is Longshawe who is speaking.

"I've hardly been outside Derbyshire, other than visiting him at Beauchief. This is already the furthest from home I've ever been. Edward, of course, he's well-travelled. He spent nearly three years at Cambridge, you know. I bet he only wrote to me twice." The two lackeys look at each other. Strelley smiles.

"I was a student there. But I never received my degree. Perhaps I'd not be heading to war now if I had. I'd be a comfortable, fat parish priest somewhere, with a flock to tend and God's word to preach." He laughs. "And a pretty mistress, perhaps."

Longshawe shakes his head. "Three years studying and he still can't tell me who's right of the Catholics and the Protestants." The two lackeys don't react to the comment, but Strelley and Pike share a brief, significant look which Longshawe notices. "I promise not to discuss religion any further, gentlemen. Since the educated can't shed any light on it..." He turns to Andrew Shepherd. "Can you handle a sword, young Master Shepherd?"

"A little," the youth replies. "My father taught me some fencing. But I learned more as a boy about how to fight without a weapon."

"That reminds me," Strelley says, "I have something for you, Guy." He hands Guy Fletcher a short fencing sword, in its own leather scabbard. "As you asked for, your own weapon. I got it before we left Doncaster. Ask James, and he'll show you how to use it."

They stop to rest their mounts and to eat. Within minutes, Longshawe is instructing Guy how to hold his new sword, showing him where to put his feet, thrusting and parrying. George Talbot approaches, watching the lesson.

"Perhaps you could show me a few of your moves, Sir," he says, as Longshawe demonstrates a low thrust. "My father hasn't encouraged me particularly to swordsmanship." Longshawe looks at him, surprised.

"I should have thought your father would engage the finest fencing master he could for his only son," he replies.

"Perhaps he did not want me to learn fencing so as to prevent me fighting duels, Master Longshawe." Talbot grins. "I hear you are something of an expert." Longshawe's eyes fix on de Winter, some distance away, speaking with the man who seems to lead Talbot's retainers. He frowns, but does not reply.

"De Winter has already told me that I shall avoid any serious fighting, and that he is charged with my safety. I should at least like to learn something from this excursion." Talbot's hand falls to the hilt of his sword.

"Very well," Longshawe replies, "Guy, put your sword away." He takes out his own, and adopts the guard. Talbot, contrary to his earlier suggestion, handles his weapon confidently, and immediately begins to search for weaknesses in Longshawe's defence. They clash, briefly, Talbot flourishing his blade extravagantly. Longshawe parries his thrusts for a few moments, before avoiding a clumsy attack and touching Talbot with the flat of his blade on the shoulder.

Talbot looks at his shoulder, surprise showing on his face. Perhaps his previous fencing master would not have dared touch him. "You shall have to show me how you did that, Master Longshawe."

Strelley hands round a few pieces of bread and cheese, and all, including Talbot, eat their fill, talking about the campaign to come. De Winter walks over and joins them, taking the food Strelley offers him with gracious thanks. The two lackeys are up, testing their sword arms, moments after their last swallow of lunch. The young men smile at their enthusiasm.

A week later, de Winter rides ahead of the others along the central avenue of the camp, through rows of tents. He does not look back, heading towards the largest of the tents over to the east side. He dismounts in a single smooth action, that of someone for whom riding is as natural as walking, and pushes the flap of the tent aside as he enters. Pike follows, with Longshawe and Strelley behind. Guy Fletcher and Andrew Shepherd have disappeared, to find a suitable place to pitch their tents, along with the bulk of Shrewsbury's levies. Talbot himself and his personal retainers have gone into Jedburgh, in an attempt to find a more suitable lodging for the young nobleman.

Inside the tent, two men are arguing, gesturing at various locations on a map. The first, a burly, ginger-haired and thick-bearded man of about thirty five years, speaks with a north-eastern accent. The second is older, and has a hint of Scots in his voice.

"This!" The ginger-haired man slams down his wine-cup, spilling its contents liberally on the map. "Brumehouse Tower. That'll show them how we mean to prosecute this war. We shall break their resolve!"

"Yes... Send a company to do it before any Scots get there to defend it. Burn it to the ground." This man, the one with the Scottish accent, is firm and resolved. He scratches his chin as he speaks.

"I agree. I will go myself." They both look up, sensing the presence of a new arrival in the room. De Winter's eyes move from one to the other, appraising. He announces himself.

"George de Winter, Sirs. I am sent by My Lord Shrewsbury, with his men."

The bearded, ginger man says, "it's high time that Shrewsbury sent us some men. I am Ralph Eure. This is Brian Layton. You can use these two, and Shrewsbury's levy," he gestures at De Winter and Pike. "I'll take this pair with me to this tower." He looks at Strelley, then for longer at Longshawe, whose considerable size and lithe movement have caught his attention. "Are you men of courage?" he asks Longshawe.

"We are, Sir," Longshawe replies, with a half-glance at Strelley.

"Good. As you are brave Englishmen, you shall join me on a mission of great significance. We march at daybreak, so get your horses and your other gear ready."

De Winter watches as Longshawe and Strelley, dismissed by Eure's gesture, turn and leave the tent. He signals to Pike to wait by him, and he waits briefly for the two commanders to acknowledge his wish to speak. After a moment, he decides he has waited long enough. "Sirs, My Lord Shrewsbury has sent his son with us. As I'm sure you are aware," his intonation makes it clear that he isn't sure at all, "George Talbot is the earl's only son, and it is imperative that he is kept safe throughout this campaign. I have personally undertaken to the earl that he will be in my care. I would be grateful for your assistance, gentlemen, in achieving this."

Eure stares at him, unsure what to say in reply to this demanding newcomer. Layton thinks for a moment. "De Winter, is it?" he says, slowly. "Well, Sir, let me be clear. Shrewsbury's son is a necessary burden on this campaign, and if you are his keeper, then so are you. Find a place to stand near the back somewhere and stay out of danger."

De Winter smiles wryly. "Brian Layton, did you say? My Lord

Shrewsbury has sent me to take command of a company of Reivers. My lieutenant, Lorenzo Calonna, has already-" Layton holds up a hand. De Winter looks surprised at this, as though he is not often interrupted. Layton and Eure exchange a weary look. Eure takes up the thread.

"Whatever your birth, and whatever command your father or your patron has bought you, when we are on the battlefield you *will* take your orders from me. Any dissent or disobedience, and you will be flogged. Be ye the lowliest peasant or some great Laird! Do you understand?"

De Winter's weight shifts back on to his heels and there is a flicker of a smile across Pike's face. Neither replies, disquieted at the way that Eure has spoken to de Winter, accustomed as he is to being addressed rather more deferentially. A quarter minute passes in uneasy, tense quiet.

Layton eventually speaks. "We'll take your silence as assent, then. You will join my army as we march northwest. Your company will need to be managed with a rod of iron, as it is composed of Borderers who, frankly, are not to be trusted. But I'm sure Calonna has told you all this. Now go to your company, and try to endear yourself to them." He waves them away. After the shallowest of bows, de Winter turns and leaves, flouncing his cloak over his shoulder as he walks out. Pike follows after a more convincing obeisance.

"Good luck with him," Eure says to Layton. "I shall ride out to this Brumehouse in the morning and raze it to the ground. That should smoke out Arran and his barbarians."

"I will take the rest of the men north to Melrose," Layton replies. "We should unite the forces there."

"Indeed. We must be wary of chasing this Scots army around the hills. We must force an engagement. Perhaps the Abbey would bring them out." Eure and Layton continue to look at the map, from their own position near Jedburgh to Melrose Abbey, each pointing and drawing lines of march to follow. We shall leave them to their planning.

Calonna seats himself between Pike and Strelley. Guy Fletcher and Andrew Shepherd have got a decent fire going, but it is still bitingly cold in the January night. They sit next to each other, and listen to what passes between the others. De Winter welcomes Calonna with a gesture. They sit around, warming themselves against the winter air, eating bread and cheese.

"Have you got the men ready to march tomorrow morning?" de Winter asks Calonna.

"We shall be ready, Sir," Calonna replies. "The men have grown restless at the lack of action." His bouncy Italian accent does not suit his grave words.

"You mean the lack of plunder," Longshawe smiles.

"I will not deny that these men like to be well-rewarded... But you are mistaken if you think they risk their lives to rape and steal." Calonna's voice has a hint of disdain.

"Truly?" De Winter seems genuinely surprised. "I thought that was the best part of soldiering!" He laughs.

Calonna's eyes narrow at the joke. "Many of the men under your command are Scots themselves, Sir. You would do well to remember that. They may not think so little as you do of burning homes and killing children. They are attacking their own people."

De Winter's top lip curls under his moustache, but he quells his evident desire to tell Calonna exactly what he thinks. Longshawe looks to Strelley, who is watching the exchange, impassive. Longshawe opens his mouth to speak, pausing briefly to think before he begins.

"We may not find ourselves doing much fighting, from what I have heard. I was speaking to some Germans and they told me they've barely seen the enemy. And when they do, the most that happens is a few shots are fired, but well out-of-range."

"You sound disappointed," Calonna replies, "and yet you should be relieved. A battle is a dangerous place for the inexperienced."

"I can handle myself!" Longshawe is piqued by the Italian's slight.

"I've no doubt you can, but that's no use if you catch a ball or a pike-point in your belly. If it is one or the other, I would rather be paid to march and burn houses than face a determined enemy on an open field." Calonna grins, revealing his teeth in the light of the fire. Odd ones are broken, but he has most of them. Longshawe nods as he listens, relieved that this mercenary is not accusing him of cowardice. "These people fight to defend their homes, their wives. Your king wants only a royal prisoner. Which of you gains from this rough wooing?" he asks, expecting no answer.

"Will we beat the Scots?" Strelley asks.

"No one is sure how many march with the Earl of Arran. But we have several thousand with us. And this campaign of terror against the borders has been going on long enough to draw them out if they felt they could defeat us." Calonna looks at the four young men and two boys assembled round the fire, before continuing, "the English army is of mercenaries, and many of them are Scots themselves. If Arran's army is bigger than ours, those Scots may not remember who is paying them." He smiles, perhaps remembering a defection of his own at some point.

They talk around the fire, speculating on the battles to come. It is only a short while before Calonna suggests that it is time to go to sleep, as all of them must awaken early. They retire soon afterwards, the Italian's earlier words troubling each in his own way.

The following morning, after Longshawe, Strelley and Guy Fletcher have set off on their march with Ralph Eure, Calonna introduces de Winter to some of the men of his company. The soldiers sit round the remnants of the fire from the previous night, and look up at the approach of their lieutenant.

"Is this our new commander, then, Lorenzo?" The soldier has a dense Scottish accent and a luxuriant black beard. Calonna nods.

"Gentlemen, may I introduce My Lord de Winter?" He gestures at de Winter, who is frowning.

"Do you not rise for your superiors?" he barks. The soldiers suppress a laugh, before standing up slowly. Calonna's eyes narrow. "Now, I am George de Winter, and I *am* your new commander, though I am no Lord. I shall have your respect, and your obedience." The soldier that answered before looks him up and down, but does not reply. The silence is strained. The Scot stands a full six inches taller than de Winter, himself a tall man.

"These men," Calonna says, "are borderers from Teviotdale. We have engaged them only recently. But they fight well, and are brave." The soldier watches Calonna as he speaks. There is an obvious respect, an appreciation of the Italian that de Winter notices immediately.

"So you are yourselves Scots?" de Winter asks, without directing it at any particular soldier.

"I am." The man who replies is short, stout with lank brown hair. "But the English pay better." The Scotsman allows himself a laugh as he says it. The smile that accompanies it is wry, knowing.

"You fight against your countrymen?" De Winter's voice is high-pitched, his interest piqued.

"I fight for whoever pays me, Sir. I do not choose to fight against Scots, but, as that is what my masters ask of me... A soldier doesn't always have the choice of whom he fights for."

"Do you never think of taking the money and doing as you chose? Surely the English don't have enough power here to chase you down if you desert-" The Scot puts his hand up to silence De Winter, frowning his disapproval.

"I'm no deserter, and I will not hear talk of it. You should not speak of it again."

"But what about your country, your king? Are you not loyal to them?"

"I would love my king as any man should. But we have no king, and until there is one, there is no king to love. Some – myself included – would have our country united with yours." He points in the general direction of the English army. "Some would say I spake treason, talking about uniting your country with Scotland. But I agree with Henry's idea. Marry our queen to your prince, then the child of the union is king of both England and Scotland. No more wars then. That united kingdom would be a real power."

"Not just pawn in the war between the Empire and France, eh?" Calonna jokes. He turns to de Winter, and leads him away with a gentle hand on his shoulder. "Sir," he begins, "be careful around these men. They are proud, and easily angered. You must choose your words carefully, even if you are their master."

De Winter nods slightly, acknowledging Calonna's sentiment. He is thinking hard as they walk. Pike is slightly behind, having offered some polite word of farewell to the soldiers before he followed.

Already some miles away, Longshawe and Strelley are riding in a company of about six hundred men, led by Sir Ralph Eure. Their lackey rides with a group of similar young men at the rear, unburdened of the weapons which the soldiers now carry themselves. Longshawe has his gun in his hands, and is talking about it to Strelley.

"It's not as good as a longbow. With mine I can hit the target at two hundred paces, and I can hit it again a moment later. This thing must take two minutes to load." His lip curls in distaste.

"But your longbow won't bring down an armoured Scot at two hundred yards, and probably wouldn't at twenty yards." Strelley reaches out his hand and takes the gun from Longshawe, holding it out in front of himself to inspect it. He sights along the barrel. "Pretty straight," he remarks, and hands it back. "If you lined up fifty of them and fired all together, not much would survive it."

Longshawe nods agreement. "I'd rather fight the man in front of me with a sword or a spear. It's fairer."

"But in a melée you're just as likely to be stabbed in the back or the side as killed by the man in front of you." Strelley jabs his elbow out, just reaching Longshawe's shoulder next to him. Longshawe keeps his balance, coolly turning to his friend.

"I shall make sure that I fight next to someone else, Edward. We're both already dead and the battle's lost in your mind." He laughs as he says it, but notices that Strelley's face is markedly pale. "We shall be safe, Edward. God will look to his own."

Strelley's features contort as he considers his reply. There are several things he might say, but none is right. Eventually, after a moment's pause, he replies, "I shall have to make sure I look after us both, James. I'm not so sure that God is an Englishman!"

5: Brumehouse Tower

Night falls as the company of which Strelley and Longshawe are part ride on towards the tower of Brumehouse. The wind whips coldly, carrying a fine, penetrating mist of drizzle. Lights are visible from a few isolated farmsteads. Longshawe speaks without turning as he and Strelley ride, their horses matching step for step.

"I'm soaked. Why haven't we stopped and made camp?"

"They're pushing on to this tower they talk about. Brumehouse, they called it. Eure talked about burning it to try to force an engagement with the Scots army." Longshawe listens to the information, whilst continuing to ride forward. His eyes do not focus on anything in particular.

He grunts a reply, which sounds like "I knew that," then there is nothing but silence. Eventually he raises his right hand to point to the horizon. Strelley looks where he indicates. A stone tower rises on a hilltop two or three miles distant, some of its windows visibly flickering with internal light.

Strelley's hair, wet through with drizzle, is matted across his forehead. He pushes it away with a gloved hand, and adjusts the hood of his riding cloak to keep the rain off. He looks back, trying to find Guy Fletcher in amongst the loose group of lackeys at the rear of the column, but cannot see him.

"I hope Guy is safe," he says, but Longshawe isn't listening. He looks out towards the tower, and Strelley follows his gaze. There is a group of lights moving towards it, only a few moments away. They disappear, as whoever has arrived at, or returned to, the tower goes inside.

"Soldiers, do you think?" Longshawe asks.

"Not enough to defend the tower against us."

"Perhaps it's the farmers." Longshawe points to the outlying farmhouses.

"Perhaps. I don't like what comes next."

"What do you mean?"

"Have you not been listening? All along we've heard nothing but talk of burning farms and churches. They – we – are going to burn this tower and I wonder what they'll do with the people inside." Strelley's voice is taut but quiet.

Longshawe's eyes narrow. He hasn't considered this part. "Take them prisoner?" He stops and thinks. "There were no prisoners at Jedburgh, were there?"

"If they're lucky, we'll kill them quickly. But this whole thing is about frightening them, isn't it?" Strelley looks ahead. Longshawe watches him, waiting for the next words, but they don't come.

Half an hour later, the company draws up three hundred yards from the tower. Eure, at the head of the column, barks orders, sending men scurrying for axes to fell the low scrub trees dotted around. He points a group of men to set up a barricade opposite the gate of the tower compound. There are two other posterns, and Eure sends men to cover them as well. As various soldiers make their way to their positions, Longshawe and Strelley come to the front of the column.

"Halt!" Eure calls, and the rest of the men come to a standstill. "Gentlemen, I have a job for you. We need fires burning. I would like you two to find some suitable kindling to get us started." He laughs. "Well, snap to it!"

Strelley looks at Longshawe, whose expression shows that he recognises both the awful fact that they are about to burn the tower, and that they have been picked to gather the firewood. Strelley sniffs audibly. During the moment that it takes for them to obey the order, Eure's face breaks into a smile.

"I see we have some delicate flowers here, gentlemen!" he laughs, drawing the attention of the other soldiers, and indicating Strelley and Longshawe with a gesture. "I gave you two an order. You obey it now or this company will have the pleasure of watching you flogged in the morning!" Eure roars, still smiling.

Strelley rears his mount and rides away, with Longshawe behind. They head for a copse about half a mile distant the crest of a nearby hill, and neither stops or slows until they reach it. Strelley shouts a curse, red-faced with unconcealed fury. Longshawe catches him up from a few yards behind, seeing him breathing heavily but deliberately.

"This is your doing!" Strelley shouts, jabbing his fingers in Longshawe's direction. "You and your uncontrollable prick, Longshawe! If you hadn't had to go and show off to de Winter's sister we wouldn't be here now about to burn Christ knows which innocent family!" He turns his horse, shouting wordlessly. After a few moments, he calms, but is still breathing noisily, the vapour visible in the moonlight.

Longshawe watches his friend, considering what to say. He makes to start several times. Finally, he settles for a simple, quiet, "sorry." Strelley stares at him, contorting, trying to regain his sangfroid. A moment passes, as each wishes himself back to the warm comfort of homes and family. All seems bleak in the Scottish Lowlands.

"We could turn back..." Longshawe says, uselessly.

"I'd rather be flogged for insurrection than hanged for desertion," Strelley replies. He forces a smile, trying to compose himself. "I apologise for what I just said. I know it wasn't fair. It's just bloody Providence pissing on me!" He laughs. Longshawe watches him, and struggles with the attempt to keep his equanimity. The brave soldier of a fortnight ago fights against tears of fear and sadness.

"I didn't know it would be *this*. Killing innocent people..." Longshawe almost whispers it. "It would be hard enough to kill a man facing him as he tried to kill you, but-" Strelley holds up his hand.

"Firewood," he says, simply. They dismount, Strelley throws his cloak on the ground and they begin to look for dry pieces of wood. As they do, Longshawe begins to speak again.

"I'm sorry, Ned. I didn't think." Strelley looks up from the ground, his eyes narrow. "Yes, I know, I don't think, do I? Perhaps I will think more in the future."

"Our actions have consequences. I've said that to you before." He pauses. "But we're not here *just* because of some amorous episode of yours... I'm sorry I shouted. I don't want to be here, and I'm no soldier." He shrugs.

"I know," Longshawe replies. "And I hope we won't be out here long."

They return to the camp outside the tower compound, Longshawe carrying Strelley's cloak full of kindling. He throws it on the ground in front of Eure, spilling some of the contents. Strelley walks past, towards Guy Fletcher, who is standing with some other lackeys near one of the postern barricades. As he does, Eure shouts at him, "I shall have a job for you in a moment, boy!"

Strelley stops. His fingers ball into a fist, then open again, stretching and splaying. He turns to Eure, silent, waiting for the next insult. Eure issues orders for various soldiers to light fires.

"Take this," Eure says, handing him an unlit torch, stinking of oil. "Get it lit, and put it through that window." He points to a glazed ground floor window, where the wall of the tower is also part of the outer wall of the compound, through which the flickering light of a fire is just visible. Strelley stares at him for too long, before turning and resuming his walk across to Guy Fletcher. Longshawe follows without acknowledging Eure.

Fletcher looks over at Strelley. "Are you full well, Sir?" he asks.

"No, Guy. I think our leader has something of a desire to torment and humiliate me." Strelley forces a smile for the young lad. "Put it out of your mind."

"He's a cruel man, Ned," Longshawe says. "Give me that torch and I'll do it."

"Thank you, James, but I must refuse. If I give him a reason, he'll have me flogged." Strelley shrugs his shoulders as he speaks, resigned.

Eure calls out to the occupants of the tower. "I am Ralph Eure, Malleus Scotorum, scourge of your pathetic people. If you wish to bargain for your lives, speak now!"

He waits for a response. A moment later, a casement opens high up in the tower. A woman's voice, firm and even, issues from it.

"There are no soldiers here, Englishman. Leave us in peace, for we have no part in your war with the Regent Arran." The casement remains open, but no face appears at it. Eure smiles malevolently.

"There you are wrong, madam. Your deaths will go a little way to persuading your errant Earl of Arran to marry his ward to Prince Edward!" Either side of Eure, fires are beginning to burn. He points to Strelley, singled out for the duty of being the first to set fire to the tower. Strelley moves towards one of the fires, holding the torch in it until it catches.

Longshawe and Guy Fletcher stand next to each other, watching as the light of the torch glints off the tears that roll down Strelley's face. Strelley walks slowly over to the window, and breaks the glass with the pommel of his sword. A voice shouts out from within, but it is unintelligible. Strelley lifts the burning torch to the broken window. For several moments, it hangs there, resting on the broken glass, the flames reflecting in the smoothly rippled surface of what is left.

Strelley pulls the torch out of the broken window, and hurls it back towards Eure, whose face, in its twisted grimace, is lit briefly. Strelley strides away, past Eure, who still has not reacted to this defiance. There is a brief pause, the soldiers all in anticipation of their leader's next move. Eure looks over to the fire, picks up another unlit torch, and goes himself to light it. Then he casts it through the broken window. He gestures, and soldiers start setting fire to arrows and loosing them at the roof of the tower. Others throw more torches through windows.

Soon the tower is burning inside, the distinctive crackle of not-quite-dry wood audible loud in the otherwise quiet night. Eure has turned away, searching for Strelley. He spots him, standing with Longshawe and Guy Fletcher, and marches intently towards them.

As he approaches, he shakes his head, and there is something of a smile on his face. "At least one of us shall enjoy our time together, young man," he gloats. "I haven't had the pleasure of lashing an insubordinate for a long time. My men told me that the last one I larruped didn't walk straight for a month."

Longshawe jerks his arm up towards Eure, but Strelley catches it before his fingers get to Eure's throat. "No, James. It won't help," he whispers.

"You!" Eure spits. "Just as bad. Give me a half a reason and I'll strip your worthless hide as well." Longshawe stares at him, eyes wide and nostrils flaring. Eure turns, and calls to a group of soldiers to manacle Strelley. They spend several minutes in search of suitable fetters, returning with a pair cruelly sharp at the edges. Strelley offers his hands to be clasped in them.

Longshawe stands by the manacled Strelley, who is now also tethered by a shackle around his ankle to a nearby tree, and they watch as the tower burns. Guy Fletcher has come over as well, and Strelley has his arm around the boy's shoulders, comforting him. The screams and shouts of the occupants of Brumehouse Tower are perceptible through the noise of the fire and falling masonry. One side of the tower collapses inwards, sending sparks flying up into the dark night sky. Eure's soldiers proceed with pitching camp a few hundred yards distant, and Eure himself watches Strelley.

As the flames begin to die down, Eure posts guards on Strelley, to stop him escaping during the night. He does not take the opportunity to taunt him again, much to both Strelley's and Longshawe's relief. Longshawe tells Guy Fletcher to pitch the tent as close as possible to where Strelley is chained. He won't be able to sleep under it, but at least he will be close by. They will hear if anything further happens during the night.

It is cold, and when day breaks a heavy mist has sunk down onto the moorland. It holds the smell of burnt wood, and there is a faint trace of meat as well. The tower has almost completely collapsed, with outer walls pulled down by teams of men and horses. Eure takes quill and ink, and makes his mark in what will become known as the Bloody Ledger.

The camp is struck, and after a sombre breakfast the soldiers begin the march north towards Melrose Abbey. Strelley, still chained at the wrist, is forced to walk. Guy Fletcher leads his horse, riding with the lackeys at the back of the column. About midmorning, a lone rider approaches from the north, and after offering a password, approaches Eure.

"A message from Sir Brian Layton," he says, handing a rolled scroll to Eure.

Eure reads. After a few moments in consideration, he turns to his lieutenant. "We'll continue our march north to Melrose, but we must be on our guard. Layton says his outriders have spotted Angus's force, and they may be heading this way."

"What of Arran, Sir?" the lieutenant asks.

"Arran is a fool and a coward, and no friend of Angus. He will not act until it is too late." Eure smiles to himself before ordering the march to continue.

That evening, before nightfall, the column stops and a camp is pitched. Longshawe watches as Strelley is bound to a tree, arms raised high above his body. His shirt is torn from his back. Eure taps his riding crop against his thigh, his eyes light with anticipation. Soldiers gather. Longshawe strains to interpret their murmurs, whether sympathetic or condemnatory, but he can't hear. He sees Guy Fletcher, and walks over to him.

"Don't watch, Guy," he says quietly. "It will do no good."

"I don't want to," Guy replies, "but I find myself drawn to it." He indicates the growing crowd.

"These are men of war, professionals in the art of killing. But show them a fellow man suffering and they will watch for pleasure. I hope I would be better than them." Longshawe shakes his head.

A few yards away, Eure readies himself to inflict punishment.

He flexes the crop, before winding up and striking with some vigour. Strelley breaths quickly, trying to stifle the urge to cry out. The second blow lands with a resounding thwack, drawing blood in a line that shines in the setting sun. Strelley's eyes close tight. Again the crop rises and falls. Strelley cries in pain. A tear falls from Guy Fletcher's eye.

Moments later, and it is over. Strelley is released from his bonds, and he stumbles over towards his friends. Neither Guy Fletcher nor Longshawe say anything, unable to find words to console him. Longshawe rubs a dampened cloth across Strelley's wounded back, trying to clean the blood off him. The pain is visible on Strelley's face.

"I'm sorry," Longshawe says eventually. "That you're here, that this has happened." Strelley does not reply immediately.

"It isn't your fault. But Eure is a vile bastard. He will lead us to ruin and we must make sure we do not go to our deaths for his cruelty."

Longshawe nods, continuing to apply the cloth to Strelley's lacerated back, his friend doing his best not to let the pain show to Guy Fletcher, who watches, a pace away. The sun sets, the hum of conversation around the camp not matched by the silence between two young men and a boy sitting around their fire.

6: A Warning

A few miles to the south of Melrose Abbey, in the early evening, de Winter and Calonna are talking amongst the tents. They have already been speaking for some time, it seems.

"The Borderers must not be relied upon, if they're all like him." De Winter shakes his head.

"Don't worry, Giorgio. The Reivers are well paid. They will fight as well as any mercenary." Calonna smiles at him.

"But they're Scottish!" De Winter gestures with an open palm, asking how it can be that Calonna doesn't agree. "Even *they* would not kill their own countrymen. We heard rumours before we even got here that they barely pretend to fight. If they turn, if they fight against us, we will be cut to ribbons."

"They will only change sides if they see an enemy army of twice our numbers. There is no such force in Scotland," Calonna replies. "Not that we know of." He offers a wry smile.

"Indeed. I suppose if the commanders are aware of some threat, they must have planned for it." De Winter's voice is high, strained. "How can it be that we are relying on these mercenaries? They will burn and loot, but how would they fight a pitched battle?" He shakes his head.

Calonna chews on a grass stalk, his eyes flicking to de Winter and then away several times. He considers his reply.

"Signore de Winter, what do you hope will come of raising this concern now? Layton will not take us back to Jedburgh until we have sacked Melrose. When we do meet some Scots force then we do not have to engage them if they do outnumber us. There is no real danger."

De Winter lowers his eyes, addressing his comment to the ground or his feet. "Perhaps we shall avoid an encounter altogether. We can but hope." He turns and walks away, leaving Calonna thinking over their exchange. The Italian lets out an expression of frustration. Pike, busy cleaning his gun nearby, has listened to the conversation and is watching Calonna.

"Our master is worried," Pike mutters.

"Not without justification, Guglielmo." Calonna has given up trying to say Pike's Christian name in English. "He's right about the Reivers. If we do find ourselves in a battle with a properly drilled Scots army, not the local militiamen... We can't rely on them. They are well paid, certainly, but they will back the winner. Beaten commanders do not honour their debts."

"George does not like the prospect of it being his company that are disloyal," Pike says.

"It is his first command, isn't it?" Calonna asks. Pike nods in reply. "I would be disappointed if my men did not follow me into battle. But your king has chosen to send these mercenaries to fight on his behalf. Most of this army is foreign to you, to your country. I have met Germans and Spaniards as well as Scots. He can't raise enough Englishmen to prosecute his campaign, it seems."

Pike continues with the task of cleaning his gun, considering what Calonna has told him. Eventually, he speaks again. "What do we do? I mean, if the Scots defect."

"Make sure that you are not at the front when the army turns to flee. You have the young Talbot to keep safe, do you not?"

"Master Talbot is our responsibility, yes. But he does not take kindly to being told where his place is. Not by George, at least. He will find his way to the front line of battle, and I will have to be next to him, keeping him well clear of any Scottish steel. His father would be murderous if we let him get killed."

"Then don't let him get killed." Calonna smiles at him.

"Talbot barely listens to George. I'm not sure he's even aware of me."

"Your master – de Winter, I mean – is shrewd enough. Whether young Talbot is keen for battle or not, he will not see any real danger. Nor shall you." Calonna notices that Pike is following someone or something with his eyes. Half-turning to look for himself, he sees Layton and Talbot, talking to each other as they stride past. Talbot's footmen follow at a discreet distance.

Layton has, it seems, chosen to indulge the young man and is listening to a lengthy description of some dangerous and exhilarating hunt of which Talbot was part. They pass before we can find out the outcome. Pike and Calonna realise together that they have been silent as Layton and Talbot passed, but neither speaks for a moment.

"Why do the Scots not retaliate? To our spoiling of their lands and burning their churches?" Pike asks eventually.

"I think it is because these border lands barely belong to any country. An infant child rules, and these lands are of no real value. No king rules these people. Perhaps if the French were here your King

Henry would be more committed. There would be a real campaign, not this..." he considers, trying to find the right word. "Teasing," he concludes, satisfied with his choice.

"But Henry wants Edward married to the child queen. So why aren't the French here, stopping this?"

"Perhaps they might be. Who knows? Perhaps they are in Portsmouth right now. We may be sent to fight there. The French have their own war to fight. My country has not been free of war for many years. Did you know? I thought not. The Emperor and the King of France do not have the balls to fight on their own ground, so they choose my Italia for a battlefield."

"Did you fight abroad?" Pike asks, interested.

"I did, in many battles. There is much work for the soldier to do. I have fought for both the French and the Spanish in the past few years. It doesn't much signify for whom one fights. Either will pay."

"What brought you to Scotland? Money? Why do you keep fighting?"

"I know no other trade. And as you can see from the fact that I yet live, I am a good soldier! A good soldier is a lucky soldier." Calonna laughs, and puts his hand on Pike's shoulder. "Look after yourself, Guglielmo. Survive your first battle, that one is the most dangerous." He turns and disappears among the tents. Pike forces a half-smile, shakes his head and returns to cleaning his gun.

Across the camp, de Winter addresses Layton. "I cannot agree, Sir. The Borderers are unreliable and if we meet a superior force they will not fight for us."

Talbot watches the exchange with some relish. He smiles as Layton replies. "Master de Winter, I assure you that we pay those soldiers well enough."

"They are Scots!"

"And some of my soldiers are Germans and Spaniards. What of it? I will relieve you of your command, George, if you continue with your bellyaching." At this, de Winter's eyes are wide in disbelief. He mutters a word of farewell and walks away. Layton shakes his head, and spits on the ground. He takes Talbot aside.

"Young Master Talbot, your guardian is beginning to irritate me. I'm not sure I can stand his whining much longer."

"Is he not right about the Reivers, though, Sir?" the boy asks.

"Not you as well!" Layton smiles. "Those Borderers are good soldiers." Talbot nods, but the look on his face shows that he is not convinced.

De Winter wanders around the camp, looking for Pike. He finds him, after a short while, sitting on the ground with his hat over his eyes, and sits beside him.

"I am beginning to think this command of Talbot's was something of a poisoned chalice, Will. The soldiers are malcontents, and at the first sign of serious fighting they'll be in the front line against us."

"What can we do?"

"Make sure that we don't end up receiving their charge."

"Calonna says that once you've survived your first battle, it gets easier after that." Pike pauses. "I'm scared, George."

"So am I."

A day later, in the gloom of early evening, de Winter and Pike watch the huge abbey of Melrose as it burns. Layton organises the camp, shouting orders and pointing emphatically, while the bulk of the soldiers look for loot. De Winter shakes his head. "One day, Will, people will visit this place and lament that we burned it." A passing infantryman smirks at the comment. "And they will call us barbarians and murderers," de Winter adds, loudly enough for the soldier to hear, but he does not respond.

A few miles away, Longshawe and Strelley ride with Eure's company towards Melrose Abbey. The column of smoke is clearly visible on the horizon, though the abbey itself still hidden by the hills. Strelley holds his shoulders high, trying to relieve the soreness of his back. Longshawe grimaces in sympathy. They look at the rising smoke. "More destruction," Strelley mutters.

"More entries in that bloody ledger," Longshawe replies.

"It can't carry on much longer. The Scots will have to confront us soon."

"Henry wouldn't have let it go this far if they were doing this to us. You're right, even with the Regent in command, we'll be challenged."

"We're going to get that battle you wanted. And I'd better not get killed, James." Strelley smiles, and it isn't forced.

"You won't. I'll look after you." Longshawe smiles with him.

The two English armies camp three hours' march apart, within sight but too far to make it in the gathering gloom. In the morning, Eure's men strike camp and advance to Melrose. The armies unite, and begin the long march back to Jedburgh.

As the column ceases its relentless progress, Pike seeks out Strelley. "Edward," he says, nodding his head in acknowledgement of Longshawe who stands by him, "George asked me to find you both. Despite his *disagreement* with Master Longshawe, he is concerned for your safety. He suggests that you join us and Master Talbot when the battle begins. We have been instructed to keep the earl's son safe, so will be away from the fighting. He also sends you this." Pike hands over the small pot de Winter's father gave him. "For your wounds. We heard of your ordeal."

"Thank him for his concern," Strelley replies.

Pike lowers his voice, leans in towards Strelley and Longshawe. "He is concerned that a bullet or blade does not find its way into either of you. He thinks that any battle with the Scots may not result in victory, and he's right."

"It won't be long before we see this battle," Longshawe whispers.

"George does not intend to be killed or taken prisoner, and he wants to make sure you two aren't either." Pike nods and turns away.

Longshawe and Strelley watch him as he disappears into a mass of soldiers. They do not see de Winter, nor the young Talbot. Strelley calls out to Guy Fletcher, who is standing talking with some other lackeys. He walks over.

"Guy," Strelley begins, "there's going to be a battle soon. When there is, we will do what we can to look after you. We must try to stay safe ourselves, and you must stay near us as you can. George and William will be with Master Talbot, and they will be somewhere near the back of George's company of soldiers. You mustn't get to the front line. Do you understand me?"

Fletcher nods, eyes wide.

"Guy," Longshawe says, "you must not be frightened of the battle. We don't want you to get hurt, and if you panic, you may put yourself in danger." He bends to lower himself slightly, and puts his hand on Guy Fletcher's shoulder. As he does so, he looks at Strelley. "Edward here will look after you." He smiles, as does Strelley.

As they march south, it becomes clear that they are being shadowed by a small Scots force. The Scots outriders are occasionally visible on the horizon, keeping their distance at around a half-day's quick march. Layton and Eure converse in the early evening. De Winter is present with George Talbot, but Layton has instructed him that he keep his peace or lose his tongue.

"Every time we stop, they stop," Layton observes.

"They don't want battle because they know they'll lose. Our scouts reckon about six or seven hundred, but well-mounted and armed. Probably friends of your lot." He points at de Winter, who seems about to respond. "I don't need you to comment, Sir."

"They're Angus's men." Eure scratches at his dense beard. "Still no sign of Arran, though. If we engage them now, we'll beat them."

"So let's get stuck in. I can't stand all this dancing!" Layton growls.

"Not yet. They've got enough distance on us to keep us chasing for a week. And we don't know the land." Eure stops, considering.

"You said yourself if we fight them, we beat them."

"But we have to fight them. And they won't want to fight. I wonder if we might tempt them to engage us." He points at the map. "Could we not split our forces and catch them in between hammer and anvil?"

Layton looks at the map. Eure is pointing to a location west of Jedburgh where the hills could trap the enemy army in a pincer movement. He nods. "We march for Jedburgh, then!"

On the afternoon of the second day, the English stop their march to make camp, north of the small village of Ancrum. The village sits on the hillside, and some inquisitive villagers look down on the English camp. The camp is a few hundred yards north of the river Teviot, where we now see Strelley and Guy Fletcher gathering water into skins.

"Mister Strelley," Guy asks, "are you frightened of the battle?"

"Yes, Guy. There are lots of ways a person can die, and battles tend to bring you into contact with lots of those ways. I'm not ready to die, yet. There are a few things left to do before that."

Guy nods. "I was hoping to live a little longer before I die, as well."

"We're not going to die, Guy," Strelley says, holding Fletcher in a one-armed embrace. They return to the camp, where Longshawe, de Winter and Pike are sitting round a substantial fire, which Andrew Shepherd has built and now fans with a piece of bark. The lackeys prepare a simple meal of hard tack and cheese, but within a few minutes of them beginning to eat, a shout goes up around the camp.

The Scots army has been sighted on the flank of a hill on the opposite side of the valley. A thousand or so horsemen are visible. The English commanders are already busily preparing their companies. Eure and Layton each bark orders, trying to get their soldiers ready for battle. As the companies begin to separate out and form up for battle, cavalry forward and infantry behind, de Winter calls to Talbot to join him in the rear ranks. Strelley motions to Longshawe to follow him to the same place. Before riding off, he turns back to the camp, pointing to Guy Fletcher where they will be. Even mounted, the boy would not keep pace with the cavalry charge and must remain behind. Strelley rushes to join de Winter and Talbot, in the rear ranks of the company of Borderers under de Winter's command. Drums beat, and the English cavalry form up for the charge.

7: The Battle of Ancrum Moor

The Scottish cavalry move forward slowly. There are perhaps eight or nine hundred. A whisper amongst the English cavalry says that they can beat these Scots. The English front ranks break into a trot, despite the order not yet being sounded to charge. The trot begins to increase in pace through a canter to a gallop, and the full force of two thousand or so English horse charges. The infantry is rapidly left behind, marching in the wake of the cavalry.

The Scots cavalry, across the valley, retreat around the hill, out of sight. As the English pursue, one or two of the mounts lose their footing in the marshy ground, throwing riders who are immediately crushed under the hooves of those behind. One body almost causes Strelley's horse to rear, and he has to use all his strength to hold the reins firmly and keep himself in the saddle.

The sun is setting behind the hill, making it difficult for the English to see. They can make out the glinting of odd pieces of armour in the distance, but as they reach the crest of the rise, the trick is revealed. The hills that Eure and Layton saw on their map have concealed a force much larger than had showed itself, and it has the English cavalry trapped in a pincer. The ruse planned by the English has been turned on them. Infantry to the English left crash into their flank, as the Scots cavalry renew their charge into the English right.

The horsemen of de Winter's company of Borderers almost immediately burst forth from the front ranks of the English army, galloping a couple of hundred yards and reforming expertly, facing back towards the English. A shouted order, and they join the charge against the English.

In the press of battle, de Winter and Pike keep themselves either side of George Talbot, and do their best to avoid the front ranks and combat, a task made much harder by the desertion of the Scots Reivers. Men shout their battle-cries and scream their last screams. Weapons clash and clatter, and horses whicker and snort. Over the noise, de Winter calls to his ward.

"Master Talbot! We must fall back."

Talbot shakes his head. "I want to fight!"

"The fight is lost already!"

A volley of musket fire catches the rear ranks of the English. Men and horses fall under the hail of bullets. Talbot turns and sees the destruction, before looking back at de Winter. His face is pale, his eyes wide. "Perhaps you are right." He turns his horse and makes his way through the rear ranks at a gallop, followed by de Winter and Pike, and a few shouted insults and cries of "deserters!". They ride around the now-formed English infantry, still some minutes away from joining the battle, despite their hurry. Eure, commanding the infantry from his fine mount, hurls threats at them as they pass. At the camp, they find Andrew Shepherd and Guy Fletcher, standing on a hill watching as the English cavalry begin to waver. The infantry march towards the combat, but the marshy ground slows their progress and they are still several hundred yards behind.

In the melee, Layton, engaged in the press with the Scottish infantry, is hauled from his horse. As he hits the ground, he is repeatedly stabbed. Within moments, his bloody head is carved from his neck, and mounted on long pike. This new standard reinvigorates the Scots, and the English cavalry are soon broken. Strelley and Longshawe, who have found themselves briefly face-to-face with the enemy, are among the last to turn, but manage to do so without being cut down by their opponents. As the English begin to flee, the Scots infantry fire their muskets, bringing down many men. Longshawe's horse is lamed, and it collapses slowly, throwing its head about in pain and fear. Longshawe leaps from it, landing gracelessly on his back. He scrabbles and thrashes until he is upright.

Strelley immediately notices that his friend is no longer beside him, and wheels back to face the Scots. He draws alongside, and Longshawe scrambles onto the croup, ducking down, as Strelley tries to break the animal into a gallop again, himself leaning low over the horse's neck. It runs, and despite dropping a few yards behind the other fleeing English cavalry, they eventually catch up into the press of riders.

Scores of men and horses were cut down in the initial engagement. Eure, determined to bring a successful close to the battle, despite this first setback, barks orders at the cavalry, which eventually reforms well enough to support the infantry. De Winter sees Longshawe, now remounted on a new horse, and rides with Pike to his side. Talbot remains with the lackeys, but only after a short and pointed exchange with de Winter.

"Good to see you alive, James!" he calls, smiling. "Perhaps God rides with us today after all!"

Longshawe claps de Winter on the shoulder as he rides alongside. "I'm almost enjoying this," he shouts, showing de Winter a bloodied cavalry sword.

"It is... somewhat exhilarating," de Winter replies. Pike and Strelley, behind, exchange a significant look, shaking their heads.

The Scots are only a hundred or so yards distant, with cavalry on each wing. The English cavalry split, but are now outnumbered after the defection of the Borderers. Longshawe points to them, saying, "aren't those your boys over there, George?" De Winter glares at him before replying.

"Not any more, it would seem. I did warn them!" At this, the front ranks of the cavalry meet the Scots a second time, as musket fire reports across the battlefield. The melee joins again.

Moments later, Strelley is bloodied, wounded across the left forearm by a Scottish cavalry sword. Longshawe brings the man down with two quick thrusts through his chest, neatly finding two gaps in his armour. Strelley closes his eyes in pain and shock, but shakes himself and recovers his focus. He begins to use his sword with more presence of mind, engaging with and holding his own against a furiously attacking opponent.

Longshawe cuts down another Scot, revelling now in his superior strength and reach, and his considerable ability with the long sword. De Winter and Pike fight together, watching each other and covering weak spots. It is only a minute or so later that the Scots begin to prevail and the English again give ground. As the battle line pulses and ebbs, the cavalry and infantry intermingle, bringing Strelley within a few yards of Ralph Eure, dismounted now and carving a bloody swathe through the nearby Scots. The English soldiers around him have fallen away, and he is on his own, surrounded.

A moment passes during which he sees Strelley, and shouts out. "Your horse, boy!" He parries a blow, before hacking away at the arm of his attacker, severing it at the elbow. The scream is revolting. "Your horse!" Eure barks, half-turning. Strelley's eyes narrow. He watches as Eure is pressed again by more Scottish soldiers, and does not move. This time Eure turns around and begins to utter a curse, but he is pierced through the chest by a spear-thrust and brought down. A second English leader is cut to pieces by the Scots, and his head mounted on the spear that killed him. Strelley forces his horse back through the ranks, bursting through and galloping away towards the camp. De Winter and Pike are already there, but Longshawe has not yet returned. Strelley winces with the pain from his arm, tosses his head back, then vomits.

The English army lasts only a few more minutes before breaking completely. Longshawe is visible for a moment, his horse rearing as he fights in the front ranks, but he disappears again as the horse is brought down and the company collapses into flight before the press of the Scots. This time it is over. There is no reserve force that can plug the gap, and the infantry is soon beaten, trapped by the Scottish cavalry wrapping around. Leaderless, they surrender, some thousand troops casting down their weapons in defeat.

The fleeing cavalry break apart, and Strelley sees Longshawe, once again mounted. He spurs his horse on, riding to his friend and drawing him away towards the camp, where de Winter and Pike wait with the two lackeys and Talbot. As one, they begin to ride, choosing a different route to the main body of the cavalry, so as to avoid capture.

The battle was fought in the early evening, and it is now getting dark. The late January air is cold, the sky cloudless. Our young men are still riding at a fast canter, despite the dark, putting as much distance between themselves and victorious Scots as they can. Guy Fletcher seems to have taken the lead, riding at the van of the seven.

De Winter and Talbot are in conversation, over the noise of the hooves. "We should head back to Sheffield. My father will look after us all," Talbot shouts.

"I have no doubt that the earl will be pleased to see his son again, after the defeat we suffered. We are lucky to be alive." De Winter smiles at Talbot, before looking round at the others. Strelley in particular has been listening to him and is smiling back, pale with the pain of his wounded arm. Longshawe is staring away into the distance, as is Pike, both lost in their own thoughts. Andrew Shepherd is riding at the fore with Guy Fletcher.

After a moment, Strelley speaks. "As long as whatever your father finds for me to do does not involve any more fighting!" He laughs contentedly. "I will shovel shit if I have to." This elicits some giggling from Guy Fletcher and Andrew Shepherd. "Perhaps he has a need for a tutor?" Strelley adds, hopefully.

Talbot shakes his head. "I am fully sixteen years, Master

Strelley. I have no need of your tuition. Perhaps if you could instruct me in the arts of war... Though that seems not to be to your tastes!" he grins.

"Indeed not, Sir. I am only the same age as you. Do you not have a younger sibling?"

"Ah, now I catch your meaning. My sister is older than I, and my brother died some years ago. I am my father's only son and heir. He has shown no sign of taking another wife."

Strelley persists, noticing that Talbot is at least taking him partly seriously. "A shame, Sir. I shall ask My Lord Shrewsbury if he can find a young scion of some noble house to for me to educate."

"Are you sure you are suitable for a tutor? I understand you had something of a falling out with the university."

"I see George has told you my story! I may not have my degree, but I have learned from William May, and hold my own against scholars twice my age. I am worthy, I assure you." He smiles. Talbot shakes his head.

"Your assurance alone may not be enough to secure you a position. But we shall speak of it further when we return to Sheffield." They ride on into the night, still led by Guy Fletcher, talking of other things.

The following day, the young men find and join the road that leads south to Doncaster. During the daylight, they have caught occasional glimpses of other stragglers in their wake, but well-mounted as they are and led by Guy Fletcher's impressive memory of the terrain, they are well ahead of any others fleeing. Pursuit seems to have been abandoned, with relatively few of the English army escaping the battlefield.

That evening, for the first time since the battle, a proper camp is pitched, a fire lit and some local wildlife caught and prepared. The young men sit about, discussing the battle.

Talbot is speaking. "I can't decide whether to be angry or disappointed. Perhaps I'm just relieved. That I didn't get to fight, I mean. I can't say that I learned a great deal about soldiering. Plenty about running away, though."

"I'm sure you'll get your chance," de Winter replies.

"I should be relieved if I were you, George," Strelley says, addressing Talbot. "I was right, there isn't much glory in battle."

"There isn't much glory for such a soldier as you, Edward!" Longshawe replies, roaring with laughter. "I found it quite... enlivening. I don't mean the killing – that isn't pleasant – but there is something thrilling about conquering your fear, standing up to another man who is trying to cleave you."

De Winter nods his agreement. "Even a duel is not the same. Though it is purer, somehow."

"I suppose you two would know," Strelley grunts. "Five hundred Englishmen lay dead on that field, and another thousand are prisoners of the Scots. You should not make light of it."

"Men live and men die, Edward." De Winter warms his hands on the fire as he speaks. "God wills it, the king orders it, men go to their deaths for a cause they may not even understand, and certainly don't care about. One thing is certain, though, that we all shall die someday."

"I shall die an old man, in my bed, tended by a wife half my age!" Strelley laughs. "I shall leave the dying on some foreign field, cut apart by ravening savages like those Scots, to you two." He shudders.

Pike, who has been watching and listening intently, says quietly, "the fate of our leaders was rather gruesome, wasn't it?"

Longshawe replies, "I didn't see much of what happened to Eure, but I saw Layton's head on a pike."

De Winter points to Strelley. "You were closest to Eure, weren't you? What happened to him?"

Strelley closes his eyes as he relives the end of Ralph Eure. "I let him die." He speaks quietly, almost reverentially.

"What do you mean?" Longshawe asks.

"I let him die," Strelley repeats. "He asked me for my horse. No, he ordered me to give him my horse. I watched as they cut him down." The others are leaning forward, listening attentively. Strelley carries on.

"He was out beyond the line, right in the midst of the Scots. But he'd got too far ahead and was out on his own. I could have saved him."

"It would have been too dangerous. You would have died yourself, and it would not have helped." De Winter seeks to reassure him, resting a hand on his shoulder.

"I could have got him out. I could have." Strelley's eyes close again. "God wills it." He is almost whispering now. "If God had wanted Eure saved, he wouldn't have sent me to do it. I shall bear his scars."

"Edward," de Winter says, squeezing Strelley's shoulder, "I was near. You couldn't have survived if you'd ridden beyond the infantry line. The Scots would have torn you to pieces." Strelley looks into de Winter's eyes for a moment, before turning away.

"Perhaps," he says, unconvinced.

The following morning, Guy Fletcher follows Strelley as he walks to a nearby stream to drink.

"Master Strelley," Fletcher says, "your arm... The wound needs to be dressed. I should like to help."

"Thank you, Guy. I don't know what we would do without your help. Now," Strelley says, gathering himself, "it will need cleaning. I know that James carries a flask of liquor. It should have some left in it. Don't return without it." He sets to washing the wound on his arm with water from the stream. Moments later, Fletcher returns with the flask, along with clean cloth and the clay pot.

Strelley takes the flask from Fletcher and pours a little of the liquid over his arm. He gasps with the pain. Then he nods his assent as Guy Fletcher scoops a little of the ointment on to his fingers and rubs it into the open wound. His eyes screw up as he tries to bear the sensation. Fletcher is about to stop, but his eyes open again.

"Doesn't hurt as much as flogging." Strelley forces a smile. "Now wrap that cloth around, not too tight. Very good." He holds up his arm, showing Fletcher his work. "That'll hold until we get home."

He and Fletcher wash themselves in water from the stream. The cold is bracing, and as they make to return to the camp, each has a bright red face. Strelley stops and tilts his head. "Guy, what shall you do? Do you intend to return to Doncaster?"

"I hadn't considered, Master Strelley."

"I'm Edward, Guy, not 'Master Strelley'. In any case, I wonder if you would prefer to come to Sheffield with us, rather than return to Doncaster?"

"I would like to come with you. Edward." He tests the name, shyly.

"I'm sure we shall find some worthy task for a mind such as yours."

"I should like to learn from you, Sir. I should like to learn about God and Catholics and Protestants. I should like to learn to read and write."

"We shall see what can be done. I'm sure James will want to continue your schooling in the arts of fencing."

"Perhaps you should spend some time learning fencing as well, Sir," Guy says, pointing to the bandage on Strelley's arm. Strelley cuffs him gently.

"You must learn to watch what you say, Guy. If we are lucky, we may find service with the Earl of Shrewsbury. He is a powerful man, you know. Perhaps we might meet others yet more powerful through him."

"I should be content to earn enough to eat well."

"Indeed. The earl is rich, considerably more so since the Abbey lands were split up." Strelley addresses the remark to himself. Guy Fletcher looks at him, waiting for further explanation. "You know that the monasteries were all closed, a few years ago? My family secured some of the lands and the Abbey building of a place called Beauchief, but the earl also took a lot of the land himself. My father is a sort of tenant, I suppose."

"But your father owns his own land?"

"He does, but he answers to the earl. And of course that land will go to my brother Nicholas."

"So you yourself have no inheritance?"

"After my disgrace at the University, I suspect I shall have been struck from the records altogether. But no, I don't think I shall inherit much at all from my father. I did read a great deal from the library at Beauchief. That's my inheritance. Once I have taught you to read, you shall read from those same books."

"I look forward to it, Sir," Guy replies.

Will Pike moves silently across the broken scrub of the moorland, following the edge of the woods, tracking his prey. He drops to his knees, then lies down, settling himself into position. He lines up the barrel of his gun, pointing it at a fat-looking goose that settled by the edge of a small stream, some thirty yards distant. His breathing stops as he lights the primer. The bang is not enough to alert the bird to the hunter, and it collapses, writhing on the ground. Pike stands and goes to it. For the briefest moment, he looks down into its eyes, before lifting his head and bringing his boot down firmly on its neck.

From a few hundred yards away, Guy Fletcher and Andrew Shepherd set off at a gentle run from the camp. Longshawe has been watching the expert hunter, and nods his head in appreciation. Strelley reads from a little leather-bound volume. George Talbot and George de

Winter are in conversation, although each looks up at the report of the gun, neither breaks off.

"When we get back to my father, I shall," Talbot is saying, "serve you all myself."

"But you are noble." De Winter shakes his head.

"A pure accident of my birth."

"You don't think that there is something that separates the nobility from the rest?"

"No more than that which separates a first son from a second. Were I to have an older brother, I should not inherit my father's title and estates. But would I be different? The blood in my veins would be the same."

De Winter looks at him for some moments. "Men obey your father. Men serve your father. We-" he indicates the group "-serve the king, and might have died in that service."

"The king is a second son."

"That is true. But he is the second son of a king."

"The last king took the throne in battle."

De Winter shakes his head at Talbot's indifference. "These people serve your father and the king because they believe in nobility and royalty. They need that."

"Because otherwise the nobility would have none to serve them? I don't see it." As Talbot gives this, his final word, Pike and the two lackeys return with the dead bird. Pike sets to and plucks it clean, Guy Fletcher starts to build a fire and Andrew Shepherd disappears into the nearby forest, returning with more firewood a few minutes later.

As the bird is cooking, Longshawe encourages the others into fencing practice. Strelley excuses himself, pointing at his wounded arm, but the others take their places en garde. Longshawe shows them a clever thrust, and also how to avoid it, then lets them loose on each other. De Winter and he deliberately avoid fighting each other, but use their skills to help the others learn. Pike steps out of the melee to check the cooking, and nods at Strelley, who looks up at him, then down at his book. With a half-sigh, he closes the book and stands, flexing the fingers on his wounded left arm.

Pike smiles at him. "You don't fight with that one," he says, and helps Strelley up.

An hour or two later, bones litter the ground around the fire. The goose has served them well, together with what little they have left of their provisions from before the battle at Ancrum. Edward Strelley stands and clears his throat noisily.

"Gentlemen, if I may... A little something to keep you entertained?"

Longshawe smiles wryly. "Something exciting." He scratches his cheek. "Not difficult."

Strelley shakes his head. "Very well, then." And he begins to recite, with the ebb and flow of the practised storyteller.

"O queen, you command me to renew unspeakable grief,

"how the Greeks destroyed the riches of Troy,

"and the sorrowful kingdom, miseries I saw myself,

"and in which I played a great part. What Myrmidon,

"or Dolopian, or warrior of fierce Ulysses, could keep

"from tears in telling such a story?"

And from memory, he recites the second book of Vergil's Aeneid, including that most famous line of all, 'timeo Danaos, et dona ferentes' in both Latin and English. He tells of Priam's death at the hands of Pyrrhus, of the loss of Creusa and the flight from Troy, occasionally switching from English to Latin to emphasise a line. The others listen, enraptured, and when he finishes some time later, they applaud warmly. As the noise ceases, George Talbot calls out a new request.

"What about a little Catullus?"

Strelley laughs at him. "I take it, Sir, that you want the lewd stuff?"

8: Francis Talbot's table

Ten days later, Sheffield Castle, the birthplace of the 5th Earl of Shrewsbury, one of his favoured residences and the destination of the group of young men, is visible in the distance. It is perhaps fifteen miles away, less than half a good day's ride. The journey has been long and has seen them in straitened circumstances, but no real danger. As they cover their eyes against the westering evening sun, George Talbot turns in the saddle, and announces to his friends, "I should like to be the first to enter the castle, if it please you all, gentlemen."

"That is of course your right, My Lord," de Winter replies, bowing his head slightly. Then, after considering for a moment, he addresses the others, indicating them all with a gesture of his hand. "We should enter together, as a sign of our fellowship. Behind Lord Talbot, of course." He receives a few nods and murmurs of approval at this, forgoing as he is his own right to enter before them, behind the earl's son.

A couple of hours later, as darkness falls, they approach the castle gate. Their presence on the road has evidently been noted: the main gate of the castle is open, and a herald loudly calls out the name of the young heir to the Earldom of Shrewsbury. His six companions ride abreast behind him, with Andrew Shepherd and Guy Fletcher in the middle.

The earl, his countenance showing signs of the cares of the last few weeks, stands in the courtyard, ready to receive his son. He is dressed in a sombre, practical way, wrapped in furs against the late winter evening chill. George Talbot dismounts some way distant, and runs to his father, who offers his hand. The son stops himself and takes the last few paces more decorously, accepting his father's handshake. Although their greeting is formal, the earl's emotion is clear in his eyes. His beloved and only son has returned. They spend some moments in silence, before George turns round and signals his companions to approach.

The earl shakes de Winter's hand vigorously, and thanks each of the others as his son indicates them in turn, naming those unfamiliar to his father. George Talbot dwells a moment or two as he introduces Guy Fletcher and Andrew Shepherd. Shrewsbury, waiting until his son has finished, says, "we had heard of your defeat, and that a thousand or more were taken. We had feared... There was so little news of the remains of the army. But you are here, safe! Tell me, is it true that both Eure and Layton were killed?"

Strelley winces. De Winter takes half a step forward. "Indeed, My Lord, both Sir Ralph and Sir Brian were lost in the battle. Many of our force lost their lives, but the greater part were captured. Perhaps a thousand escaped, perhaps only a few hundred. I could not say. We did not have chance to survey the battlefield afterwards." He rushes the last few words, dipping his head.

After the brief pause that follows, a voice calls out from across the courtyard, speaking with a familiar bouncy, musical accent. "Gentlemen! How good it is to see you all safe! God smiles on you and keeps you, it seems."

Strelley and Longshawe exchange a look. De Winter goes across to him and shakes his hand. "I told you – and I told Layton – that those bloody Reivers would desert us!" He smiles, and Calonna smiles warmly back at him. "It's good to see you again, Lorenzo. And you beat us back, I see."

"Ah..." the Italian says, stroking his beard. "Experience in battle gives you experience of defeat. And survival." His comment provokes much laughter among the others.

A retainer ushers them inside, and sees to it that they have fine, fresh clothes. Strelley requests hot water to bathe. The footman who brings it does not comment aloud, but his frown indicates that he regards Strelley's unusual habit with some suspicion. It is not long later that they gather to dine, and Shrewsbury has provided the very best of his larders and his cellars to celebrate the return of his son.

At table, the conversation is lively, and, encouraged by the earl himself, with little regard for formal deference. It breaks into pockets, so that several people are speaking at once, but no one is put out. The earl's heir is complaining loudly, although with more than a hint of a smile, that he was denied much action by his protector, de Winter. The earl is asking Longshawe and Strelley about themselves.

"So you, James, wish to spend your life soldiering? I have served on the borders myself Have you not seen enough of it to put you off?"

"I know the dangers now. But what else can I do? I'm not like Edward. He can read the Bible in Greek, and other languages besides."

"You are learned in tongues, Master Strelley?"

"I am, My Lord. I learned from some eminent scholars at the

University." He looks around the table, almost furtively. "Even though I didn't receive my degree, I am competent in the classical languages, and a few more modern."

"Anything else you can do?" the earl asks, interested.

"I am a keen student of the scripture, Sir. But I also know a little natural philosophy and medicine."

"Indeed." Shrewsbury chews a mouthful, thinking. "I know of someone who might make use of a young man like you. How old are you?"

"I shall be seventeen years this summer, Sir."

"Do you write well?"

"Tolerably, Sir. I pride myself on celerity, not presentation."

"We shall arrange a meeting for you. I am in contact with a tutor, and he may need assistance in his work. It would be the least I can do for you. After your care for my son..." Talbot sits back in his chair, contented.

"Begging your pardon, Sir, but who is this tutor?" Strelley asks.

"He's a Cambridge man himself: Grindal."

"Ah! I think I know him. A humanist? Evangelical?"

"You should beware of that word in this house, Master Strelley. A Protestant is an unusual being round here." Longshawe jabs forcefully at a morsel with his knife. Shrewsbury notices, eyes drawn by the flash of the blade, but continues, unruffled. "But yes, so far as I know he is an advocate of the reformed faith. I can't say that such things occur to me."

Strelley is surprised by the comment, which shows briefly on his face. Longshawe looks from him to the earl, who, after a brief moment, lets out a loud laugh.

"We all must come to God in our own way, gentlemen. My faith differs, it seems, from King Henry's. It does not signify. I shall organise for Grindal to see you. But I make no guarantees. I hope he does not view your failure to acquire a degree as significant."

"I thank you, Sir, for your consideration." Strelley says, managing to hide his excitement by sipping at his wine.

"Remind me and I shall show you my library tomorrow." Strelley's delight breaks out in a wide, honest smile. The earl turns to Longshawe.

"The war is over for now, Master Longshawe. I am not asked for more men. But there will be a chance for you soon enough."

"I too thank you for your consideration, Sir." He lowers his head in deference. "I should like to keep Guy Fletcher as my lackey."

"Then we shall have to find something to occupy him as well." The earl smiles at Longshawe, pleased with this exchange.

George Talbot has now finished complaining about the lack of fighting he saw. He asks de Winter, "and what shall you do with yourself, Sir, now that our brief period of military service seems to be over?"

"I shall not be returning to the battlefield. Something more... safe." He wrinkles his nose.

"Safe, you say? What about service in a noble household?" Talbot asks.

"Such as this? I would consider serving the king himself."

"Your ambition is extraordinary." George Talbot continues to look into de Winter's eyes for several moments, challenging him to respond. De Winter is not riled.

"Perhaps it is. Nevertheless I should like to pursue the highest calling I can. My father is of the nobility himself, although *I* shall not inherit his title. Perhaps your father will secure me an introduction."

"What about one of the girls?" Talbot asks, his enthusiasm for the conversation returning.

"What do you mean?"

"The princesses! Mary and Elizabeth."

"Their father does not acknowledge them," de Winter replies flatly. "They are not princesses."

"Indeed not, so it may be easier to find you a position in their households. I shall ask my father, if you wish."

De Winter ponders Talbot's offer. "I would be grateful if you did. I could serve the Lady Mary. *She* is a good Catholic. My conscience would not allow me to take a position with the boy prince or Boleyn's girl."

Talbot nods. "I understand."

Longshawe is vividly recounting his valiant fighting at Ancrum against the Scots, which captures the attention of George Talbot, and a moment later of George de Winter. Thrusts and parries are reenacted, drinks spilled and chairs knocked over, each near miss relived. Edward Strelley is quietly contemplative, not joining in with the others. Guy Fletcher goes over to him and sits by him, but does not say anything. Instead, he listens and watches as the others enjoy themselves.

The following morning, Francis Talbot shows Edward Strelley his magnificent library. "Some of these volumes were rescued from Beauchief, you know?" Talbot says.

"I had made that connection. My father's collection did not seem adequate for the Abbey."

"It was a great shame. I cannot say that I did not profit from the king's dislike of the religious orders. As did your family."

"Indeed they did, Sir," Strelley replies. "Were it possible, I should like to borrow some of these books."

"My library is at your disposal, Edward. For now, you must consider yourself part of my household. And would you try to get my son to learn some of your Latin and Greek? He pretends to me that he learns his lessons, but he doesn't. He is more interested in hunting and hawking." The earl smiles to himself as he speaks. Strelley disappears into the library. Shrewsbury walks out into the courtyard of the castle, to find his son fencing with de Winter. Longshawe stands to one side, watching the earl's heir carefully. Pike, Guy Fletcher and Andrew Shepherd are sitting on some stone steps leading to a doorway, also watching and talking occasionally.

"Try to keep your wrist rigid," Longshawe remarks, as the young Talbot makes a thrust at de Winter. "Look: if you do touch him, you'll lose your blade." Longshawe waves the sword in his hand to illustrate the point, before stepping away. De Winter probes Talbot's defences, testing his balance, his awareness and his movement, the use of his weight to his advantage. Talbot is talented, but despite only being a little younger than de Winter and Longshawe, he fences with poorly controlled aggression, over-reaching himself frequently, and thus exposing himself to counter-thrusts.

Eventually, Longshawe stops him. "Watch," he says, before taking guard facing de Winter, who smiles and offers him an exaggerated bow. They circle each other, footwork careful and measured, blades some distance apart. They look into each other's eyes, responding to the slightest movement, covering their own weak spots and looking for an opportunity to exploit. It is Longshawe who tests first, but De Winter avoids the thrust and touches him on the upper arm.

Longshawe turns to Talbot. "Did you see? George could only get at me when I attacked him. The advantage lies with the defender. Be balanced, be patient, and wait. You won't win any duels charging in and leaving yourself open."

Pike stands and disappears briefly, before returning with an armful of practice fencing swords, with blunt tips and edges. He hands one each to Guy and Andrew, and taking one for himself stands before Longshawe, who nods his head and takes guard. Six young men test themselves and each other, swords clash and spark.

It is perhaps half an hour later when Strelley joins them, taking a sword himself and practising for a short while with Longshawe, and then with Guy Fletcher. He sits down after allowing himself to be touched on the thigh by the point of Guy's sword, and reads his book, keeping half an eye on the martial pursuits as they continue.

A few minutes pass, before Guy comes over and sits next to him. "What are you reading?" he asks Strelley.

"This is part of a poem by a Florentine called Dante. I have seen another volume of it somewhere before, but never found the whole thing together. This copy is in Italian, of a sort, which I can just about read but some of it I can't immediately understand."

"So you're reading a book that you can't make sense of?"

"I have to think about it. This way, I learn to fill in the gaps in my knowledge. Let me show you. I'll find a section that I remember from reading before in translation." He flicks the leaves of the book, trying to recognise the relevant passage. "Here. I may not know the exact words, but I can see that this word means 'sun', this word means 'silent'. The words in this are often almost identical to the Latin, but sometimes I can remember a passage from reading it before and fit meanings to the unfamiliar words."

Guy watches, fascinated. The others continue their swordplay.

"The easiest thing is to find Bible passages in other languages." He takes out another volume, concealed in a pocket. "That way, you can go from one language to another, but still be aware of what it all means in English."

"Will you show me how to read?" Guy asks.

"I shall indeed. Do you know your Bible passages? A psalm, perhaps, or a story about Jesus?"

"Not really, Sir. The priests always spoke in Latin when they read from the Bible at Church."

"Never mind, I shall show you."

He reads aloud from his other book, a tiny copy of Tyndale's English Bible, showing Guy the words as he reads them. "See how they are formed from the letters, so the sounds I make correspond to the letters?"

"So this is a 'b'?" Guy says, pointing to the initial letter of 'beginning'.

"It is. We shall have you reading Vergil and Homer by the end of the week."

The Earl of Shrewsbury, who has been watching the fencing from the other side of the courtyard, strolls over and joins Strelley and Guy. He reads over Strelley's shoulder. "That looks like Tyndale's work, Edward. Be careful to whom you show that."

"I shall guard against heresy, Sir," Strelley replies in a bantering tone. The earl returns to watching the fencing practice, and Strelley reads to Guy Fletcher. George Talbot is learning quickly, his ready eye and hand beginning to be matched by balance and composure. Andrew Shepherd, strong in the arm, is already accomplished and has landed blows on both Longshawe and de Winter, to much cheering and whooping from the others.

The earl calls out. "Tomorrow, gentlemen, we shall hunt at the Manor."

Sheffield Manor lies at the top of Park Hill, looking out westwards over the castle, and commanding a view of the higher ground to the south and east of the city. The hunting lodge is a simple three-storey building in the yellow stone common in the area, with a crenellated roof and a round tower another ten feet high, which sits apart from the main manor building. To the north west, down the hill in the valley, Sheffield Castle sits at the confluence of the rivers Don and Sheaf. Tracing a line south from the castle, it is also possible to pick out the Ponds Hall, a timber-framed building surrounded by ponds teeming with birds, from which it takes its name. A hart has been spotted in the deer park south of the Manor lodge, and the pack of hunting dogs is made ready. They signal their keenness with a cacophony of barking, but the hunting party is already awake, dressed, and preparing. De Winter stands next to Pike, who has loaded his gun and is aiming it at a wood pigeon some forty or fifty yards distant, perched in a tree.

"You can't hit it from here," de Winter laughs.

Pike lifts his concentration, turning briefly to de Winter, but saying nothing. Then, focusing himself, he closes one eye, steadying the long barrel and applying the match to the pan. The report of the gun sets other birds flying. Pike lifts his head from the gun barrel and looks at de Winter for a moment, before pointing to the ground at the base of the tree. Andrew Shepherd runs over and picks up the dead pigeon, neatly beheaded by the ball. He holds it above his head, a look of victory on his face. De Winter claps Pike on the shoulder. "Extraordinary," he mutters.

"Good shot, Will," Longshawe says, nodding. The Earl of Shrewsbury and his son have also been watching, and each echoes Longshawe's words. A group of retainers lead mounts out from the stables, the finest of them reserved for the earl and George Talbot. De Winter is offered the best of the others, as Longshawe picks a sturdy horse to bear his considerable frame. Strelley walks around to show himself to his, stroking down its muzzle. Pike helps Guy Fletcher to climb up into the saddle before leaping into his own. Andrew Shepherd puts the pigeon into a cloth bag and drags himself up.

The Master of the Hounds sets the animals off, and they streak forward, across the open ground around the lodge and into the sparse forest that surrounds it. The earl allows his son the privilege to ride at the fore, staying at his shoulder, followed by the six other hunters and a handful of retainers, carrying knives, bags and spears.

The chase is long, leading many miles into Derbyshire, but the hunters pursue relentlessly. The party has passed the village of Norton and is on its way to Coal Aston when the prey is brought to bay. The dogs snap at it, but are afraid to get close, as it swings its antlers to defend itself. One of the retainers offers a spear to Francis Talbot as he dismounts, but he refuses it, pointing to his son. George Talbot takes the spear, and focuses on the stag. Pike aims his gun, offering some degree of protection if the kill goes awry. Talbot drives his spear in to the deer at the shoulder. It sticks fast, but the wound is not fatal. The deer heaves and snorts, thrashing about and driving the spear further into its flesh. George Talbot takes another spear, edges carefully around to be away from the head, and drives it into the opposite flank. The deer collapses onto its rump, then falls sidelong.

Francis Talbot hands de Winter a long hunting knife, to deliver the coup de grace. De Winter takes it, smoothes his moustache and steps forward. He plunges the knife into the neck of the stag, and red blood spits from the wound as the deer expires.

Later that evening, Longshawe and Strelley are sitting outside the hunting lodge. Longshawe is talking. "I must go and see my father. His welcome will not be as warm as the earl's, but I must let him know I am still alive." Longshawe is contemplative, thinking his thoughts out loud, as much to himself as to Strelley.

"I'm not sure Sir Nicholas will be interested in my safe return. I don't think his own experience of the borders was one he would wish to repeat," Strelley replies.

"Nonsense, Edward. He'll be delighted to see you, and to hear your stories. As will your mother."

"I think dear mamma at least will appreciate my coming back." Strelley laughs as he speaks. "I wonder if any of my brothers even noticed that we'd been away."

"I doubt it. Perhaps I should pay George's sister a visit!" Longshawe leans back and joins with Strelley's laughter. "I'm not sure George has completely forgiven me yet."

Strelley frowns at him. "Let's not get started with that again."

Longshawe stops laughing, and looks out into the night, focusing on nothing in particular. "No," he says quietly. Strelley does not hear the sigh that follows.

9: A Royal Appointment

A few weeks later, Edward Strelley nervously awaits his visitor. The Earl of Shrewsbury has arranged for Grindal to come to Sheffield to meet him. He sits in a withdrawing room at the Ponds Hall, where the Porter Brook and the Sheaf empty into the Don. He reads from a small book, beautifully illuminated and bound. The others are out hunting wildfowl in the ponds around, and occasionally the report of Pike's fowling gun can be heard reverberating across the dale. In the distance, a lone rider appears over the brow of the hill, riding from the south east.

A footman greets the rider as he arrives at the Hall, and takes his horse away to the stable. The rider, neatly bearded and dressed in the almost-ecclesiastical garb of the scholar, enters the room where Strelley sits. Another retainer announces him.

"Doctor Grindal, Sir."

Strelley rises and offers his hand, which Grindal shakes warmly.

"I understand that you too studied under Dr Ascham?" Grindal says.

"Amongst others, yes. I did not complete-" Grindal raises his hand, stopping Strelley speaking. Strelley frowns.

"The earl has informed me of your situation. My mind is open, Master Strelley, and what interests me is your abilities, not your degree." Strelley, his face regaining its look of enthusiasm, nods appreciatively, and gestures Grindal to a chair. The fires are burning high despite the returning warmth of early spring. Strelley opens a casement, and the fresh air drifts into the room.

"Doctor Grindal, what is it that you would like to discuss?" Strelley asks, sitting down again. His nerves are evident by his constant fidgeting, curling and uncurling his fingers, chewing his lips.

"The earl tells me that you are a capable linguist." Grindal sits very still, his eyes fixed on the more mobile young man.

"Indeed, Sir. I can read several languages and write in most of those. I do not speak them so fluently for lack of practice." Strelley's agitation starts to show again as he waits for a reply. Grindal is slow in making it, but it is positive, appreciative in tone.

"Useful. What is your handwriting like?"

"Not always pristine, but it is fast."

"That is to the purpose. You may be required to scribe quickly.

How is your knowledge of the Bible?"

"I am well-versed, Sir." He smiles at his own joke. "I do not quote like a pastor, but I can recall what matters."

"Indeed?" Grindal's previously measured voice has a hint of amusement for the first time. "And what do you consider to be *that which matters*?"

"Well, Sir, it is the teachings of Christ that matter," Strelley ventures. "Not the glosses or the ornamentation of the scholars."

"And yet you came to the University to study exactly that which you now say does not matter. The logic of the schoolmen."

"If I may, I must correct you, Sir. I came to the university to study grammar, rhetoric, philosophy, *humanism*, not doctrine."

"Ah!" Grindal's exclamation is enthusiastic. Strelley has said the right thing. "And what did you learn?"

"A great deal," Strelley says. "What is it that you wish me to recount?"

"Do not trouble yourself to recall your lessons verbatim." Grindal smiles. "It is not necessary if one can carry a text with him. It is your analysis that I am interested to hear. What you think that isn't what someone has told you to think. I should like to know your thoughts on the Humanists."

"The schoolmen have obscured Scripture for a thousand years. The common man should hear the word of the Lord, not someone else's interpretation. I have read Erasmus, his dispute with Luther. The letters-" Grindal interrupts with a gesture again.

"Master Strelley, before you proceed further, might I ask what is your opinion? Are the Catholics in the right, or the Evangelicals?" Grindal asks.

"I should like to know that I speak without fear of the consequences before I make my answer, Sir."

"You may speak freely, young man. This shall remain between God and ourselves."

"Then I shall speak my mind, Sir. It is my opinion that the Catholics base their religion upon a small and insignificant part of the Bible. It says in Matthew: *'And I tell you that you are Peter, and on this rock I will build my church, and the gates of Hell will not overcome it. I will give you the keys of the kingdom of heaven; whatever you bind on earth will be bound in heaven, and whatever you loose on earth will be loosed in heaven.'* But the Catholics have bound on Earth what God would not bind in Heaven."

"And yet this is the word of God, is it not?"

"It is written by the hand of a man. There are other words of God, and there are other words of Jesus. The Gospels do not speak of buying Masses or indulgences. In such matters I think Luther is right."

"Perhaps. Do you mean thereby that the Pope is not Peter's successor, head of the Church, given the authority to speak to man on God's behalf?"

"Pardon me, Sir, but the Church is not the Pope's, but the Lord's?"

"I should think even the Pope himself would agree."

"But is it right to assert that the Pope is unerring on account of his being Pope? Does the institution grant the man his infallibility, or is he infallible and so becomes Pope?"

"A subtle distinction, I grant you. To what purpose do you propose to put it?"

"The point," Strelley, realising he is getting louder and more animated, lowers his tone with a pronounced effort, "is that there have been some Popes in the past who would not, to my mind, find their way past St Peter at the gates of heaven."

"Perhaps the office of Pope, chosen by men, is sometimes offered to the wrong man? I think I follow you. Your thoughts do you great credit, Master Strelley. Do you propose, then, that the evangelical religion is the one we should follow?"

"The reformers seem to have the same problem as the conservatives."

"What do you mean?"

"Well, Sir, they read the Bible, and what they see from it is the detail. The message of the new covenant is to love your neighbour."

"Do you think salvation is in acts, then?"

"Not on acts alone. Not just in the sacraments, at least. Why should a good man be refused entry to heaven because he did not have faith in Christ?"

"What if that good man were a heathen? A Moslem?"

"God created the Moslems just as he created us. Can they not attain heaven, if they are God's creation?"

"They do not believe that Jesus Christ was the son of God."

"No. But they are capable of piety, of learning, of agape."

"So salvation *is* in acts?"

"Good actions spring from good motives. God would see that even a generous act done purely for the purpose of entering heaven is selfish. But it cannot be faith alone. A pious man does good, doesn't he? In any case, the Evangelicals are just as diverted as the Catholics, and our king, by the question of *how* to worship God, and they ignore the reasons why we do so in the first instance."

"You should be careful to whom you say that, Edward." Grindal laughs, his face lighting up with a sort of perverse pleasure in the grim thought of the punishment for heresy. "You have some interesting ideas, I see. What is that you are reading?"

"Pliny, Sir. I found this volume in the library at the castle. I don't think the earl will ever read it."

"Perhaps not. Now, Edward, I have to tell you: my student will be a person of the highest calibre, someone of great importance who must trust us totally. You have been entirely candid with me. Shall you be so with her?"

Strelley raises an eyebrow at the feminine pronoun. "I did not anticipate having much contact with your student."

"You are correct, of course, but your position would require the greatest tact, diplomacy and discretion. You must learn to control your humours. Have you read Galen?"

"A little, Sir, and Avicenna. I rather enjoy the study of the human body. I wonder how it is that Aristotle could be so obviously wrong about so many things and yet his echoes mislead us even now."

"The Church does not of course encourage the study of the brain. I assume you refer to the primacy of the brain as organ of control?"

"I do. What could be a greater project than understanding God's greatest work? To know how the body functions would allow a healer to cure-"

Grindal stops him. "I have a book that will interest you, by an Italian professor called Vesalius. There aren't many copies in this country to my knowledge, indeed, I should be surprised if there is another. His work would not – could not – be understood by the average parish priest. Much less would they endorse his quest for knowledge of man."

"Surely knowledge is the goal of mortal life?" Strelley says excitedly.

"Only in that it leads to salvation. Remember that. My student

78

is, as you have no doubt realised, Lady Elizabeth, King Henry's daughter. I begin my engagement with her in a few weeks. The Earl of Shrewsbury has asked me to find some task for you. I am sure we can put a mind such as yours to good use."

Strelley nods, his eyes shining, but does not reply.

After a moment, Grindal speaks again. "You must put your affairs in order here, Master Strelley. I shall need you to travel with me the day after tomorrow."

"I shall return to Beauchief to inform my father."

"There is no need to rush. Once the earl and the others have come back, we can discuss our arrangements. For now, I should just like to talk."

Before the earl and the rest of the party return, Strelley and Grindal discuss poetry, philosophy, history. Grindal, betraying somewhat his prejudices, confesses himself surprised and impressed by the younger man's learning. In spite of not having passed his degree, Grindal says, it is clear that Strelley has benefitted as much or more from the education as many others who did.

The shooting party returns around midday, each of them carrying several wildfowl. As they approach, they converse about their morning's work.

"I can't understand how you can hit anything so small with a ball at that sort of distance," George Talbot says to Pike. "I can barely hit them with shot."

"It's this rifling. It makes the ball fly straighter." Pike shows the gun to Talbot, who takes it in his hands, sighting along the barrel, checking its straightness. He feels the gun's weight.

"It looks like there are grooves cut into the inside of the barrel," Talbot remarks, holding the muzzle to his eye.

"That's right," Pike replies. "It means you have to clean the barrel of grime more often, but the ball flies straighter."

Talbot hands the gun to his father, who inspects it with interest.

"We shall have to have some made for ourselves. Where did you get it?" the earl asks.

"My father knew a gunsmith at Bradfield who cast dead straight barrels and then cut these grooves into them. As far as I know, he still works there..." Pike takes the gun back from the earl, and begins to clean it by wrapping a rag around his ramrod and drawing it slowly and carefully up the inside the barrel. "If only the powder didn't leave so much soot, I wouldn't have to clean it so often," he says, to himself as much as to the others.

De Winter and Longshawe have both been watching the conversation, impressed with Pike's shooting and allowing him his moment to impress the earl. As the Talbots withdraw inside, they remain outside with Pike as he continues to clean.

"How was the baron?" Longshawe asks de Winter.

"Delightful company, as usual. I think he was pleased that we had all returned safe, but it's hard to tell through the drunken nonsense that he talks most of the time. He has a little more time for my oldest brother than he does for me, of course. And my sisters." Longshawe's brow furrows, unsure what comes next. "Caroline asked after you."

Longshawe allows himself the merest hint of a smile, before replying, "I hope you passed on my best wishes to her. I'm sorry for the insult, George. I was acting the fool."

"I know. Perhaps we shall both remember to act honourably in future."

Pike listens to the exchange whilst continuing his process of tending to his gun. De Winter and Longshawe are watching him, fascinated by the care and precision of his work. After a half-minute of watching, de Winter speaks, without turning to Longshawe.

"Did your father celebrate your return?" he asks.

"We dined together, but he isn't well," Longshawe replies.

"What is it that ails him?"

"I don't know. He doesn't like to admit any frailty, so he doesn't look after himself properly."

"I wouldn't trust my health to practitioners of physick. I sometimes wonder if their remedies don't hurry people into the grave."

"You should talk to Edward. He reads all sorts of books about it. I'm sure he's told me that some of it proves your point."

"Ah, but they sent him down from the University for that sort of thing, didn't they?" Longshawe's face contorts. "You didn't think I knew? News gets around fast, I suppose. I heard that he was suspected of heresy approaching atheism."

"He doesn't hide the fact," Longshawe mutters. "But an accusation is no proof, is it?"

Pike speaks up. "Edward is no heretic. He knows the Bible better than the three of us together."

De Winter laughs. "I'm sure he does, but if he and his family persist in ignoring the commands and instructions of the Pope, they will burn, whether in this life or the next."

"You are not to refer to him as *the Pope*, George." Longshawe delivers a friendly but thudding blow to de Winter's shoulder. "He is *the Bishop of Rome* or some such. Else they'll be waving your cock at you as you watch the rest of your innards make their way out of you. The king won't have it." The three of them shudder at the thought of the brutal punishments meted out to traitors.

"If that is the price of avoiding eternal damnation... Anyway, do you really accept that Henry is the head of your church?" de Winter asks, a note of incredulity in his voice. "A man who has executed two of his wives? More? Cromwell, bastard though he was? Bishop Fisher?"

"Well..." Longshawe hesitates. "I confess that I do not perceive a great deal of difference, whether the king or the Pope – whatever he is – decides how I should worship."

"It's fortunate, then, that you grew big and strong, and handy with a sword, eh?" De Winter returns the blow from moments ago, palm against shoulder blade. "Perhaps you should try attending Church every so often. You might notice a few things have changed."

The hunters eat together with Strelley and Grindal, the earl's servants having prepared a hearty meal. De Winter and the two Talbots are deep in conversation on one side of the table. Across from them, Longshawe tells Strelley about the shooting, but it is clear that despite his forbearance Strelley is not altogether interested. His royal appointment occupies his thoughts. Occasionally, he glances across at Grindal, as though he is checking that the scholar is still present, and this sight confirms somehow the content of their earlier conversation, the extraordinary fortune that it represents.

Longshawe begins to notice Strelley's lack of attention. "Edward, have you listened to anything I've told you?"

"Hmm...?" Strelley's eyes focus on Longshawe.

"I just told you that Pike shot a Phoenix."

"What? I was just thinking."

"About what? This great scholar who barely speaks to us?" He flails a gesture in the direction of Grindal.

Strelley shakes his head. "You haven't given him much

opportunity to do so."

Longshawe turns to Grindal, a sly look of feigned guilt across his features. "I apologise if I spoke over-enthusiastically of our morning's hunting, Sir. My friend," he looks pointedly at Strelley, "has previously shown some enthusiasm for *venery*." Longshawe smiles at this rather inappropriate and inaccurate joke.

Strelley frowns at the double meaning. "Doctor Grindal is to tutor Lady Elizabeth," he says, quietly.

"Elizabeth who?" Longshawe replies, sizing up Grindal, who sits impassive, his head slightly aslant as he tries to fathom Longshawe. Grindal's eyebrow barely flickers at the question.

"Elizabeth Tudor, James. Anna Bolena's daughter. King Henry's daughter," Strelley answers him.

"Jesus Christ!" Longshawe exclaims rather too loudly. "And you are to assist him?"

"Indeed." Strelley grins, and finally Grindal's face also, finally, cracks into a wide smile.

"Fortune favours you, it seems," Pike interjects.

"Fortune, and George's strong hand in protecting young Talbot," Strelley replies. "Which reminds me: how are Guy and Andrew?"

Pike considers his answer. "The earl has found them work. They are both healthy, and look well in their uniforms."

"He has them for servants?" Longshawe asks Pike.

"I think he wishes them to learn properly their duties as a gentleman's footman, but plans to release them: Guy to you, Andrew to de Winter, once they have shown him their worth."

"The earl truly has our best interests in mind..." Longshawe mutters. Shrewsbury puts out his bottom lip and nods.

"Would you know how to train a footman properly?" Strelley asks Longshawe, smiling.

"Of course not," Longshawe replies, stung. "I appreciate the intervention, but I enjoyed having my own servant."

"Guy was no ordinary servant, James, he was our lackey." Strelley shakes his head. "And he had enough about him to lead us all back through the borderlands." Grindal watches the exchange, his eyes flicking between one speaker and another. He is perhaps twenty eight or thirty years old, with the peculiar waxy look of one who spends a great deal of his time indoors.

Longshawe holds his hand up, palm outwards, demanding

permission. "I just mean that if I were to serve again, I should prefer to have Guy at my side. More so than you!" He points to Strelley and laughs.

"No, war and I were not comfortable bedfellows. I shall enjoy engaging myself in something more constructive." He looks over to Grindal, who nods in confirmation. The meal continues long into the afternoon.

The following morning, Longshawe enters the stables at the Manor. The stable-hands recognise him as a guest, and ask him what he wants, to which he replies simply that he wishes to borrow a mount to ride for the morning. Seeing nothing untoward in the request, the servants prepare a horse for him, and a few minutes later, without any ceremony, Longshawe sets off westwards towards Sheffield Castle.

The journey is only short, and Longshawe covers most of it at a fair trot. The horse he has borrowed is a sturdy animal, tall and broad rather than finely built, and it bears Longshawe's large frame with ease. He reigns it in a hundred yards or so distant from the castle gate, and dismounts, leading the horse in-hand up to the gate. A few words are exchanged with a uniformed guard, and a more important-looking servant arrives a minute or two later.

"Can I help you, Master Longshawe?" This steward recognises the young man, and is deferential in his tone, although his lips and eyes retain the slightest hint of a sneer throughout the exchange.

"I have come in search of Lady Caroline de Winter. I have reason to believe she might be here at the castle."

"I am sorry to disappoint you, Sir, but she left the castle a few days ago and set out for the de Winter residence at Byron Greave."

"Truly? And you think she is still there?"

"I cannot speak for her, Master Longshawe. She is not a part of this household."

"Is her father here?"

"For once, no." The retainer raises an eyebrow at the question and his own answer. "He is at Holmfirth. Business, he said."

"Thank you for your help." Longshawe shakes his head as he remounts his horse in the castle courtyard. He rears the animal extravagantly and unnecessarily, but does not get the reaction he is after as the steward is absolutely still, unmoved. Longshawe looks over his shoulder as the animal gallops out of the castle gate, and sees the steward still standing motionless, one eyebrow raised.

Byron Greave, or Burngreave, lies to the north of Sheffield Castle, on the rise that leads up to Pitsmoor, perhaps a mile distant. Once out of the castle grounds, Longshawe slows his pace to a canter, then a trot, then a walk. He looks around, back towards the castle, then south-east to the Manor. In his contemplation, he allows the horse to stop altogether. For a half-minute, he looks out in the direction of Byron Greave, his breathing deep and slow. He lowers his eyes, then closes them and allows his head to fall backwards on his shoulders. After another half-minute of this silent thought, he wheels around and sets off at a gallop in the direction of Sheffield Manor.

10: Departures

Edward Strelley rides back to his family home, a large stone house nestled in the hills above Beauchief village. He is greeted neither by family nor retainers, so he rides around to the stables, where he tethers his own horse, pats it and gives it a handful of oats, before entering the house through a rear door. He walks through the servants' quarters at the back of the complex, where one of the domestics stands straight and acknowledges his presence with a murmured "Master Strelley".

"Do you know where Sir Nicholas is, Daniel?" Strelley asks. The servant's face registers surprise that his first name is used.

"The Master is at his business in his study, I believe, Sir," Daniel says, then adds quietly, "welcome home, Sir." He gets on with his work, removing cobwebs and sweeping, as Strelley passes through the long corridor. Eventually he comes to a heavy oak door, in front of which he stands motionless for a quarter minute. Then, after a deep breath, he opens it without knocking.

Sir Nicholas Strelley sits in a comfortable-looking upholstered chair, reading through papers laid out on a desk. The light through the glazed windows is bright enough for him to read without a lamp or candle. He looks up and sees his son, and then returns to the papers for a brief moment, before putting them aside. "Sit," he says, gesturing to another chair. Strelley does so.

"Father," he begins, "I have-" he pauses, then puffs himself up, "-secured a position which will engage my skills."

"Good." Sir Nicholas's voice is contemptuous, almost dismissive. "I trust that it does not involve anything that will bring further disgrace to this family." He emphasises the word 'further' with a sneer, then he looks at his son for a few seconds, his expression glowering, before turning his head back to the documents on his desk.

"Um... Indeed not, Sir." Strelley shifts around in his chair, as though he regrets his decision to sit down and give up easy escape. "It seems that our adventures with the earl's son have not gone unnoticed." He carefully injects his words with the enthusiasm so lacking in his father's, trying to seem casual in the face of indifference. Nicholas Strelley has not looked away from his papers while his son spoke, nor does he when he begins to speak again himself.

"I should hope so. The earl sends his only son on some foolish mission to that dark pit of a place with just you and your friends for protection, and he returned alive. I cannot think what possessed him... They would not have let children like you fight the Scots in my day. I would have sent you back home. Bad soldiers cause more harm than no soldiers at all." Nicholas Strelley strikes through a line with his quill-pen and raises his eyes to his son again. "It is well that your noble charge survived your expedition. What is this *position*?" Again, Nicholas Strelley's sneered emphasis reveals his contempt.

"I am working for a tutor, by the name of Grindal. I think I met him at-"

"Don't mention that place, please," Strelley's father interrupts, waving his hand palm-out.

"In any case, I shall be going away. Possibly for a long time." Edward Strelley has found a reserve of firmness. "South. To court." By the pauses he leaves, he offers his father the opportunity to inquire, but it is not taken up.

"Grindal. Never heard of him. Speak to your mother before you go."

"I shall, Sir." Edward Strelley rises, leaving his father seated at the desk. Sir Nicholas watches him go, then dips his quill and begins writing. After a moment, he raises his eyes to the door by which his son left, shakes his head, then returns to his papers. We shall leave the old soldier to his work, and follow the son.

Strelley makes his way through the house, looking with curiosity at its fixtures, its plaster walls and wooden doors, as though he has never truly seen it before. He has passed to another part of his house when he enters a withdrawing room, this time very deliberately knocking to announce his presence. He waits for the door to open, and the maidservant holds it open as he passes through, but she doesn't speak. Two women are sewing. One is young, perhaps only twelve years old, and the other is in her late thirties. Both look up at the sound.

"Edward!" The young girl cries, leaping up and casting her sewing about the room. She rushes over to him and throws her arms around him.

"Elizabeth! Have some decorum, girl," the older lady calls out as Elizabeth Strelley buries her face in her brother's shoulder.

"Sister!" Edward Strelley greets her warmly, returning her embrace. He looks over at his mother. "My Lady," he says, his warmth clear but kept carefully controlled, pushed back beneath an exterior of calm. He goes to her, leading his sister by the hand.

"I am your mother, Edward, not your lady. With your sister, well, you're almost shameless! But with me, your mother, you're cold!" She smiles, belying the implication that there is no love between her and her son. She takes his free hand in hers and traces her thumbs across the back of it. Edward Strelley focuses on her for a moment, holding her gaze as they wordlessly exchange thoughts. Then he looks down at his sister and smiles broadly at her.

"I am to be engaged to help with the lessons of the Lady Elizabeth," he says. Elizabeth Strelley thinks about this for a moment before she realises to whom he refers.

"The princess? How so? That is excellent news, brother," Elizabeth Strelley says, flashing him a proud smile.

"We are not to refer to her as 'princess'," Edward Strelley replies, "but yes, King Henry's daughter. The earl arranged for me to meet her tutor, and he has agreed to employ me. I do not know whether Talbot applied any pressure, but-"

Elizabeth Strelley interrupts him, raising her voice to be louder than her brother's. "Nonsense, Edward, you are the most learned young man in Hallamshire. Even a queen would be glad of your instruction." His sister's compliment makes him blush, but he cannot avoid his mind wandering to contemplation of whether it is true, which shows on his face as his eyebrows rise. The silence grows before he replies.

"I shall be leaving tomorrow morning. I may be away for some while." Strelley's eyes meet his mother's. "Wish me well on my way. I shall remember you in my prayers."

"You haven't prayed for years, Edward," his mother says, laying her hand gently on his shoulder. She tries to force a smile, but she is weeping without sobbing.

"You've only just returned, dear brother," Elizabeth says. "Can you not extend your stay?"

"I cannot. I should not. In time, you will leave Beauchief just as I have, Lizzie." Strelley takes his sister's hand. "Father will find you a suitable husband."

"Perhaps the earl could marry his son to our Elizabeth?" Strelley's mother suggests.

Edward Strelley shakes his head. "I think George Talbot's father is aiming him at royalty." He turns to his sister again. "Let us hope that you find a propitious match."

"I do not want a husband," the young woman says, bristling. Her mother shakes her head, and wraps an arm around the girl's shoulders.

"Forgive me, sister," Edward Strelley says quietly, "I did not mean to offend." He turns to his mother. "I shall remain at Beauchief to dine, but will ride back to the Manor before nightfall." Strelley's mother listens to him, weeping once more, but not speaking. His sister pouts at him, and he responds by putting his hand over his mother's on Elizabeth's shoulder. Let us leave them for now, and return to the Manor.

There, de Winter and Longshawe are once again engaged in fencing practice, watched by George Talbot and William Pike. De Winter's father, the Baron of Sheffield, sits at a table opposite the Earl of Shrewsbury. They are discussing a letter that the earl has received, gesturing, sighing and frowning. Longshawe is demonstrating a thrust that, he says, he has read about in some fencing manual.

"You read about this in a book?" de Winter asks, laughing, stressing the question with a pointed finger. "Are you certain it wasn't Strelley that read it, then told you?" Longshawe looks sheepish. "It was!" De Winter laughs again, his head rocking back on his shoulders. Longshawe ignores him with a sniff, flaring his nostrils. He turns to Talbot, then shows him the steps and the movements leading to the thrust. Talbot tries it himself, his blade cutting through the air with a whipping noise. Undoubtedly he has improved as a fencer, even in the few weeks since they returned from Scotland.

Pike takes up a sword, and attempts to parry the thrust that Talbot is trying to perfect. The blades ring together, Pike turning the final attack aside with a flourish to suggest he was in more danger of being touched than he was. Breathing heavily, he says to Talbot, "you nearly had me then, Sir." Talbot, also recovering his breath, looks out from beneath knitted brows, unconvinced.

"George!" the earl calls out. De Winter and Talbot both respond, turning to him. The earl addresses himself to his son, tapping the paper in one hand with the back of the other. "A letter from the court!"

All of the young men walk over to the table, and Talbot goes around behind his father, reading the letter. De Winter and Pike stand respectfully distant, Pike with his eyes lowered, de Winter straining to see what it is that has sparked this interest. Longshawe rather casually saunters around the table, sheathing his fencing sword and stretching his neck from side-to-side.

"The French!" George Talbot barks. "Haven't we just dealt with them in Scotland?"

De Winter closes one eye in thought, then replies, "their allies, perhaps. And I think it would be more accurate to say that they dealt with us." A ripple of laughter greets the remark. "What does the letter say?" He opens his hand, palm up, conjuring calm indifference.

George Talbot is almost spitting as he speaks. "The French are mustering an invasion force. All England must be ready to serve to send them back home. We are summoned south."

"*You* aren't going anywhere this time," Francis Talbot says, pointing to his son. "Others can handle this. George. William. James." He gestures to each in their turn. " You must be ready to serve if the French invade. I shall organise a party of men from the estates to serve with you." He considers for a moment. "I shall release your lackeys from my service. It is a shame that I did not have more time to perfect their skills." He turns to Longshawe. "Find Calonna. He is usually in a tavern somewhere. You and he shall take a company to Portsmouth. Wriothesley seems to think the French shall invade at the Isle of Wight. Take young Fletcher with you. There isn't time to spare. Go!" The earl waves him away. Longshawe turns to leave, shrugging his shoulders, then heads off into the Manor to find Guy Fletcher.

"George," the earl continues, now addressing de Winter, "I want you to be my eyes and ears in London. Go to Shrewsbury House at Chelsea, and be ready to serve the king in whatever way he wishes. I shall put my best men there at your command."

George Talbot has been watching, his frustration evident in his face. "Father-" He begins, but the earl raises a hand.

"No. I shall not put you at risk again," Shrewsbury says, carefully emphasising each word. George Talbot sighs, turns on his heels and disappears into the Manor in a foul temper, following Longshawe. His father watches him go, shaking his head a little, but he does not rise. The Baron de Winter tries to arrange his face neutrally, neither condemning nor endorsing the young man's anger, avoiding commitment to either view. He waits for the earl's next words.

"That boy does not know his own importance," Shrewsbury mutters.

"Indeed not," the baron confirms. There is a long silence. George de Winter taps Pike on the shoulder and motions him away.

They trudge off, taking a different route into the Manor buildings to the one used by Longshawe and George Talbot.

Once out of earshot of the earl and the baron, Pike rubs his chin, and says, "I don't like the sound of this. I am no court intriguer."

"No," de Winter replies, "perhaps not. I don't think there will be much in the way of open space in this new posting. But it could be worse."

"You mean dodging French bullets in battle?" de Winter nods. Pike sighs, but carries on, "at least then either side can get a good look at the other. Look the enemy in the eye."

"Then blast it out with a half-ounce of lead," de Winter laughs. "I did not think you had any taste for soldiering."

"I don't. But I have even less of a taste for a city and having to spy on folk."

"Have you ever been anywhere bigger than Sheffield?" de Winter asks, a wry smile on his face, knowing the answer before it comes.

"No," Pike says, shaking his head, "and I don't like the idea. All those people in one place. It must stink."

"Yes, Will, it's going to stink." De Winter jostles Pike, who forces a reluctant half-smile.

That evening, Strelley rides back from Beauchief to Sheffield Manor. He is greeted some way outside the gate by Longshawe, who has ridden out to meet him. Longshawe immediately begins to recount the day's events, detailing the earl's letter from Wriothesley, the summons it contained, and finally their various destinations.

"Calonna, Guy and I shall be at Portsmouth. The fleet is there. Everyone seems to think that the French will invade through the Solent or land on the Isle of Wight. I don't know... I think I might prefer to be in London with de Winter and Pike," he says, scratching his beard. "At least you can look the enemy in the eye on the battlefield."

"More fighting? I am glad to be out of the earl's service."

"Don't be so sure. There won't be much use in you teaching the king's daughter when the French invade. Not unless you're teaching her fencing." Longshawe smiles, and Strelley returns it. "Shrewsbury said that the French are more likely to land further west, so we're being sent there to bolster the local forces. If the French have mustered a real invasion army, *every* man will have to serve. Even you."

"My contributions to our last campaign have not put the earl off engaging my services as a soldier a second time, then?"

"We shall see. You seem to be excused for now. Your new commission may just keep you away from service." Longshawe angles his head. "That and your lack of willingness."

"We must hope that it does." Strelley allows himself a wry smile.

"How were they all?" Longshawe asks, changing the subject.

"Mother and sister are well. Sir Nicholas managed to speak a few civil words in my presence. He's not even interested to ask for whom I shall work. And I don't think he said anything at all to me at dinner. Christ, James, how can anyone be so *choleric*?"

"At least your father understands..."

"What? What it is like to go on campaign? He sat behind the walls at Berwick for ten years."

"He was on the front line."

"I'm not sure how much actual fighting he did. About as much as me, probably..." They laugh together. "So... Sir Longshawe..."

"Let's not talk about him now, eh?" Longshawe says, and points to the door. They make their way indoors, where the Earl of Shrewsbury is entertaining a group comprised of Calonna, the Baron de Winter and his son, Pike, and the two lackeys, who are no longer wearing their Talbot family liveries. The earl's son is present, but is sitting in a corner, nursing a tankard, in a deep sulk. As Longshawe leads Strelley into the room, the anecdote finishes, and several of the assembled company laugh heartily. Calonna smiles wryly.

"Good evening, Master Strelley," the earl calls out. "Your man Grindal is in my library, if you need to speak to him." Strelley shakes his head. "Good, join us in a drink then before you all go away again. I shall summon Doctor Grindal forthwith."

"I shouldn't bother," the baron guffaws. "The man will refuse to drink with us."

Strelley glares at him, as does George de Winter, but the looks go ignored, or perhaps unnoticed altogether. The earl strokes his beard, considering. "Perhaps if you didn't bully him so he might not feel so discomfited in our presence. Call in Doctor Grindal." He signals to a manservant, ready at the door, who nods, then turns and leaves.

Strelley and Longshawe seat themselves, as far away from the baron as they can manage. He watches as they make their way, his contempt thinly disguised. Grindal arrives a few minutes later, by which time the conversation has struck up again, this time about the situation at court.

"So Boleyn's girl, Elizabeth, is it right that she is restored to the succession?" the baron asks.

"She has been for twelve months, my dear baron," Shrewsbury replies. "But, as I have told you more than once, Henry does not recognise her as a legitimate daughter. She is not 'princess'. One hopes that she shall never have to be queen, though she shall have her role to play in the future of this country, one way or another. Perhaps her brother will see things differently when he is king. Thank God for him. Anyway, she shall be a better match for some ambitious foreign prince than her sister." This comment reverberates around the room, the silence building for a few moments.

It is George de Winter who replies. "The Lady Mary is a devout, God-fearing Catholic, My Lord."

"Yes, and if you were a duke or a prince, is that what you would want?" The earl laughs. "Or would you perhaps prefer the daughter of the great bewitcher Boleyn?"

"She is a daughter of England, Sir," de Winter says, nettled. "She is not some pawn to be passed back and forth in a game of power."

"I'm sorry to have to tell you that she is exactly what you deny. The king may deny her legitimacy, but she is still second in line to the throne. Her devotion means she may not be much of a match for anyone. Not at her age. Elizabeth at least has her youth on her side." Shrewsbury sits back, awaiting someone to take up the case, eventually settling on Grindal, whose eyes narrow as considers his reply. Heads turn to him, anticipating. Eventually, he speaks.

"The king has made his decisions. The two ladies are his heirs, but not his legitimate daughters. It is only if Edward dies without issue that their role in the succession matters. The king may change all of this in his will in any case. No one can predict... He continues in his break from Rome, but not in his pursuit of reform of the litany. The earl is right, they may not be thought to be such a good match unless they are restored to legitimacy. No one should marry them assuming that he will rise to the succession himself. The difference in their personal qualities is rather marked. Lady Elizabeth is one of the most extraordinary people I have met. Her learning is astounding." He looks at Strelley as he says this. Strelley smiles back at him. The conversation moves on to other matters. Strelley and Grindal both leave early to bed, knowing that they must rise and set out early in the morning. The others, with less pressing on them, or perhaps less observant of their duty, stay up into the night.

The following morning, Strelley and Grindal are up by dawn, readying themselves. Both have considerable packs, bulging with unread books from the earl's library. The rest of the household is slower to rise, despite the bright spring morning. As they prepare to ride south, others start to pass out of the Manor house into the courtyard. De Winter, first out, takes Strelley's hand.

"You've done well for yourself, Edward."

"I have. The earl has, we should say. I hope he finds something equally rewarding for you."

"Perhaps. He seems to know the great and the good. Though they are not necessarily the same," de Winter laughs. Behind him, Pike has made his way to say goodbye as well.

"Keep well, Edward. We shall meet again soon, God willing."

"Let us not leave it in the hands of God. You know where to write to me?"

"We do," de Winter replies. Guy Fletcher stands at the edge of the courtyard, uncertain, waiting for some signal to approach. Pike waves at him to come over.

"Master Strelley," Guy says, a little hesitant, "I thank you for your care for me. I shall be eternally grateful for your coming to Doncaster, and for all that has happened since." Strelley smiles at this obviously rehearsed speech, and presses the young boy to himself in a gesture of genuine affection. A moment passes, and Strelley begins to look about the courtyard. Guy notices, and runs back inside, calling out, "I will rouse him and bring him, Sir!"

Longshawe is already on his way, though, and Guy comes back half a minute later, a few paces in front. "Leaving me again, Ned?" Longshawe calls. "Perhaps you shall see out this engagement."

Strelley flashes an obscene gesture, unnoticed by Grindal, which Longshawe returns. As Longshawe walks over, the smile on his face fades. "I had just got used to having you back. Write to me."

"I shall. And you must write to me. Perhaps you could dictate to Master Fletcher..."

They embrace. The earl and his son, the baron, Calonna, and several retainers of the Shrewsbury household, have gathered to see off Strelley, who is now mounted and ready to leave. He is obviously popular with the servants. His polite deference, even with the footmen and domestics, has not gone unnoticed. He and Grindal ride together, already deep in conversation on some topic of undoubtedly great philosophical import.

It is the next day when another party leaves, this time of de Winter and Pike, Calonna and Longshawe, each pair with their lackey, at the head of perhaps fifty other men from the earl's estates. They are equipped not with books, but with the armour, the guns and the long cavalry swords of the mounted warrior. Their departure, in contrast with Strelley's the day before, is subdued, as they march once again to war. Despite their different destinations, they set off together to ride south, their journeys only set to diverge many miles hence. Both Francis and George Talbot wear their finery, as a token of respect and the honour of those departing. The Baron de Winter sheds a tear as his son leaves him again, although George de Winter does not see. Both Andrew Shepherd and Guy Fletcher have been given their own campaign equipment from the earl's stores, and each looks pleased with himself.

As they ride southwards beyond the earl's lands, a single rider can be seen occasionally on the hilltops to the west, watching their progress, but never approaching closer than a couple of miles away. After an hour, the rider disappears and they do not see him again. They stop at a coaching inn for the night, the men filling the rooms and spilling out into the stables. Fletcher finds Longshawe and mentions the apparition.

"Did you see that someone was watching us?" he asks.

"I did," Longshawe replies. "You don't know who it was...?" Guy does not need to ask out loud. His expression carries his question. "It was Sir Harry Longshawe, Guy. My father. Who does not, I think, approve of my second departure to war."

"He fears losing his son, perhaps?" Guy reflects.

"Perhaps indeed. If I let him make my choices for me, I would never ride, shoot, fence. I'd never leave the comfort of my own bed."

Calonna watches this exchange, interested. "Do not let your

father's attitude make you reckless, James. It would be a shame for you to catch a bullet or a blade now." The Italian smiles through his beard. "Don't die for your defiance."

Longshawe's expression is one of surprised confusion. The Italian's words have caught him out, somehow, exposed a truth that he hadn't faced before.

"Look at you!" Calonna says, laughing. "Had you never considered that the life you have chosen is your answer to your father's..." he considers the right words, "...conservative nature?"

"Thank you for your counsel, Lorenzo," Longshawe says, with hint of a frown. "I shall mark it well."

11: The Lady Elizabeth and the good man Gilbert

A month later, and Calonna and Longshawe have arrived at Portsmouth with their band of men, ready to cross the Solent to the Isle of Wight if the spies are right and that is where the invasion will begin. They are billeted on a wealthy merchant in the centre of Portsmouth, and are looked after well by the merchant's wife, who seems to show a particular interest in the exotic, weathered Calonna. The merchant himself is a busy, fastidious man who leaves the house at a crushingly early hour each morning to make the best of the day's trade. It is now mid-morning, and the unhurried soldiers, self-consciously wearing a few parts of their battle-gear to accentuate the image, lounge in the buttery.

Longshawe has received a letter, handed to him by a messenger a moment ago. He breaks the seal without looking at it, and begins to read, as shall we.

My dearest friend Longshawe,

It is with the greatest pleasure that I take this opportunity to write to you of my first fortnight here in Lady Elizabeth's household, and to inform you of my good fortune in finding myself in her service. Now, rather than curse Him, I rather thank God that he sent me the opportunity to serve in the North, as it led directly to my engagement with Grindal and the lady herself. Grindal is the perfect master, and she is the perfect mistress. Despite her youth, she is already greatly learned, as we had heard, and yet she retains a modesty and amiability that belies her station. She is certainly a fine daughter of the noble house of Tudor.

She is a worthy and pleasant student, and has kind words for all those who help her and serve her. She acknowledges me in her lessons, and has even addressed a comment of praise on my handwriting when I have acted as her amanuensis, though I think this was rehearsed. My writing has never been praiseworthy. Indeed, I wonder that any person of royal blood should deign to speak to me, for whatever reason. It seems that as she warms to Grindal, she is more inclined to speak openly with me as well. Grindal himself has shown some inclination to consult me on points of language, and I begin to think that he may even consider me a worthy equal on some of the ancient tongues. The lady excels in French and Latin, has some Italian and Spanish, and is making progress, albeit slowly, on her Greek. Grindal is widely read in these languages, and I find myself learning from him as well. I have even had the pleasure, on a few occasions, of correcting his gloss.

It seems, from what I gather from the other members of the household, that Grindal's appointment was in response to some inability, real or perceived, I do not know, of her governess, a rather delightful woman by the name of Campernon, to teach her these languages. This governess, whom they call Kat, had been responsible for the education of the lady until recently and I cannot help but feel she resents our presence, though she has shown me no ill will personally. Grindal does his best to be civil to her, but I suspect he thinks her to be obsessed with trifles and of no further use to the lady. He does not trouble himself to speak much with her. I do not agree with him in his appraisal of her value which has led to him ignoring her. This governess seems to have encouraged Mistress Elizabeth's affable humour. She has spoken to me directly and always takes time for pleasantries, though she is given to gossip and even ribald talk. I like her, and I shall do what I can to reach accommodation with her.

There are, it seems, many others about court who would have Lady Elizabeth behave as the daughter of a Tudor and a Boleyn, high, mighty and superior. But Elizabeth does not forget that she is herself human, nor does she give herself the airs and graces that even the minor nobles seem to hold so important. Though it is not, of course, for me to decide the education of an heir to the throne, it seems that Campernon has played a good part, and has a part to play yet in the development of this girl into a woman. Elizabeth would make a fine queen at some powerful European court, but it is her ability to understand the people and make herself one among them that will make her strong.

I have not yet encountered the king himself, although the members of the household think we may be summoned to court at some point. From what I hear, his wound troubles him, and there is much manoeuvring at court to find favour with Edward. Whilst it is supposed to be treason to foretell his death (a matter which you and I have considered at some length), it does not seem to warrant the same charge to conduct oneself as though the king might die at any moment. Grindal talks of men trying to acquire the king's favour, such that they might be named Protector of the Realm when he is no more. It must be hoped that Henry finds for that role a strong and good man, willing to relinquish power when the time comes, though there must be few enough of those.

Prince Edward, so the rumour says, has been educated by some of the more committed Protestants, which sounds like the doings of the queen, though the men whom the king trusts are not of that party. Catherine is, it seems, committed to her evangelism, though she steers a careful course with the king. Now that he is readying himself to meet God, he does not seem quite so sure that he wishes to continue these departures from the old ways. The nation will not be ruled, though, by the boy prince for many years, so there is yet time for the counter-reformers to make their mark. Prince Edward may be influenced by their conservatism, although Grindal says he is already beginning to make up his own mind. He is very much his father's son. One hopes that, whatever the provision for the succession, it does not lead to civil war.

The Lady Mary occasionally visits, and though I do not find her, even in her young adulthood, to be the equal of her sister in learning, she has the sort of fervour that was supposedly so lacking in the religious houses of this country. She tries to persuade Elizabeth to Catholicism, though I wonder if My Lady is aloof to such doctrinal concerns. I have already heard her telling Grindal that "There is but one God, Master Grindal, and how a man comes to him is between God and that man alone. I shall stand before Him at the judgement, as shall you, and He will not ask of us 'Did you believe that the wine really was the blood of Christ?' God has no need to ask us these questions. He sees what is in our hearts, and no amount of good done will disguise this. I will not believe he is fooled by those who do good just to enter the Kingdom of Heaven." I suppose that aligns her with the Reformers, but she still attends the Mass. Mary spent hours last time repeating the argument that God can only judge what a person does, but neither shifted an iota in their beliefs. I shall not bore you further with details of these subtle arguments, though. It will be enough to say that you would not be interested in most of what passes for lessons here.

I trust that you keep yourself well. Remember me to Lorenzo, and to Guy. I wish you all fortune and safety, whether you find your war or not. I shall be visiting Chelsea in a few days, to stay with de Winter and Pike. I will remind George to write to you.

Yours

Strelley

Longshawe folds the letter and puts it away. Calonna asks if the news was good news.

"Edward has fallen on his feet, it seems. He has done well to find himself in the service of royalty."

"You are jealous?" Calonna asks, the bluntness only partly because of his unusual accent.

"In a way. Edward's *position* is not what I want. It's his closeness to the king, and the future king as well... I wish that I had his luck. It's like you said, I don't want to take a ball in the guts and die on some God-forsaken field on Wight. I don't relish killing, but perhaps soldiering is what will put me in front of King Henry. It's what I'm good at... I don't have Edward's talent for knowing things."

"Few do, James." Calonna pronounces Longshawe's name with two distinct syllables. "Eduardo has a prodigious mind. You have the strength of your body."

"But he can exercise his mind in front of a roaring fire, in the home of one of the royal family. I must resign myself to showing what I'm worth by spilling blood in battle. It had best not be my own blood!"

Calonna laughs. "You have passed the hardest test already. You have seen one battle. The rest will be much the same. But you must learn *when* to fight!"

"When the king is watching..." Longshawe smiles.

"And when to preserve yourself. I have not survived thirty battles without learning when the fight is done. Watch me, and I shall teach you. You must not let your fire lead you to your doom."

Longshawe listens, reminded by the mention of his rashness of their conversation a month ago. "I should like to see my father again. We, um... We did not part on friendly terms."

"And yet he came to watch you march south?"

"He did. He would have preferred me to remain at Longshawe Hall, take a wife and live like he has. But I can't become him. The bucolic life does not suit me."

"Bucolic? You have been studying. Why then did he ride out to see you?"

"I don't know. Perhaps he thought he might not see me again."

"Then you must make sure he does. Come. We must join our company for our drills." They rise together, thanking the merchant's household servants for their breakfast as they leave. Longshawe smiles at the lady of the house. Calonna elbows him through the threshold, then turns for a long look of his own.

Some eighty miles north and east, Strelley prepares for a morning's lesson, copying and construing a passage from Vergil. He hands the manuscripts to Grindal, who checks it over briefly.

"It seems accurate, Edward. I would not wish to chastise the lady, then find it was your mistake, not hers."

"Indeed not, Sir. I have checked the copy of the text, and the translation, twice. I am rather pleased with it."

"You must try to make your handwriting more regular. Perhaps Elizabeth could teach you to form your letters more carefully."

Strelley smiles. "That passage took me half an hour, Sir. In your hand, or My Lady's, it would be a day's work."

"Do not be too proud of your quickness of hand. Some things are worth taking the time over. Thank you. In any case, here is a list of items that you are to pick up from Gilbert." He hands Strelley a scrap of paper, which Strelley reads before folding up and putting in a pocket of his doublet.

"Tell me again where I will find him."

"Gilbert's warehouse is by the river, three streets along from St Paul's. It is easy to find, since outside it has the word 'Gilbert' painted in green letters three feet high! Be on your way, or else I shall not let you go to see your friends at Chelsea on Thursday."

"I shall return this afternoon."

Grindal waves Strelley away, and continues reading the translation alongside the copy of the passage in Latin. A moment or two passes before Strelley turns and leaves the room, closing the door behind him. Grindal's face screws up, before breaking into a smile. He lets out a gasp of satisfaction. Not only is the translation accurate, it expresses well the idea and sense of the original, and clarifies the difficult sentences.

Strelley walks west from Greenwich to London Bridge, crossing and continuing west towards St Paul's, which is at this time not how it will eventually become. Rather than Wren's domed Baroque, it is the Norman Gothic spired Cathedral which towers nearly five hundred feet above the surrounding buildings. Strelley's journey takes him perhaps an hour and a half, and at its end he stands in front of a large warehouse building with its own wharf. A small seagoing vessel is docked, and a team of stevedores is unloading it. Strelley looks around, trying to decide whether a small door under the painted letters Grindal described to him is where he should enter the building. He approaches the door, which opens before he reaches it, emitting a short, cloaked figure who scurries away clutching a package, about the size of a cat, wrapped in dark cloth. Despite the already-strong smell of the city, Strelley's nose wrinkles noticeably as this stranger passes. A voice issues from inside the door.

"Come in, will you? We might attract the wrong sort of attention with you outside the door." Strelley looks through the open door, to see a man of about thirty seated behind an elaborately carved wooden desk. He has a pointed beard that accentuates his chin, and is dressed in stylish black and grey. He holds in his hand something brown, with a glowing orange tip. "Well, come on then!" he says, waving his other hand.

Strelley enters, looking about him as he does so. The man points him to a wooden chair placed opposite the desk, facing his own. "Be seated, and let's discuss your requirements. I'm Gilbert, by the way. Tom to my friends. So you can call me Gilbert, for now." Strelley's eyes narrow, but a hint of a smile is visible on his face.

"Not my requirements, Sir, but Master Grindal's."

"Ah!" Gilbert exclaims. "You're Grindal's new boy. I understand, now. We don't get many dressed in such a... shall we say, 'provincial' manner. Not among our regular customers, in any case. Do you have any proof of your association?"

"I don't understand."

"I'll kill Grindal next time I see him," Gilbert mutters. Aloud, he addresses Strelley. "I need some sort of evidence of your connection, you see, as I need to know that I'm giving Grindal's merchandise to the right person. There are some things that we need to keep among friends."

"I see," Strelley confirms, and hands the list over to Gilbert, who takes it and reads.

"It's a good job you've got this written down, lad, because you wouldn't get the half of this off us on your first visit otherwise." He lets out a grunt of something like laughter. "Is this for that royal bastard that he supposedly educates? Half of these books are heretical, and the half that aren't used to be." Strelley says nothing as Gilbert puts several books and a couple of bags and parcels on to the desk. "Well, now, I don't have this-" he points to the list "or this. He'll have to wait for those." Gilbert puts the brown object, like a cylinder with a bulging middle, to his lips, closes them and seems to suck. The tip glows more brightly, and he exhales a stream of grey-white smoke. Strelley, caught unawares, coughs vigorously.

"Tobacco. From the New World," Gilbert says. "It'll never catch on, though. It's not as good as that stuff Grindal has." He points to a wrapped package on the desk. "In fact, it's not much good at all," he says, throwing his cigar onto the stone floor and grinding it with his foot. "Remind him that if he gets caught with that, it's nothing to do with me. And you might want to make sure you don't get searched by any guards on your way back into the palace."

Gilbert eyes Strelley warily, searching for some evidence of a future betrayal. "You don't say much," he notes, although more to himself than to Strelley. Strelley nods slowly but does not reply, considering whether Gilbert is in earnest or merely bantering him. "You're not simple, are you?" Gilbert asks, brows furrowed. Strelley inhales sharply, but makes no response. Gilbert angles his head. "No? Do you understand this: where's my money?"

Strelley takes a purse from inside his coat. "Can I have that list back?" he asks. Gilbert pushes it across the desk to him with a broad smile, showing teeth stained brown from his recent drinking of tobacco smoke. Strelley spends a moment thinking, before removing a handful of coins from the purse and putting them on the desk. Gilbert looks at them.

"Where's the rest?" he says.

"That's for what you've given me. I'll pay for the other books when I get them. The expensive ones. That you haven't got."

Gilbert's face shows the slightest sign of frustration, before relaxing into a grin. "Hmm. You know your stuff. I could use someone with your skill at reckoning. I'd pay better than Grindal, let me assure you."

"I'm sure you could. I shall take my leave of you now." Gilbert remains seated as Strelley gathers the various items and puts them into a satchel, before turning and leaving the warehouse. As he does so, Gilbert watches him. "Strange lad," he says to himself, before returning to his accounts book.

Two hours later, Strelley returns to Greenwich, entering the palace through a postern gate with barely a challenge from the armed guard at the door. He walks through corridors until he finds the room where Grindal is tutoring Lady Elizabeth. He knocks, and hears the instruction to enter.

"Where should I leave your... purchases, Sir?" he asks, whilst making a deep bow of obeisance to the Lady Elizabeth, who lifts a hand to acknowledge him, before returning to her study. Strelley is familiar, but not of any great interest, to her.

"Give them here," Grindal replies, and takes the satchel Strelley hands to him. "Thank you for that, Edward." He checks the contents of the bag.

"Gilbert told me he did not have a couple of the books you asked for, but will soon." Elizabeth looks up at this.

"Never mind," Gilbert replies. "We shall get on to them when the time is right," he says, to the young girl. Then he turns to Strelley to say, "we found a few barbarisms and at least one solecism in your translation, but it was a good effort." Strelley considers replying aloud, but decides against it. Instead, he raises his eyebrows at Grindal, but the teacher does not seem to notice.

Later that day, when Lady Elizabeth is no longer with him, Strelley approaches Grindal. "Barbarisms and solecisms?" he asks, without preamble.

"Well, the girl didn't like your translation in a couple of places."

"That doesn't make it wrong."

"Nor, for that matter, did I. But you did well not to point that out in the lady's hearing. She is not yet quite able to accept her own fallibility. Though she does learn quickly."

"You must point out where she errs," Strelley says, surprised.

"I do. And I am pointing out where you err as well."

Strelley sniffs at Grindal's admonishment. "I shall be glad to gloss my next translation for you."

"You do not need to. No one is right all the time. Do not dwell on it." Grindal puts a paternal hand on his shoulder, then shuffles off to some other task.

"I am not dwelling on my errors," Strelley says to himself after Grindal has moved out of hearing, "but yours." He takes some of Elizabeth's papers, and underlines a few of the words, scratching tiny notes between her beautiful lines.

12: Invasion!

"Arise. We are summoned." Calonna's voice sounds clear, alert. "The French are in the Channel, and the Isle needs its defenders." Longshawe struggles to rise from his comfortable-looking bed. It is now past midsummer, and the morning is bright and warm despite the early hour.

"How many?" Longshawe asks, stretching himself and casting about for clothes.

"Over two hundred ships." The Italian is agitated by Longshawe's dim morning wits, fiddling with his overcoat and gloves. "Perhaps twenty or thirty thousand men. A reasonable challenge for the militia on Wight."

"They won't all land there, will they?"

"No. But a beach-head there will be disastrous for England. Get up, James, or we shall miss the boats." Longshawe pulls on an undershirt and puts his breeches on.

"And are we two the men to turn them back?" Longshawe asks, stung.

Calonna turns and walks out of the room. In the time it takes Longshawe to dress and gather his small pack of things, Calonna visits the lady of the house. A few minutes later, he leaves the room again, a smile on his face. Longshawe joins Calonna, who is sitting with his booted feet up on a table, some fifteen minutes afterwards. Calonna has already fetched Guy Fletcher, who has been billeted elsewhere. He, like the Italian, has been ready for some time, their discipline in sharp contrast to Longshawe's lethargy. The bulk of their baggage and equipment is in three packs, a large one for the young boy to carry, two smaller for the men destined to do the fighting.

"However good you are at fighting, James, you are no soldier yet. If we miss these boats across the Solent you will be flogged. Or shot." Calonna clicks his fingers and rises. "Onwards. Your sword can do no good if we are not there on the battlefield."

They leave the house, and pass through Portsmouth to the docks, where a large number of small craft have been requisitioned to pass soldiers across the water. Despite being late, the queues of armed men awaiting their passage are still long. Calonna spots a group of the men that the earl sent with them from Hallamshire, and leads Longshawe and Fletcher over to join them. One or two of them offer Longshawe a half-hearted salute, perhaps piqued that their supposed captain is the tardiest of all. They only wait a short while, as a larger merchant ship is brought into the dock, with room for perhaps a hundred and fifty men, nearly as many as are waiting there. As they sail out, they pass some huge warships, including the pride of the king's navy, the *Mary Rose*. She is a huge 700-ton carrack, overbuilt to allow an extra row of guns on each side, with a towering mainmast well over a hundred feet tall. The men point at her as they pass, murmuring in their admiration for this impressive instrument of war.

Two hours later, Longshawe leads a company of about thirty men south out of the village of Ryde. The Isle of Wight is considerably fortified, with tall watch-towers erected at strategic points along the coast, in sight of each other to allow rapid communication. Armed men appear all about, standing at their stations or practising their fighting technique, and there is an occasional piece of cannon at the bigger towers. Fishing boats are at their moorings, rather than out in the Channel. As they march, Calonna talks to Longshawe.

"There are no more than two thousand fighting men on this island," he says. "We can only hope that the French don't land a big force or we shall be overwhelmed. There isn't much cannon, and it is spread out across the island. If they are determined and clever, they will have landed and razed the island before we can gather. We must pray for good fortune."

Longshawe's face shows his concern. "What else can we do?"

"Hope that these watch-towers do their job. If the system of getting messages across the island is good, the entire body of men could be brought to any place within the day. It may be fast enough, it may not. I'm not sure about the guns, though. They are slower, and I haven't seen much ammunition. An oversight on the part of the garrison commander, I suspect." He chews on a grass stalk, contemplative, eyes narrow against the bright sun. "We must hope the ships do their job."

That evening, the band of thirty make a camp outside a small village called Sandown. The summer sun and long daylight succeed in conspiring to make the men almost happy, although their ration of beer, bought by Longshawe with the earl's money from the village, may also have contributed. The prospect of a hugely superior French force landing doesn't seem to dampen their spirits especially.

Longshawe goes over to Guy Fletcher, who is writing. Guy notices Longshawe is reading his words, and stops.

"Who are you writing to?"

"I keep a journal of our campaign. Perhaps one day people will read it, as they do Caesar's commentaries. I have written a letter to Master Edward as well. Would you like to read it?"

"No. Once this battle is done, perhaps I shall add my small contribution to it."

Calonna notices them talking and joins them. He scratches his arm with his hand as he speaks.

"Gentlemen!" he greets them enthusiastically, "I have been talking to the locals. They say that they have seen sails in the distance out to the east. They couldn't see whether the ships flew any flag. Perhaps the king's navy is even now putting the French to the sword."

"Have you ever fought at sea, Lorenzo?" Fletcher asks him.

"Once or twice. I avoid it if I can. It is just one more thing that can take you in battle. There are enough dangers without drowning added to them."

"We shall be well-enough occupied with trying to avoid thirty thousand French bullets soon enough," Longshawe frowns. There is a moment of silence. Guy Fletcher looks from Longshawe to Calonna then back again before breaking it.

"I have prepared your powder and shot, Sirs. Your swords are oiled, and I have checked the strapping on your armour. It shall not be for want of preparation if anything goes ill." Fletcher speaks with pride, puffing his small chest out. "I should like to to be near you when the battle takes place."

"I shall make sure of it, Guy," Longshawe says, putting his hand on Fletcher's shoulder. "I did not bring you here to let you die alone."

Calonna watches them. "Make sure you stay close to me, Guido. Your guardian has not yet learned all the tricks for surviving battles." He laughs, cuffing Longshawe on the upper arm. Longshawe scowls at him, but after a moment the tension breaks and he too laughs.

The three continue drinking and talking for several hours, until after dark has fallen. Several times, Calonna suggests that Longshawe go to sleep, if he finds it so difficult to rise with the sun. It is only when the Italian pointedly declares that he himself is turning in for the night that the others return to their tents and sleep.

In the morning the continue their march south, past Shanklin to the tiny village of Ventnor. No sails are visible, but a report has reached the band of men already stationed at Ventnor that the full might of the royal navy, some eighty or so ships, has passed and is sailing east to engage the massive French force. The captain there, a rotund, red-faced fellow who goes by the name of Fyssher, tells them that the bulk of the men, under the command of Worsley and Bellingham, are billeted in the more considerable town of Cowes, off in the north.

"That's ridiculous!" Calonna exclaims, when told. "It'll take them at least a day's march to reach here."

"Indeed, but there isn't enough for them to eat here. They can't stay here permanently, like," Fyssher replies. "Sir Worsley does have the men well-organised, though. And we can summon them by lighting the beacons."

"I wish I had your confidence, Captain Fyssher," Longshawe grunts. "How many men do we have here?"

"With yours, perhaps a hundred," Fyssher answers slowly, as if counting the soldiers in his head.

"Perhaps?" Calonna exclaims in a high-pitched voice. He shakes his head, and climbs up to a high point, looking out into the Channel.

"You must excuse Signore Calonna," Longshawe says quietly. "He doesn't tolerate disorganisation on the part of others."

"Indeed not. We are not disorganised, though, Master Longshawe. Should the enemy arrive you will witness the full power of this island's defences."

"I hope so. Come, Guy." He follows Calonna up the hillock, and joins him in looking out east.

Calonna points to a distant blur on the horizon. "We had better hope that your king's navy has the beating of the French. If not, they will be on us in less than a day, if this wind holds."

The wind does not hold, but nevertheless, by mid-morning a small expeditionary force of four French ships lands just north of Ventnor. The beacons have been lit overnight, although the sizeable force promised by Fyssher has not yet arrived, other militia stationed on the coast have come, bolstering the English force to around three hundred. Fyssher starts issuing orders, but it is soon clear he has little authority amongst the men. For a minute or two, Calonna and

Longshawe stand watching, waiting, for some semblance of purpose and organisation to emerge, but it does not. Longshawe's face shows his dismay. Calonna, calm but alert, taps Longshawe on the elbow. "You could lead them," he says, quietly.

"Why not you?" Longshawe whispers back.

"You've already got Talbot's men at your back. Speak out and lead *them*. The others will follow. I will assist you." Calonna nods as he finishes talking.

"Listen!" Longshawe shouts, surprised by the almost-immediate silence among the men. "We must be ready to face these French, or we shall all face God sooner than we would wish. Follow me!" His men form up instantly, and the others soon follow, the discipline shown by Shrewsbury's band proving infectious as Calonna predicted.

Longshawe orders the militia as best he can, forming groups armed with guns interspersed between those equipped for hand-to-hand fighting with pikes on Calonna's advice. They march up the hill out of Ventnor, trying to take the high ground before the French can get there. After reaching the crest and forming up, they watch as the French disembark. There is a report from the guns of one of the French vessels, which draws the attention of all. A held-breath moment passes, but the ball lands several hundred yards short of the English position, kicking up a storm of earth. Longshawe calls out to the men to be steady.

The French force of perhaps five hundred forms up and begins the march up the hill. Confident in their superior numbers, despite the ship's guns being out of range, they come up quickly, calling out challenges and insults to the English as they advance. Some of the English soldiers return the jeers, and one or two who know a line or two of French give back some ribaldry of their own. Longshawe sends Fyssher away to the rear of the line, and puts himself with Calonna in the front line of pikemen, with Guy Fletcher behind and between. They ready their guns, each to fire once before joining the combat.

The French fire first, and one or two balls hit home, felling Englishmen in the front ranks. Longshawe waits, his gaze fixed on the French advance. Moments pass. Calonna turns to him, eyes wide.

"Fire!" Longshawe shouts, and fires his own weapon. The English volley is much more effective, as many as fifty of the French soldiers are struck. "With me!" he calls. The English soldiers, well-drilled despite their poor local commander, advance in well-formed rank and file. Calonna is smiling as they engage, relishing the clash of weapons and the thump of body against body.

The French, less disciplined, are caught on English billhooks without disrupting their enemies' formation. The English gunners join the melee, and for a few minutes the combat hangs in the balance. Fyssher joins the combat on the English left flank, and is rapidly lost amid the press. The French ships' guns fire again, the balls still falling far too short to change the battle.

Calonna and Longshawe, strong and well-armed, cut a swathe through the French middle. They fight in a gap of their own creation amongst the English pikes, protected by the vicious billhooks of the soldiers to their left and right several feet behind, fending off any attempt to get around their flanks.

Ten minutes have passed since the fight was joined. The French, exhausted by their uphill assault, fall back, taunted by the English with obscene gestures and shouts of victory. Their commander runs up and down the line, rallying them, and eventually they form up for another attack. This time they do not use their guns, preferring to advance as quickly as possible. Despite their initial success, the English have suffered perhaps eighty casualties, to the French hundred and twenty. The French still have numbers on their side and their leader intends to make his advantage pay.

Longshawe barks out orders. "Hold your lines! Gunners! On my command!" Again, he waits, this time until the French are practically upon the points of the English pikes. "Fire!" he shouts. The French lines are torn to pieces by the close-range volley. "Send them to hell!" The English march forward, together, beating off the second wave.

The remnants of the French army turn and run for their boats. The English have sustained many casualties, at least a hundred, among them Fyssher, whose body has taken enough bullets and blades to kill him ten times. Some of the men stand over him, lamenting his passing. Their commander had not been effective, but he had at least been friendly. There are maybe two hundred Frenchmen left behind on the battlefield.

Longshawe sits on a rock as the men take their booty. Calonna walks over to him. "A natural commander, it seems... I thought we were beaten for a moment."

"We must thank God. There were more French than English alive when they broke."

"True, but they did not have your courage. They are on foreign soil. Your men are defending their homes." He gives Longshawe a half-smile. "Look. Out in the sea, towards the north-east." Calonna points to the ships that must have left the harbour at Portsmouth. "The rest of the ships have sailed. The French must be near at hand."

Both men look out into the sea, but they cannot see the French navy. From a little way off, the small figure of Guy Fletcher trots over and stands with them, shielding his eyes as he tries to follow their gaze.

Two days later, Longshawe's men remain stationed at Ventnor, but he, Calonna and Guy Fletcher have returned north to Cowes. Sir Richard Worsley receives him personally, handing him a letter that, Worsley says, shall get him an introduction to the king for his valour. Rumour has spread fast about an English victory against a superior French force, and for a day Longshawe revels in the glory of his achievement, lauded by his superiors and feted by the soldiers for his bravery and skill in turning back the French.

Now, though, a new threat looms. The French navy has entered the Solent, and the English are about to give battle. Clear in the waters east of Cowes, the English navy has sailed from Portsmouth and is firing on the French at long range. No significant damage is done by the exchange, although one of the French ships, a large galley with a distinctive flag flying, appears to be stricken. During the firing, the flag is lowered and appears some minutes later on another vessel.

Calonna points this out to Longshawe. "That is the Admiral D'Annebault's flag. I met him once, in Marseille. A good man, good soldier. His luck with his ship does not appear to have held, though."

"Luck must play a big part in battle," Longshawe says, more to himself than to Calonna.

"One can persuade luck to be on your side, with the right preparation. That ship has not been hit by cannon-fire. It must have been holed sailing from Havre." Calonna points. The French ship appears to be righted, but has fallen back to the rear of the line.

A couple of hours pass as the ships fail to close in the low wind. Eventually, the English navy retreats out of range back towards Portsmouth to anchor overnight. The French do not pursue, but remain in the open waters north of Cowes. One or two shots are loosed in the direction of the town's docks in the evening, testing the range, but they fall well short.

The following morning is calmer still, and the English navy, watched again by Calonna and Longshawe amongst others from the higher ground behind Cowes, struggles to make its way back out to engage the French. As they close, the French galleys start to manoeuvre, putting the English fleet in danger of taking fire without being able to return it. The great new warships built by Henry come to the front of the line, their sluggish progress cheered on by the English spectators ashore. They make it through and position themselves broadside to the French fleet. The cannon-fire begins again, the crack and fizz of the balls dulled by the distance.

It is late afternoon, and although the engagement is indecisive the French have the upper hand. It is only when a breeze strikes up as the air cools that the English navy finds itself able to bring its full weight to bear. Several ships throw up sail, and suddenly the battle turns. French ships scatter, taking heavy fire from the long English guns. Amid this renewed cannonade, one of the English vessels, which the watchers recognise as the *Mary Rose*, wheels about to bring the broadside to bear. As it does so, it tilts wildly in the wind, then, masts and rigging shrieking from the strain. A great shout goes up as scores of men throw themselves clear of the doomed vessel. Once the gunwale is below the waterline, she goes down rapidly, the heavy broadside guns clattering against each other and the sailors desperate to get away. Beyond the damage caused by the loose cannons, she does not appear significantly damaged as she sinks.

Calonna points. "Another ship lost to bad sailing," he says, wryly. Despite this loss, as the evening gets cooler and darker, it is clear that the French have been turned back. They begin to retreat as the light fades, a score of their ships foundering. The English leave behind perhaps ten, including the carrack sunk without apparently taking a hit. The Battle of the Solent is over, for now, the cries of victory from the English sailors mingling with celebratory cannon fire audible over some distance.

13: Henry VIII and his Court

Edward Strelley rides west from Greenwich Palace, staying south of the river, avoiding the City of London. He crosses the Thames at Westminster, riding past the old palace and out into the fields on his way to Chelsea. He dismounts in front of a large brick house laid out as three sides of a quadrangle, with the familiar design of a lion rampant over the oak door. The door opens before he gets to it, and he is ushered into the house by a liveried retainer as another whisks away his mount around the house and into the considerable stables.

"Master Strelley?" the servant asks. Strelley nods. "I will show you through. Masters de Winter and Pike await you in the earl's library."

"Another library?" Strelley says to himself. "Thank you. Has my horse-"

"Your mount will be in the stables to the rear of the house when you need it again." The servant leads Strelley down a hallway, wood-panelled throughout with intricately carved scenes and figures, then through a heavy studded oak door. Beyond, de Winter and Pike are sitting on comfortable-looking, fabric-upholstered chairs, finely fashioned from more dark oak. De Winter and Pike rise to greet the new arrival.

"Edward!" de Winter greets him warmly, taking his hand and shaking it firmly. "It is good to see you again. We have many questions for you," he says, without further preamble.

"I'm sure you do, George," Strelley replies, eyebrows raised. He turns to Pike. "Will. I trust you are well?" Pike nods. He is dressed more finely than he has been before, and there is a hint of agitation about him, as though the stiff collar and tight hose discomfit him. Strelley sits in a third chair, his back to a wall of ancient-looking volumes entitled *A History of the English People*.

"How goes it with the Lady Elizabeth?" Pike asks.

"Since I saw you last – what? Two months ago? - the lady has grown less reticent around us. She has begun to talk to Grindal not just about her lessons, but also seeks his thoughts on matters of state. She knows a great deal about the king's affairs, in particular those concerning the government of the country. It is quite interesting to hear her take on how we should be governed. She holds forth without compunction."

"Does she?" de Winter asks, then he carries on without waiting for further comment. "Good. That shall make our task easier, at least."

"What do you mean?" Strelley returns. De Winter leans against the back of the chair, considering how to reply. Pike speaks first.

"The Earl of Shrewsbury has charged us with reporting to him on the current affairs of the court, including the king's own."

De Winter carries on for him. "And since we have little access to the court out here in the middle of nowhere, we trust that you can help us with that."

"I can, but I'd like to know what the earl intends to do with the information." Strelley frowns slightly in thought. "He's not ambitious, is he?"

"It would seem not," de Winter says, "though he intends for his son to take a more active part at court than perhaps he himself has done. I wonder if he does not have it in mind for the boy to marry-" He stops himself abruptly, and ponders. After a quarter-minute has passed, a long silence uninterrupted by Pike or Strelley, he carries on. "He might have ambition for the boy to marry your charge, although that strikes me as unlikely to happen." He points at Strelley.

"Indeed it is," Strelley laughs. "The girl would not much like George Talbot."

"Why not?" Pike asks. "How can you be sure he is not suited to her tastes?"

Strelley closes one eye for a moment, before answering, "I don't think she will be impressed by someone as dedicated to the hunt, and to all those *manly* occupations so favoured by the earl's son. She would find him... Coarse, I think."

"Coarse?" de Winter exclaims. "He is, from what I hear, rather akin to her beloved father, His Majesty the king. Though one might forgive her for not wishing to marry a man like her father..." He smiles, his lips twisting and curling.

"She is of a serious cast of mind, not like Talbot. But she's a great prize, since she has been returned to the succession. If the king is going to marry her off, it will be to some foreign prince, who can stave off invasion by the French, or the Spanish. We can discount the possibility of her union with the House of Shrewsbury, for now at least."

"The earl will be disappointed with this analysis, but he will not be surprised." De Winter twirls his moustache. "It can't be any news to him. But that is not all the information we seek. The king seems to be growing aware that he will not survive long enough for the prince to attain his majority."

"That I cannot say for certain. I don't see him often, and have not yet had the pleasure of addressing His Majesty. I *can* tell you a little that the earl may wish to know. The Lady Elizabeth has asked Grindal's counsel on something germane, and I heard from both a few things that shall be of interest."

"Though you cannot yourself confirm the truth of what you say?" De Winter leans forward eagerly, hands clasped and fingers intertwined.

"It's as I have said. You must explain that what I have told you is rumour, the intercourse of a girl and her tutor. I am no spy, George."

"Nevertheless, we shall hear your story." De Winter relaxes again, sitting back and putting his hands behind his neck.

"It seems that the boy prince is educated by a man called Cheke, a reformist. It isn't clear to me whether he was chosen specifically by the queen, but he certainly holds her favour. This man teaches the boy Latin and Greek, as well as other of the humanist subjects. Prince Edward is no papist, and it seems the rest of his doctrine is anti-Catholic, although neither he nor his educators embrace the reformed faith publicly."

"You think they practise it in private?"

"I have only the rumour I report to you, but it seems to be true. Queen Catherine is without doubt a reformer, though whether she believes fully the doctrines of Luther and Calvin or not is not clear. There are times when she and the king dispute over doctrine. Though the king is not always prepared to listen to her extol the virtues of Luther or whoever she is espousing. I have heard it said that she has angered him on occasion."

"So the king does not know that his only son is being educated thus?" de Winter asks.

"Indeed not. Much of what passes in the court goes without him noticing. The king is frightened of dying, and I think it occupies his thoughts. So he finds comfort in trying to appease God by returning to the old ways. I wonder what influence his elder daughter exercises in that regard. She is... *committed*. In any case, it seems that queen and prince lean towards further reform, even if the king does not."

"Who are the other men about the prince?" de Winter touches

the tips of his fingers together, once again alert.

"I don't think there are any, beyond his teachers. The king keeps about himself a number of counsellors, though each I think is careful not to find himself sharing in Cromwell's fate. None is willing to try to guide the king. "

"So each awaits the king's pronouncement and essays to be the first to agree," de Winter says, half statement and half question.

"That is true. They pretend that they were of the king's mind all along, so no one will venture an opinion before the king has spoken. Not one of them wishes to contradict Henry regardless of what it is he says."

"Does the king think he will die soon?" Pike's question is quiet, almost reverential.

"It is forbidden to speak of it. His leg troubles him still, and he is grown fat as he barely rides, and never walks. But he assembles men around him, and it seems that he is gathering some sort of council for his son's minority. Even King Henry can't cheat death, so he moves to secure the future."

"But what future? Who are these men he gathers round him?" De Winter is eager again, as though this question is the nub of the matter.

"The earl's friend Wriothesley is among them. How is it that he does not hear from him?"

"Wriothesley is his own man, with his own ambitions," de Winter replies.

"In any case, it is he, Norfolk, even Gardiner. The king seems likely to appoint these as a regency council."

"Not just one man but many?" Pike asks. Strelley nods. Pike continues the thought, "he educates his son as a reformer, but those are the conservatives he's trusting with Edward's minority. Has the king lost his wits?" He addresses his question to de Winter rather than Strelley.

"Perhaps," de Winter replies. "One might more profitably ask why the king thinks to appoint a council, rather than a single man. If this council is composed of conservatives as you say, then it can only be to forestall any ambition Prince Edward may conceive of towards further reform. It may be the king's way of lessening the influence of this tutor and the queen..." de Winter stops and thinks again. "It may be that the king simply does not have a clear idea of what he wants after his own death."

"One might say," Strelley adds, "that Henry is unused to considering, and so afraid of, his own death that even to contemplate it robs him of his reason."

"No man can think himself immortal," Pike says, pronouncing each word carefully.

"Henry has torn to pieces the links with Rome, he has rejected the Pope's authority as head of the church. Not only that, he has stolen-" de Winter glances at Strelley as he speaks, checking his friend's expression, but Strelley is impassive - "stolen the wealth of the monasteries, used their lands to gratify himself and his chosen elite." The vigour subsides slightly. "The king is afraid to stand in front of Sainted Peter and give his account of himself."

"The king's never troubled himself over his conscience, has he? With the Howard girl and Anne Boleyn... He's had two of his wives killed," Strelley says. "He wasn't interested in Anne trying to instruct him before and he isn't attentive to the ministrations of his current wife. I think that he just can't bring himself to think about his own end."

"Whatever the truth may be," de Winter replies, "it seems that should a man wish to gain influence over the king, now is the time. We shall pass on what you have told us, and ensure that the earl knows the information has come from you."

Strelley thanks him as a servant enters with a tray of drinks. For now, we shall leave our three as their discussion turns to more prosaic matters, and instead return to the story of another of our young men as he enters London.

The following day, some eight miles to the east, two riders approach the king's palace at Greenwich. One is dressed richly, almost to a fault of ostentation, in a doublet of bright blue moire with a matching hat. The other is less distinct, more weathered. As they approach, the guards who stand on the gate stand to and challenge them to identify themselves.

"I am James Longshawe, and this is my companion Calonna."

"What business do you have at the palace?" one of the two guards, a heavy-set, stout man with an odd, moustache-less beard, asks.

"I have a letter of commendation to the king." Longshawe trots his horse backwards then forwards a couple of paces.

"Indeed. May I see this letter?"

Longshawe draws out the sealed letter given to him by Worsley, and leans down to hand it over. The guard examines the imprint in the seal, shows it to his fellow guard, before speaking abruptly. "Wait here."

He disappears through a smaller door in the larger door, leaving the other guard outside. This one is taller, leaner than his compatriot, and much younger. Longshawe looks at his uniform, pristine green and white. "Tudor colours?" he asks. The second guard looks at him, considering whether to answer the question. He deems it harmless enough and nods his confirmation.

"How does one join the palace guard?" Longshawe continues. The answer is interrupted as the first guard bustles back through the door, clashing his halberd against the plates of his armour.

"Dismount. Inside, please."

Longshawe and Calonna do as he says, dismounting and following him through the door. Once inside, he asks them to leave any weapons at the gatehouse. Longshawe unbuckles his sword-belt, handing it to him. Calonna frowns, before offering several concealed knives, two pistols, his sword and a knuckle-duster. The guard smiles cynically at them, before leading them across a courtyard and into a dimly-lit room. At the desk sits a man with a rich chestnut-brown beard, clad in the ermine-fur of nobility.

"Rizzley," he says, rising. "Interesting letter, this." He points to the letter recently handed over by Longshawe, which lies open on the desk. "Sit down."

"Sorry, I didn't catch your name..." Longshawe says as he seats himself.

"W-r-i-o-t-h-e-s-e-l-y." The nobleman spells it out, before confirming the pronunciation, "Rizzley." Calonna shakes his head, smiling. Longshawe tries not to look across at him. "Well, Master Longshawe, it seems that the king has much to thank you for in your defence of the Isle of Wight. He has only just beaten you back to Greenwich, after watching the French navy turned back in the Solent." Wriothesley speaks while reading the letter, eyes barely flicking up at his interviewees.

"The king was there? At the battle?" Longshawe asks, wide-eyed.

"He dined with the Lord Admiral the night before the battle," Wriothesely says, with a sort of curtness that betrays his distaste for this encounter with the common soldiery.

Calonna considers. "Then he saw that great carrack go down without being hit?"

"What was your name? Calonna? Might I suggest that you do not mention the *Mary Rose* before His Majesty. It is still a sore point with him. Whatever, the king has heard already about your contribution on the island. He is eager to meet a man who took command of a company not his own, and beat off a French force larger than his own."

"The men were brave and disciplined," Longshawe replies. "And I had the help of a master of these matters." He gestures towards Calonna, who is now chewing on a grass stalk, listening.

"I am no commander," Calonna says to Wriothesely. "What Signore Worsley did not see was how the men fought for this man. How he made them brave." Longshawe turns to Calonna, but does not say anything. These brief but honest words of compliment evidently mean much and have not previously been spoken.

"Indeed. It seems that you should both be rewarded. I shall try to arrange an audience for you with His Majesty. He still likes to meet courageous men from among the ranks. Where are you staying?" Wriothesley continues to look at the letter rather than the men who sit opposite him.

"We do not yet know, Sir. My lackey is charged with arranging our accommodation in the city."

"Very good. In that case, let me ask you to return hence on – what day is it today? Tuesday? - Thursday, in that case. If His Majesty will not receive you on that day, I shall have something for you, whether a time for an audience or some token, by then."

"I thank you for taking an interest in us, Sir," Longshawe says, rising and bowing.

"Listen: when you present yourself to the king, do not let your Italian friend do much of the talking. The king likes to think his armies are composed of loyal Englishmen. You must let him keep that illusion." Wriothesley takes a little time to appraise Longshawe. "The king will like you, Master Longshawe, so it is in both of our interests that you do this well."

"And I thank you for your counsel," Longshawe says. "Might I have my letter back?"

"Of course." Wriothesely hands him the letter, folded again. They turn and leave Wriothesley behind in his office. He scribbles on a piece of paper, reminding himself of this conversation and the potential for gaining just a little favour from the king by this presentation. Longshawe and Calonna walk out of the palace by the way they came, accompanied by the same guard who led them in. Their horses are returned to them and they ride off into the city in search of Guy Fletcher. Calonna has told him to meet them by the gates of the Guildhall, and it is there they find him. He leads them off to an inn where he has secured lodgings for all three of them.

"Guy, did you ever send that letter to Strelley?" Longshawe asks after they have eaten a hearty meal at the inn. Fletcher shakes his head. "Do you think you could write me a letter to him?"

"I could, Sir, if you get me the materials."

"Well, here they are," Longshawe says, passing him quill, ink and parchment. "I took the trouble of asking Mine Host for these earlier." He raises his eyebrows at his adolescent lackey, as if to admonish him for his doubt over his master's organisation.

"What do you wish me to write?" Guy says, gaze fixed firmly on the paper to avoid Longshawe's teasing.

After a moment, Longshawe abandons his banter and says, "address it to Edward Strelley, at the Court of His Majesty King Henry VIII. Then write:

My dear Edward,

Since last we corresponded, I have been involved in a great battle on the Isle of Wight. 'Great' indeed, for I am summoned to the presence of the king. I should be most gratified it if you could divert yourself to being in attendance during my audience. It may be Thursday, or it may be later. We are in contact with *Rizzley* for our appointment. I shall send Guy to find you at the palace, and you may send your answer, be it verbal or written, with him.

Yours,

Longshawe."

Guy continues scribing for a minute or two after Longshawe finishes dictating. "I shall go to the palace immediately if it please you, Sir. I should like to see Master Strelley again."

"It does please me, Guy. Do not take no for an answer, even if he is the tutor of Henry's daughter. Tell him to bring her along, and that Grindal fellow!"

"I shall, Sir." Guy Fletcher folds the letter and leaves the inn, heading back south towards the river. The walk takes him an hour and a half, pleasant enough in the early afternoon sun of late July. When he arrives, the same guard with the beard-without-moustache is on the gate.

"Can I help you, young Sir?" the guard asks, leaning over slightly.

"I have a letter to deliver."

"I'm sure you do. Who is it for?"

"Well, it's for a gentleman of the Lady Elizabeth's retinue, by the name of Strelley. But I should like to hand it to him personally."

"Strelley, you say? I think I know him. Amiable chap, bit scruffy? I shall see if I can fetch him here." The guard disappears into the palace again, and five minutes later Edward Strelley appears through the small door within the larger, heavy doors across the gate.

Strelley takes Guy Fletcher in a warm embrace. "Master Turner," he says, turning to the guard. "Guy is a friend of mine. Do I have your leave to take him inside the palace for a while?"

"Keep an eye on him," Turner the guard replies. "I should not like to have been responsible for allowing an assassin into the palace. Even a miniature, innocent-looking one."

Strelley leads Guy inside, where we shall leave them to tell each other their stories. We only need know that Guy returns later to the inn where Longshawe and Calonna await him, and gives the reply: "he says he shall be there."

14: Henry VIII

Thursday morning dawns to find Longshawe already awake and up, dressed finely in another new outfit, this time beautifully cut to show off his fine physique in a striking purple cloth. Calonna, with his customary indifference, is dressed smartly but has not gone to the lengths of acquiring new clothes. He watches as Longshawe styles himself carefully, smoothing his doublet and fingering his moustache, which now shows clear on his upper lip as the rest of his beard is shaved away. His hair is oiled, styled to accentuate his strong jawline.

"It is still early, James," Calonna laughs, pointing at him.

"I have not been received by my king before, Lorenzo. Perhaps *you* are well acquainted with royalty...?"

"Indeed I am not, but the king is a man just like any other."

"He rules the nation!" Longshawe exclaims.

"That is true. He rules, but if I ruled, would that make me a different man?" Calonna smiles, stroking his beard. "I would still be Lorenzo."

"But you *are* Lorenzo. He is King Henry."

"His father was a usurper. He won the throne, he did not inherit it."

"Be wary of saying such things in his presence. You should avoid speaking treasonous nonsense like that even to me." Longshawe studies himself in a glass as he speaks, checking that his eyebrows are even.

"Do you deny the truth of what I say?" Calonna is still in good humour, though one of his eyes is partly closed as he speaks, giving him a sardonic expression. Longshawe, taken by surprise at this curt reply, thinks briefly before speaking again.

"Surely it was Gloucester that was the usurper. God would not have allowed Henry's father to win at Bosworth if he was not the rightful heir."

"You are not normally given to piety, James. God did not win the battle at Bonchurch. You did, with your brave Englishmen. And me."

"Perhaps. Do not speak your mind before the king."

"Fear not. I shall keep my counsel. This is your moment, not mine, so I shall not embarrass you."

Longshawe does not reply, still concentrating on his appearance.

A moment later, Guy Fletcher bustles through the door of the room they share.

"I have groomed the horses, Sir, and fettled and polished the tack. We shall resemble three great knights of King Arthur."

"His Majesty will be pleased with that. He fancied himself as a flower of chivalry in his youth," Calonna says.

"I think he still does, Lorenzo," Longshawe replies.

In the familiar room at the palace, Strelley stands by the door as Grindal speaks to the Lady Elizabeth. It is still morning, but the sun has risen high enough so that the windows cast light only close to them. Strelley's eyes are narrow against the brightness, which goes some way to disguise the fact that he is concentrating on the young lady.

"Your father the king has requested your presence, as well as your sister's and the prince your brother's. You shall receive a hero of the defence of the Isle of Wight, and His Majesty wishes that you attend." Grindal's voice carries a tone of admonition, as if he delivering a finger-wagging telling off. His hands, though, are firmly by his sides.

"I have no love for these men of war, Master Grindal. Nor do you." Elizabeth is curt, dismissive of the tutor.

"The king has decided that his three children shall be present. He favours this young man as a flower of English chivalry," Grindal counters, not quite managing to hide his exasperation with the teenager.

"My decision is made for me, it seems."

"Perhaps so, My Lady." Grindal offers her a genuine smile, and she returns it as best she can. He rises, and continues, "I shall take you to the presence chamber, with Master Strelley here. Be ready in an hour." Strelley stands by as Grindal bustles out of the room. Grindal speaks to the ladies-in-waiting, and a moment later they enter, ignoring Strelley, who watches for a moment as they prepare to ready the girl for Longshawe's royal reception.

Strelley bows his head, turning to leave. "Stay a moment, Master Strelley." Elizabeth holds up her hand to stop him. "I would speak with you."

"My Lady?" Strelley says, discomposed for a moment.

"This hero that Grindal speaks of, he is your friend, is he not?"

Strelley recovers himself. "He is an old and very great friend of mine, yes, My Lady."

"And is he such a hero as Grindal describes?"

"Madam, I have fought alongside him only once, and I must confess that my wits were diverted to keeping my own skin intact."

"You have never struck me as a warrior, Edward." Elizabeth smiles at him, the slightest hint of coquettishness about her. Strelley's eyes widen as she speaks his Christian name. Her ladies surround her, painting her face from various pots. They untie her hair, and one begins brushing it through. It shines copper-gold in the light from the windows. Strelley thinks how to reply, watching the activity surrounding Elizabeth. His mouth curls a little as he considers that it is only as an insignificant servant that he might be allowed to see this toilette. Eventually, he arrives at his careful reply.

"For my king, Madam, I have fought. But I am no soldier. I can handle a blade to fence, but the press and the noise of pitched battle..."

"I have read of battle, Master Strelley, but I fear I shall never see one. Master Grindal and his books cannot answer my questions as you can. I should like to know what it is like."

"What can I tell you, Madam? As I said, I am hardly able to describe events even that took place around me." Strelley's face goes pale, remembering the last moments of Ralph Eure. "I was no more than a hindrance to better men on the fields of Scotland. You should ask Longshawe. He may be able to answer your questions more accurately."

"You disappoint me, Master Strelley." Elizabeth's tone has returned to its former curtness, but she looks happy enough nevertheless. "I hope your friend is more forthcoming. I did not speak the truth to Grindal just now." Strelley nods, unsurprised by the revelation. She continues, grimacing as the brush catches on a knot. "I am of course no lover of death, but I find the men who deal in it rather fascinating. Such bravery to disregard danger!"

"Rather, Madam, you might say that they fail to value their own lives..."

"I think that the good soldier must set the price of his life very high, else he should die forthwith." A wicked smile flashes across her face.

"It is true that the presence of an enemy lends a certain focus to ones actions. But I care not for such dubious pleasures. James – Longshawe – seems to revel in it. But he is a stronger man than I, and more courageous."

"We shall see, Edward. Leave me now whilst I ready myself."

She waves Strelley away, and he bows again, before turning to leave.

Later that morning, the Royal Family assembles in the presence chamber at Greenwich. Henry seats himself, with help from his footmen, in an ornately-carved wooden chair raised on a wide dais, with the boy Prince Edward standing next to him. Elizabeth and Mary are further to the side, next to Queen Catherine. Each is dressed well to the point of ostentation, with many jewels and much gold cloth adorning their outfits, but it is the boy and his father who stand out, resplendent in their regal trappings.

Strelley stands with Grindal in a corner of the room, some distance back behind other, more important courtiers. They watch in silence as the family prepare themselves to receive their guests, who wait outside in an anteroom. Longshawe is among them, voice just about audible from inside the presence chamber, with Calonna and Guy Fletcher. There are others, higher-ranking and therefore preceding. Quiet descends on the room as the crowd of people notice movement by the entrance.

"His Grace the Earl of Shrewsbury, and his son the Earl of Waterford," a herald announces. Francis Talbot and his son George stride forward, bowing to the Royal Family. As they pass, both turn their heads slightly, and acknowledge Strelley and Grindal with a nod. The king does not rise to meet them, but exchanges pleasantries with the elder Talbot. A few minutes pass as they converse, Shrewsbury asking banal questions and getting equally banal responses from Henry, before they stand aside, positioning themselves near the front.

"Masters Longshawe and Calonna, and Squire Fletcher." The herald's strident voice sounds across the room. The three of them enter the room together, although Longshawe leads the others before the king. As he speaks, Henry's voice is heavy, grating in his throat.

"My brave soldiers!" he grunts. "It is with the greatest pleasure that we receive you. I am told that your actions on the Isle of Wight were of great significance in pushing back the French assault. You are to be congratulated and commended. It is a long while since we won Boulogne, and since Norfolk and Suffolk left it without a garrison to defend itself, a victory against them is most welcome. Tell me, Master Longshawe, how you turned the French back."

Longshawe takes a breath, puffs out his chest, and begins, trying to muster a suitably grand tone. "Your Majesty, I am deeply honoured to be in your presence." The king holds up a hand, silencing him.

"You may dispense with formality, Master Longshawe. I wish to hear your tale, not your obeisances." The king laughs, as does Prince Edward. The boy's eyes flick from Longshawe, to Calonna, and then to Guy, who, having previously fixed his own gaze on the prince, lowers his head in deference.

"Indeed, Sire," Longshawe continues, "I took men from the Earl of Shrewsbury's lands to Portsmouth, from where we were summoned to defend the Isle when the French were spotted in the Channel. I marched south, where we joined a larger company. After a few days, French ships landed, and their troops disembarked. We assembled on the high ground, and fought off their charge with musket and pike. Many brave Englishmen..." He pauses and lifts his head, before persisting. "Many brave Englishmen were killed, but more of the French. They took flight, but reformed and charged again. This time there was more fighting hand-to-hand, but we prevailed, and sent them back to their boats, leaving behind the greater part of their force on the field."

"England is indebted to you, Sir. Approach!" Henry commands. Longshawe moves to the edge of the dais where the king's throne is placed. Henry stretches out his hand, and whispers, "for your bravery, Sir. Share it with your companions." He drops a gold ring into Longshawe's palm. Longshawe closes his hand tightly, and withdraws, still facing the king, bowing low.

Henry speaks again to the whole assembly. "I should like these brave men to dine with me today. See to it that places are set for them." Footmen scurry about, passing the message to where it needs to be heard. "I shall speak to your master about your future employment."

Longshawe and Calonna withdraw. Guy Fletcher stares in awe at the king and the assembled Royal Family for a moment before following them out. As soon as he can, Strelley leaves the presence chamber and searches for his friend in the anteroom, a much bigger hall where many are gathered, some still in anticipation, some having already been received. Grindal does not follow.

Longshawe sees Strelley first, and steps forward to greet him, calling his name out. "Strelley! Edward!" They clasp hands. "It is with the greatest pleasure that I see you," he says, recalling the king's words from a few minutes before.

"It was the greatest pleasure for me to see you being received by the king with such honour and grace. He gave you something, as well." Longshawe nods, holding out the ring in his palm. It is set with three diamonds, and sparkles in the light from the windows.

"One for each of us, I suppose!" Longshawe laughs,"but it would be insignificant compared to a permanent summons to the court."

"What do you mean?" Strelley asks.

"I've said to My Lord Shrewsbury that a place in His Majesty's Yeomen of the Guard or another of the palace guards would be, shall we say, of interest to me. I want the earl to see to it that I am stationed here. This is where I want to be, near the king. In the middle of it all. Henry himself said that he would speak on my behalf."

"Then we may be happily rejoined here." Strelley turns to Guy Fletcher. "I knew you were a good lad, Guy, but did not foresee you a hero so soon! You are greatly honoured."

"I have done naught but what I was bidden by Master Longshawe, Sir. We owe our being here now to him, to his being brave and leading us well. Perhaps we owe him our lives," Fletcher replies.

"I thank you for your kind words, Guy," Longshawe says, aware of the formality of his tone, so to break the tension he claps him on the shoulder. Calonna has been watching the exchange, following the conversation, and it is now he chooses to speak. When he opens his mouth, the three others listen intently.

"Your friend is brave, Eduardo. But it is that when he commands, men obey. That is significant." He takes Strelley's hand. "I trust that your occupations here have suited you better than warfare?"

"They have. I have learned a great deal from Master Grindal, and a little from the lady herself. She is markedly accomplished in many ways, more learned than many twice her age. I am more than content in her service." As Strelley speaks, Longshawe shares a significant look with Guy Fletcher.

"Do not forget how to handle a sword, Eduardo," Calonna says, looking into his eyes and holding them for a long moment. "This land is destined for strife, and you must not be lost amongst it."

Strelley now exchanges a glance of his own with Longshawe, who shrugs in response. "Do not speak of strife now, Lorenzo," Longshawe says. "Let's celebrate our victories whilst we can, enjoy our renown for what it is." He casts his eyes around the room. Several young women are looking at him, and he returns a few of their smiles, paying particular attention to the prettiest. "I could be more than content here as well, Edward."

Later that afternoon, a great feast is served, with spectacular dishes of venison and various exotic fowls, posed on their serving platters as they might have appeared in life. The king dines heartily, as he has always done, but his now-considerable bulk leaves him sweating and short of breath as he eats. Strelley nudges Longshawe when he notices that his friend is staring overmuch at the king.

"Don't watch him like this, James. He does not like to show his infirmity. If that is the right word."

"He is not healthy?" Calonna asks, from the other side of Longshawe. Longshawe turns and eyes him, shaking his head just a little. Fletcher, mouth full of some viand or other, chews slowly as he awaits Strelley's reply. It is some moments coming, as Strelley considers his answer.

"He has these bouts of rage. Sometimes we hear him shouting in anger, and he has been known to direct such moments of wrath at the queen." Strelley sits back in his chair, calculating if any can hear their conversation. Sat in a corner of the great dining hall as they are, there is little chance of his words carrying further than those for whom they are intended. He carries on.

"The queen is a reformer. Of that there is no more doubt, and the man who educates the boy, Cheke, he is the same." He looks round, still sitting straight and tall in his chair, as the others bend in to listen. "Those articles of Henry's will be overturned when he dies if the boy has reached majority. That isn't in doubt either. But the king is going to die before and the realm will be governed by some regent, or worse, a council, so all will remain undecided. I don't know whether the king is fully cognisant of his son's Protestant education. From the little I know of the prince himself, he is already as much of a fanatic as his oldest sister, but on the opposite side of the battlefield."

"This tutor is a Protestant, then?" Longshawe asks.

"Cheke? He is firm in his convictions. And they are for the reform, yes. The talk is that the queen took great pains to persuade His Majesty of the skill of this tutor. They – the king and Queen Catherine – argue over matters of doctrine. From what I have learned from the gentlemen of the chamber, the queen tries to persuade the king towards reform. But he gets angry when she contradicts him. If I were her, I would be more prudent. It is not as though Henry has tolerated much licence in his previous wives, is it?"

Longshawe considers this information. Calonna is little moved by it, allowing himself the ghost of a smile at Strelley's seriousness. Guy Fletcher watches all three at intervals, trying to gauge their thoughts. Eventually, it is he that speaks.

"What of the prince? Is he strong? Healthy?"

Strelley's brow creases, and he speaks whilst looking into the bottom of his wine-cup. "The king wants him kept locked away, protected from any and all evil. He fears the plague in London, and foul airs, assassins, and God knows what else. It leaves the prince healthy in one sense, and not in another. He is practically forbidden all those things that the king himself enjoyed so much in his youth. No riding, no jousting, no fencing. So he is intact, Guy, but he is not *healthy*, as you say."

Longshawe has been considering another enquiry during Strelley's speech. Haltingly, he asks, "has the archbishop made no difference to the king's thoughts? He is a thoroughgoing Protestant, is he not?"

"Cranmer is some kind of Lutheran, yes. Married, too, from what I hear. Though the king has an affection for him which is undimmed by their differences on matters of doctrine. One wonders whether Cranmer has a special power over the king. He has had his litany approved, even though he denies the six articles in private..." Strelley stops at the approach of a liveried footman, looking up at him as he falls silent.

"Lady Elizabeth requests your presence," the footman says to Longshawe, whose eyebrows rise. He gets up, shoots a significant look at Strelley, and follows the footman.

"Your mistress summons James. Interesting." Calonna's smile is wicked.

"I think she is rather taken with this buccaneering soldier image. It's Longshawe through and through. She spends her days in study, but she's still her father's daughter. Adventure stirs her. James' adventure on Wight in particular," Strelley replies, flashing his white teeth back at Calonna.

The three of them watch as the tables are cleared and the king's own company of tumblers performs a series of impressive tricks. They cannot see Longshawe, disappeared to some other dark corner of the room, nor the king and his queen. Lady Mary watches the tumbling, dark eyes following as the acrobats dash across the floor. Prince Edward is sitting with his sister, listening as she points out particularly spectacular feats.

It is only after the performance comes to an end that Longshawe returns to his companions. "By Christ, your mistress is a bloodthirsty young lioness! She was more enthusiastic for the details of the battle than her father."

"She asked me about our time in Scotland as well, you know. She was very disappointed when I couldn't tell her much about what went on."

"Too preoccupied keeping your hide unpunctured, I suppose?" Longshawe laughs. "Well, she wanted to know about that as well. You might get one or two more questions to answer about that tomorrow."

"Well, I thank you, James. All I've wanted to do since we returned is relive that battle," Strelley sighs. "It could be worse. At least I don't have to fight again."

"No," Longshawe answers, "nor me, it seems. The king has it in mind for me to join the Warders. Among his personal guards."

"So you shall be joining us here at Greenwich?" Strelley asks, eagerly. "What of Guy? And Lorenzo?" He points to each in turn.

"Guy, I'm sure, could still be my lackey. Calonna I think has had enough of court already."

"I shall return to Europe when I can. With my share of that shiny bauble your king gave to James. Italian women are worth travelling for." Calonna makes an obscene gesture, causing the English young men to laugh. Guy Fletcher is bemused.

Longshawe points to several young ladies who surround Mary, and others who seem to serve the queen, although they are currently gathered chatting. "I shall take my fill of English women before I sample your Italians." He rises, and swaggers over to the knot of women, watched by his friends.

"I'm not sure he's really interested, you know," Strelley says.
Calonna nods. "In women?"
"No. In those women. I don't think his heart's really in it."
"It is already given elsewhere?" Calonna asks.
Strelley confirms by pursing his lips and giving a slight nod.

15: The life of a guard, the life of a tutor

Some weeks later, Longshawe attends the palace at Greenwich with Guy Fletcher. Calonna is no longer with them, disappeared to indulge his desire for Italian women, perhaps. Strelley meets him at the gate, leading him and Guy through to the royal presence chamber. The herald announces them, and this time the king receives them alone. Strelley doesn't enter with Longshawe, but disappears quickly along a corridor once he has seen his friend into the room.

"Ah, Longshawe. The hero of the Isle of Wight. Yes, I wish to have men of wit as well as valour as part of my guard here at the palace. You seem to be such a man." Henry waits, the echo of his words dulled by the heavy tapestries that surround the chamber. They depict great warriors, hunts, battles. The king himself looks at those scenes as he allows himself time before continuing to speak. "Perhaps one day future kings will gaze upon my likeness in their great halls, and wonder at the deeds of Henry. I wish that it will be so." Again, the king lets his words settle before carrying on his thought.

"More than myself, it is for my son that I need strong men... and true. Will you be that? Edward will need your prudence as well as your bravery. I shall not live to see my son reach an age when he can govern for himself. You may be but a soldier, but you can look to his interests, protect him from the evils of the greedy men who surround him even now, furthering only their own ends? Bah! I do not expect you to understand." The king has worked himself up into something of a fervour, almost spitting his words out in anger and fear. His colour has risen to a bright red, but he spends a moment mastering himself, and he gradually pales.

"I should not wish to show my apprehensions to many of these supposedly great men of court, Master Longshawe. Can you see why? They would see it merely as an indication that they are about to come to power. But I will not have civil war again. You may not be able to prevent that on your own, but you will swear to me always to act in the interests of my son, and not the men who may think to make themselves king after I die. Will you swear your loyalty to Edward, Sir?"

"I swear loyalty to Your Majesty, and to His Royal Highness Prince Edward. I shall act only to further the interests of the House of Tudor." Longshawe's voice is calm despite the gravity of his words.

"Good. I value your oath, Sir, but it is your deeds that shall matter. See to it that they accord with your promise. To me as well as to my boy." From a concealed recess behind a tapestry, at the back of the dais on which the king's seat is raised, the Prince Edward emerges. He is reasonably tall for his eight years, but is not possessed of the same vigour as his father had in his youth. He stares wide-eyed at Longshawe, his gaze searching his character, though fixed firmly on his face. Longshawe bows a low obeisance. Guy Fletcher, standing slightly behind, lowers his head.

"Your Royal Highness," Longshawe says to acknowledge the prince.

"Master Longshawe, my father the king recommends you to me as someone who will serve me loyally." The boy speaks with affected dignity, bordering on pomposity.

"That I shall, Sir," Longshawe answers. Edward nods, and stands by his father.

Henry says, "your friend should be able to show you to the armoury. You can collect your uniform and other trappings there. Wingfield may assign you a specific duty, though I suspect he delegates even that duty to some other officer."

"Pardon me, Sire. Wingfield?" Longshawe asks, hesitantly.

"I forget how unfamiliar you must be with my household. Your office means that Wingfield is your captain. He has responsibility for organising the household guard, though, as I say, I wonder if another ultimately effects that task. Wriothesley may have something for you to do, as well. You met him on your first visit, I believe. Seek him out before Wingfield. He may have some useful advice for you on life in the palace." The king dismisses Longshawe and Guy Fletcher by a gesture. Two sets of footsteps are audible, one quiet and leading away into the Royal chambers of the palace, one heavier and leading back towards the antechamber. As Longshawe and Guy Fletcher emerge, Strelley has just reached the same location, returning via the same corridor through which he left a few minutes ago.

"Well, lads," Strelley begins, "it looks like I shall be seeing more of you." He takes Longshawe's hands in his. "I am glad that you are not going to war again. Both of you." He releases Longshawe, and puts his arm around Guy Fletcher.

Two days later, Strelley visits the merchant Gilbert again, sent to fetch more books and supplies by Grindal. Longshawe accompanies him, finding a gap in his duties. He is dressed spectacularly, not in his guardsman's uniform but in a finely cut silver-grey doublet and matching slashed hose. As they walk through the streets of the city towards the warehouse, Strelley pinches the material between his fingers and rubs it gently.

"This must have cost you everything you got for that ring. Did you save anything?"

"I have a few coins left over. Besides, it's important for someone of my station to look the part."

"What do you mean, your station? You're a guardsman!"

"Ah, but I'm a Yeoman of the Guard, you see, not just any guardsman. I've already stood while the king dined, and I'm assigned to the receiving room tomorrow. There's foreign ambassadors and all sorts of nobles going to be there."

"Good for you. What will you do if you catch the eye of some duke's daughter?"

"Hmm..." Longshawe contemplates the conquest of some fresh-faced noble maiden, then changes tack entirely. "This guy had better be worth the walk."

"He will be." Strelley raises his eyebrows to show his enthusiastic anticipation.

They arrive a few minutes later, and this time Strelley approaches the door with confidence. It is closed, and there is no sound from within. After a moment, a muffled voice issues forth.

"Try the handle. That's what it's for."

Strelley allows himself a half-smile at Gilbert's raillery, and looks at Longshawe before opening the door, fixing him with wide eyes. He enters ahead, and Longshawe follows, stepping slowly past the threshold.

"Grindal's boy again! And you've brought someone to speak for you this time? Excellent. What shall it be?" he says, addressing Longshawe, whose eyes have been drawn to some ornately carved swords that lie on a trestle table down one side of the room. "Ah, those. Expensive. Although, for a man like you..." Gilbert stops, and focuses on Strelley again. "Do you have Grindal's list?"

Strelley hands him a sheet of parchment, which elicits a series of hums and hahs from Gilbert. He points to an entry towards the bottom of the list. "This is banned. If you get caught with this, they'll cut your knackers off for witchcraft."

"Grindal said he was working on a poultice for the king's leg," Strelley replies.

"Treason as well as witchcraft, eh? Well, as ever, I didn't sell it to you."

"Indeed not." Strelley smiles at him, head tilted to one side.

"Your friend...?" Gilbert begins, watching Longshawe as he fingers the hilt of one of the ornate swords. "Is he... rich?"

"Not especially. But he will buy." Strelley strolls over to Longshawe, and picks up a sword. He unsheaths it, tests the balance and feel, the blade whipping through the air with a vicious snicking sound. Longshawe watches, eyes following the movements of his friend's hand.

"May I?" he asks Gilbert.

"Be careful with those. They're expensive. Don't blunt them. In fact, don't let them touch. They don't look as nice when we've had to whet them," Gilbert says. "They're not really for fighting, those." Longshawe gives him a quizzical look. "Some of our richer customers *wear* a sword... But they'd have someone else to do the dirty work for them."

"But you must make a lot of money from selling them these swords with all this gold on the hilt?" Longshawe asks. Gilbert nods. Longshawe frowns at him, nonplussed. "Do you have swords good for fighting?"

Gilbert laughs, and fetches a wooden bucket of plain-looking blades. Each is dark, almost blue, contrasting completely with the silver look of the others. "Toledo steel," Gilbert says, reverentially. "If you meet someone and he threatens you with one of these, run. He'll know what he's doing. Not for show-offs." Longshawe's eyes narrow. Strelley takes one, unsheaths it and shapes a few cuts and thrusts. It is light, well-balanced, a natural extension of his sword-arm.

"You'll be wanting a poniard? I have some from Sheffield in here." Gilbert passes them another shorter bucket containing a selection of short knives, some thin, some with heavier blades. Strelley picks one with two long extrusions, one either side of the thick blade, over a heavy wire basket hilt. "That's a real brawler's weapon. Snap almost anything if you catch it right. Good choice." Strelley returns the weapon to its sheath and tucks it into his belt, on the right side. He takes the Toledo sword and fastens that likewise to his belt, but to his left.

Longshawe agonises over his selection, eventually finding a

more ornamented Toledo blade that catches his attention. It is, according to Gilbert, the most expensive in the shop, but a fine piece. Longshawe's purse is much lighter when the matter is settled. "A pleasure doing business with you gentlemen. Now let me fetch your things for Grindal." He takes the list off Strelley, and disappears for several minutes into the main warehouse, occasionally appearing between two crates or shelves. During this time, two burly men stand near the door, relaxed-looking but alert, ready to prevent any ill-conceived attempts at thievery.

Gilbert returns, with a handful of books and other wares, but a concerned look on his face. "Did Grindal really ask for this?" He points to the bottom of the list. "I know he has odd taste in literature, but this is way beyond his usual stuff. Very rare, as well. Expensive."

Strelley maintains a straight face for a moment, before it cracks into a tacit admission of guilt. Gilbert laughs at him, patting him on the shoulder.

"For you? My silent friend, this is most interesting request, and one that you should have thought very carefully about writing down. Be careful, boy, or you really shall be fed your balls by the executioner. I have it, of course, but tell me: why should I sell it to you?" Strelley fights to master himself, colouring only slightly. Longshawe can only look on, wondering what volume the exchange is about.

After a moment, Strelley replies. "You shouldn't. But you can't read it yourself. Perhaps, when I have translated it, I shall read it to you."

"Ah, I should like to hear you read such a volume. But your voice may not have quite the same allure as the illustrations. Very well, you shall have it. Keep it hidden from that master of yours. I'm sure King Henry has his own copy, well-thumbed indeed I don't doubt."

After more money has changed hands, the two young men eventually leave the the warehouse. Gilbert smiles extravagantly as they do so, cheered by the sport he has had with Strelley as much as the sales he has made. As soon as they round a corner, Longshawe stops Strelley and demands to know what the book is.

"You can amuse yourself at your leisure perusing the pictures, James."

"But what *is* it?"

"I don't really know. I've read about it in some other books. But rest assured that if I can decipher it I shall tell you. No doubt your interest will be piqued."

"I'm sure it will."

The following day, Longshawe stands guard in the king's receiving room. A series of dignitaries and nobles are introduced, each with their own matter to bring to the king's attention, occupying him for most of the morning. Some plead a legal case, others try to curry favour, but Henry is listless and disengaged. None of them makes much headway. When they are gone, Wriothesley enters and begins speaking to him.

"Your Majesty, I have some warrants for you." The king begins to sign them on a small table set by his chair, looking at each only briefly before applying his pen. "Sire, your foundations are progressing well in each of the Universities. I should also bring to Your Majesty's attention that we have arrested several heretics who have refused to attest the six articles-" Henry stops him, waving his hand.

"Sir Thomas, please. I am weary of it." The king drops his head on his hand, resting it there for a moment, and takes a long, slow breath. "I had thought this heresy was on the wane."

"It seems that Luther has attracted some followers among the common folk, Sire." Wriothesley is cautious, non-committal. "The articles are accepted by most of your loyal subjects."

"Ah, Thomas. I thank you for softening the blow. There may not be many open Lutherans at court, but I do not doubt that many have learned to dissemble. Perhaps they do so out of loyalty, perhaps fear. The queen does not always take that trouble. Perhaps she does not fear me."

"Your Majesty?"

"I wonder if she is more committed to the reform than she would dare admit to me. She sometimes argues that way with me. I also suspect that Edward's tutor is a Lutheran. I would not have my issue fall into heresy, Thomas. You must take care for his soul when I am gone."

"I shall, Sire. But if Your Majesty is unhappy with Prince Edward's tutor, why not remove him?"

"Cheke *is* a good man, and he seems to have taught the boy wit and intelligence. With whom would I replace him? Gardiner? He is a firebrand. Pole? The absent Cardinal? Papists, the pair of them. Neither of them would accept the nomination. I agree with more of what the most extreme reformers say than these flatterers to the Pope. So

Norfolk and you will have to guard the prince's conscience. And that of the nation, which, of course, must not be ignored."

"Sire... I shall do my utmost to ensure your son's spiritual well-being," Wriothesley says, with an air of dignity that isn't quite unforced. "If Your Majesty is called to God, we shall govern after your fashion. We shall not allow the Bishop of Rome to dictate to us, nor shall we let the people fall into heresy."

"Indeed not. I appreciate your devotion." The king signs the last warrant, and passes it to Wriothesley. "My son will need you soon enough," he says, a significant look on his face.

Across the palace, Grindal is discussing the same six articles mentioned by Wriothesley with his young charge.

"So it sounds as though these articles essentially confirm Catholic doctrine?" Elizabeth asks, perplexed. "I had thought my father embraced the reform. What about Cranmer? Did he not influence my father?"

"He does, to an extent," Grindal answers. "Though your father once had more zeal for the reform than he does now. He seems to have lost his desire for change since his son was born."

"But this is all Papal nonsense, isn't it?" Elizabeth offers, tapping the sheet of paper with the back of her hand. Strelley, across the room looking at some of Elizabeth's work from earlier, raises his eyebrows. Elizabeth does not see, but Grindal does.

"My Lady, your own father has written on the subject," Grindal answers. "Master Strelley, have you read the King's Book?"

"I have, Sir. The king professes that the Church is one, united, but that it is not the Pope's Church. He writes rather of God's Church. Though it is true that his most recent doctrine matches closely that held by the Catholics."

"The king, remember, is supreme head of the Church in England. He is searching his conscience, asking God for the right answers." Grindal smiles as he speaks.

"His most recent doctrine?" Elizabeth says, eyeballing Strelley. "Anyway, were I to be queen, would I be the supreme head?" Elizabeth smiles wryly, knowing the effect she will bring out. She is in line to the throne. Her question elicits sighs and coughs from Strelley and Grindal.

"You must not speak of being queen, madam, for it is treasonous to foretell the death of the king," Grindal answers.

"And yet my brother is prepared all his life for his duties as king. Is that not treasonous, Master Grindal? No one countenances a woman as head of the church." Elizabeth leans back in her chair, satisfied that she has outwitted her teacher.

"It is not treason to prepare a future king for his reign, no." Grindal's brow creases. His tone suggests that he wishes Elizabeth would not pursue the matter.

"And yet to do so anticipates the death of the king my father, does it not? Whence this exception to the law, I wonder?"

"Pardon me, Madam," Strelley answers her, filling Grindal's silence. "Your brother's education does anticipate his future as king. It foresees the king's death without foretelling it."

"And this is enough to save my brother's tutor from a charge of treason?" Elizabeth says, sharply.

"Madam, I do not judge." Strelley does not entirely hide his smile, which Elizabeth notices.

"And yet it seems you do, Master Strelley. You judge me shrewd, I think."

"Your argument is sound, as far as it goes," Strelley answers.

"But you are unwilling to cross me, are you not?" she says. Strelley's eyes narrow. "Master Strelley, you are as much my tutor as Master Grindal." She gestures to Grindal, who is watching the exchange carefully, unsure of whether or not to intervene. He allows it to continue.

Strelley considers his reply. "I should not like to contradict you, Madam, unless it were for your own benefit."

"Well, Edward," she stresses the name, drawing attention to her unusual decision to use it, "I should like you in future to speak your mind to me. Do not equivocate, even if you think you might offend me. These lessons are a sanctum in which I wish to learn, to argue, not to be obeyed without question. Master Grindal, it should please me if you were also to correct me when I err."

Grindal, stung by the comment, speaks in a firm tone. "Might I remind Madam that it is her father, not herself, that is our employer?"

"Do not play such a coward, Master Grindal. My father employs you to educate me, not to tiptoe around me in such a way that I could think myself always correct. You allowed me to use two solecisms in our translation this morning. Do not think I don't know, Sir." The girl touches the tips of her long, gracious fingers together, satisfied with her victory. Strelley can barely contain his amusement.

"I shall be more exacting in future," Grindal says quietly.

An hour later, lessons over, Grindal talks to Strelley after the lady has left. "Be wary, Edward. Whatever Mistress Elizabeth says, it is always to her father that we must answer. I might have allowed her a little too much leeway, which I shall now reduce."

"The lady is blessed with a faster wit than either of us, Sir. And greater."

"That may be, but we must not over-indulge her high opinion of herself. She may be the daughter of the king, but we shall both be for the block if she proves too shrewish for whatever princeling she is destined. We must rein in her cunning so it does not lead her to say something all three of us may regret."

16: The Prince's Uncles

"Who?" Strelley asks. He is sitting in a comfortable upholstered chair in the mess room. Longshawe, sitting across from Strelley and dressed in his guard's uniform, thinks briefly about his reply.

"Thomas Seymour. Apparently he's back from some sort of embassy to the Low Countries. I don't think the king was pleased to see him." Longshawe cracks his knuckles.

"He wouldn't be. I've heard that the queen and he were destined to be wed before the king took an interest in her."

"I didn't realise that. The king barely acknowledged him, despite their family ties."

"Hmm. What about the other? Was that the other brother?"

"Hertford. Yes, the brother. He had much to say to the king."

"Tell me. I should like to know what he is planning." Strelley folds his arms and listens intently as Longshawe speaks.

"Hertford – he's called Edward as well, isn't he? - spoke to the king about the prince. He was trying to find out what the king has in mind if he dies before Prince Edward reaches his majority. I think Hertford was angling to be named sole protector. It sounded as though he doesn't wanted his brother involved, but I couldn't really tell. He was subtle, not saying what he really thought. In any case, the king talked about forming a council of wise men who would guide his son until he was ready to rule in his own right. Hertford took great interest in that. He was asking the king for names, names of these men who would form this regency council, that's what he called it."

"A man of lesser standing would be dismissed for insolence. But the king suffered him to speak of death, his own death..."

"Yes. Henry said that he doesn't want the Lutherans to become powerful after his death. He was talking about how Gardiner is a true believer, but Cranmer's Protestantism is a burden to him. If I were Cranmer, I should take great care around the king. Surely he speaks his mind at the risk of his neck!"

"Henry seems always to take Cranmer's side, despite their differences on these matters of faith. Henry still believes in the doctrine of the Catholics, even if he doesn't acknowledge the Pope – the Bishop of Rome, as we must now say – and he will go to the grave with that now. The king seems to have lost any desire to pursue further reform."

"That is true. But Cranmer can't escape the royal wrath forever."

"The king's favour will last. He needs Cranmer to maintain this idea of Royal Supremacy. Gardiner and the others would return us to Rome. That's where Cranmer gets his power. The king can't get rid of him because the conservatives would have us back to the jurisdiction of Rome. Cranmer got him his break, and Cranmer creates the rules that the king needs to maintain it."

"That may be so. I hadn't thought about it. Anyway, he praised Hertford for his campaign in Scotland, which can't have been the same one that we were part of. He at least seems to have met with some success. But they haven't got hold of this Scots princess. 'She proves elusive', Hertford said, and 'it is easy to hide a tiny child in the vast expanse of the Scots kingdom.' I'm not sure Henry totally believed him."

"What about his brother? I'm sure he was made Warden of the Cinque Ports, so he can't be totally out of favour." Strelley rubs his chin.

"Honestly? He thinks very highly of himself. Spent the audience adjusting his clothes and twirling his moustaches, looking for people to impress. I don't know if he holds some honorary position. As I say, the king barely spoke with him. They don't get on."

"I don't doubt I. I have heard it said that Catherine would gladly have wed him. More gladly than she wed the king."

"So this Seymour has an interest with the queen? She must not have been pleased at the king's desire for her."

"Be careful what you say, James. It must be treason to question the king's manly attractiveness. Even compared to the flower of chivalry that is Tom Seymour."

"But he was a boor!"

"Perhaps to you. But there must be some truth in the rumours about the queen and him. It was around the time that Henry despatched his last wife, and this Seymour and Catherine Parr, as she was then, became close. Perhaps she welcomed the king's affection. Now she is one of the most important women in the kingdom, even if she didn't marry Henry for love. In any case, the king sent Tom Seymour to the Low Countries to be rid of him."

"Interesting."

"Indeed. We must keep a close eye on them both."

"For what? What difference does it make to us who has power? We'll still be subjects, whether a council rules or Edward Seymour on his own."

"That may be true, but it is wise to be forewarned." Strelley pats his friend's knee. "Would you rather serve the king or his protector?"

Longshawe looks at the clock, then rises. "I have to go to see Wriothesley."

"Luck rides with you as always. What does he have you doing?"

"He likes to know what goes on in the presence chamber. I tell him odd details, which seems to keep him happy."

"Be careful what you tell him. Limit yourself to reporting what people say in the presence chamber, not in private audience. Wriothesley could be a powerful patron, but he will not think that he owes you anything yet."

"I shall. Adieu."

"Good day, James."

Longshawe leaves the mess room, his steps audible as he strides away. Strelley pulls out the book that he and Longshawe bought at Gilbert's, and a manuscript already a foot-and-a-half long. He begins to thumb the leaves of the book, but looks up at the door to the mess room, thinks better of it and packs his translation away, taking it elsewhere, hidden from the prying and judgmental eyes of those who attend or work in the court.

"Did you meet the Seymours yourself?" Elizabeth is as close to giddy as she gets, eyebrows raised slightly, fingers on display, straightened out upwards and touching at the tips.

"I had that pleasure, Madam," Grindal replies, "I have spoken with Hertford before, although he did not seem to have much time for me on this occasion." Strelley watches from across the room, his eyes subtly lifted from the roll of paper on which he pretends to write.

"Hertford is Edward?" Elizabeth asks. Grindal nods. "And his brother, Thomas. He is the one whom Queen Catherine rejected for my father?"

Grindal coughs loudly at this, and takes a moment to compose himself. Strelley smiles, and Lady Elizabeth notices. She turns to him, and asks with a hint of sharpness, "and what would you know of the matter, Master Strelley?"

"I know very little, Madam. The king your father chose Queen Catherine for his wife after she was widowed." He allows himself a moment, face wry, before delivering the punchline. "For the second time."

"I have already counselled you on the matter of speaking your mind, have I not?"

"You have, Madam."

"Well then, speak your mind. I order it." Elizabeth's command issues from her accompanied by a twitch in her hands, bending her fingers at the knuckle. Strelley looks over at Grindal, who crumples his bottom lip in a gesture that says 'you're on your own'.

After a pause, Strelley begins to speak. "Well, Madam, before the erstwhile Lady Parr was aware of your father's interest in her, she may indeed have formed an attachment with Thomas Seymour."

"About that much we can be certain, Master Strelley." Lady Elizabeth's voice has lost some of its sharpness, now adopting a more bantering tone.

"Indeed. Though it seems that the king made provision for her to forget him – Seymour, I mean – as quickly as possible."

"You refer to his diplomatic mission?"

Grindal speaks up. "The lady's wit is beyond reproach as always," he addresses his charge directly. "Madam, you must be careful what you say. Your father is quick to anger. The queen herself has felt the sharp edge of his tongue on occasion, for much less a transgression than you threaten to make, so you must never think yourself beyond reproach."

"I do not consider myself thus, Master Grindal, rest assured. I am aware of my father's temper. And I thank you for your candour, Master Strelley." Strelley nods in acknowledgement. "Both of you, gentlemen, I would ask you again not to treat me as though I am a child. I do not need to be protected from the world."

"No, Madam," Grindal replies, chastened.

"And what of Hertford, then?" Elizabeth picks up her own earlier thoughts, "he comes to beg my father the king to be appointed to some regency council, does he? I'm not sure that my father wishes to have Lutherans such Hertford as part of my brother's council. Though the queen might."

Grindal and Strelley exchange a look. Grindal sighs heavily, puffing out his cheeks, and so it is Strelley who speaks. "With respect, Madam, I think Hertford presses your father to be made the prince's sole protector."

"Ah!" Elizabeth exclaims. "Hertford expects to rule in my

brother's stead. It saddens me that those born outside royalty are so eager to claim power in whatever way they can find. Your friend, Master Strelley, the one who is a guard. Did he tell you all of this?"

Strelley is thrown for a moment. Eventually, he replies. "He told me little more than we have discussed, My Lady."

"I do not believe you, but I shall press you no further. Come, let us resume our lesson." Elizabeth waves her hand, her gesture signalling the recommencement of Grindal's teaching, and a reduction in the tension between the three of them that comes from Elizabeth's chaffing. There we shall leave them.

Across the palace, Longshawe stands guard in a corridor, outside a suite of royal apartments. Inside a room a few paces from where he stands, the voices of the Seymour brothers can be heard, raised in anger. The door is slightly ajar. Without noticing himself doing it, Longshawe leans ever so slightly towards the sound.

"For heaven's sake, Thomas, forget her!" Edward Seymour growls.

"She does not want him. She wanted me, and she still wants me now."

"You will get us both killed. You're an imbecile, Tom."

"I can't stand in front of him while he lords it over me. I can't, and I won't."

"He is your king. You will kneel before him if he commands it. Kiss his boots."

"*You* don't kneel before him." There is a brief silence, before Thomas Seymour continues in a sneer. "Do you, My Lord? He will never have you for the boy's protector."

"Not if you continue in this manner. Now you will hold your tongue, or I shall cut it out." The door slams shut, and though the argument can still be heard, the words are no longer distinguishable.

A few days later, Elizabeth is joined at her lesson by the queen, Catherine. Grindal has prepared some impressively dense Latin work for her to translate, and Strelley sits with an annotated translation of his own, together with a blank sheet to record Elizabeth's version. However, the lesson is distracted as Catherine begins to ask Grindal questions about his acquaintances.

"So you studied under Ascham at Cambridge?"

"I did, Your Majesty. I learned much about scholarship from him. He thinks as the humanists do, though I could not say if he actively practises the reformed faith. He is rather above such matters, concerned ideas and principles, not the mundane."

"It does not signify, Sir. There are men of the reformed faith who are Godly, and those who are not. Just as there are men of the Catholic faith who are Godly, and those who are not."

Elizabeth has watched this exchange, and is considering adding her thoughts. She sets off slowly, "surely, Madam, there can be no doubt that either the reformists or the Catholics have claim to be Godly, but not both. One or other party is right. My father the king sides with the Catholics on matters of doctrine."

"He seems to," Catherine agrees. "It is difficult to know what the king thinks. He is of such commanding intellect that I cannot always follow his arguments." She lets out a stifled laugh as she says this, and then looks around the room at the the two men and the young girl with her, as though she is trying to call back the sound, erase the blunder, however slight. Strelley and Grindal succeed in remaining impassive, watching with great interest as the dialogue plays itself out.

Elizabeth frowns at her stepmother. "Do you mean that he outwits you, Madam? Or are you dissimulating? He is not of such great age as to have descended into decrepitude, is he?"

"Your charge knows not when to hold her counsel, Master Grindal," Catherine laughs as she speaks, but Grindal at length pales visibly. Strelley's eyes, unwatched by the queen, flick from Elizabeth to Catherine, then to Grindal.

"I thank you not to speak ill of me in my presence, Madam," Elizabeth snaps. "My tutor treats me like a child, and my father encourages him to, as you and I both can tell. Master Strelley is not afraid to speak his mind, when he speaks. Which is not often enough, Sir." She turns to Strelley to address him. He gulps and his eyes widen, although there is more than a hint of sarcasm in his expression. Elizabeth catches his gentle mocking, and continues in as even a tone as she can muster, "do not worry, I shall not press you for your opinions before the queen. I know when I am defeated, Master Strelley," she declares, before carrying on with her translation in a sulk. The adults exchange glances but don't say anything further, wary of setting off another rant.

Queen Catherine, humbled by her stepdaughter's outburst,

listens to Lady Elizabeth, following the Latin as she construes it. She is evidently impressed, but does not speak to say so.

Half an hour later, the lesson is finished. Elizabeth, still glowering over Catherine's criticism, stands and leaves the room. "I shall speak to her later," Catherine says, after Elizabeth is gone. "I did not mean to upset her so. You must be congratulated on her remarkable progress, Master Grindal. She outmatches many scholars twice her age."

Grindal smiles. "She is a most able pupil," he says.

"I would ask you, Sir, what you know of the prince's tutor. Master Cheke."

"Cheke was tutor to Ascham, as Ascham was tutor to me. I am sure you know that already. Cheke is a good man, and a great scholar. He will see the Prince Edward is raised fit for his duty as king."

"I do not doubt it. Where do you think his sympathies lie?"

"Madam?"

"For a man of such learning, Master Grindal, you are stubbornly insensitive to my meaning. I ask you if he is a reformer or a Catholic."

"Ah. I could not tell you."

"You have told me all I need to know." Queen Catherine looks past Grindal, concentration on the conversation lost in her thoughts.

"What do you mean?" Grindal asks, pulling her focus back to him.

"You know as well as I do that the conservatives have the king's backing. You know one way or the other, and as you do not tell me, I infer that you have reason to hide your knowledge. Cheke is a Lutheran." At this, Grindal draws breath sharply through his nose, and the rushing sounds louder than it should. "We both know that. I am just testing your willingness to dissemble. And I see that you are not made for court life, as you dissemble so poorly!" Catherine laughs.

"I am Lady Elizabeth's tutor, Madam, not a politician. If I am involved at court it is as a servant. I do not aspire to be a part of the court myself."

"Nor should you. It is not a safe place. Certainly not if you disagree with the king."

"Might I counsel that Madam should not, then, disagree with him?" Grindal speaks slowly and carefully, as one who fears to stoke up further anger.

"I thank you again, Sir," she says. There is a knock at the door, which Strelley, who has been following this talk without letting either of them realise that he has, rises and answers. A young girl of perhaps eight years stands there, hands clasped in front of her. She is just about to speak when she remembers herself and offers a well-rehearsed courtesy.

"May I speak with Her Majesty?" Strelley nods and ushers the girl into the room.

"Jane? What is it?" Catherine asks.

"There is someone who wishes to speak with you, Madam. He called himself Seymour."

"I must deal with this. Master Grindal, please... Do not speak of this to anyone." Grindal nods, and the queen bustles out, conducting the young girl through the corridors.

"Thomas Seymour visits the queen in the king's own palace," Strelley mutters. Grindal slaps his hand on the table.

"Master Strelley!" He shouts, and Strelley's face immediately betrays his surprise at the outburst. "It is bad enough that Lady Elizabeth knows not when to be quiet, but you as well! Learn to hold your peace. If Seymour wishes to visit the queen, that is between him and her alone."

"It is true that Seymour and the queen were involved," Strelley says, quietly. Grindal frowns.

"What do you mean? Speak, Edward."

"I mean what I say. Before the king married Catherine, there are rumours that she and Seymour had an affair. Hence Seymour's removal to the Low Countries on some redundant diplomatic mission."

"Perhaps Catherine would tell you that, unlike me, you *are* made for court life. So, it would not merely be a matter between Seymour and the queen should they meet?"

"Indeed. The king would likely have Seymour's balls-"

"Enough. You must also learn to control your vulgarity, Master Strelley."

Strelley smiles, celebrating his victory. "I shall try harder in future."

"Master Strelley, isn't it? I have something for you." Lady Mary hands Strelley a letter. "It is from your friend, George de Winter. I shall let you read it for yourself."

Strelley takes the letter and begins to read, sitting himself as he focuses on the words. Mary addresses herself to her sister, who is studying a passage with Grindal. "Dear sister, what are you reading?"

"The Aeneid, My Lady," Elizabeth answers. "Do you know it?"

"Very little. You know I have nothing approaching your zeal for this learning." The two sisters share a smile. Mary's is kind, warm. Elizabeth's has a little more of condescension, despite her youth. Strelley lets out an excited gasp.

"Master Strelley?" Grindal asks him, looking up from his work. "I trust all is well."

"More than well, Sir. George writes to say that he has been offered a position with the Lady Mary and that he hopes to join us at court within the month."

"He has the offices of the young Talbot to thank for that," Mary says. There is a colour to her cheeks that was not present moments ago. "Indeed, I believe the earl himself speaks very highly of Master de Winter. Your friend is an honourable young gentleman, Master Strelley."

Strelley offers Lady Mary a nod of his head in lieu of a bow, seated as he is. She listens intently as her sister reads in Latin, then herself offers a version in English. Strelley waits until Mary has left to correct a few minor mistakes.

"Does he mention Pike at all?" Longshawe asks, later the same day.

"He writes that Will is going to join His Majesty's hunt at Hampton Court. Perhaps we shall get to see him if the court removes there," Strelley replies.

"I look forward to it. It will be a great pleasure to see them both again."

17: The King's Wishes

Edward Seymour, Earl of Hertford, is once again in the presence chamber, petitioning the king. Longshawe stands guard, silent, staring ahead but noting the words carefully.

"My brother has returned to the Low Countries, Your Majesty. He, um, does not wish to neglect his mission there." Hertford looks at the king, and then away from him quickly, as though he does not wish to meet his gaze.

"He cannot stand to see me with the queen. He makes no secret that he wishes she had married him rather than me." Hertford shapes to interrupt, but the king silences him with a forceful gesture. "No, Your Grace. I will speak my mind. Your brother does not find it easy to kneel before me because I married the woman he thought belonged to him. It does not signify for you, though. I do not hold you accountable for your brother's sins of arrogance, pride and malice."

This time Hertford succeeds in interrupting. "Majesty, I do not agree that my brother is malicious. Proud, arrogant perhaps, but not malicious."

"No? You deny that he wishes me dead? I have had some shrewd counsellors in my time, Edward, and *you* are not so acute as to deceive me in this matter. Nevertheless, your brother's folly is not your folly. But you must understand that he does not please me."

Hertford is all contrition, apologetic. "Indeed, Majesty. And I shall do all I can to reduce your displeasure."

"All I ask is that you remain vigilant on my behalf. Affairs of the heart can lead men to terrible – and foolish – crimes. All of that is of minor import, however."

"Majesty?"

"I grow concerned that I am not well-served, Your Grace. My counsellors do not tell me what passes in this palace, let alone what goes on abroad in my realm. I know not whether to trust Archbishop Cranmer, whose continual pressing for the Lutheran cause is close to intolerable. Gardiner is nearly as bad."

"Sire? Gardiner is a staunch believer in the Articles."

"I do not doubt it. But he refuses to recognise my authority as head of *my* church." The emphasis is clearly pronounced. "You must find some better spies, Master Seymour. On matters of doctrine, Gardiner seems to me to be in the right, at least close. But as far as the

Church itself is concerned, he refuses to acknowledge exactly what Cranmer allows, namely that I am rightful Supreme Head of that Church."

"So Your Majesty wishes that Gardiner would acquiesce to you as the Act of Supremacy requires?" Edward Seymour wrinkles his nose, considering.

"I wish you to grasp the subtlety of my problem, Hertford. It is not a simple matter of acquiescence. Unless and until the likes of Gardiner truly believe that I am Supreme Head of the Church there shall always be this unbearable stain of Popery that so confuses my people. The so-called Pope is nothing more than the Bishop of Rome, a parish priest, not some supreme emperor. His claim to rule over all the princes of Europe – to rule over me, Edward – is nonsense. Unsupported by the scripture. An invention to grasp power." The king has grown more aggressive during this speech, spitting the last words, and he finishes it by pointing fiercely at Hertford, whose eyes widen slightly. Longshawe's eyes flick across to take in the scene, but he keeps his head still. Eventually both king and subject master themselves, and Longshawe returns his gaze to straight ahead.

It is Hertford who speaks next. "Your Majesty speaks the truth. What can I do to aid you, Sire?"

"You are the future king's uncle, Edward. You may be called on to look to his welfare, spiritual as much as temporal. But for now, I should like your help in more immediate matters of state. It cannot have escaped your notice that I am no longer healthy. Indeed, my descent into decrepitude alarms me and I do not foresee that I shall live out the next year. I do not wish my Privy Council to be composed of grasping, self-interested men. Men who may use the opportunity of my demise for their own gain."

Hertford's face shines with satisfaction. "Your Majesty has every right to expect your council to serve only you, and thereby your people." He allows himself a smile that he does not think Henry notices.

"I do have that right. And I shall value your assistance in, shall we say, pruning out the bad." The king looks melancholy. "I truly loved your sister. Of all of them... The son she bore me is the most precious life in the kingdom. You are his uncle, and you must ensure that when he comes to rule he is kept safe."

"I shall, Sire."

"Do you truly understand what I ask? The boy must not fall into heresy! He must rule in accordance with what is right. He must not condemn himself to the eternal misery of damnation. I suspect his tutor of inculcating the boy into Lutheranism, though the queen defends him. I have reason to suspect the queen herself on matters of doctrine. I can trust no one, it seems, even those closest to me."

"Your Majesty may trust me without fear or doubt."

"Fine words, Your Grace, but they must be acted out. I still rule, and you shall obey."

"Sire?"

"You shall be my eyes and ears about this palace and this realm. If any speak ill of me, I wish to hear of it. Do not spare me the difficulty of being told that I am not loved or respected." Hertford nods, slowly. "Have I made myself clear to you, Edward? If *anyone* speaks ill of me. Whoever it is."

Hertford bows low, and the king dismisses him with a gesture. Once Hertford is gone, the king turns to Longshawe. "Master Longshawe," he says, quietly, "I grow weary."

"Your Majesty wishes me to call for assistance?"

"No, my boy. I wish merely to speak with a man who has no desire for power, no agenda that I cannot divine, and most of all nothing to take from me without my knowing it. I am weary of those about me dissembling, and I no longer have the energy to play such games. My son is but eight years old and I fear for him if I die. I must impress on you the need to protect him."

"I would give my life to keep His Highness from danger."

"Perhaps. But I would have something else, not your life. I wish only that you bend your wits to his safety. He is all that stands between this realm and chaos. I cannot countenance the thought that his sisters should rule. The elder would return us to the curse of Papistry, and the younger is no more than a child herself, though she has wit enough. I believe your friend has no little part in that." Henry smiles, though his eyes well with tears. "You, and your friend... You promised loyalty to Edward. My son. Would you fight against Hertford were he to use his connections to take power to himself?"

"Your Majesty, I am entirely your servant. As you know. And I shall serve Edward as I serve you," Longshawe replies quietly.

"If only I had men of your fibre for the prince's uncles. Find me paper, and I shall write to your friend."

Moments later the king has scribbled a note on a scrap of paper and handed it to Longshawe. "When you are dismissed, deliver it to him. I shall expect him here tomorrow."

Several hours later, Longshawe finishes his duty and heads straight for Strelley's quarters, where Strelley is reading from one of his many books. Longshawe glances down at a long roll of paper on the desk, recognises a few words and laughs.

"This is how you occupy yourself? Translating ribaldry?"

"That work is among the finest I have ever read," Strelley replies. "Perhaps you might like to read it yourself...?" Longshawe dismisses the suggestion with a wave.

"I have something infinitely more interesting for you." Longshawe hands Strelley the king's note.

"Is this your idea of a joke, James?"

"It's real." Strelley returns to reading the note, which he does several times. "The king gave it to me himself, to give to you."

"Extraordinary," Strelley says. "Well, I shall have to dress myself appropriately!"

The following morning, before Lady Elizabeth's lessons begin, Strelley attends the king, dressed as neatly as he can manage. He smoothes his doublet as he enters. Henry sits still in his chair, only his eyes move to show that he has noticed Strelley arrive. Longshawe stands to one side, with a guard Strelley does not recognise on the other. Both look straight ahead, not watching him.

"Good morning to you, Master Strelley. I see you have read my note. I hope I do not encroach upon the lady's education."

Strelley bows. "You do not, Your Majesty."

"I hear that my daughter progresses rapidly. Indeed, it seems that she is more than a match for her father." Strelley is thrown, unsure what to say. "Do not feel the need to flatter my opinion of myself, Sir. I have had enough with flattery, deception, and all that it brings. I must not be deceived in these matters. Well?"

"Lady Elizabeth is as intelligent as any man of Your Majesty's court. She shows great aptitude for her studies. Grindal teaches her rhetoric and argument, as well as languages. She argues with great precision and perspicacity."

"You do not think her shrewd?"

"The lady has a sharp mind, Sire, but her manner is gracious."

"Your loyalty to her is commendable, Master Strelley. Both the queen and her lady mistress have reported that my daughter is headstrong, even ungovernable." Henry smiles as he says this.

"Lady Elizabeth is learning to control her passions, Sire."

"Judiciously put, Master Strelley. Nevertheless, she is of great importance. Her learning is secondary to her compliance. She may be required to wed a great prince of Europe." Henry emphasises the words, speaking each one carefully. Strelley does not reply. He throws a glance at Longshawe, but his friend doesn't alter his straight-ahead gaze.

"Master Strelley," the king says, "your silence signifies. But what? Do not dissemble, even if you think to protect me, or indeed her."

Strelley considers for a moment. "Your Majesty, Elizabeth is not likely to be ruled by any man, prince or not. She could not be consort, even to the Emperor or King of France."

"And why not?"

"Your Majesty, she is..." He stops, still unsure of the ground.

"Master Strelley, I have told you already to be honest. I shall have you whipped if you deceive me," Henry laughs.

"She is like you, Sire. She would make a fine king herself."

Henry's eyes narrow. "I would tell you that you had forgotten your place, Sir, but that I had asked you to speak openly." Strelley bows again, as he has nothing to add. "It does not matter, as Edward shall be king when I am gone. And it is to that that I should like to turn. I have your friend's promise of his loyalty, to my son as much as to myself. Can I expect that same loyalty from you, Sir?"

"I do not understand Your Majesty."

"There are many about this court who would use Prince Edward's youth to their advantage. I wish you to turn your mind to his protection. Indeed, I want you to be loyal to him, whatever may be offered by those who seek to gain advantage."

"Your Majesty fears that someone will try to usurp the throne?" Strelley asks.

"That is a possibility. I anticipate also that some member of the council may try to accumulate power to himself. I do not wish this to transpire. There is to be a council, but each man is to have his share and no more."

"How am I to help?"

"Your counsel may not be sought, but you must offer it. Elizabeth may be a suitable mouthpiece for your thoughts, or Edward may seek you directly. I would like you to put your learning, your wit and intelligence, to the protection of my son's interest."

"Your Majesty flatters me greatly, but I have nothing to contribute to affairs of state."

"You must permit me to disagree, Sir. I have conversed with my daughter, as I have with Grindal, with her governess and her mistress, and she does not derive the unusual depth of her insight from them. They try to teach her by the book, but her lessons teach her more than just what she realises. I do not see that it is Grindal, for all his learning, who has shown her how to, shall we say, disagree...? Her inability to behave in the manner of a princess of the realm might lower her value in making alliances, if I cannot marry her as I wish. But it seems you have certainly shown her how to be a prince, and I commend you for it. Let us pray that she never has to rule in her own right, but I can rest in my grave knowing that she would be capable if she was called upon."

Strelley offers another obeisance. "I shall offer what I can to Prince Edward."

"I should like you to join Cheke as he delivers certain of the boy's lessons. There is another thing I would ask of you."
"Sire?"

"I fear that my children are being taught heresy. I would like you to find out what it is that Cheke teaches the boy and report it to me. Equally, I should like to know what is taught to Elizabeth."

"Lady Elizabeth has studied Your Majesty's articles at great length. She is as pious and devout as could be wished."

The king's voice is raised slightly, with an edge that was not there before. "Master Strelley, I will not have her believing in heresy!"

Strelley breathes slowly and deeply, as he contemplates his reply. "Your Majesty, Lady Elizabeth is no heretic."

"No, but her tutor? The queen chose him herself, and I wonder at the motivation for her choice."

"Grindal encourages the lady to question everything, so that she might understand better. But he does not lead her to heresy."

"You are sure that he is no Lutheran?"

"He is no Papist, but neither is he a Lutheran. He believes in Your Majesty's supremacy."

"I doubt that greatly. But he inspires your loyalty, so he must be a good man. You will relay to him my concern. I do not wish Elizabeth to be aware that I have influenced him, nor do I want the queen to know. You must ensure this."

"I shall do my best, Sire."

"Your best, Master Strelley, had better be good enough." The king smiles at his descending tricolon. "Now, you may go and commence your lesson with Elizabeth. Should you be summoned to Edward, you must leave Grindal to his work with my daughter." Strelley nods and leaves the presence chamber. Longshawe's face has broken into something of a smile, but he remembers himself as the door closes and arranges his expression into sternness.

Walking along the corridor, reflecting on the content of his meeting with the king, Strelley doesn't notice as a footman walks the other way. The footman makes to stand aside, which shakes Strelley out of his thoughts. "My apologies," he says to the servant, who bows his head. Purposeful now, Strelley makes his way across the palace to the room in which Elizabeth takes her lessons. It is cold, as autumn breaks into winter, and his breath is visible in the air before he enters.

Elizabeth looks up at him as he opens the door, fixing him in her gaze for some moments. He nods his head, and seats himself across the room at a writing desk. Still watching him as he takes out quill and ink, Elizabeth licks her teeth and frowns.

"Master Strelley," she says, eyes glinting with a sort of devilish naughtiness. "Where have you been this morning? Master Grindal has missed you, as have I. We have failed to construe a single line of our translation." Her tone is bantering.

Strelley looks at Grindal, whose countenance is once again arranged to indicate that Strelley is very much on his own. Resigned, Strelley says, "My Lady... I have been summoned by the king."

"Indeed? My father wished to speak to *you*? You are not much more than amanuensis for Master Grindal. I wonder what he could wish of you."

Strelley considers. Then, emphasising his words deliberately, he says, "His Majesty the king merely wished to engage me in certain aspects of the education of your brother, His Highness Prince Edward."

"Congratulations!" Elizabeth exclaims, not without a certain irony. "It seems you have moved up in the world, from the bastard daughter to the only son and heir." She slams her book against the table.

Grindal's eyebrows raise, but he does not intervene. Strelley allows Elizabeth a moment, before offering his reply. "The king thinks very highly of you, My Lady." She moves to interrupt, but Strelley raises his hand to request that she continue to listen. "His Majesty spoke of your princely qualities. But you must be wary, My Lady. The king is greatly exercised over matters of religion, and regardless of your true beliefs, you would be wise not to cross him in this."

"I thank you for your counsel, and your flattery." Elizabeth has calmed. "My father told you not to speak to me directly of religion, I suspect. And yet you do. Why?"

"My Lady's judgement serves her well. I can do more to the good by offering you and your tutor this warning against the king's wishes, than I can by respecting them."

"It seems you are willing to commit treason for the sake of policy," Elizabeth reflects.

"Not so. You're wise enough to know how your father can be quick to anger. Learn to dissemble, Madam, such that no man may judge the depth of your perception." Elizabeth stares at him, brows knitted. Grindal sits back in his seat, watching intently.

"I shall heed your warning. Now to work!" Elizabeth says after a moment, then bows her head over her paper and flourishes her pen pointedly.

18: Ambitions

Edward Strelley and James Longshawe travel out to an inn outside Westminster, riding leisurely despite the winter chill. Guy Fletcher, dressed in a new fine outfit and with his new sword at his belt, all bought for him by Longshawe, rides with them. They talk about their lives at the palace, and how things have changed since Ancrum Moor. When they arrive, they hand their mounts to a stable boy and seat themselves in the main room of the inn.

"Mine Host!" Longshawe calls out. "I shall have beer, and lots of it, as shall my companions. Prepare your finest wine for my friends who are yet to arrive."

"Do you think Andrew will be with them?" Guy asks.

"De Winter kept Andrew Shepherd as his own manservant. We can hope that he is also coming." Longshawe lays a hand on Guy Fletcher's shoulder. The innkeeper comes out from a back room with a large jug and several cups. Longshawe picks one up and looks at it, then at the innkeeper. Strelley puts his arm across him before he speaks up.

"Just let him alone. We'll drink from earthenware. We've no need to show off to George and William, have we?" Longshawe smiles in reply, and pours himself a generous measure of beer, before offering the same to Guy, then to Strelley. The innkeeper disappears again, furtling around in his cellar, and all three of them drink deeply.

A few minutes later, George de Winter enters the inn, with Will Pike a step behind and Andrew Shepherd following. Strelley goes to Pike and shakes his hand warmly. Longshawe bows to de Winter, a grin on his face. De Winter returns the bow with his own mocking obeisance. Guy Fletcher approaches Andrew Shepherd and they greet each other quietly.

"Gentlemen!" de Winter says, loudly. "It's a long-awaited pleasure to see you all. How well you look." He looks at Longshawe for a moment. "I hope the king doesn't dress all his palace guards thus, James. How is His Majesty?"

Longshawe casts about for a witticism to return, but de Winter is tastefully dressed, beyond reproach indeed, underneath another black riding cloak. Eventually, he settles for actually answering the question. "The king is alive, but he makes his preparations for passing."

"And what would a guardsman know of such matters?" de Winter asks, smiling.

"His Majesty has had the pleasure of addressing me on a number of occasions." Longshawe looks to Strelley, seeking his approval for this little joke. Strelley rolls his eyes, then Longshawe continues, more serious. "The king has asked us both to look after the interests of his son, now and in the future. He has made us swear our allegiance to the prince directly." De Winter looks impressed, as does Andrew Shepherd.

"What does he want you to do?" Pike enquires.

"It's not obvious. He wants us to make sure that we support the boy when he has died, to make sure that powerful men in the kingdom do not become over-mighty. Else they might try to rule the country themselves," Longshawe replies.

Strelley takes over. "The king is aware that there are many about the court, surrounding himself and the prince, who would use his passing to try to secure their own ends. Henry knows he is going to die, and doesn't anticipate living until the boy reaches his majority. He sees men like us, loyal only to him, as the way of protecting his son. Everyone else has something to gain – or to lose – when Edward ascends the throne, and each will seek to protect his own interest. So we are a part of his insurance against such a thing happening, in our own little way. So... tell us about your new position, George."

"I am to act as a sort of equerry, though I haven't yet been fully appraised of my duties. I have met the Comptroller of the Household, but he didn't seem to know what to do with me. Talbot's influence extended to finding me employment, but not to defining its nature." His eyes follow the innkeeper, who places wine on the table. Both he and Pike take a draught, although Andrew Shepherd takes a cup of beer, which he sips quietly.

"That disappoints you?" Longshawe asks him.

"It may be that the lady chooses to take me into her inner circle, or it may be that I see her only once or twice in a month. I do not yet know what to expect. Will at least knows what will occupy him." De Winter gestures to Pike, who smiles and begins to explain his appointment.

"The Master of the Hunt at Hampton Court requires someone to manage the park. I may be able to ride with the King's Hunt. If he is ever well enough to ride out again of course..."

"You must be pleased," Strelley says. Pike nods, his face lighting up with a broad grin.

"Fortune, it seems, has favoured us all," de Winter says. "And yet what are we?" He looks out of the window of the inn into the distance, eyes unfocused in his contemplation.

"What do you mean?" Strelley demands, surprised by the tone.

"Only that whatever heights we might rise to, we are still and will remain insignificant. No one will recall us when we are gone. No one will write our history."

"'Quod in vita facimus, resonat in aeternum.' What we do in life echoes in eternity. I forget where I read that," Strelley answers him, conjuring some finality in his tone that is supposed to close the matter. "And each of us will stand before St Peter to account for his deeds." He smiles, casting his gaze at each of the assembled companions, before continuing, "is that not what we're supposed to think, to fear? That God watches everything?"

"I wonder sometimes that He does not find it within himself to see to your end, Edward. You insist on testing him so. Anyway, do you not crave something a little more temporal than God's approbation at the judgement? Something more tangible, here and now?" De Winter waves at the innkeeper who has reappeared from the cellar. "Wine, my man. The finest you have."

"Wine again! We have already alerted the good host to your preferences," Longshawe sighs. "Anyway, aren't you pleased to be part of Lady Mary's household? What better role could there be for you? Or do you think that the king should choose you, and let's remember that you are the son of a minor nobleman, and the second son at that, to guide the nation's tiller?" He accompanies this last with a derogatory wave of the hand, which de Winter watches with his head tilted and a wry smile just dragging his lips into a curl.

"He chose Cromwell, did he not?" de Winter says. "The son of a brewer. I am at least of noble blood. Should my brother die, I may become a baron myself. Why should I not have such ambition?"

"Be ambitious, George," Strelley offers. "But remember that Cromwell paid with his life."

De Winter looks at him for a moment, eyebrows creased into a frown. "I would not wish to succumb to such a fate. Perhaps it *would* be wiser to wait for calmer seas on which to sail." He puts his hands together as in in prayer.

"Perhaps," Strelley agrees. "But it seems to me that if you want to make a name for yourself, that will be easier to achieve now, or at least whilst the future king is still a minor. This king has had a habit of cutting down those who have risen too high."

"That's true," de Winter says, the thought coming out slowly as though it takes a little time to penetrate into his mind. "But it might be easier to serve a king who ruled as Henry has done, always at his own behest and following his own... muse, I suppose. At least you would need to please only one man. A council of regency would dilute any influence one might accumulate."

Longshawe eyes de Winter carefully before breaking the moment's silence by responding, "I should content yourself with what you have for now if I were you. I like my head where it is, as ought you."

"You must see how lucky you have been, though, James? You have fought for His Majesty only twice, and yet you somehow found and indeed find yourself in his presence chamber." De Winter opens his hand as he speaks, then rolls his fingers into a fist.

"Fortune has smiled upon me particularly, I agree. Though there are many in my position to whom the king has barely spoken in years."

"Perhaps His Majesty has a little weakness for you?" de Winter laughs. "I congratulate you, Longshawe. And you, Edward. I am little more than a rider for Lady Mary, but it seems that you have a much closer association with the Lady Elizabeth."

"I am involved in her lessons daily, though Grindal still does not like to allow me to lead. I wonder sometimes if he is... I don't know... Jealous?" Strelley hesitates as he speaks, struggling to find the right idea.

"Jealous of you?" Pike asks. "Why?"

"He teaches the lady all sorts about languages and history, though he will still refer to me for the finer points of the ancient tongues. But it is the attention of the lady... She will ask me questions that she would not ask him. As though I were an older brother, and he still her tutor. She seeks my counsel on matters beyond our lessons, even though she does not speak to me outside them."

Longshawe claps him over the knee as he finishes speaking. "Well, Ned, perhaps she'll marry you and one day you'll be prince consort, or even king."

"Do not joke about such matters," Strelley chastises him, batting his hand away. "I have no wish to attract her interest in the way that you might. She is still a child." Guy Fletcher's ears prick up at this.

"Do you say *I* am yet a child, Master Strelley?" he asks, smiling.

"You have travelled to the farthest ends of this island, though, Guy. Elizabeth has sat at home being tutored into being a princess, or whatever she is," Longshawe answers. "You have earned the right to be a man. She has not had your experiences."

Fletcher sits back, pleased with Longshawe's praise. De Winter takes up the questioning. "Well, then, is it true, Edward, that your duties have extended to include tutoring the future king?"

"To a point. The king has rather appointed me chief spy on the boy's tutor, rather than his assistant. He has taken it into his mind that Cheke is a reformer – which is true enough – and that he fills the boy's head with Protestant doctrine, which I don't know one way or the other. The king fears that the boy is doomed to fall into the Lutheran heresy, as he sees it."

"Good," de Winter replies. "I am pleased to hear that the king thinks Luther is a heretic. It is time that we were taken back into the good graces of the Church of Rome."

"But the king will not succeed," Strelley answers. "Whatever he plans for the education of Edward, there isn't a scholar who will tolerate the king's position. He cannot find a willing Catholic, who would have to allow that the king's doctrine is correct but that he is also supreme head of the church. No Catholic of conscience will consent to teach the prince that this is right."

De Winter nods. "That's true. So the king cannot find any who agree with his thoughts on the Eucharist who will also allow that he is legitimately head of the church."

"Indeed not," Strelley confirms. "So the men available to him are all, to a greater or lesser extent, hoping that their willingness to tolerate the king as head of the church will gain them some sort of concession when it comes to modes of worship. Even Cranmer only gets to have his say on doctrine because he supports the royal supremacy. Cheke is no rabid religionist, nor is Grindal, but the king fears that they are indoctrinating his children to the opposite effect of his own teachings on the subject. Henry wants his own salvation, but he wants his power on Earth all the same. Cranmer lets him have it. Gardiner wouldn't."

"But the king asks you to spy on Cheke?" Pike asks. "Do you report what you see?"

"I have been careful to warn both Grindal and Cheke that their positions are subject to the king's suspicion. We all know what he is capable of, and these men are friends and colleagues, and they are good men, whatever their religion. I do not wish to bear responsibility for good men being burned."

"Do you not fear your disloyalty could be your own downfall?" de Winter says, grimacing. "You are running a great risk if the king finds out from another source."

"Yes, I may be. But I should prefer my choices to affect me, and not the lives of others. I do not fear death. I have made my peace with God, and I do not doubt that He will accept me as I am. But I do not wish to consign others to a death for which they are not prepared."

"You've made your peace with God? What do you mean?" Pike exclaims.

"Only that when we were fighting, I found myself able to speak to God in a way that had been denied to me until then. I feared death because I feared God, but now I do not fear God."

"Then perhaps you should," de Winter says, nodding, before his tone changes from friendly banter to something much more serious. "Bah! It does not signify. God is a merciful being, is he not? Then we should live as we wish, and repent when we are done."

"I'm sure God would not agree," Pike tells him, before taking a long draught of beer. "You cannot repent a sin then commit it again," he says into the silence.

"Well, then, one should not repent of the sin until one is done with sinning!" de Winter laughs uproariously. "Do not trouble your conscience over me, Will. I shall meet St Peter at the Gates and I shall meet his eyes, and say to him that I have lived in the faith of Christ."

"And he will reply that the company you keep is enough to deny any man entry into Heaven." Longshawe laughs in his turn, as do the others. It seems to relieve the tension, shoulders noticeably dropping and faces relaxing into half-smiles.

De Winter puts his wine-cup down, and fixes Longshawe with a stare. "I should like to ask another question, but for this one I want an honest answer. Can you give it?"

"That depends on the question."

"Indeed. Then I shall ask it. What influence does Seymour wield at court?"

"You mean Hertford?" Longshawe asks. De Winter nods. "I wonder for whom this information is intended? Our old master or your new mistress?"

"Shrewsbury would like to know how the land lies, as it were. Though it stands me in good stead with Lady Mary, should I have a little gossip to give her."

Longshawe thinks for a moment before replying. "The king wishes that his son be free to rule as he should wish. Though Henry recognises that he will die long before the boy reaches his majority. Seymour pushes the king, trying to have himself named Protector."

"And does the king acquiesce?" de Winter leans forward to ask.

"He does not. The king has some trust in Seymour, but he will not go so far as to name him sole Protector. Rather, he wishes that the office be fulfilled by some sort of council," Longshawe answers.

Strelley watches de Winter's face, which remains dispassionate, as he hears this and after a brief pause, speaks. "George, the king is frightened that Seymour will try to take over after he dies. It's not what he wants. Henry is making people swear that they will look to the interests of the boy prince after he dies. And that includes Longshawe and me."

De Winter's eyebrows rise at this. "The king speaks to you of such matters?"

Strelley puffs out his cheeks, then blows the air through pursed lips. "He does. There are few people that he trusts at court. His wife he suspects of heresy, and of teaching his son that same heresy. Each of his advisers has his own agenda, the nobles would seek to gain whatever they can for themselves after his death... We must seem to him the perfect loyal subjects in contrast to the more august personages of court."

"Then I shall take heed of your successes, and be myself a listening ear to the lady," de Winter says, with a hint of irony. "Before we drink overmuch, read this letter from My Lord Shrewsbury."

De Winter passes round a letter, bearing the Talbot seal.

Gentlemen,

I hope this epistle finds you all well, and that you are satisfied with your various stations. I intend to visit Greenwich to seek an audience with the king, and I hope thereby to be present at the New Year celebration. I shall, if I can, present my son to His Royal Highness Prince Edward. It shall be of the greatest value to me if you should each consent to meet me before I see His Majesty, as I have much to ask about the men and women at court. If you are willing, please pass on by courier a sign of your willingness.

"Even Shrewsbury wishes us to spy for him!" Longshawe says. "I do not know whom I can trust."

"Shrewsbury expects a good return on his investment in us," de Winter replies. "His influence put us in these positions, and no doubt he could have us removed just as easily. He simply wishes to reap whereof he has sowed."

"But beside the king and Prince Edward, I do not know with whom to dissemble and with whom to be honest," Longshawe protests, frustrated. Strelley smiles wryly at him, looking out from under his brows, and shaking his head at his friend's vexation, exaggerated though it is.

"Perhaps you should limit your trust, James, to those with whom you speak now. Reveal nothing to anyone unless it is in your own interests to do so." Strelley waves a finger vaguely as he speaks. "Keep what you know to yourself."

"But share it with us, of course!" De Winter pats Longshawe on the shoulder. "Perhaps we four-" He looks over to Andrew Shepherd and Guy Fletcher, deep in conversation together "-six, even, could become... important." He nods slowly.

"I have no desire to be important, George," Pike says. "I ask no more than a warm bed, a full belly, and the love of a good woman." At this, Longshawe, unnoticed by the others, stares long at de Winter. He fingers something in his pocket, wonders about saying something, but does not. The others laugh together. Longshawe seems to forget whatever it is that troubles him, and joins in. The merry drinking carries on for some hours before they retire.

19: The Education of Guy Fletcher

Edward Strelley and Guy Fletcher are hunched over a book in the room that Grindal normally uses to teach Lady Elizabeth. It is daylight, but late; the sun is low, its light entering the room at a low angle. The room is bathed in coloured light from a stained-glass window. Fletcher is reading tentatively. He stumbles over words in several places, but is able to decipher them after two or three attempts without help from Strelley.

"After the eight articles of our belief, in which we knowledge God's might and power in the creation of the world, his mercy and goodness in our redemption, and his spiritual benefits, exhibited and given, to us by the Holy Ghost, followeth the ninth article, in which we declare, that we do believe and confess the manner of God's working, in calling us to have fruition of him, and to be made partakers of his said benefits."

"Very good, Guy," Strelley congratulates him, "your progress is very impressive. What do you think of the King's Book?"

"I think it is mostly well-reasoned, although it professes too much of the old faith by my reckoning. Salvation in acts? Through the sacraments? Isn't that all the old Papist thinking?"

"True enough, Guy. If you agree with the reformists, that salvation is through faith alone... The king seems to hold quite orthodox views in these writings. I am not sure it is still so."

"Why do you say that?" Guy asks.

"The queen must have *some* influence on the king's thinking. Although if I were her, I would consider the wisdom of pressing matters of religion with him. She shall feel the sharp edge of his anger if she pushes against him too hard." Strelley mimes a chopping gesture, imitating the execution of two of Henry's wives.

"So what *does* the king think?" Fletcher angles his head and leans in to Strelley.

"I don't know if even he knows that, Guy. There are men around him who try to change their views as his change, and there are others who persist in their own interpretation regardless of the king's current thoughts. The king has bound himself tightly to Cranmer, as he is the only senior one among the ministry who supports the king's break from Rome. The Bishop of Winchester has tried endlessly to turn the king against him, but failed."

"I think I understand."

"Then you do better than most, Guy, myself included." They laugh together.

There is a rustling sound at one side of the room. Strelley looks over in that direction, narrowing his eyes. His expression is one of wary uncertainty. He focuses on a portion of the wall, aware that there is a hidden door on that side of the room, and he rises quietly and approaches it by following the edge of the room. He carries on talking to Guy Fletcher as if nothing unusual has happened, maintaining the illusion that the intrusion is unnoticed.

"The king is difficult to fathom, but we owe him our service as King of England, whether we believe that we owe him service as Supreme Head of the Church or-" At this, he reaches the hidden door and thrusts his arm in, grabbing a handful of the clothes of whoever is listening to them speak. As he recognises the eavesdropper, he lets out an exclamation of genuine surprise and falls over his heels back into the room.

The Lady Elizabeth steps out from the passage behind the secret door. "Ah," she says to Strelley, supine on the floor. She tries to smile sweetly, taking a moment to compose herself before adding, "I did not know you were aware of this corridor." Strelley frowns at her, before altering his expression to offer her a wry smile, raising himself on his elbows. Then he rises to his feet and offers the lady a nod of his head. He turns to Guy Fletcher, brushing off his clothes demonstratively. Fletcher gets up from his seat and bows his head.

"Guy Fletcher, may I present to you Lady Elizabeth..." He turns back to the young girl. "What are you doing?" he asks, no anger in his voice but a great deal of wonder.

"Listening."

"I can see that for myself." Strelley moves aside as she makes her way into the room.

"Good day, Master Fletcher. I trust that your tutor is to your liking." Elizabeth sits herself in the chair that Strelley had occupied. "The King's Book! Do not let Master Strelley lead you on matters of religion, Sir!" She has a broad smile on her face as she admonishes, rescuing some dignity. "He would mislead you into heresy!" She flourishes a hand to accompany the last word, and stands by the chair, defiant, awaiting a response. Fletcher says nothing, awestruck at the novelty of the situation.

Strelley coughs. "My Lady... It is not seemly for you to listen at secret doors, even if that to which you listen is harmless."

Elizabeth looks at Strelley for a moment. "As ever, Sir, you have my welfare at heart. I do not know where I should be without you acting as my guardian."

"My Lady, I do not wish to instruct you-" Strelley begins, but Elizabeth interrupts.

"Well then, don't. I shall answer for myself should anyone who matters in this palace take exception to my behaviour." She speaks without looking at either Strelley or Fletcher, eyes now fixed again on the book they were reading before her unusual entrance. As she finishes, she sits down.

Strelley sits by her in Guy's chair at the reading desk. He glances at Guy, who is still quite unable to speak and stands motionless with head bowed low, before speaking again to the lady.

"Elizabeth," he begins, and his failure to address her formally catches her attention. She is about to stop him again, but he carries on despite her attempt to interject. "Listen to me, please, My Lady. *I* do not object to your conduct. Indeed, one might – generously – say that it is a positive sign of your unwillingness to be directed, at which your father can hardly protest, given his own temperament. But you must not test the patience of those who *do* wield power in this palace. Should you succeed in directing their attention towards you, you may find yourself unable to charm your way out of danger. At best, you would darken your name. At worst, the king may not forbear to inflict some more telling punishment should you inadvertently find some subject which rouses his anger." He stops, and realises that he has leaned in towards her. He sits back, watching Elizabeth closely. She has her head down, her hands together. After a moment, he realises that she is crying.

"My Lady, you must not allow this to affect you," Strelley says, quietly. He considers taking her hand in his own, even putting his arm around her shoulder, but thinks better of it. That this comforting gesture is forbidden is only part of the reason. She notices his slight movement and raises her head.

"My father," she whispers, putting great stress on the three syllables, "sent my mother to the block. Do you know how *that* feels, Master Strelley?"

"I don't. Of course I don't. And I don't envy you your position, nor do I begrudge you your grief. But this is not the way to express it."

He rises, and walks over to a cloth bag in which there are several books. He picks out a manuscript and brings it over to the table.

"It is my own translation," he begins, "and I think you would find it instructive. Do not be prejudiced by what you have read elsewhere. It is the journal of someone who lived through times yet more troubled than these. Someone with much wisdom to offer you, advice of which you might take heed."

"I thank you, Edward. Do not think ill of me." She stands. "And it is a pleasure to meet you, Master Fletcher." She offers him a low courtesy and a genuinely warm smile. "I apologise for the manner in which we came to be introduced." Elizabeth turns and leaves the room, through the still-open door she from which she entered five minutes previously.

"So that is the Lady Elizabeth?" Guy asks, smiling.

"Indeed. I shall have to try to keep her safe from herself." He pauses. "Remember that Shrewsbury and his son are coming tomorrow. They have requested your presence. It would be wise to keep this incident to ourselves."

"I have made the necessary arrangements. I'm not sure Master Longshawe would have recalled the meeting had I not mentioned it."

"That does not surprise me. Ensure he is not late."

"I shall."

"Now go, and think on what you have learned today." Guy Fletcher stands and leaves the room, closing the door behind himself. Strelley runs his fingers around the jamb of the not-so-secret door through which Lady Elizabeth entered. He pulls it open, and takes a couple of paces into the corridor, looking upwards, to each side, then directly forwards. He continues along, the light from the room giving him just enough light to see. A few yards further down the passage, he hears something, voices that he recognises. Elizabeth is speaking, though the sound is too muffled for him to hear what she says. A moment later, another voice takes over, older, more assured. The voice belongs to the queen, Catherine. She does not sound as if she is admonishing Elizabeth. Strelley listens for a few minutes, satisfying himself that his pupil has not found herself in trouble with her stepmother. Then he turns round and returns, closing the door quietly but firmly behind himself.

The following day, Strelley, Longshawe and Guy Fletcher ride out of the palace westwards towards Chelsea, towards Shrewsbury's house, which the reader will remember as bearing a design of a lion rampant on the door. The three of them dismount and their horses are taken by a footman, dressed in the distinctive Talbot uniform. Another servant opens the front door and ushers them inside, leading them to the same library as Strelley has seen before. Inside, de Winter is seated in the embrasure of a window, and the Earl of Shrewsbury and his son sit opposite, just out of the line of light that the glass allows into the room. George Talbot rises and welcomes the new arrivals. De Winter and Francis Talbot remain sitting, watching as Strelley, Longshawe and Fletcher seat themselves, chairs pulled around to form a sort of circle.

"Gentlemen!" Shrewsbury exclaims as they settle. "It is the greatest pleasure to see all of you, though I note that Master Pike has not yet joined us."

De Winter sees Guy Fletcher looking around the room. "Andrew is with the servants, Guy, if you wish to see him." He points to a door, not the one through which Guy and the others entered. "Through there. You should be able to hear them." Guy nods and stands, bowing as he walks past the earl. He closes the door behind himself.

"Now, I should like you to elaborate on what George here has been telling me," Shrewsbury says, his face animated with interest. Strelley and Longshawe both look at de Winter, who offers them a shrug and a pout of his bottom lip.

"I have spoken of My Lady Mary's devotion to her religion. And that she seems to think of little else. Although the queen seems to hold her in high esteem, despite their differences."

"What differences?" George Talbot asks.

"The queen is... The Lady Mary is of the opinion that the queen and she do not share similar views of questions of faith," de Winter replies.

"You mean that she is a reformer? An Evangelical?" Shrewsbury takes over from his son. "A matter of some significance, I shouldn't wonder, and I confess I had always suspected it. Does she make much of this with the king?" Shrewsbury directs the question at de Winter, but he does not offer an answer other than another shrug of his shoulders. A moment later, Strelley speaks.

"The queen makes a sort of sport of her discussions with the king. She does take the Protestant cause in those arguments, but she is capable of bending before the wind. The king does not like to be vexed on such matters, indeed he does not like to be vexed on any matter."

"What do you mean?" asks George Talbot.

"The king is wary of all of his courtiers. There are those among the court who would try to use Edward's youth to their advantage, and the king is increasingly concerned for his welfare. After he is gone..."

"Indeed," Shrewsbury answers. "What do you think is the king's position on matters of doctrine?"

"It is difficult to say. His most recent professed orthodoxy is under strain. He continues to rely on Cranmer to support his authority as head of the church, and his wife pushes him, gently as she can, towards further reform. His elder daughter may have retained her strictly Roman Catholicism, but the son? He is educated by a Protestant, without doubt. One can only imagine that Protestant is what he will turn out to be."

"Who is this tutor?"

"Cheke. I knew of him at Cambridge. It appears that he was chosen by Catherine, rather than Henry himself. The king would not have tolerated such clear conviction, though Cheke is without religious fervour. He is principled, not zealous."

"And what of Prince Edward? Who shall govern in his stead, before he is of age?"

Longshawe answers, "the king says that he's going to form a council of equals, so that no one man may have the power of a king until the boy can rule in his own right. Norfolk and Gardiner think that they have his ear, but the king seems to have more time for Seymour."

"You mean the Earl of Hertford?" George Talbot asks.

"Hertford, yes. Now that his brother is gone again, the king places his trust in the prince's other uncle," Longshawe tells him, before looking at Strelley for his contribution.

Strelley picks up the thought. "I'm not sure how far Henry trusts Hertford, but it would not surprise me if the king elevates him above the others. Though even with him there is some misgiving, a concern that he will use Edward's minority to take power to himself."

"A Regency Council would be preferable to the king," Shrewsbury answers, noting but not responding to the last comment, "but he may find it impossible to impose such a solution when he is gone. If his wishes were known, made public... But there are those who will do what they can to keep the details of the king's will secret."

"You suspect Seymour is capable of such... treason?" George

Talbot inquires of his father.

"I don't know," Shrewsbury says quietly. "I am acquainted with Hertford from our service together, and I have met his brother Thomas, but I could not say I knew either of them well. Let us hope that Hertford is a good man, but let us not be be complacent in expecting it. What do you know of him?"

Longshawe considers. "He is ambitious, I think. I heard him speaking of these matters – the succession, I mean – to the king. He will continue to put doubts in the king's mind. He preys on the king's fears that the boy will not be acknowledged, or that civil war, like the one that got his father the crown, will happen. And so he slowly persuades the king that others do not share his care for the prince."

"Very interesting. Do you think he will succeed in being named Protector?" Shrewsbury leans forward, hands clasped together. His eyebrows are ever-so-slightly raised, indicating the depth of interest of this normally impassive man.

Longshawe looks to Strelley, whose expression says nothing more than that Longshawe is free to give his opinion, so he does. "I cannot say. There are others who try to prevent it. And though the king tolerates Seymour speaking of the future, he has little patience for it. I don't think he likes to be reminded of his mortality. It might be that Seymour's hectoring actually puts the king off the idea."

"It might." Shrewsbury leans back again, and folds his arms. "Though equally it might not. I should like to know what you can tell me about this Seymour. Does he hear the Mass?" Shrewsbury looks at Longshawe, but his shake of the head diverts the earl's attention to Strelley. Strelley's eyes widen, and he thinks for a moment before speaking.

"He does not, My Lord. Though this is not commonly known, I think. He avoids dispute with the king on matters of faith. He may well have had some influence in the choice of Cheke as Edward's tutor, and that was not in ignorance of Cheke's views. May I speak freely?"

Shrewsbury offers a nod of encouragement. Strelley continues after a pause, during which he looks to Longshawe, who frowns, and sighs, but does not discourage his friend from commenting. "My Lord, I wonder whether the king holds firm in his doctrinal views as once he did. His wife, his archbishop, his son's uncle, his son's tutor, his son himself... all are more or less in favour of Luther's reforms."

"I understand what you are saying, Master Strelley,"

Shrewsbury replies. "Though from what I know of the king, his mind in these matters is very much his own, and he is not much susceptible to the arguments and opinions of others. I don't doubt the firmness of his convictions, whatever they are."

"Sir..." Strelley begins again. "What you say is true. But may it not be that the king no longer has the energy to dispute, that he will accede simply because he is tired?"

"You may be right, Edward," Shrewsbury nods. "And that may bear out in the king's last days as he chooses who will govern, and how. For now, though, let us go and find a drink."

"I understand that Master Pike is not expected until later," de Winter says as he rises. "He has fully four leagues to ride to get here, and duties that seem far more onerous that any of ours!" He laughs as he leaves the room behind the Talbots, followed by Strelley and Longshawe.

Later that day, William Pike arrives at Shrewsbury House. He is well-dressed, more impressively than he has been before, though still with the quiet good taste of the outdoorsman, not the ostentation of the city dwellers. He rides a strong horse with fine, expensive-looking tackle. When he gets to the house, he dismounts smoothly, handing the reins over to a waiting footman, and strides confidently indoors. A retainer leads him to a withdrawing room, where the earl and his son, together with de Winter, Strelley and Longshawe, sit about at ease on several couches. Pike glances around, acknowledging his friends and his mentor with a nod, and pulls up a wooden chair. As he sits, he takes off a pair of leather riding gloves that, whilst unadorned, are of high quality. He puts them across his lap and leans forward.

"Well, gentlemen, it is good indeed to see you all!" He sits back again, smiling as he looks from face to face. De Winter has a slightly raised eyebrow, but his face breaks after a moment into a broad grin. He smoothes his moustache.

"Will! You have moved up in the world, it seems."

"The steward at Hampton does not allow the huntsmen to go without. The king likes everything just so. He is not to see anything that might displease him, and a poorly-dressed keeper would no doubt cause him some distress." He laughs at the thought. "Not that the king has much use for his pack and his deer park any more. I don't think we expect to see him..." He stops, remembering himself and the meaning behind his words.

De Winter puts a hand on his knee. "You are among friends, Will."

Shrewsbury takes over. "Indeed you are, Master Pike. Your hunt has not been made ready for the king since you went to Hampton?"

"No, My Lord." Pike's confidence has returned, and he looks Shrewsbury directly in the eye. "I believe that Secretary Wriothesley has written to the majordomo at Hampton, suggesting that we should manage the park as though the king will not have need of it for some time." He glances at de Winter as he finishes, who nods slowly but says nothing.

"Interesting," Shrewsbury replies. "It seems, from what you have told us, that you do not expect to pay host to the Prince Edward soon either?"

Longshawe laughs. "Edward? Shall he be allowed to join the hunt?"

Shrewsbury and his son both look at him, enquiringly. Strelley takes up the story. "The king does not allow Prince Edward much opportunity to develop his manly strength. I understand, though, that he has a little bit of a taste for it, like his sister. Though she is subtle enough not to express it."

"Elizabeth has a thirst for blood, does she?" George Talbot asks.

Strelley nods. "She is interested in our war stories, certainly. She does not have much opportunity to get out hunting as the king is no longer able to do so."

Shrewsbury waves his hand. "Let us talk of other matters." He signals an attendant servant. "Fetch more wine, please, and a cup for Master Pike. Now, Will, how are you?" For now, we shall leave them to their conversation, turning as it is to small-talk of no significance for our story.

20: A Proposal

Henry VIII awaits a visit in the receiving room at the palace of Westminster. He sits with his chin cupped in his hand, shifting his wounded leg uncomfortably. Longshawe stands to attention at one side of the entrance to the room, with another guard at the opposite side. A herald enters, and announces: "His Grace the Duke of Norfolk, and the Earl of Surrey!"

A few moments later, Norfolk and Surrey enter together. There is a recognisable family resemblance, though Norfolk is clean shaven and his son wears his beard fashionably long, cleft at the chin. Norfolk is old, perhaps sixty-five or seventy years of age. His son is around thirty. Each of them comes forward and bows. Norfolk only lowers his head slightly, but Surrey flashes an elaborate low obeisance that the king watches without moving.

"Your Grace," the king welcomes Norfolk with a restrained gesture of his hand. "I trust you are well. Your request for an audience has set me wondering. Do you come to me with tidings of deeds done, or a request of your king? I should like to hear some good news of your family's exploits, which of late have been less than pleasing to me." Henry watches as the duke tries to arrange his face, caught out by the king's bluntness in highlighting the Howards' lack of recent success.

Norfolk composes himself and forces himself to smile, showing his polished ivory false teeth. "Your Majesty is as perceptive as ever. I do not come to you to sing the praises of my own deeds or those of my house. Indeed, Majesty, it may be said that those deeds speak for themselves-" the king waves his hand, silencing the old courtier Norfolk.

"I do not wish to listen to this. Speak your mind, Your Grace, or do not speak at all," Henry says, abruptly. Into the growing silence, the king frowns. Surrey looks at his father, awaiting his response with impatience, disappointed at this early negative turn.

After another moment taken to master himself in the face of the king's forthrightness, Norfolk begins again, "Your Majesty, I come to propose an alliance that will strengthen both of our Houses when we are called to God." Henry responds by sitting forward in his gilded chair. It creaks as he does so. He holds up his hand, fingers pointing towards the duke.

"I reckon, Your Grace, that an alliance between our houses is a route we have already tested several times, and found it wanting on those occasions. Besides that, I am already married. Happily, I might add, for the first time in several years."

"I do not propose a lady of my house as Your Majesty's queen, Sire," Norfolk replies. "I present to you my son, the Earl of Surrey." Surrey repeats his ostentatious bow.

"Ah yes, you. I have recently had the pleasure of reading a little of your work. It is not without merit, though it has too much in common with Wyatt's for my tastes. We are well rid of him. Though I should not let that alter my judgement of you. Your failures in France are proof enough of your character." Ignoring Surrey's attempt to interject in his own defence, Henry returns his gaze to the older man. "Your Grace's intentions are...?" Henry lets the words fall with a tone of haughty indifference. Surrey frowns at his father.

"Sire..." Norfolk hesitates. "I propose an alliance of marriage."

Henry looks from father to son and back again. "It cannot have escaped your notice, Your Grace, that your son is already married."

"A pretext could be found..." Norfolk begins, then stops. He draws breath, then begins again. "Your Majesty must be aware of the perilous position of your esteemed house at this time. Your son and heir is yet young, and his succession not without its perils. Sire, the dangers that surround him are great." Norfolk's face settles into a serious expression that is not entirely feigned, and he maintains a steady gaze at the king.

"He is indeed young, but that in itself does not signify," the king answers. "This alliance you propose, it is between your son and whom?" Henry eyes flash, but he does not smile, instead engaging Norfolk in the contest over whose eyes will fall first.

"Between my son and your daughter, Lady Mary." Norfolk still keeps his eyes fixed on the king's.

Henry laughs out loud, bursting the tension. "You propose your son as a suitable match for Mary?" Norfolk nods, his expression calm. Longshawe, standing facing Norfolk and Surrey, twitches his nose, then straightens himself, standing up tall.

"Majesty, as the Lady Mary is not acknowledged as a legitimate daughter, she has not found a suitable partner for a marriage alliance at home or abroad. Yet. My son is the perfect match for her, ours is a family of royal descent and noble blood."

"Your Grace, your son has much to gain by marrying my

daughter, but Mary seems to have little to gain from your son." Henry leaves the words hanging, a challenge awaiting a reply. Norfolk breathes slowly and deeply before replying, trying to gauge the king's attitude.

"Sire, I do not presume-"

"Oh, but you do, Your Grace. You presume that as Mary has reached the age of thirty that any proposal of marriage from a noble house will be welcome, and you hope that by this alliance your house will stand to gain the ultimate prize. I tell you, your son shall not be king!" His face has grown red. "I grow weary of every one of my nobles grasping what he can. I am not yet dead, nor shall I be soon. You would do well to remember yourself, Your Grace."

"Your Majesty is settled on the matter," Norfolk says, as much to himself as to the king. "Very well. The offer remains, should your attitude to this matter change."

"Your Grace's presumption is monstrous!" Henry spits. "Your son is married, and yet you have the temerity to *offer* this to me. Watch your words, Sir, or I shall have you removed!"

Norfolk's brow creases into a frown as the king's outburst subsides. "Your Majesty will remember that the support of our noblest of houses will be vital to the stability of your son's reign. Your son's enemies – your enemies – might use his minority to their own ends."

"So it would seem," Henry says sarcastically, as he shifts himself in his chair. "And you count yourself among his friends. I shall be frank, Thomas. My son will be king of this realm for many years. Thus marriage to the Lady Mary would not elevate your son to the succession, even were I to sanction it. I suggest that My Lord Surrey should consider his own family, rather than striving to become part of mine." Norfolk is quiet, desperately figuring how to turn the situation to advantage.

Surrey has been watching this exchange, his countenance openly displaying his frustration with the rebuff their proposal has received. He takes a small step forward to signal his wish to speak. Henry turns to him, and says, "I do not know what you could add, Sir, but I should like nevertheless to hear it."

"Your Majesty," Surrey begins, bending himself to express contrition in his tone, "the Lady Mary has little time for English men. Were you to allow her, she would leave England altogether and marry some Spanish prince. Should Prince Edward accede, she may do exactly that, without the consent of her sovereign king, your son, or your permission."

The king listens to this exordium, his patience and serenity seemingly returned. He does not interrupt as Surrey develops his argument.

"Sire, it is imperative that England should not be subjected to the rule of the Spaniard. Mary will seek an Imperial match. Her place in the succession means that Edward's reign, as he is yet too young to be married, and thus likely to be childless when he takes the throne, may be challenged by..." He waits to grow his emphasis, lowering his eyes as he feigns to search for the correct word. He finds it and delivers it with a sneer. "Foreigners." Surrey's final flourish is accompanied by a deep sigh.

Henry allows the words to settle before speaking. "My Lord Surrey, you are indeed right that it is my duty as king to protect my realm from the incursion of foreigners, and from the influences of Papists and traitors." He pauses, breathing heavily in and out several times. "Very well, I have considered the matter. Go to Mary. Announce your interest in her. If I should hear from her own mouth that she wishes to marry, and that she has decided upon Surrey for her husband, then I would consider this alliance, despite the impediments."

"Sire, I thank you for your interest," Surrey says.

"You may leave me now, Sirs." Henry waves Norfolk and Surrey away. Norfolk shuffles out, and Surrey offers a third bow before leaving the room almost backwards, trying not to turn his back on the king.

Once they are gone, Henry summons Longshawe, who approaches the dais and stands close. The king leans forward and whispers, "fetch your friend. I would send a message and I need someone I can trust. Make him wait in the corridor, out of sight." He looks over at the other guard, and aloud, he says, "go and find Wriothesley, and make him aware of what has just happened. I shall speak to him later. When you have finished with him, bring My Lord Hertford to me." The other guard nods and leaves. Longshawe waits until his footsteps have receded, before exiting through another door and going to Elizabeth's apartments.

He finds her deep in conversation with Grindal about the relative merits of Seneca and Cicero as model rhetoricians. Strelley stands to meet him, noticing the serious mien of his friend and giving him a questioning look. Longshawe leans in close to him and passes on the king's request in a low voice. Elizabeth's eyes flick to Longshawe, before returning to Grindal. She does not otherwise acknowledge him. Strelley bows and says, "I am summoned."

"A greater duty than my education calls you, no doubt," Elizabeth says, without looking up at him. She extends her fingers before flicking them towards the door in a gesture that says 'go, and I shall trouble myself no further over you.' Strelley does not reply, only bowing his head a little to Elizabeth and casting a brief but significant glance at Grindal, then he follows Longshawe as he leaves.

They walk quickly across the palace, and Strelley, having to take four strides to the much taller Longshawe's three, tries to ask his friend questions without attracting the attention of any of the courtiers or servants they pass.

"What did Surrey say?" he asks, a little breathless.

"Just that Henry needs the Howards to look after the country when he's gone."

"That's brave of them. Do you think he really went for it?"

"Hard to say. He can't ignore it, can he?"

"Did they threaten to be disloyal after Henry dies?"

"Not quite, but not far off. Look, we're here." Longshawe points at the door. "This is big, isn't it?" he says, and Strelley nods in confirmation.

A few moments later, they stand together before the king. "I thank you for your expeditiousness, Longshawe," Henry says, his tone lively and his manner alert. "Now, Master Strelley. I need to send a message to the Lady Mary, without it attracting the attention of any of my, shall we say, *dedicated* servants. Do not write it down. Speak only to the lady herself, and do so, if you can, alone. I do not wish any other than she to hear what I wish to know."

"Sire?" Strelley lowers his head, expectant.

"I wish to know how Norfolk and Surrey broach the subject of marriage with her. Specifically, I wish to know whether they claim to have my approval in raising the matter with her. I did not explicitly give it, so I wish to know if these Howards assert that I am the engine of this connivance. You may also tell Mary that I would not approve of Surrey as a marriage match, even were he free to marry. But it is imperative: she must allow him to speak of it before she stops him." Strelley frowns. "Speak, then, if you see a flaw in my stratagem!" the king commands.

"I see only that the Lady Mary may not wish to have her honour tested in this manner," Strelley says, slowly, picking his words carefully, appreciating the danger of angering the king.

"I appreciate your concern for my daughter," Henry replies, "but as she will reject the proposal out of hand, her honour is not impugned. Nor is mine, provided this trick remains secret. And as it is not in Surrey's interests to make public the failure of his suit, I trust it shall." Henry sucks his teeth. Strelley looks at Longshawe, whose face is serious, composed, declaring himself ready.

"Sire, Longshawe and I have a friend in the Lady Mary's service," Strelley says.

"And?" the king asks, solicitous.

"He may be able to help you with the information you seek if the lady herself is not forthcoming." Strelley accompanies this with a twisting gesture of his hands, as though he is himself figuring out the labyrinth of plotting that has been laid before him.

"She shall obey her father!" Henry asserts bluntly. "I will not have it else than thus."

"She may protect Surrey if she understands your trap. She may tell you otherwise, or even tell Surrey himself of your wish to snare him." Strelley lets the king ruminate on his suggestion.

"I trust to your judgement. I wish only to know the extent of Norfolk's ambition for his son, or Surrey's own. Now go. You must be away before Seymour arrives. I would not have him know of your message either." At this, Strelley bows and leaves, before heading for the stables. Longshawe watches him go, taking slow, steady breaths. Once the door is closed behind Strelley, Longshawe steps close to the king. Henry nods at him.

"Return to your post at the door, Master Longshawe," Henry says, quietly, "I thank you again for your assistance with this delicate matter."

Longshawe stands to attention by the door, regaining control of himself. It is a full two minutes until the other guard returns, by which time both Longshawe and the king have assumed neutral expressions, totally belying the intrigue that has just taken place. The newly returned guardsman bows as he says, "My Lord Hertford, Sire." We shall leave the king to his discussion with his son's uncle, and instead follow Strelley, who passes through the stables, visits the kitchen and eventually heads across the palace unwatched to Lady Mary's apartments.

He is greeted there at the door by a footman whom he asks to find de Winter. A minute or two later, de Winter appears, and steps outside. He questions Strelley with a look, and the response he gets tells him immediately that great matters are afoot. De Winter closes the door behind himself, and ushers Strelley away from it.

"Wouldn't want anyone to hear anything they might not need to know..." he whispers.

"Indeed," Strelley replies. "I bring a message from the king. He wishes you to do something for him." De Winter raises an eyebrow and leans closer. "You know Norfolk and his son are here at the palace?"

"I didn't, but I do now."

"Well, it seems that Norfolk has conceived the idea of elevating his son to the succession."

"Really? And how does that concern me?"

"The king wishes you to find out how Norfolk and Surrey approach the lady." Strelley's whisper forces de Winter to tilt his ear very close. Strelley looks out past him, watching for signs of other people moving about nearby. There are none.

"A marriage proposal?" de Winter replies. "I would imagine that they would begin with her father."

"They did. Norfolk has already been to ask him, not fifteen minutes ago. Henry told him that the lady had little interest in marriage and that they were wasting their time. And, of course, there is the small matter of Surrey's wife. But he told them to take their proposal to Mary directly. He wants to know what they do."

"Surrey is already married? Then this can go nowhere, surely? Regardless of that, the king still seeks some foreign marriage for her, I suspect."

"I'm not sure. She's more use to him unmarried."

"What do you mean?" de Winter frowns.

"I mean that anyone who marries her gets himself into the succession. And if the king meets God before Edward reaches his majority..." Strelley's raised eyebrows indicate the significance of this eventuality.

"Civil war?" de Winter says, himself looking each way down the corridor to check for the presence of others. Still there are none.

"Civil war. So it's not in his interests to marry Mary off to some

180

foreign prince now, because it only introduces another claimant. He suspects Norfolk of exactly that sort of ambition."

"Norfolk has no royal blood."

"Well, it's a very old line, but he does. And Surrey does through his mother. She's a descendent of King Edward."

"Which Edward?"

"Edward the Third. A weak claim as well, but nevertheless, a claim. Henry doesn't want anything to prevent his son succeeding to the throne unchallenged. Whether or not Norfolk and Surrey profess their great loyalty, Henry has a lot to lose by giving them a pretext to block Edward's accession. But if he rejects their alliance out of hand, they could make life very difficult for Edward when he is king."

"Of course, so Henry has to at least let them play their hand. But what about Surrey's proposal? What should we anticipate?" De Winter jerks his head around, looking over Strelley's shoulder as he asks. Whatever he heard, he cannot see anyone about in the corridor, and he turns his head back so that Strelley is able to whisper directly into his ear. He nods as Strelley tells him the plot.

"Surrey will come to the lady, I don't know when, and he will ask her for her hand in marriage. Henry has not given them his blessing, but he wants to know if they claim to have it. Henry told them both that if he hears from the lady herself that she is settled on marrying Surrey, he will consider the alliance, regardless of the difficulties."

"Why would he say that?"

"He knows full well that Mary will send Surrey away with his tail between his legs. Or not, as the case may be!" Strelley mimes the act of cutting with a knife. They both smile, some of the tension dissipating at this crude gesture.

"I don't know," de Winter says, "she seems to have some interest in marrying."

"Perhaps she does, but it wouldn't be to a Howard." Seeing de Winter's quizzical look, Strelley continues, "Anne Boleyn was a Howard."

Recognition spreads across de Winter's features. "So the king has done nothing more than set Norfolk a trap?"

"It seems so. Mary will reject Surrey out of hand, although Henry wanted me to tell her explicitly that he forbade their marriage. You can pass that on to her if it will help. But what he wants to know is how they approach this proposal, not the outcome, which he thinks is foregone. I reckon that the trick is this: if Surrey claims the approval of the king, which he is not above doing, that would show their ambition extends to the throne."

"It does, doesn't it?"

"I suppose it does. I don't think Surrey has the patience to woo Mary, to actually win her affections. But he also thinks the king is dying, and that his move must be soon or it will be in vain."

"So my task is not to intervene, but merely to report this conversation between Surrey and Lady Mary?"

"It is, unless you wish to warn Mary of his coming. If your luck is good, you may be able to speak to the king directly. He is with Hertford now. Hertford will no doubt be telling the king that the Howards are traitors. He wants no opposition to his nephew. I wonder whether he plans to take power himself."

"Whom does the king trust?"

"No one. Not of significance, not of the nobility. He suspects them all of following their own agenda. Though Hertford seems to be able to speak more freely than most. Since he sent Thomas Seymour back to the Low Countries, Hertford seems to have risen in the king's esteem. Indeed, Henry rather celebrated Hertford's return from Boulogne."

"That other Seymour... He was involved with the queen at some stage, wasn't he?"

"Yes, he was. That is their weakness in this game. Anyway, the king wants you to tell him whether they tell Mary that he has already sanctioned the marriage, or whether they try any other underhand method of persuading her."

"Then I shall listen out for it."

"You should go. They may already be on their way."

"How am I to report to the king?"

"Find Longshawe. He seems to be able to get people admitted!"

Strelley turns and walks away, again looking around the corridors to ensure the conversation has not been overheard. De Winter stands outside the door for some moments, breathing steadily, before drawing himself up and re-entering Lady Mary's apartments.

21: Surrey's Gambit

Later on the same day, Henry Howard, Earl of Surrey, approaches the apartments of Lady Mary Tudor. His father is now absent, but Surrey has assembled several gentlemen of his household around him. He is extravagantly dressed, wearing several jewelled rings about his hands, and has a great deal of silver and gold in his clothes. His hose are artfully arranged to show off the curve of his calf. Before he enters, he signals to one of his entourage, who holds a looking-glass before him. He smoothes his beard and moustaches with fingers and thumb, and his face breaks into a satisfied smile.

"Good," he says, to himself. "We shall enter together, but you gentlemen will allow me to approach the lady alone. I would not have her in fear that any should hear what I have to say to her." He flashes another signal, and one of his men raps the door. It opens almost immediately, and the man who knocked on it leans inside. There is the sound of some commotion inside, but after half a minute a retainer in the lady's service, who wears a version of the Tudor green-and-white livery, announces the earl. Surrey strides into the room, swaggeringly confident.

Lady Mary is seated, surrounded by several of her ladies-in-waiting. She glances up at Surrey, who repeats the extravagant bow he gave the king, but this time with an additional flourish of the hand. She looks down again, and Surrey, lifting his head, realises that she has returned to her needlework. He remains bowed for a second or two, before standing straight again. He watches her, eyes following the careful movements of the lady's hand, flicking to her face once, and again, waiting. His face glowers at the rebuff. His agitation begins to reveal itself even in his breathing, loud and aggressive, and he looks away from Mary, from side to side, sweeping the room for a way to break this silence. He sees several of the lady's men standing ready to serve her about the room, one of which we will recognise as George de Winter, standing with his feet apart and his hands behind his back. De Winter maintains a straight-ahead stare, allowing himself to observe the earl only when he can do so without being noticed. Each time Surrey's attention is elsewhere, de Winter trains his eyes on him, but de Winter is sharp enough to return his eyes to straight ahead before Surrey looks at him.

"My Lady," the earl says, finally, "allow me to present myself. I am Henry Howard, Earl of Surrey, Earl Marshal of England." Mary stops her needlework this time, and looks at Surrey. Her face is neutral, perhaps a little unimpressed.

"Ah, yes. We have met before," she replies. "You are welcome, Your Grace, but I cannot divine the purpose of this visit. What do you wish of me?"

Surrey is thrown as Mary once again focuses on her needlework and not him. He coughs, and she ignores it. He starts to speak. "It is a matter of the greatest importance to your Highness-" Mary holds up a hand, bringing him to an abrupt stop.

"I should have thought, Sir, that as an officer of the realm you would be aware of the correct forms of address."

"Indeed I am, Madam-" She interrupts a second time.

"Then you must not address me as 'Your Highness', for it cannot have escaped your notice that I am not, according to *His Majesty* my father, I repeat I am not a princess of royal blood but a mere bastard." She stares at him, her breathing slightly more heavy than previously. Surrey winces, then forces himself into a flattering, obsequious smile.

"Then you must excuse my slip, Madam, for it is not my intention to confound the king in these matters. Though Madam will own that for all she is not *called* 'princess', she is nevertheless the king's daughter and thus entitled to deference from his subjects, of which I am the most humble." He allows himself a more genuine smile, flashing white teeth through his carefully-arranged beard and moustache. "And as it is as a most humble subject that I appear before you now."

"Your Grace flatters me. I cannot help but wonder why." Mary smoothes her skirts, forcing herself to look away from the earl's face. He continues to watch her, now that the game is joined he has found a motivation and intensity that were previously absent.

"Madam, would you accompany me on a walk through the gardens?" She looks nonplussed, and doesn't answer.

"I can see that my presence is not pleasing to you, My Lady." Surrey bends on one knee, bringing his face down level with the lady's. "Though I would have it otherwise." She turns to him, charmed perhaps by his soft tone and his undoubted physical refinement.

"We shall take a turn, then, if it please Your Grace. I have no desire to offend one of my father's trusted officers." She rises, and turns to a lady-in-waiting. "Susan, you will accompany us on our walk through the gardens."

The lady that Mary addressed as 'Susan' nods her head and bustles out of the room, returning a few moments later with an elaborate gable hood which she ties over Mary's hair. De Winter steps forward and offers to assist by a gesture, which Susan refuses by a shake of her head. Her headgear securely attached, Mary shuffles into another room where other ladies-in-waiting attach her jewellery. Surrey, meanwhile, leaves the room and waits outside with his gentlemen. One of them raises a quizzical eyebrow as his master reappears. Surrey smiles, and says quietly, "so it begins."

In Lady Mary's room, de Winter again approaches Mary's lady-in-waiting. "Mistress Clarencieux," de Winter begins in a solicitous tone, "allow me to accompany you on our lady's stroll this fine afternoon. I should be most honoured were you to accept. And it would be seemly for a man of Lady Mary's household to accompany this outing."

Susan Clarencieux looks de Winter up and down, considering him and the mixture of appeal and warning in his request. She frowns, but after a moment comes to a conclusion. "Very well. George, isn't it? Keep yourself at a discreet distance from the lady. I do not need to remind you not to speak unless you are spoken to. Make yourself useful and fetch some drinks for them from the kitchens. The lady enjoys perry, or mead. Go!"

De Winter leaves, following Surrey's men along a corridor briefly, their conversation audible but frustratingly unintelligible, until he turns towards the kitchens. He enters, and a few minutes later he emerges, carrying a basket with several bottles poking out from underneath a covering cloth. His smile is broad as he takes a morsel from under the cloth and chews on it.

De Winter walks alongside Susan Clarencieux, some yards behind Lady Mary and the Earl of Surrey. Surrey plays his part well, first gazing into the distance, waiting until the lady looks at him, and then looking her in the eye when he turns, forcing her to turn away for modesty. Surrey takes the lead, showing off his graceful stride and shapely leg. He keeps himself half-turned, walking almost sideways, looking across the lady now.

"My Lord Surrey," Mary says, not allowing her eyes to meet his, "I still wonder at your request to walk with me. I did no more than remark your unwarranted flattery inside, but now I demand an explanation."

"Very well, Madam," Surrey begins, his voice smooth. "I do not offer my praises lightly, but My Lady warrants them more than-"

"Your Grace, I will not have more of this. I would know what it is that you would have of me?"

"My Lady, I shall be frank. Your father finds that he cannot tell his enemies from his friends. I am his friend, and it is my wish to secure this friendship beyond that which it is now."

Mary stops walking. A pace later, so does Surrey. De Winter and Clarencieux wait, a few yards away.

"My Lady," Surrey begins again. He takes her hand, which causes her to frown. He smiles, letting out his breath in what might be a sigh, or might be a laugh. "You cannot be ignorant of your charms, nor your worth."

"My Lord Surrey, I do not wish to misconstrue your meaning."

"Then I will delay no further. I wish to marry you, My Lady. You are the great jewel of the king's family, and there isn't a lord in the kingdom who wouldn't wish for your hand. But I propose this marriage in the hope that you may see me as a fit husband, unlike the many who might contest with me for your hand."

Mary holds her hands together across her belly. Her discomfort shows as she twists her fingers together. "My Lord, I see that it is no longer possible for me to be unsure of what it is you desire."

"No, indeed it is not. I should have liked to have more time to make my suit more carefully, and to gain Your Highness's love by showing you my affection, my devotion, my desire to be your husband. But this could not happen."

"Uhhm." Mary offers him the ghost of a forced smile to go with her exhalation.

"No!" Surrey warms to his theme, gesticulating and growing in volume. De Winter stares straight ahead, listening without moving. "No, I say. The king would not allow it! I pleaded with him, to allow me to *win* your hand, to woo you as His Majesty could only wish for his daughter. But his desire to see the match made, and made quickly, means that his haste can only be satisfied by immediacy. I would not have it so."

Mary continues to listen, her face pale.

"I said to the king that you would not receive this well, and so I demanded of him that he allow me to be the one to bring this joyous news to you."

Mary's eyes narrow. "This joyous news? You speak as if we are already wed."

"Well, Madam, all it needs is your acquiescence. The king expects me to return with news of your consent given, as he has already given his blessing."

"My father has blessed you to be my husband?"

"Why, yes indeed. He has." Surrey's tone shows that he is worried, that he has overlooked some crucial fact or overplayed his hand.

"Then he has no memory for history." Mary smiles, this time genuinely. "Or perhaps he has chosen to forget, I know not. I shall speak with him forthwith."

"I do not understand." Surrey tries to take her hand again, but she pulls it away.

"My Lord, you may have forgotten, but I have not. It was one of your Howard kin who broke my father's marriage to my mother, and it was she who cast me out from my father's affection. I may no longer be a princess, but I am not thereby grown into a dupe, nor shall I assent to marriage with that which I cannot abide."

Surrey drops to one knee. "My Lady, you must not judge the man by those others of his family who have done you wrong. I am not my father."

"That is true, Sir, but you are his son, and I cannot look at you without seeing her. It is my only comfort that she burns in hell as the traitor she was. The witch!" Mary's eyes seethe with the passionate hatred she feels even now, more than ten years after Anne Boleyn's death. Surrey rises, trying to rescue something from the situation.

"I see that I do not find Madam receptive," he says, contrite.

Mary's voice rises in tone and volume. "You shall not marry me, Sir. Even if my father orders me, I shall refuse, and I shall go to my grave before I lay with you."

Surrey struggles to maintain his sangfroid, offering Mary a low bow and turning away. He walks directly towards the palace, flouncing his cloak over his shoulder as he goes. Mary turns to Susan Clarencieux, and gestures that they shall return whence they came. We shall return to them in a moment. For now, let us follow Surrey. He approaches the palace and enters, as footmen guarding the door offer him the slightest of bows. He returns, his footfalls thumping out his anger, to his quarters, where his father and several gentlemen of his suite are seated, playing at cards.

Norfolk looks up at him, seeing his deep colour and his exaggerated frown. "I take it your efforts of this morning are not well rewarded, my son...?" Despite himself, he finds the indignant manner of his son faintly amusing, and his smile sets Surrey's fury to an even higher pitch.

"No they are not! This plan was of dubious merit, father."

"What mean you?"

"The lady rejected my suit immediately. She would not marry a Howard, it seems."

"Ah." Norfolk puts his cards on the table, face down. "She has not forgotten the late Queen Anne's association with my name, then." He maintains a quiet, even voice in the face of his son's fuming.

"Apparently she has not. It is time to change our target." Surrey's breathing is still heavy with the frustration he feels, but his new plan seems to settle his mind a little.

"It may be. But you must show a little more patience with this one. She may be our last hope to secure our positions after the king passes. We must hope that we have not exhausted our credit with him."

"I shall begin my work tomorrow." Surrey sits down, and pours himself a cup of wine.

Meanwhile, Mary returns to her apartments with Susan Clarencieux and de Winter. She seats herself, removes her lace gloves and places them across her lap. Her composure disintegrates, and she weeps.

"How dare he?" she says, as Clarencieux kneels by her and takes Lady Mary's hands between her own. Mary looks at her lady servant, who returns her gaze with a sympathetic look but does not speak. "How dare he forget that it was his cousin... That *she* was his cousin! I shall speak with my father. There is more to this than might appear. There must be. I cannot believe that even he would be so ignorant."

"No, Madam, it must come as both surprise and shock." Clarencieux wipes Lady Mary's tears with a soft handkerchief.

"Did you hear him claim the king's blessing? Indeed, he said that the king was so deSirous of our marriage that Surrey had to present his proposal immediately, rather than woo me as he no doubt considers proper for a gentleman of his standing. No, he expected that mention of my father would win me. I wonder... Does he have any intercourse with the queen? Perhaps she has put my father up to this. Though I doubt her capable of such intervention. She is no longer brave enough to try to direct my father. In any case: why?"

"I agree with you, My Lady. The queen would have had no part in this. Perhaps your father genuinely wished that you would take Surrey as a husband and be happy." Clarencieux busies herself, fussing around Mary, the activity a thinly disguised ploy to defuse Mary's anger.

"Perhaps," Mary replies. "I shall speak to His Majesty when I can."

Some time later that day, de Winter finds Longshawe lounging around in the quarters assigned to the Yeomen of the Guard. Longshawe wears his undress uniform, black with red trim. He had been listening to the other off-duty warders regaling each other with war stories, but leaps to his feet when he notices de Winter. He rushes over and leans in close as de Winter begins to speak.

"He did it. Surrey. He went to the lady and he asked her."

"Have you told the king?"

"Not all of us can get before the king at will, James."

"I see. You wish to be admitted?" De Winter nods. "The king is receiving tomorrow, in the morning. I shall see to it that you are allowed to speak with him before he engages in the business of the day. I am sure he will be most interested in your news."

"I would be most grateful for the opportunity to be presented to His Majesty."

"Just be careful. You're telling him what he already suspects, but it will make him angry."

De Winter nods in agreement. "He may already know by tomorrow. The lady herself intends to confront him over this. She objected to his choice of a Howard as her husband."

"The king will deny saying any such thing. Do you not think so?"

"It had not occurred to me that he would dissimulate, but it would save his honour and that of the lady if all the blame is placed on Surrey."

"Nevertheless, you shall be admitted. The king wanted to know your news, and he shall hear it." De Winter shakes Longshawe's hand and leaves the mess.

"What is it, Mary?" Henry asks his daughter. "You appear agitated." He sits alone in his study, facing Mary across a beautiful oak desk on which a few pieces of paper are neatly arranged.

"And well I might, father," she answers. "You must be aware of the test that has been made of my honour as a gentlewoman today."

"No, my daughter. I do not understand of what it is that you speak." She looks at him for several seconds, searching his impassive face, trying to find a trace of insincerity.

"My Lord Surrey has come to me today with a proposal of marriage."

"My Lord Surrey is already married."

Mary looks down, confused. "I thought that you had sanctioned this proposal."

"My dear daughter," Henry says, smiling, "why would I do that, when I know that Surrey is already married? Besides, he would not be pleasing to you, I should think."

"Indeed not, Sire. I-"

"You are bemused by his words? I doubt it not. But My Lord Surrey appears to be trying his best to find a way to be important when I am gone. It is no surprise to me that he has resorted to such trickery in an attempt to win your hand. Perhaps he would have returned to me tomorrow and told me that he had secured you consent, and that you had said that it was your heart's desire, if only your father would allow it."

"So I am thoroughly deceived? I had not thought myself so naïve."

"Nobody does until the deception is revealed. Do not dwell on it, dear daughter. I shall deal with Surrey. His ambition is becoming intolerable."

Mary turns to leave. She looks over her shoulder as she passes through the door, and thinks that she catches a broad smile on the king's face. He notices as she turns, and arranges his face into one of quiet rage on behalf of his elder daughter, but she is not convinced. She leaves, and returns to Clarencieux, to whom she reports this conversation immediately, word-for-word.

22: Unprincipled

It is early, but the king is already up, closeted with his Lord Chancellor, Wriothesley. Longshawe stands guard at the door, facing into the room, having informed the king of de Winter's wish to see him. Henry is red-faced, heavy with sleep. Wriothesley shows the alert sharpness of the slick political operator that he is, his movements calm and measured.

"She will not speak?" the king asks.

"I have not yet heard her confess her sins. Though Your Majesty is aware of my suspicions." Wriothesley uses his tone to highlight the accusatory undercurrent.

"Thomas... My Lord Wriothesley, must you persist in your designs to find some route to attack the archbishop? He is no heretic, nor is he abroad organising the scum of London in their heresies."

No, Sire, I do not speak out of a personal desire to see His Grace brought low. Your Majesty already knows the extent of his refusal to comply. Though you do not see fit to punish him." The last sentence is matter-of-fact, the challenge in it disguised by Wriothesley's deliberately flippant attitude.

"I do not! Cranmer is on my side!" Henry grunts. "I could do with you on my side as well, Thomas. Do not use this preacher of heresy to undermine my authority."

Wriothesley is visibly struck by the king's words, pulling a contrite face. "Sire, I act only in your name and on your orders."

"If she gives you names, I want to know. But I want to know first, so before you speak of this to anyone – and I mean anyone, be it the humblest servant or our risen saviour himself – you come to me and you tell me whom she names. And then *I* shall decide how we will proceed. Do you understand?"

Wriothesley does not speak as he rises, but instead offers a deep bow, signalling his acquiescence. As he stalks off through the palace, we shall follow him briefly to learn where he goes, and a little of what he is thinking. He seeks out Norfolk's apartments, and joins the duke and his son, who are awaiting his return.

"Well?" Norfolk asks him, without preamble.

"This does not go as well as I would have liked, Your Grace. The king does not want his favourites implicated in heresy."

"I should imagine he doesn't. That, My Lord, is precisely why they must be. We must use this opportunity to our advantage." Norfolk rubs his hands together. "Have you threatened her? Tortured her?"

"That is our next move. She has already been told that she must die, so it is a question of the ease of her passing. A full confession and she might escape the purifying fire..." Wriothesley shows a certain relish as he speaks, curling his upper lip.

"I am delighted that you can find such pleasure in the torture of a heretic street-preacher, Thomas. But you must see that there are challengers for our positions close to the king. Challengers who will not pass up any opportunity to do us down." Norfolk sits forward, his hands on his knees.

"No one is more aware of that than I, Your Grace," Wriothesley sneers. "I should think that you would appreciate my efforts more... Or perhaps you would prefer to take matters into your own hands? Ah! This work is too dirty for a duke's delicate fingers, is it? We shall have Cranmer, over a barrel if not in the fire. And with that achieved, we can move on to the queen and her women, and that bastard neophyte son-of-a-peasant Seymour."

"Your fervour is admirable, My Lord, but it must produce results. If this woman goes to the stake without naming names, we may be passing up our best chance." Norfolk thinks for a moment. His son, Surrey, sits by him, stroking his beard, then smoothing his moustache. Surrey takes a deep breath, and speaks.

"Can we not simply report to the king that this Askew woman has named Cranmer, the queen, and whomever else? Put the names into her mouth. Add the two Seymours' names to your list as well, while you're about it?" His father turns to him and frowns. Wriothesley smiles patiently, and takes up the explanation, his heavy articulation that of someone explaining a simple rule to a child.

"Your suggestion has been considered, My Lord Surrey. But there are too many who are not so ready to help our cause that they will tell the story we wish them to tell. And even the slimmest chance of our deception being revealed is intolerable. It could lead us all to the block. So no, we must have it from Askew herself, and we must have it before witnesses."

Surrey does not look impressed. "Grease palms. Use your authority! For heaven's sake, Wriothesley, have you no imagination? Torture her in private if you must."

Wriothesley draws breath slowly, and looks to Norfolk, who

scratches his chin. "Son, your thoughts show your ingenuity, but we have considered this matter in some depth. We need others, others whose integrity is beyond question, others who, in the king's mind at least, have no agenda, belong to no party. Is that clear?"

Surrey huffs and turns away. Wriothesley addresses his father.

"So, Your Grace, I shall speak to the Constable forthwith, and we shall have what we need."

"Do that," Norfolk says, then he considers, tipping back his head. "My son's suggestion... If the Seymours-"

"I understand Your Grace," Wriothesley interrupts. "Now, if I may, I do in fact have work to do for the king's Majesty." He nods the smallest of bows, and leaves. Norfolk looks at his son, eyes narrowed, but says nothing, breathing in and out evenly for a quarter-minute before he stands and sets about some other business.

Let us for now rejoin the king, who is preparing to receive George de Winter. Longshawe brings him in, bowing to the king and speaking de Winter's name aloud. Longshawe withdraws to the door, but watches intently as de Winter approaches the king and bows deeply. De Winter keeps his hands clasped in front of himself, as though unsure what to do with them in the presence of His Majesty.

"You are my daughter's footman, are you not?" Henry booms.

De Winter nods, and opens his mouth to speak. "I am My Lady's Esquire of the Body, Your Majesty."

"Well, Sir, whatever your position I welcome you. I have need of my subjects' loyalty, and I would value yours."

"It is frankly given, Your Majesty."

"Good. I understand that your father is a baron in the North. I don't recall meeting him."

"He is not given to travelling, Sire." De Winter stifles the urge to speak further and reveal the full extent of his father's limitations.

"It does not signify, Sir. I shall judge you on your own merit, not on your father's. Master Longshawe here tells me you served together in Scotland."

"We did, Sire," he says, turning and nodding to Longshawe, who has had the presence of mind to be staring straight ahead, not watching. "Although our campaign was not one of great glory. I believe My Lord Shrewsbury was grateful for the safe return of his son."

"Talbot is most careful of his son's welfare. A father

understands the need for his heir to be protected, you see. They are at court, are they not?"

"I believe they are, Sire."

"Now, Master de Winter, I charge you to explain Surrey's behaviour with my daughter. How did he broach the subject of their marriage? Did he claim my blessing?"

"I did not hear every word that was spoken, Your Majesty, but I think he not only claimed your blessing, but that you wished the marriage to be undertaken expeditiously. He claimed that Your Majesty had refused him time to woo the lady." De Winter's eyes flick around the room, from Henry to Longshawe and back again. He adds, in a quiet voice, "he played the devil of a trick."

"I thank you for telling me. I shall ask you frankly: Do you think him ambitious?"

"Surrey wishes to marry your daughter, Sire. He wishes to do this for his own advancement."

"No doubt what you say is true. Now answer me another question. Do you think he is capable of treason?"

"I know not, Your Majesty. Indeed, I am not sure I follow your meaning."

"It is quite simple, Sir. Do you think him capable of trying to make himself king when I die? Do you think his ambitions extend as far as the throne itself?"

De Winter's eyes open wide. His head twitches as he considers his reply, recognising that there is great significance attached to his response. "Your Majesty, I do not know. I have seen and heard little of him, until today."

"Well, Master de Winter, in any case you have been useful. However, it seems that as my daughter has given Surrey every reason to avoid her company in future, he will not be back again to trouble you." Henry looks up at de Winter, holding his eyes on him for some moments. "I wonder... Master Longshawe!" he calls. "Fetch your friend, Elizabeth's tutor, if you would. I would speak with him."

Longshawe bows and makes to leave, and as de Winter turns to watch him, he nods conspiratorially. After he is gone, the king waits a few seconds before he carries on with his questioning of de Winter.

"Master de Winter, there is another matter that I would know of. My daughter tells me that she is all obedience, but I cannot help but fear that she still acknowledges the Bishop of Rome as head of the Church.

What think you of this?"

"Sire, I know little of the lady's private business. She sees Van Der Delft occasionally-"

"The Imperial Ambassador?"

"Yes, Your Majesty. Though I do not know if she corresponds with others of the Imperial Family."

"I have little doubt that she does, through the Ambassador or otherwise. I would have you find that out for me, if you can."

"I shall do what I may, Sire."

"Good. God forbid it should come to pass, but if Edward were to die without issue, she would be queen. I must know if she is persistent in her Papistry, such that it might be altered, as she is so little concerned with its being forbidden. Now, speak to me of other matters." Henry leans back in his chair. "I would know a little of you."

"Your Majesty?" De Winter bows, unsure of himself.

"Well, I would know a little of your history. How come you to be in my daughter's service?"

"I served with Longshawe and Strelley in Scotland. We were sent by the Earl of Shrewsbury to accompany his son on campaign. It is as I have already had the pleasure of telling Your Majesty."

"Yes, I know young Talbot. A sturdy young fellow, though still in his father's shadow, I'll warrant. I confess I did not know that Francis had sent him to war."

"I think the earl wanted his son to gain some experience, to learn how to handle himself."

"As all good young men should, Master de Winter. How was he on campaign?"

"George Talbot?" de Winter asks unnecessarily, buying himself time to think about his answer. The king nods as de Winter marshals his thoughts. "He is brave, Sire, but has a hot head. We had to persuade him to stay clear of certain dangers..."

"If only I had had a few more like him in France. This country needs its heroes, and there are too few left. I despair that my supposed best nobles are loyal only to themselves, and not to me."

"Your people fight for you." De Winter draws himself up tall as he speaks, puffing out his chest to accentuate his meaning, taking the opportunity to ingratiate himself by flattering the king.

"Some, perhaps. But with just a few good men, Sir, what could be possible! It is to my great regret that my body will no longer allow me to lead this nation into battle. King Francis grows over-mighty in my absence, it seems."

"War in Scotland, Sire, was difficult to prosecute." Now de Winter drops his gaze, making his point almost regretfully, taking the wind out of the king's bluster.

"You sound like one of my generals," Henry says, but there as a smile on his face. "War is difficult for those who prefer to make excuses, like Norfolk. I have never heard such nonsense as he gave me when he lost Boulogne. That is not how one serves his king." Henry rubs his hands together. "I would make this nation great, but I am always told that there is some trifle that prevents it. Wolsey dealt with France. Cromwell preferred to use his power to promote his disgusting Lutheranism. Wriothesley tells me there is no more money."

De Winter does not reply, but looks nervously about the room, not wishing to act as the conduit of the king's anger. The trick works and it wanes after a moment, then Henry's tone softens.

"These are not matters to concern you," Henry says. He thinks about reaching a hand out to de Winter, but does not. Instead he rubs his thigh thoughtfully. "It seems that the only men I can trust are those who do not stand to gain by my death."

"Your Majesty can trust Shrewsbury and his son."

"They are your patrons. It is no surprise that you promote their interest. But I think you may be right. I shall consider them both when I have need of loyal and good men. And I shall recommend them to my son."

De Winter smiles, but does not speak.

"I did not ask you how you fared in Scotland." Henry opens his hands.

"Your Majesty... It is a little embarrassing."

"How so?"

"I was in command of a company of riders, but they were hired mercenaries, and their allegiance was flexible."

"I know a little of the flexibility you speak of. It is to be expected in war. War tests the courage of the best. That it might be the breaking the courage of the least must be anticipated."

"I did anticipate it, Sire, though those who were in command did not share my apprehension."

"No general likes to be told that his troops are anything other than loyal."

"Even if they are not?" de Winter replies, somewhat shortly.

"I see you are mindful of your reputation, Sir. It is well. You may rest assured that I do not think the less of you for your experience of war." He looks up at the noise from the door. "It seems your friends have come."

Longshawe opens the door, and Strelley follows him in. Both of them look quizzically at de Winter, who gives them the merest affirmatory nod.

"Well, Master Strelley," Henry says, "I have a favour to ask of you."

Strelley cannot help himself as he flashes a glowering look at Longshawe, screwing up his face. Longshawe tries to ignore him.

"Another favour, yes," Henry says. Longshawe smiles without looking at either Henry or Strelley. The king continues, "it is a simple matter, one that a man of your intelligence and discretion can handle without trouble. But it does require subtlety."

"I am at your service, Majesty." Strelley bows a little, hiding his expression by looking down.

"It has come to my notice that one of my subjects has rather forgotten himself." Henry lets the words ring out. "I would have you put your wits to finding out if this is true."

"Your Majesty wishes to know if Surrey designs to marry Elizabeth?" Strelley asks.

"How-" Henry begins, but stops himself. "You are indeed perceptive. That is why I wish your aid in this matter. You must not give the lady ideas, and you must not question her directly. I do not want Surrey warned of my displeasure with him before I find the extent of his treason."

All three young men wince at the word, knowing the consequences, even for the highest of nobility, of the offence. The king does not appear to pick up on it, or if he does, his degenerating body does not register it, and it does not find its way on to his face.

"Yes," Henry says, "I wish you to find out the whether Surrey approaches Elizabeth. And as you are here, Master Strelley, allow me to ask of you how you understand the religious convictions of Lady Elizabeth's tutor."

"Grindal is a good Christian man, Sire. He comprehends the arguments of such as Luther and Calvin, but he is in accord with Your Majesty's feelings on the subject."

"So what do you take my feelings on this subject to be, Master Strelley?"

"Well, Sire, I have read your work. I... We believe as Your Majesty does in the True Presence, and that no law of the Church of Rome is greater than that of God."

"So he is no Papist?"

"No, Sire, he is no Papist. The same can be said of Cheke, the prince's tutor."

"Can it indeed? I wonder that such scholars have not their own thoughts on these matters. Though it would avail them little. I have found that God speaks clearly on these matters to me. They are not themselves Lutherans, then? They believe in the Presence?"

"As subjects, we accept Your Majesty's words. We believe as you do."

"I should not like to have to extract anything you wish to conceal, Master Strelley. I find it odd that such men as have studied at those dens of sedition do not disagree with me."

Strelley's eyes flick from the king to Longshawe, and then to de Winter. "Your Majesty's subjects believe in your supremacy, Sire." He masters the struggle to control his face, concealing whatever it might be that he truly thinks behind a mask of calm and honesty.

"Good. It must be so." Henry considers. "I have matters to attend to, but I thank you all for attending me this morning. You may leave, Sirs."

Strelley and de Winter leave, doing their best not to turn their backs on the king as they do so. Once through the door, de Winter catches Strelley by the shoulder.

"Be careful, Edward. The king may see through your deception if you do not dissemble better than that."

"He may. He may not. I am not sure he is deceived, though."

"He acts as though he is."

"He does not want to think that his son, his daughter and his wife all oppose him on the Faith. He is willing to be deceived. A partner in it."

"But you will lose your head for it!"

"I would," Strelley hisses. "But you would lose yours for your loyalty to the Pope, would you not?"

De Winter pales, then colours. "I am not-"

"And yet, you serve as committed a Papist as there is in

England. We must all watch our step, George. Until the king goes, everyone – and I mean everyone – is vulnerable. Do what you must to stay alive."

"Do you not have any faith, Edward? If the king sends me to the fire for my belief, I will have the succour of eternal bliss." George de Winter accompanies this statement of his creed with a fierce gesture of his hand.

Strelley shakes his head. "Do you fear death?"

"I fear pain. But not death."

"Perhaps you should, then. What if Luther is right?"

"What do you mean?" de Winter frowns, baffled by his friend's line of argument.

"I mean what I say. What if your loyalty to the Pope, your keeping of the traditions of the Catholic Church, your worship, everything you believe in... What if all of that meant nothing, because it was nothing but the work of men?"

"I do not understand you, Edward."

"I know." Strelley forces a smile. "You must act as your conscience dictates, after all. One could not die in peace if not. The king is frightened, George, and he's frightened because he has realised that all of this, this new Church of his, his supremacy, all of it was for nothing more than a woman. And that woman gave him no son. God has abandoned him."

"Do not let anyone else hear you speak thus, Edward. I wish you had not spoken of your thoughts to me." He looks around, checking to see whether there is any chance of their being overheard.

Strelley licks his lips, focusing himself firmly on de Winter, ignoring his obvious agitation. "Forget what I say about the king, then, but remember what I say about keeping your head. Try yourself, George. Find yourself a candle, see how it would feel to die in the purifying fire."

De Winter looks at Strelley through narrowed eyes. After a while, he laughs. "I had not thought you so *unprincipled*!"

23: Anne Askew

Wriothesley throws a bundle of papers on the table. "Strelley, isn't it?" he says. Edward Strelley nods in confirmation. "Well, sit down." He is alone with Wriothesley, in the office we have seen once before when Longshawe visited it. "I must tell you, Master Strelley, that I do not see how I am beholden to your Master Grindal, and thereby why I ought to humour you."

"With respect, My Lord, it is not my master who has made this request."

"Lady Elizabeth herself, then...? Interesting. The king knows nothing of this, I presume?"

"He does not, Sir." Strelley plays the dedicated servant, passing on the request of his superior without comment and without betraying any emotion in his appearance or tone.

"So you propose to take his daughter out to the Smith Field without so much as an armed guard and you will be responsible for her?" Wriothesley shakes his head, a droll smile on his face.

"The lady will come to no harm. She merely wishes to witness the death of a heretic."

"We all wish to see such vile heretics as Askew dead. Though I still do not see what I stand to gain from allowing this." Wriothesley raises his eyebrows, expectant.

"She will be guarded. Longshawe is, as you know, a palace guardsman, and he will be there."

"Do not deviate, Master Strelley. What is in this for me?"

"The lady offers her gratitude." Strelley smiles, aware of the inadequacy of the bribe.

"I shall be able to earn her gratitude in no end of ways that do not risk my being an accomplice to this... treason!" Wriothesley folds his arms, challenging Strelley to push him further if he dare.

"My Lord is confused. I cannot commit treason by act or omission with the lady, as she is not a princess." Wriothesley stares at Strelley, not quite baffled but nevertheless taken aback by his line of reasoning. "In any case, she has taken it upon herself to find a way to Smith Field. As My Lord knows, she is ingenious and persistent, and it would be better for her to be under our protection than not."

"I shall lock her up if I have to!" The sardonic smile has returned to Wriothesley's face.

"You may have to. The lady, of course, will not appreciate it. Perhaps she shall speak to her father about My Lord Wriothesley, how he comports himself about the palace without the king's knowledge. The company he keeps may not find him in the king's favour soon enough."

"What say you?" Wriothesley snaps. "Are you threatening me?"

"With what?" Strelley holds Wriothesley's gaze for a long time. "I only ask that you allow the lady this freedom." He sits back, calculating that the victory has been won. "And I offered you a word of advice."

"Your obfuscation is not endearing."

"My Lord is unclear as to my meaning? Do not prevent Elizabeth's attendance at this execution. That is the first matter. As to the second, think carefully about where your loyalties lie. Do not throw in your lot with the wrong party." Strelley's bluntness partially disguises his fear that he has not made a strong enough case. Wriothesley eyes him contemptuously, and when he opens his mouth to speak it is not in a harsh voice, but quietly, as though scolding a miscreant child.

"I have never known such insolence. You are a tutor, Master Strelley. Indeed, you are not even a tutor, but a servant to a tutor, and you seem to forget that you address your superior."

Strelley leaps up, banging his hands on the table, throwing everything at one last gamble, raising his voice to something close to a shout. "Have you listened to nothing I have said? You risk everything by your connection with Norfolk and his clown of a son! They will commit a real act of treason soon enough if they haven't already." Strelley sits himself back down, holding his head between his hands. Wriothesley watches him for a quarter of a minute before speaking.

"The king knows...?"

"More than you would imagine. He certainly knows that Norfolk will stop at nothing to marry his son to a Tudor daughter." Wriothesley's face lightens visibly, brows unknotting. Strelley notices, and narrows an eye as he considers the meaning of this.

"He finds the Howards... over-mighty?" Wriothesley says, the turbulence of a moment ago forgotten.

"He considers the Howards a threat to Edward's succession. And he will do what he needs to neutralise that threat." Strelley's breathing has slowed so it is no longer audible.

Wriothesley leans back and touches the tips of his fingers together. "Why do you tell me this?"

"Because I, and the lady I serve, have much to gain from you."

"Very well. Take her to Smith Field, but it will be on your head if anything untoward should happen. I take no part in it, and you may be certain that I know nothing of it," Wriothesley nods his head, as though he is persuading himself, "should anyone think to ask. I thank you for your advice. Know then that I shall look to Elizabeth's welfare. And your own, should it be in my power."

Strelley rises, slowly this time, and bows slightly. "I thank you on My Lady's behalf." He turns and leaves, closing the door behind him. Once the latch has caught, Wriothesley flicks through his bundle of papers, selecting four or five pieces. He passes his eye over them briefly, then throws them in the fire, watching them burn before returning to his desk.

Wriothesley stands in the receiving room in front of the king, who listens as the Lord Chancellor speaks. Longshawe stands guard across the room, watching the exchange. The king's interest and Wriothesley ignorance of him conspire to allow him to drop his usual rigid stare.

"Indeed, Sire," Wriothesley is saying, "she did not implicate anyone else in this heresy. I understand that Your Majesty was concerned that some of those closest to him might have had some involvement. I can assure you, Sire, that they did not." Wriothesley has all the conviction of someone with a great deal to hide. His sly look at the king from under his lowered forehead goes unnoticed by Henry, but not by Longshawe.

"This is most welcome news, Sir," the king grunts. "I had wondered whether my household itself harboured heretics, but you have brought me some peace of mind." His tone is almost uninterested, definitely unconvinced.

"The torture did not seem to have a great deal of effect on her. She gave no names at all. No doubt this signifies that she had no accomplice." Longshawe nods his head slightly at this comment. Wriothesley does not notice, and carries on, "I understand that her sentence is to be executed forthwith."

"Your efforts are to be commended, My Lord."

"My thanks, Sire. I have another matter to bring to your

attention."

"More business? A matter of state, I hope."

"Of sorts, Your Majesty. You must be aware of the ambition of your subjects, Sire." Wriothesley smiles broadly.

"Speak clearly, Wriothesley, or I shall lose my temper. To what do you refer? Your own ambition?"

"My own ambition is more than satisfied already, Your Majesty. I speak rather of the ambition of your nobility."

"And what do you think I need fear from my nobility?" Henry asks, mouth upturned in a grimace.

"I come not with a warning, Majesty, but a proposal. I have of late come to know that the Howards-"

"Norfolk has been a loyal servant for many years. His record in war may be questionable, and his son is a fool..." Henry trails off.

"But Your Majesty suspects them of a more heinous crime than these?"

"I understand that they are friends of yours."

"Your Majesty is mistaken. I am acquainted with the Howards, though I find my affection for them has waned." Wriothesley smiles again. "I wonder if they have not over-reached themselves. Surrey's proposal to your daughter was too bold."

"What know you of Surrey and Mary?"

"Only what is common knowledge about the palace, Sire."

"Well, then, what of it?" Henry leans back, folding his arms across his great frame, looking down his nose expectantly.

"Your Majesty is more than aware of their ambition, but I offer something different. I offer you proof of their disloyalty."

"Their disloyalty? You accuse this great noble house of treason?"

"*I* do not accuse them, Sire. It is their own actions that implicate them."

"A marriage proposal is not in itself treason." Henry is impassive, waiting for more.

"No, Sire. But I can show you that the Howards' intentions are greater than an advantageous marriage."

Henry considers this. "The throne?"

"The throne."

"And what can you show me that establishes this?"

"I have letters, Sire, that I have come by... I have allowed

Norfolk to think that I side with him, in order to see the full extent of his treachery."

"That prove Norfolk's ambitions for his son extend to the throne?"

"Exactly that, Sire."

"I shall ask you for these documents when the moment is right." The king scratches his chin, deep in thought. Wriothesley stands, bows, and leaves the room, a triumphant smile written across his face.

A few days later, Strelley and Longshawe ride out towards Smith Field. Between them is a third rider, smaller and swaddled in a cloak that obscures all features, despite the summer sun. Guy Fletcher follows a few paces behind, mounted on a black horse with a white patch across its face. Longshawe has his hand on the hilt of the sword he bought from Gilbert, watching each passerby. He follows one running street-child with his eyes, turning his horse slightly across, barring the way, protecting the rider between him and Strelley. The child shies away at the sight of Longshawe's weapon, even in its scabbard.

"We should not be doing this," Longshawe says quietly.

"Do not draw attention to us, James," Strelley whispers to him. "We are just four young men out to watch a heretic burn."

Longshawe laughs. "Four young men, you say?"

The figure in the cloak shifts in the saddle. Strelley turns, addressing this mystery person. "Say nothing. For your own sake."

"I will speak as I please, Master Strelley," Lady Elizabeth's voice hisses from within the cowl. "This is ridiculous. No one knows who I am."

"Not out here perhaps, but there will be those attending who might just recognise someone of your importance."

"Then, Edward," Longshawe cuts in, "You will be presented with your balls."

Strelley shakes his head as Elizabeth chuckles. He warns his friend, "think about what we are doing, James, please. And whom you serve today."

A few minutes later they arrive at Smith Field. Guy Fletcher remains on his mount, takes the other horses and remains at some distance. Strelley and Longshawe walk either side of Elizabeth, each looking around and sizing up the other people in the crowd.

Elizabeth, still hidden under her cowl, coughs and splutters. "The smell is unbearable!" she hisses.

"This is what you wanted to see. The smell comes with it," Strelley says, flatly, without turning his head to her. "Let's go over there. The crowd looks a little thinner."

They push and shove their way to a spot where they can see the execution clearly despite Elizabeth's diminutive stature. As they stand waiting for the prisoners to be brought out, a man strolls through the crowd with two heavy-set minders clearing a path for him.

"Bollocks!" Strelley curses, hiding his face. Elizabeth giggles at his exclamation. "Gilbert!" Strelley hisses, which prompts Longshawe to stand on his tiptoes to see.

"James, you fool!" Strelley rasps, but it is too late. Gilbert has recognised Longshawe, and is walking towards them.

"Ah, gentlemen!" Gilbert calls when a few paces away, "I am always pleased to see such good customers as yourselves out and about." He leans in towards Strelley, adopting a confidential tone. His whisper is audible to all around. "Have you finished my translation yet? I haven't had anything salacious for a while." He licks his lips ostentatiously.

A moment later he notices Elizabeth, who is silently staring out at him from underneath her hood.

"I didn't know you kept lepers at that palace of yours, gentlemen. Or perhaps Grindal has had his legs-" He stops abruptly as his thoughts catch up with his banter. "Not Grindal, then? Never mind, lads, your secret is safe with me." He nods to Elizabeth. "Not every day that one such as me meets one of your station." He makes the smallest of bows at Elizabeth, holds it for a moment, raises his eyebrows at her, then draws himself upright. "Come on!" he calls to his minders, and they move off through the crowd.

Elizabeth looks from Strelley to Longshawe, pushing the hood back over her forehead with her hand. "Well?" she asks. "Are we safe?"

"Gilbert has no interest in revealing you. Now *please* be quiet!" Strelley answers, pointing to the place where the execution is to take place, "and keep your face hidden."

They look on as four prisoners are brought forth from somewhere beyond the pressing crowd. One, a woman, is carried on a sort of chair by several men. Another can barely walk. His legs appear not to bear his weight, and he struggles to haul himself along using the other prisoners as support. They are ragged, broken people, whose skin is ravaged by torture. The guards surrounding the place of execution push back the throng, encroaching as it is, swallowing the space set aside.

A well-dressed figure pushes forward through the crowd. As he emerges, we can recognise him as Thomas Wriothesley. "I come to offer you a pardon, if you recant your heresy," he says, loudly enough for many of those assembled to hear. The chatter ceases, bringing a tense silence to the crowd.

It is Askew, still seated on her chair, who responds. "I come not hither to deny my Lord and Master." She speaks calmly, quietly, all the while watching Wriothesley. Her look suggests that she recognises him. But as she finishes, a great cry goes up, drowning out Wriothesley as he tries to speak again. He waits for the noise to die down, before repeating himself.

"The king is your Lord and Master, and as you die now, you die in your heresy. May the cleansing flames avail you."

Askew is raised from her chair by her warders, and dragged from it to her stake. She is chained to it, her arms above her head supporting her weight. The others to be executed are equally roughly handled, bound to their stakes. The faggots of sticks are thrown around them. While this happens, several men and women try to get close enough to throw black powder at the prisoners, but they are beaten back by the guards. One of these is struck a fearful blow with the butt-end of a halberd, and falls to the ground, bleeding and unconscious. No one else steps forward to assist as a guard stands over the prone body.

There is a brief lull before the fire is set, as people watching settle into the horrific theatrical display. Their murmurs do not drown out Askew as she prays loudly, invoking God to forgive those who do wrong in his name. Wriothesley stares at her, impressed by her coolness as her death approaches. The fire grows, throwing out black smoke which stains around the mouths and noses of the condemned. The three men around Askew let out cries of pain as the flames begin to scorch their skin. Askew herself closes her eyes, her prayer increasing in intensity and speed. The crowd around watches, fascinated by her, quietened by her fervour but not quite silenced as whispered comments are exchanged.

Strelley turns to Longshawe, who pulls a sort of brief smile. He then looks down at Elizabeth, still hooded such that her face is barely visible. He notices that her breathing is fast, shallow, excited. A moment later, she is aware that he is watching her, and her head tilts slightly towards him. For a moment, Elizabeth contemplates Strelley, before focusing again on Askew. Strelley does not lift his gaze away from her for half a minute, before finally returning his own attention to the fearsome execution of the death sentence.

Whatever gunpowder was thrown at Askew has not helped her. The flames rise to her waist, and the smell of burning skin and blood becomes quite distinct amongst the stink of the assembled crowd. She does not scream, but her prayer is fast and quiet, a look of stern concentration on her face. She has been in the fire for five minutes or more, her legs barely recognisable charred stumps.

The noise of the crowd begins to grow again, shouts of support and condemnation equally audible. One of the others lets out a long cry of pain, then falls unconscious. Askew looks at her fellow victim, her face too weary with her own suffering to show any pity. The crowd surges, but is pushed back again by the ring of armed guards. Strelley puts his arm instinctively around Elizabeth as he feels her being pushed away from him.

She stifles her surprised cry. "Perhaps we should leave?" Strelley asks her, urgently. He tries to catch Longshawe's attention, but he is fixated by Askew's continued impassivity. "James!" Strelley hisses. "Shall we move?"

Longshawe turns to them, and surveys the crowd. "We'll be safe. It's hardly Ancrum Moor, is it?" The crowd shifts again, leaving them with more space.

Elizabeth Tudor laughs, and smiles at Longshawe. Strelley's eyes narrow, and though he releases the girl from his grasp, he stands very close to her and looks at her frequently. Finally, Askew cries out as the flames engulf her, the crack and hiss of her body being consumed briefly drowned by the crowd's answering gasp. Her head slumps forward, her prayer finally over.

Her flesh continues to burn, though her eyes are closed and her ordeal is over. The crowd begins to thin as the entertainment is over, the other men long having since died. As people walk away, another familiar face is visible.

De Winter stands by another figure, hidden away in the folds of a cloak just as Elizabeth is. Strelley and Longshawe look at him, and he looks back. Recognition flashes across all three faces. They close, acknowledging each other without drawing attention to themselves. The two incognitos pass by each other, marginally behind their chaperones.

A few moments later, Elizabeth raises her hand to her chin, flashing long, thin and white fingers. "That was my sister," she says. Strelley grunts in agreement.

"She and you apparently share an interest in the morbid," he says. "You would be wise not to speak of this with her. Do not let on that you recognised her."

"Indeed not, Sir," she says, an officious tone in her voice. "I shall be a model of subtlety." She pauses. "I have learned my lessons from you well, Master Strelley, and I do not need to hear them again."

"No, Madam, it would seem so," Strelley sighs. "Now home, before any more of hoi polloi recognise you."

Elizabeth considers a moment. "Let us rejoin hoi oligoi, then." They leave Smith Field, unnoticed among the crowd, other than by Guy Fletcher, who restores to them their respective horses.

24: The Queen's Defence

Queen Catherine sits opposite Thomas Wriothesley, her hands grasping her knees. Wriothesley sits behind a desk, on which there are a set of papers that he pushes around. Norfolk and his son Surrey are to either side of the Lord Chancellor, and Edward Seymour sits at the back of the room, watching. He is sullen and looks out from under a furrowed brow, partly hidden in the gloom. It is daytime, but the shutters are closed across all the windows, and what little light there is comes from a pair of candles highlighting the features of the accused queen.

"So you do not possess any of these banned volumes? And you swear that you have never possessed them?" Wriothesley looks up from his papers to the queen. She shakes her head.

"I do not, and I have not, Sir," she replies. "Indeed I am shocked that you wish to ask me. Were my husband the king to hear your..." She considers a moment, wondering how hard to press her case. She decides on a defiant challenge. "Were Henry to become aware of your insolence, you would be sorry, I warrant."

"Your Majesty will appreciate that the king does not wish to have a heretic in his household. Nor of course do any of his loyal servants." Wriothesley offers a smile which he tries to make as friendly as he can, and which the others in the room do not see. "In any case, Madam, if you have done nothing wrong then you need not worry."

"My Lord, if you are convinced that I have done nothing wrong, then I need not be here." The queen folds her hands demurely across her lap. "And I should be given my leave immediately. I warn you, Sir," her voice contorts into a sneer, "that whilst you may think your position secure, the king may not."

"Madam, forgive me. I do not wish you to feel intimidated. You are not under formal investigation, we merely wish to establish the truth. There are others in the Royal Household who may not be able to read these works without being unduly influenced by them, and we wish to protect these innocents."

"As we have established, Sir, I do not and have not possessed such works." The queen shifts in her seat, looking to the shuttered windows and then returning her gaze, narrow-eyed and dry, to Wriothesley. He doesn't react as she carries on, "if you wish to accuse me of some other crime, please do so, such that I can answer your charge. Unless you clarify you position I cannot defend myself."

"We have no wish to confound Your Majesty," Wriothesley says, "and as such we do not have any further reason to detain you." Again he smiles at her, his warmth perhaps only partly feigned.

The queen stands, a confused look on her face. A maid who has been waiting in the shadows at the edge of the room steps forward and they leave together, Catherine casting one more questioning look back over her shoulder at Wriothesley as she goes. The guard who opens the door and closes it behind is Longshawe, whose eyebrows are raised almost imperceptibly as he returns to his stance, tall and straight. He focuses on a painting on the opposite wall as the others begin to speak. Seymour rises and draws a tapestry curtain to one side. The king is seated in a chair in an alcove, previously hidden behind the curtain. He has heard the whole conversation.

"There, gentlemen," he says, a broad smile on his face. "I need not repeat my position. The queen is beyond reproach, neither heretical nor oppositional. I would appreciate it if you would let her alone in the future."

Wriothesley looks at Seymour, their eyes meeting for a moment. Norfolk twists his aged shoulders, his face contorting as he settles himself to speak, gathering the assault on the queen's innocence.

"I do not believe her," he says, simply. The words reverberate around the room. Wriothesley cannot hide a flicker of a smile, but in the darkness it is invisible to the others. Seymour is impassive, but his gaze flicks from the king to Norfolk, to Surrey. Surrey is earnest beside his father, leaning forward.

"She has sworn," the king says, slightly louder than necessary, "and you, Thomas, whatever your opinions, must not suspect those who are above suspicion. My queen is loyal to me and to England."

Norfolk watches the king, circumspection written across his features. "You believe her? Your Majesty must surely realise-"

Surrey raises his hand to stop his father, and takes over. His tone is more measured, more even, as though he has rehearsed these lines many times already. "My father's concern is that Your Majesty is deceived by your queen, as is your Lord Chancellor. She would have much to lose if she were to be uncovered as a heretic." Henry listens, his breathing heavy. Surrey continues. "The queen is well-known to sympathise with the Evangelical cause, Sire. Her fear of your just retribution has led her into dishonesty. A crime of great significance.

Treason." He lets the word hang, satisfied with effect on the king's expression.

"Your lack of faith shows you are no better than your father, Sir." It is Seymour who says these words, not the king, and both Norfolk and Surrey turn to him and scowl. "If the queen says, swears indeed, that she possesses none of these books, she must be believed."

Surrey bristles at Seymour, his hands clenching into fists. His chair scrapes on the stone floor as it moves, but Surrey does not rise from it, instead fixing Seymour with a look of absolute hatred. "Your opinion, Sir, is not required," he sneers. "I wonder whether your presence here is of any value at all." They all look at King Henry, who comes to some sort of resolution only after looking each one of them in the eye.

"My Lord Hertford is not only welcome, but you shall learn to respect him, Henry, and you shall learn to value his judgements." Surrey stares at the king, mouth open, but does not reply. He suppresses his urge to shake his head at the decision. After a silence of a quarter of a minute, he turns to Seymour, who returns his aggressive glare with a wry smile.

"His Majesty does not need your fomentations, My Lord Surrey." Seymour cannot keep the trace of a smug laugh from his voice, enjoying his victory. The king raises his hand.

"Do not demean yourself by gloating, Edward. Norfolk is among my oldest friends. I value his counsel as well as yours."

Norfolk seems to have recovered himself, as he resumes the role of the flattering courtier. "Your Majesty's perspicacity is infallible, of course. If you have no worry over the queen's beliefs, then we shall think no more of it. The matter is closed." He rises, slowly and deliberately. "Allow us then to take our leave, if you will." The king nods his assent. Surrey offers a cursorily short bow to the king and stomps out, followed by his father, stick clocking against the stone floor. Longshawe shuts the door behind them.

"You must not," King Henry begins, "set out to try to elevate yourself at the Howards' expense, Edward." Henry's tone is avuncular, counselling. "If you are to be responsible for guiding my son during his minority, I would have it that you would be a humble-" Seymour lets out a breath at the king's unintentionally ironic choice of word, "-leader, able to accept the contribution of others. Remember you are not a king yourself. Nor shall you be when it is no longer my time."

Seymour arranges himself in his chair, leaning forward and placing his hands on his knees, absorbing the king's words. "The Howards are trying to stir things up, to make Your Majesty feel the need to rely on them."

"The Howards have long been a prop to this realm, Edward. Despite their failings, I need them to be on my side and I need them to be on my boy's side when I meet God. You – and my son – can not, must not allow civil war!" His voice has risen to an angry grunt. "I will not have my work undone by your grubbing for power." Henry's lungs rattle as he fights to calm himself. Seymour watches him, considering.

"Surrey intends to marry into the Royal Family," he says, matter-of-factly, testing the water again.

"We have had this discussion before. If he is guilty of treason, that will become apparent. As it stands, he has done nothing for which he deserves death."

Seymour raises one eyebrow. "Treason," he says, "may be committed by intention as well as act."

"Speak to me no further of treason, Hertford, or I shall begin to suspect you of it. Now, I would see my queen alone. Help me up."

Edward Seymour steps forward, as does Longshawe, alert to the king's request. They escort him as he limps out of the room by a different door to the one by which the Howards left. We shall leave them for a moment.

A short distance away, Surrey and his father Norfolk stand at the junction of two corridors arguing with each other. A few yards away Strelley stands hidden in a doorway, listening to their conversation whilst pretending to read from a small leather-bound volume.

"Listen, my son!" Norfolk is saying, exasperated. "Your scheming will land us all in the Tower, if not in the Tower's charnel house. You must use your energy for some other project than this to which you aspire."

"I shall not be denied, Sir!" Surrey hisses, in a whisper that is more than audible. "Would you have this Seymour, of this family of neophyte..." He stops to think, trying to find a suitably foul insult. After a moment he gives up and settles on: "Farmers! Earl of Hertford! He is a novice nobleman, without dignity!"

"I shall tell you this once, and no more," Norfolk says, "keep your opinions on Hertford to yourself. Even I grow tired of hearing them. If you persist, the king will lose his patience. Besides, once the king is gone he will be the closest living relative to the new king. Do not underestimate the power that will bring him."

"So we must intervene! Father, I cannot stand by and let him fashion the future that he desires with himself as king while the boy prince plays with his toys."

"Enough." Norfolk focuses his bloodshot, rheumy eyes on his son. "Do not test the limits of my protection. My credit with the king is already damaged by your incompetence in France. I will not have it." Surrey harrumphs and flounces his cloak around himself as he walks away. Norfolk watches his son, before turning and stumping away in the opposite direction. Strelley remains focused on his book, carefully just hidden in the embrasure of the door, the pages resolutely unturned throughout the Howards' conversation, until Norfolk has disappeared. He turns and lets himself through the door, disappearing into the room and out of the corridor.

The king, supported on one side by Seymour and the other by Longshawe, whose long halberd is discarded for this royal duty, shuffles into a long, bright room. The autumn sun casts a series of long shadows, all at the same angle. At one end sits Queen Catherine, on a beautifully upholstered chair of gilded wood. Beside her is Lady Elizabeth, and talking to them across the table is Grindal. As the king enters at one end, Strelley, doing his best to be discreet, shuts a door behind himself as he comes in at the other. He bows to the king, and catches Longshawe's eye as he does so, flashing him a broad, victorious smile. Henry does not notice, his attention fixed as it is on Catherine.

"My dear!" he calls to her. "I can only apologise most humbly to you for those who have cast your honour and loyalty into doubt. Accept my supplication, such as it is, on my own behalf and for those whose zeal in ensuring the spiritual health of the nation and its head-" His breath gives out momentarily. Elizabeth looks worried. Catherine sits serenely. Grindal, now risen, watches without moving. The king groans, then spits. After a moment, he carries on as if there had been no interruption. "-Has led them to make false accusations about Your Majesty." Longshawe manoeuvres him towards Grindal's empty chair. It creaks as he and Seymour lower him into it. Seymour's face is red with exertion, mixed with a sort of impressed surprise that Longshawe appears barely to have strained himself. Longshawe backs away, positioning himself by the grand double-doors through which they entered.

"You have no need to apologise, Your Majesty," the queen answers him. "Indeed, I have the same zeal for Your Majesty's spiritual welfare. I could not and would not commit heresy for this reason alone, even were I otherwise so inclined."

Henry looks puzzled. Grindal, now behind the king, allows himself a satisfied smile at Catherine's sophistry. Elizabeth observes her father, showing no concern despite his obviously failing health. He has lost the handsome vigour of his youth altogether, and his face is now bloated and covered with sore patches of dry skin. The heavy smell of the perfume that he wears doesn't quite disguise the underlying stink of his unhealed leg wound. Elizabeth looks from him to her stepmother, attractive and still relatively youthful. Her face betrays her wonder at the relationship, at the queen's forbearance. Strelley narrows one eye as he sees Elizabeth's expression, trying to warn her that she is revealing her thoughts.

"Whatever the cause..." the king begins, before reconsidering and starting again. "I am glad that I can trust you, Madam," he says, curtly. "You will dine with me tonight." Henry gestures at Elizabeth as well as nodding at the queen. "Lady Mary shall be in attendance, as shall Prince Edward. It is time we behaved as the family we are." The king summons Seymour again, and Longshawe, silently efficient, is by the king's other side immediately. They haul him from the seat and walk him out of the room.

Grindal's attention moves from the queen to Elizabeth, and back again. Catherine falls back in her seat, sighing. Strelley watches Grindal, alert. It is Elizabeth who speaks. "My father is not well served. Every man about him sows a seed of doubt in his mind about some other of his servants."

Queen Catherine inspects the backs of her hands. "There is much to be gained from having the king's ear. As there is much to be gained by painting a black picture in his mind of your rival."

"Even at the expense of that rival's death...?" Elizabeth asks the question without looking at the queen, focused on some distant point out in the grounds. She doesn't wait for an answer, taking up herself the thread of her thoughts. "Seymour will have the king's ear when the king is Edward, not Henry. I should not like to be Norfolk or Surrey then."

Catherine rises. Strelley bows in response, and Grindal pushes himself out of his seat and lowers his chin to his chest. The queen smoothes her skirts, then speaks. "Do not become involved in such intrigues, Elizabeth. Were it not for Jane and a few minutes warning... I should not like to think of the consequences." She indicates a prettily dressed girl-in-waiting, who performs a perfect courtesy. She is the same Jane as we have met previously in the queen's service.

Catherine strides down the long hall, soft shoes making the barest of noises as they touch the polished wood of the floor. Her maid follows her, taking two steps to each of the queen's. Strelley waits until she has left before sitting down in the chair the king occupied until a few moments ago.

"The ice thaws?" he says, mostly to himself. Elizabeth starts, as though shaken out of deep thought.

"The king," Elizabeth says, "my father has recognised, no doubt, that the future must be secured. He intends to confirm the bonds between us, my brother, my sister and me."

Grindal answers, "no doubt." He speaks slowly, deliberately. "There is safety, for your brother, in his family."

"Master Grindal," Elizabeth asks, "do you think that my father looks unwell?"

"He does not have his usual vigour about him," Grindal replies. Strelley coughs, hiding his face with his hand..

"You have something to add, Master Strelley?" Elizabeth's voice is sharp, as he recovers himself.

"Am I to speak honestly, Madam?" He bows his head in a deferential salute. She nods her permission. "His Majesty is dying." Grindal rises, anticipating. Elizabeth holds her hand across him, requesting his silence.

"Continue, Edward," she says. Her calm has returned.

"The king is ill, Madam, as he has been before. But he will not recover this time. His body is broken, and this is the final descent into death."

"Your words are treasonous." Elizabeth does not look at Strelley. "As well you know."

"No, Madam, I am not imagining the king's death. I am merely speaking the truth of its imminence."

Grindal forces himself into the conversation, despite Strelley's gaze being firmly fixed on Elizabeth, and her studied indifference. "Madam, may I apologise for my apprentice's poor behaviour? He will be punished, of course, and removed from your service if you wish."

"No, Master Grindal. Strelley is right. The king is dying, and we cannot ignore it any longer. My brother will need those about him to act in his interests alone. I am prepared to serve him as king."

"Your brother," Strelley adds, looking at Grindal, "is wise beyond his years, and will be a good king." The door through which Strelley came opens noisily. Through it steps a woman of perhaps forty years, dressed well but not flamboyantly, who immediately approaches Lady Elizabeth, ignoring Grindal and Strelley. She is at once deferential and maternal, someone who has known Elizabeth as a little girl as well as the young adult she is now.

"Good afternoon, Kat!" Elizabeth exclaims happily.

"My Lady," she bows as she walks forward, "I understand that you will dine with the king tonight. The gentlemen will pardon us if we take a little time to prepare you."

"Well, my boys," Elizabeth says, at which Grindal and Strelley exchange a look, Grindal's exasperated and Strelley's wryly amused, "I expect I shall see you tomorrow!" She lifts herself out of her chair and follows Katherine Campernon along the hall.

Grindal watches her leave. When the door is closed, he turns to Strelley, and there is anger in his usually calm voice. "You forget yourself, Edward. You are apprenticed to me, and I am therefore responsible for your conduct." He points at Strelley, accusingly. "If you expose me to the possibility of a charge of treason-"

"Stop, William." Grindal's face contorts in surprise at the use of his Christian name. "The lady will not accuse me of treason."

"I admire your confidence," Grindal says, unimpressed.

"Be assured of it. She and I... We trust each other."

"You have not done anything-"

"Of course not, William. She, perhaps, has been guilty of indiscretion."

"Do not speak in riddles, Edward." Grindal's tone has softened. He seeks Strelley's meaning in his eyes, but cannot divine it.

"I cannot say further," Strelley says, "but Elizabeth will not betray me. Or you."

"Your judgment had better be sound. There is much at stake."

Strelley pulls a face to say that it is indeed. He leans in to Grindal, and whispers. "The king has asked after you, and Cheke. 'Are they heretics?', he asks. He wants me to be his ears, his spy. And I play my part. But you are still here, unburned, head on your shoulders. Are you not?"

"I-" Grindal hesitates.

"Indeed you are!" Strelley smiles, teasing his mentor. "I am gratified that my loyalty was thus repaid, offering to remove me from the lady's service." Grindal waves his fingers in a gesture of contrition.

"Edward, your mind moves too quickly for me to follow your strategy. But please be careful."

"I shall." He stands, putting his hand on Grindal's shoulder. "And I shall not betray you. But you must ensure that you navigate the stormy waters of the king's religious pronouncements without attracting any further interest."

25: God on his side

Edward Seymour sits across from the king, dealing cards. The third player is a man whom we have not previously encountered of about forty years of age, with the powerful physique of a professional soldier. He is wearing a pointed beard that accentuates the angularity of his face. Several retainers scurry about the room bringing food and drink. Longshawe stands at a door, listening without his eyes straying from a point on the far wall, controlling his expression to remain blank.

The king is speaking. "Well, Edward, John, I am greatly enthused, despite my ill health." He taps his right index finger against the card table, reinforcing his point. "It is in the company of loyal men such as yourselves that I begin to see how the future of this great nation will develop. I no longer fear for my son with you as his guardians."

Seymour puts a card down on the table. "Your Majesty must not speak with such resignation. There are many years of life before you."

"Now, My Lord Hertford, you insult my intelligence. I am dying, as well you know! Ah, Edward," he says as he sees Seymour's grimace, "I cannot commit the treason of foretelling my own death, can I? The matter now shifts from loyalty to me, to loyalty to my son, the prince. And as his uncle, we can rely on you to act in his interests."

The third man, whom Henry called John a moment ago, looks up from his hand. "With respect, Sire, it is more than likely to be a matter of our strength abroad as at home. There will be foreign princes with their eyes on your daughters, and we must be able to deal with the threat of a usurper from abroad." He dwells on the word 'usurper', extending it well beyond its usual length.

Seymour turns his attention to this man, saying "Dudley, what a bloodthirsty, war-hungry cur you are!" He laughs, a little too loudly. "Do not trouble the king with these cares."

"Edward," Dudley replies, barely opening his mouth and hissing out his words, "there isn't the money for another foreign war. That is true now, and it shall be true..." He doesn't finish the thought, instead directing his speech to the king. "We were lucky to beat off the French at Portsmouth, Sire. We must consider our borders."

"Scotland again?" Henry grunts. "After our failures in the past?"

"Not by force, though," Dudley says. "Were Prince Edward to marry the girl-" The king stops him by lifting a hand.

"This is a route that has been tried," Henry replies, his words slurred by alcohol and his own degeneration. There is a faint trace of drool around the corners of his mouth.

"A swift and decisive strike is required, Sire." Dudley speaks rapidly, fired by enthusiasm, accompanying the words with by chopping one hand into the other. "We could lead a force to victory in two months."

"Perhaps, but not in winter. Scotland is no place for a campaign in the frost and snow," Henry says, with an air of finality that says the argument is not to be continued. Dudley studies his cards. Seymour throws a coin on the table, then leans in to speak, ignoring the king's implicit command. Henry's lips purse, but he does not interrupt.

"You'd need twenty thousand men, and two dozen pieces of cannon. But after Ancrum Moor there is much to be gained from a show of strength. The Scots are a threat whilst ever they ally themselves with France."

Dudley takes up the thread. "We put Edinburgh to the sword two years ago. It can be done, Sire."

Henry nods slowly. "It could. You will undertake it, I don't doubt, next summer. But it is not time now. Winter comes to the country, and to its king. I no longer have the energy to campaign with you. Boulogne was my last."

Seymour and Dudley share a significant look, but do not comment. The card game continues in silence for a few minutes, until there is a knock on the door. Longshawe opens it, turning himself in such a way that the three men seated cannot see who it is that has arrived. After a brief and inaudible discussion, a page steps past Longshawe into the room and bows to the king.

"His Grace the Archbishop Cranmer!" the page announces. Cranmer follows the words in, dressed in his customary white silk and covering cassock in vibrantly deep red. Cranmer nods to the Earl of Hertford and Viscount Lisle, whispering their titles partly to himself. He drops his head more significantly to the king, raising a hand to his mitre to prevent it slipping..

"Your Majesty," he says. "I trust you are not gambling with these men. It is deleterious to the soul." He smiles at the king, and takes a moment to examine the other two. His expression settles into neutrality as he awaits the king's reply.

Henry grunts out a laugh. "Your Purple Eminence," he jokes, "how wonderful to see you."

Seymour looks Cranmer up and down, smirking. "Archbishop Cranmer has forsaken his rise to the cardinalship in your service, Majesty."

"And I shall be reminded of it at every turn, it seems. But then, the Pope is not my overseer, nor the king's. My Lord." He adds the title as an afterthought, before turning to the king. "Your Majesty, I have a matter I wish to discuss with you."

"As does just about everyone else, Your Grace," Dudley cuts in, a trace of a snarl in his voice. Henry raises an admonitory finger.

"Gentlemen," he says, addressing Dudley and Seymour, "I shall see you once more in the morning. For now, I have matters of a more spiritual nature to attend." The two of them rise, and back out of the room, beaten. The page who introduced Cranmer cannot quite prevent a hint of a smile flashing across his face. Dudley notices, and his shoulders tense. He is just about to upbraid the young man when Seymour takes him by the arm, shakes his head at him, and leads him away.

Longshawe closes the door as Archbishop Cranmer seats himself in the chair vacated by Seymour. One of Longshawe's eyebrows is slightly raised; his head a little aslant.

"Sire," Cranmer begins, "the execution of the heretics Askew and Lascelles... It seems that Your Majesty's subjects are disappointed by these events."

"Thomas," Henry says in a soothing sort of voice, "my subjects are struggling to understand the true path to God, as are we all. They must be shown that a man – or woman – who strays from that path is apart from God. The fire, Thomas, it shows the pain of eternal damnation, and it brings them back. I hear that Askew did not repent, and went to her death a sinner."

"Your Majesty need hardly tell me the purpose of the fire!" Cranmer is stung by Henry's comment, unnecessary as it is, but his reproach doesn't seem to change the king's expression. "Indeed Askew was not converted to the true faith by her ordeal. She was strong to the end, and her followers saw much that pleased them."

"The death of this unrepentant heretic is a tragedy, Thomas, for her own soul. But the persistence of her followers in their recalcitrance is a matter to be resolved with the greatest urgency. I will not see the degeneration of religion in my country!" Henry spits as his fury rises. It subsides again. "You do not *share* the attitudes of these people?"

Cranmer holds the king's eye. "Your Majesty knows full well that I accept your supremacy in matters of religion. Askew and Lascelles were a threat that Your Majesty needed to deal with."

"Is this what you came to speak to me about?"

"No, Your Majesty. I have a rather more delicate matter to raise. The Earl of Surrey, Majesty... It appears that he has announced his father as your son's protector. After your..." He does not finish the thought.

"After my death," the king takes up the thread. "In what manner?"

"It seems, Your Majesty, that Surrey interrupted your son's lessons. Cheke told me-"

Henry reddens, his nose wrinkling in his anger. "Surrey has told *Edward himself* that Norfolk is to be protector?"

"So I have been told." Cranmer attempts to arrange his face in a solemn manner, but in doing so cannot suppress an expression of pleasure.

"Tomorrow, Your Grace, we shall meet. I must discuss this matter with... trusted advisors..." The king is thinking as he speaks. "You shall summon Lord Chancellor Wriothesley, as well as the Earl of Hertford. And Lisle. He should attend me as well. You must ensure that neither Norfolk nor Surrey is aware of this council."

"Your Majesty plans to arraign the duke and his son?"

"I do not *plan* anything, Thomas. I shall consider, and then I shall act."

"Sire." Cranmer nods his assent to the king's words. "I do not wish to lay cares on Your Majesty that overburden an already laden mind."

"Much will rest on how I deal with this matter. I will not hand the kingdom to my son with it on the brink of civil war. Leave me, Your Grace."

Cranmer stands, bows, and walks out. Longshawe closes the door behind him.

"Master Longshawe," the king says, "there are days when I wish I were not king. But I must remind myself when I have that thought that there is no better man for the role."

Longshawe bows deeply, hiding his eyes quite deliberately. Henry, oblivious, carries on with his thought.

"I wish to speak to your friend again. Ensure that it happens tomorrow. He may attend me after my break-fast. I will personally discharge you from your duties, and he from his, if needs be."

Longshawe nods, and straightens himself at the door. The king calls for his groom.

The following morning, Strelley is summoned before Elizabeth's lessons begin. Longshawe goes to his garret room, and leads him away towards the king's presence chamber. Strelley has dressed himself soberly, and carries himself with unusual agitation. As they walk, Longshawe slaps him on the shoulder.

"Edward... What ails you?"

"I am not ill, James. A little matter between myself and the lady..." He frowns.

"You haven't-"

"I'm not you, James." Strelley looks around, and seeing nobody about, he continues. "Elizabeth... You already know I caught her spying on Guy and me. But I have said things before her, to her... She could have me roasted alive if she's gone to the king with them." He lowers his voice. "I thought I could trust her."

"You haven't been summoned for that. I don't think so, at least. The king asked to speak to you after Cranmer came to him."

"Cranmer?"

"The archbishop."

"I know who he is. What were they talking about?"

"Cranmer visited the king last night. He said that Surrey told Prince Edward that Norfolk will be his protector after the king dies."

"Truly? Did Cranmer hear that for himself?"

"No. He said that Cheke had told him." At this, Strelley stops walking abruptly, and the colour drains out of his face. "What?" Longshawe asks him. "I cannot follow your scheming, Edward."

"No. Indeed I promise myself: no more intrigues."

"What is it that frightens you?"

"The king will ask me if he can trust Cheke's word. If I say he can, I condemn Surrey to a charge of treason. If I say he can't, Cheke, Grindal and I are all in danger."

"How does Cheke being disloyal affect you?"

"The king, rightly or wrongly, associates Cheke with Grindal. And the queen, as they are her men as far as he is concerned. I don't know if I can separate myself from them in his mind. Nor whether I want to."

"Ah." Longshawe holds Strelley's arm. "You will know what to say. You always know what to say." He smiles at his friend, trying to restore his calm.

"I can see no way out. Either Surrey goes, or I do."

"Save yourself, then." Longshawe lets out a stifled laugh.

"I may have to..." Strelley says. "I do not want to have another death on my conscience."

"What do you mean? You still dwell on the death of Eure? He did not deserve even your pity."

"Perhaps. But I don't want this, I don't want to feel like I'm condemning him."

"If he said it, he condemned himself." Longshawe lays his hand on Strelley's shoulder, desperately trying to lessen the burden on him. "You do not bear responsibility for his actions. The king is not angry with you."

"No? How do you know?"

"The king trusts you, doesn't he? Why else would he summon you?"

"I hope you are right." Strelley forces a smile. Longshawe pats him on the back as he holds open the door to the king's room. As they enter, King Henry is reading a bundle of papers.

"A gift from my daughter. She gave it to me last night," he says. "Although she admits that the translation is not all her own."

Strelley starts. It is the translation he gave to Elizabeth.

"You recognise this, Master Strelley?" The king asks with a raised eyebrow. "I don't doubt it. Whoever translated it is a capable linguist. Although I wonder if the musings of a man widely held to be an idiot are appropriate material for a daughter of the king, or the king himself."

Strelley considers a reply, but cannot think of one. He bows deeply.

"Are you dumbstruck, young man?" The king laughs, breaking the tension. "You seem to have a talent for this sort of thing," he says, waving the papers, "But for now I am interested in another of your talents. I need your judgement."

"Majesty?" Strelley whispers. The king seems to notice his quietness, his lack of composure.

"My son's tutor, Cheke. He is a powerful intellect, no doubt, but is he a good man?"

"I don't know a great deal of him, Sire. I can tell you that his lessons to the prince are of the finest, most moral and pious quality you could imagine."

"He is a good Christian?"

"He believes in the goodness of God and of Jesus Christ, our Lord."

"What about the Presence?"

"He believes, Your Majesty," Strelley repeats.

"But he rejects the tyranny of the Bishop of Rome?"

"He despises the Pope and he repudiates the Pope's authority over this kingdom, as we all do."

"Good. It is important that I can trust him. The prince needs to be taught properly so he can rule when the time comes."

Strelley tries to look round at Longshawe, but the king carries on, keeping his eyes fixed on Strelley's, not allowing him this little comfort.

"Master Strelley, what is your opinion of My Lord of Surrey?"

"Your Majesty..."

"My daughter tells me that you are one of the few of her servants who has the grace to speak to her honestly. I would ask you to do the same for me now. I repeat: what is your opinion of My Lord Henry Howard, Earl of Surrey?"

"I have little to say of him, Sire. I have not had the pleasure of his company. I do think that he fears to be left out when it comes to the..." He winces as he speaks. "Umm... The succession."

"Ah!" the king exclaims. "Have you heard him speak of such matters?"

"I have..." Strelley realises his error, casting around for a way to backtrack, but he is committed. "I heard him speaking to his father. He dislikes the Earl of Hertford, Your Majesty."

"In that you are correct. There is a great enmity between the houses of Howard and Seymour. I think that each sees itself as the second family in the kingdom. The Howards object to the Seymours' rapid rise. The Seymours find that the Howards look back, resting on their historical achievements rather than now. I think Hertford is tired of chasing round after the Howards and correcting their mistakes."

"My Lord Hertford has had more successes in Your Majesty's campaigns." Strelley is relieved to be on common ground with the king.

"Indeed. The Howards are disappointed that my marriages within their family have not produced a male heir."

"Your Majesty's daughter Elizabeth is a Howard-"

Henry stops him with a palm-out gesture. "There are certain subjects which even a Royal Fool must not broach with his king. Instead, answer me this, Master Strelley. Are you aware of anything that Surrey or his father Norfolk have done which might be considered treasonous? Do not spare details, I wish to know."

Strelley swallows, and breathes in and out slowly before he begins. "Surrey intends to contract a marriage with one of your daughters. It sounds as though he failed with Lady Mary, and is planning to move his attentions to Lady Elizabeth."

"And why would he do such a thing?"

"His ambitions extend..." Strelley trails off. "I do not wish to be the instrument of his arraignment."

"I understand. I ask only that you tell the truth as you see it. I have made no decisions about what happens next."

"I believe his ambitions extend as far as the throne, Sire. He wishes to be part of the royal line, and would marry a daughter of the crown for such a purpose. I do not know his attitude to the prince."

"The prince will be king sooner than I would like. He must have strong men around him, and there must be none who will contest his authority before or indeed when he comes of age." Henry opens and closes his fist.

Strelley does not have a reply, but nods his head to acknowledge the truth of the king's words.

"Do you know where you can find the Lord Chancellor?" Henry asks. Strelley nods.

"Summon him to me. I would speak with him."

Longshawe opens the door as Strelley moves to leave. As he passes, Longshawe flashes him a smile that says 'well done'.

Once the door is closed behind Strelley and his footsteps have become inaudible, Cranmer emerges from a booth behind a tapestry. The king watches as he seats himself.

"What are your thoughts, Thomas?" the king asks.

"The boy speaks the truth, Sire. Surrey will not cease to scheme after your death."

"Then I must take some action. I cannot allow my son to be exposed to such dangers."

"I shall find My Lord Hertford." The archbishop sweeps from the room.

Henry allows himself a wry smile. "Master Longshawe, am I doing the right thing?" he asks.

Longshawe bows, summoning the correct words. "Your Majesty has God on his side."

Surrey paces the corridor. His lips are working, as though he is testing out ways of saying something. His retainers stand away, watching him, but trying to avoid him noticing that they are doing so. Some of them are frowning, exchanging a few worried words. After a few turns, Surrey stops, repeating the same phrases over to himself.

"Hertford is a traitor. He intends to be king himself. He will deny you your kingdom," he whispers. Aloud, he speaks to his entourage. "We shall be presented now."

One of the men of Surrey's party steps forward and raps his knuckles against the door. It opens, and a brief and inaudible conversation takes place. A moment later, the man beckons Surrey forward. As he moves, the servant inside the door calls out to those inside the room.

"My Lord the Earl of Surrey!"

Surrey walks in to find Prince Edward sitting at a low table, with a set of documents and writing equipment set out before him. Across the table is his elder sister, Mary, and facing him, at the third side, is Cheke. He is inspecting two sheets, careful not to look at the earl. Prince Edward and Lady Mary are already turned towards the door, expectant. De Winter stands by the wall, observing the scene, dislike of Surrey radiating from him as heat does from a fire.

Edward smiles as he sees Surrey come into the room. His sister, by contrast, wears a neutral expression, but her nervous eyes betray the tension she feels. Her nod to Surrey is almost imperceptible. He does not return it, focusing instead on the boy.

"Your Highness!" Surrey musters all his enthusiasm. "It is such a great pleasure to see you at your learning. I understand that you would have grown up to become an eminent scholar were it not for your more illustrious destiny." He approaches the boy. Mary follows him with her eyes, and leans away from him as he bends to pick up something from the table.

"I was never much for Latin." Surrey flashes his teeth at Edward, a conspiratorial tone in his voice. "Your Highness, I hear, shows much ability."

"I thank you for your praise, My Lord Surrey, but it is unnecessary. Learning is its own reward." His voice is high, clear, and pompous. His sister smiles at the the remark. Surrey glances at her, blowing the air out through his nose.

The prince rises, handing Surrey a sheet that is covered with handwriting. "I am considering writing a record of all my business, My Lord Surrey. I intend to keep for posterity those things that I consider to be of significance. What think you of this?"

"Your Highness is wise beyond his years, as you already know. Your journal would be of great interest to your descendants." Surrey looks at the sheet, arranging his expression carefully to appear impressed by the boy's composition. "I see that you have been busy. I do not know a half of the names that you mention." He reads on. As he does so, Lady Mary watches him carefully.

She raises her hand to her cheek, conspicuously feigning artlessness. "My royal brother has recorded a very interesting conversation he had with Your Grace." She laughs as she speaks. Surrey's attention is suddenly diverted to her, an urgent look about him, recognising the threat in her words.

"What do you mean?" he snaps at Mary.

"I mean that My Lord Surrey seems to have told my brother that it shall be his father, the Duke of Norfolk, who will act as his protector should he find himself king."

"I..." Surrey is flummoxed. "I may have said that my father would be the best man for the job," he says, regaining a little of his sangfroid, "and I stand by that. As an old man he has nothing to gain for himself by taking the reins of the state."

Edward clasps his hands, fingers intertwined. "My Lord Surrey, I believe that you told me that my father the king had selected your father, the Duke of Norfolk, as my protector. I do not think you gave a reason." Surrey turns to the prince, his eyes narrow, flashing annoyance now mixed with a measure of contempt.

"My boy..." he begins, but Edward's expression registers the breach of protocol. "Your Highness..." He changes his tone, mastering his fury, and Edward too seems to relax. Surrey says, "Your Highness has mistaken my meaning. I may have said that my father is a great servant of the king and of all England... I would not presume to speak to you of such matters as this."

Prince Edward shakes his head. "I have written it here." He points to a lower part of the page. "See: 'My Lord the Earl of Surrey has visited. He spoke to me of many things, and told me of his loyalty to my father and to me. He explained that my father intends to appoint the

Duke of Norfolk as my protector should I require such a person."

Surrey has read ahead, and speaks aloud quickly but quietly as he reads. "Although my father the king has many years of life ahead of him, and I cannot see that the duke will live beyond him. The duke is old and does not have God's favour as the king does. I wonder that my father does not choose my uncle Hertford as my guardian. He would be a better choice..." Surrey throws the paper away. It crackles as it falls. He points his finger at Mary.

"You put him up to this!" he shouts. De Winter steps forward. Surrey is just beginning his next sentence when de Winter stands between him and the lady.

"My Lord will remember in whose company he finds himself," de Winter says, quietly but threateningly. His physical presence seems to further anger Surrey.

"Get out of my way, you ignorant peasant!" Surrey shouts, trying to force himself past with both hands on one of de Winter's shoulders pulling him aside. A palace guard, wearing the same uniform in which we have previously seen Longshawe, steps forward, sword threateningly drawn. Surrey bristles, but does not press further. Instead, he turns and storms out.

His retinue, some of whom have been drawn to the door by the noise of the shout, scatter away as it opens. Surrey marches through, face red with anger, battering a few bodies out of his way. The entourage to a man wear worried looks as they follow him on his stamp through the palace.

Surrey slams the door behind himself as he enters his father's apartment. "We are lost!" he shouts. "That idiot child has recorded a conversation I had with him... He says I have named you as his future protector... We are lost! God's Blood!" He throws his gloves away, then picks up a lavishly decorated vase and throws it at the wall. It shatters loudly, and the noise takes a few moments to calm to silence, punctuated only by Surrey's heavy breathing.

Norfolk watches his son. "I told you, Henry. I told you to be careful. Now you have brought us to this..."

"I did not say that which he has written... Besides, he wrote in his own hand that Hertford would be a better choice than you!"

"Henry!" Norfolk shouts, finally roused to meet his son's anger with his own. "Stop this! Whatever we hoped to achieve must be abandoned. There is no ambition after death, Henry. Save yourself."

"I must return to Kenning Hall. I cannot stand to be here when Hertford hears of this."

"Then fly, Henry. I will join you when I have secured your future with the king."

"Do not talk to me as you would a child, father!" Surrey growls. "I shall manage my own affairs with the king."

"Is that so? You have not managed your own affairs with any great success thus far," Norfolk sighs. "I would that it were different, Henry, but you do not find yourself in the king's favour. I will be hard-pushed to rectify this mess."

"Is it not your ambition as well that we elevate ourselves?" Surrey asks, astonished.

"Indeed. But perhaps we – you – should have paid heed to history. Men like us do not choose how we benefit from the king's largesse. Nor does history teach us that we are wise to marry into the royal family."

"No," Surrey spits. "Perhaps not. Then I shall wait out my penance elsewhere." He scowls at his father.

"Please do. Do not, by act or omission, make my task any more difficult than you have already. I shall join you when it is safe for me to be away from the palace."

Surrey offers his father a bow. "I thank you, Your Grace," he says, bitterly, "and I look forward to your arrival at Kenning Hall."

Later that day, de Winter, Longshawe and Strelley are talking in a corridor.

"I think he would have struck her had I not intervened," de Winter says. At this news, Longshawe whistles and Strelley puffs out his cheeks. "You have to wonder why he persists in his designs after the setbacks that he has suffered."

Strelley nods. Longshawe replies, "ambition... Obviously Surrey can't be satisfied with anything other than the very highest position in the land."

"Perhaps." De Winter scratches his chin. "But it will lead him to his downfall. The king knows, doesn't he? That he has announced his father as Prince Edward's future protector?"

Strelley takes up the thread. "Yes, he knows. Cranmer found out from Cheke. And he told the king." Longshawe confirms with a gesture, pointing to his ears to indicate that he heard it for himself.

Strelley again picks up the story. "The king wanted to know from me whether Cheke was trustworthy. I confess that I found myself torn."

De Winter looks at him, eyes aslant. "Torn?"

"Had I told the king the truth, that Cheke is an Evangelist, a committed anti-Catholic and leading his precious child towards and into Lutheranism, both Grindal and I would be in great danger. Instead it is My Lord Surrey who is at risk of his life."

"So your decision to condemn Surrey was selfish?" de Winter laughs. "With such high principles as yours!"

Strelley frowns. "As you said, James, Surrey has condemned himself by his behaviour. His proposal to Lady Mary, his persistence in putting forward his father as the rightful holder of the position of protector, these things are not of my doing. If my words are the trigger for his fall, he is the architect."

De Winter puts a hand on Strelley's shoulder. Longshawe holds Strelley's gaze for a moment before speaking. "Do not be troubled by that over-active conscience of yours. God will protect Surrey if he is innocent."

"God?" Strelley exclaims. "Did God protect me from being beaten in Scotland? Did God protect us from defeat at Ancrum?"

"No," Longshawe replies, in a soothing, conciliatory tone. "But we are alive and we find ourselves in the royal service. The good is not to be ignored amongst the bad. Have you not got much that you wished for?"

Strelley breathes in and out twice before making his reply. "Perhaps. But I don't believe that I've had God looking after me all this while." De Winter removes his hand from Strelley's shoulder and folds his arms, tilting his head before speaking.

"You two are the most irreligious heathens I have ever heard!" he laughs. "Neither the one nor the other has worshipped since I came to the palace! How can you expect God to be on your side if you are not on his?" He looks from Longshawe, whose expression is one of restrained amusement, to Strelley, who is perplexed. "If either of you believes at all, of course," he finishes. Strelley gives him a wry smile in reply. Longshawe waves his hand, finger pointing nowhere in particular.

"My belief is in God, not in priests and idols, not in sacred relics," he muses. "I may not take the sacrament very often, but when I do, I remember Our Lord Jesus as we are meant to do. And I pray..."

De Winter shakes his head. "Your faith is none of my business, James, beyond that you are my friend and I would not wish your soul to end up in the Hellfire. Nor is yours, Edward. But be careful that you do not try to lead where you really should follow. I do not doubt that the king's religion is confused, even vague, but why go to the stake for such a thing as what you say?"

Strelley throws his head back and laughs. "And you call me unprincipled!"

"Well," de Winter replies, "would you speak the truth before the king? I could, in conscience, speak my faith to him. I may not gain from such a conversation, indeed I would stand to lose more than just my station. Yet you... I wonder if you would have anything at all to say on the matter."

"You suspect me of atheism?" Strelley's bottom lip protrudes in a quizzical expression. "That I am not. I just see a little bit more of man's ways of finding God than either of you two."

"That may not be the best way of navigating this subject with the king," Longshawe snorts. "I'm not sure that he would appreciate being gainsaid on a subject he holds so dear."

"In any case," Strelley changes the subject, "all will change when Edward accedes. His beliefs are Evangelical, not just anti-papist but anti-Catholic."

"His sister does her best to alter his beliefs. I have seen her try to persuade him that his ideas are wrong..." de Winter says. "Though she does not get far. He seems to see her as more of a jester than the older, wiser sister she is."

"Edward does not yet recognise his own fallibility," Strelley confirms, "though Mary is staunchly Catholic... She seems equally immune as her brother to the argument and reason of others as far as her faith is concerned. Both think they are right, and Edward has the peculiar problem of his position... Not many have the confidence to tell him he is wrong. Cheke is very careful to allow him to correct himself with gentle guidance."

Longshawe adds, confirming the idea to himself, "Edward will not be persuaded by his sister, much as she will not be persuaded herself. Of whom does that remind me?" He smiles at his own joke, looking from one to the other.

De Winter sniffs, twists his moustache, closes one eye in thought, and replies, "your Lutheran proclivities... You do not see that the boy is headstrong and arrogant? You do not see that Cheke leads him astray, away from the true faith? When he is king, the country, its people, will suffer for his fervour."

Strelley holds up his hand. "We shall get nowhere with this. The queen drives the prince's education. It is in no one's interest now for her to fall out of favour with the king. And Edward's beliefs will be second to Hertford's, I think, whilst he is young."

"Indeed," Longshawe says. "It shall be Seymour that is named protector. He has the king's ear, and his trust."

"Seymour is a Lutheran," de Winter says, flatly.

"He is," Longshawe answers. "And no doubt the people will be told that they have to share his beliefs when Edward is crowned. He may wait many years before he is king in anything but name, though."

Strelley and de Winter laugh quietly. De Winter is the first to speak. "It seems that whatever direction the beliefs of these powerful men take, we are to follow. I had thought religion was a matter of conscience. Shrewsbury does not blindly follow the king against the Pope, nor does he consider the heresies of these..." he chews his top lip, trying to find the right word. "Germans." He satisfies himself with this choice, and smiles.

"Germans or not," Longshawe says, "they have actually advanced the cause of religion, have they not? Surely even you can't believe that simony is acceptable? Or that God will listen to Masses bought with money taken forcibly from the poor by rich men? Could God be persuaded by such transparent means?"

De Winter watches Longshawe as he speaks, shaking his head, face contorting into a sardonic smile. "When did you acquire such conviction?" he asks. Longshawe raises an eyebrow, but de Winter continues, "I do not disagree with all the matters that Luther raises. But his attack on the Church is motivated not by a desire for reform but for his own advancement by the removal of the old structures. He desires to be Pope himself."

"Truly?" Strelley snorts. "Have either of you read the theses? Or the twelve conclusions of the Lollards?"

De Winter and Longshawe share a glance of exasperation.

"No?" Strelley continues. "Then perhaps you should content yourselves rather with an admission of your ignorance, and a resolution to reduce it." He pats Longshawe on the back. "I shall meet you halfway, dearest James, by some warlike act – punching the next man I meet in the face, perhaps – and you, George, by crawling to the Cross next time I attend Mass, should either of you wish to trouble yourselves with the effort of familiarising yourself with the content of these two texts. I recommend the Lollards on account of their relative brevity, though my Luther is at least in modern English."

"The last book I saw you reading, Edward," Longshawe sneers his name, "was some blasphemous Mohammedan nonsense. Perhaps you should keep your counsel on matters of religion, lest you attract the attention of those for whom atheism is not a matter for merely sending you home from university but sending you back to God himself." He returns the pat Strelley gave him moments earlier, all condescension. "And while we're at it, shall we agree to disagree and put matters of faith aside?" Strelley sighs, but nods.

De Winter's eyes flick from the one to the other, before he mutters a quiet "Yes". After a pause, he brightens. "Have I told you that we're going to Hampton Court? I received a letter from Pike yesterday. He says the preparations can only be for a Royal visit to the palace."

"I hope we are all invited. I have missed Will." Strelley's eyes shine.

27: Hampton Court Palace

There is a great ferment at the king's royal palace of Hampton Court. Men hurry about, variously carrying and fetching, bringing and taking. There are several guardsmen about in the red of the Yeomen of the Guard, armed and proudly displaying polished metalwork. They barely contribute to the activities of the household, preferring to watch at a sort of half-ease, neither alert as they would be for the royal household itself, nor fully relaxed.

A flustered retainer liveried in the Tudor green and white walks up to a guard. The reader will immediately recognise the guard as James Longshawe by his dirty-blond hair before even seeing his face, which, on inspection, reveals a broad grin, showing off straight white teeth. Longshawe stands with his feet apart, resting his weight on the haft of his halberd, shining in the autumn sun. He towers over the servant, who shades his eyes against the sun to look up at him.

"Would you please move your *soldiers* out of the way, Sir!" the retainer grumbles.

"With respect, Sir," Longshawe replies, "they are not my soldiers but the king's. As well you know. And you should get used to our presence."

"I hope not," the manservant huffs, looking over his shoulder. "If you're not going to move, can you at least help to prepare the palace?"

"Well, since you ask with such grace..." Longshawe points a finger at two other Yeomen, summoning them. "Do as this man asks, and tell the men to obey him if his orders do not contravene the Captain's."

"You are not the Captain?" The servant eyes Longshawe, suddenly unimpressed.

"He rides with the Royal Party. I am sent ahead to ensure your preparations are to the king's liking." Longshawe thinks for a moment. "Why do you not wish to host King Henry and his family?"

"Their presence requires a great deal more... precision... on the part of the staff. I fear that some may not be quite as assiduous in their duties as they ought to be."

"Do what you can. If the Yeomen can be of assistance, tell me. Once the party has arrived, you'll have to ask Captain Wingfield himself."

The retainer breathes out with a certain resignation. "Your coming here was long since declared, but I must confess never really expected. The king... I do not think we anticipated his travelling."

"You would do well to keep opinions of that sort quiet. But no, the king is not in the greatest of health. I do not know if he rides or if he travels by litter."

"He does not intend to join the hunt himself?"

"Hmm. No. He has it in mind for the prince to lead the hunt, I think."

"He has never encouraged such sport in Prince Edward before."

"I wonder if My Lord Hertford, or perhaps the queen herself, has not had a hand in it."

"We have been told Her Majesty is with the party."

"I hope you have prepared suitable rooms for her. She wishes to be near the two Ladies, Mary and Elizabeth."

"That is as I have been instructed."

"Good. Now be about your business! Could you direct me to the Master of the Hunt?"

The retainer points at a set of low buildings partly hidden by the majestic hedgerows of the formal gardens. "If you want the hunters, they're making their preparations over there."

Longshawe shakes the man's hand. "Your name, Sir?"

"Astley, Sir."

Longshawe leaves his companion guard and makes his way across the grounds. On his way, he finds Guy Fletcher, smartly but plainly dressed in grey canvas with a leather overcoat. He is seated on a step, stoning the sword that Longshawe bought for him. The stone makes a crunching noise as it passes along the edge, spitting sparks.

"Guy, would you like to see if we can find Master Pike?"

"I would!" He leaps up, sheathing the sword, and follows Longshawe as he swaggers confidently through the Palace gardens, each glancing occasionally as a comely serving girl bustles past. Longshawe smiles at Guy when he notices the young man's eyes following a particularly shapely young lady.

"No harm to be done by looking, Master Fletcher," he laughs.

"Perhaps you could instruct me..."

"In how to make an approach...?" Longshawe asks, feigning disapproving shock. Guy Fletcher turns a bright shade of red.

"We have to get that nervous streak out of you, Guy. You've fought His Majesty's wars, by Christ!" Fletcher chuckles at Longshawe's swearing. "Very well, once we are settled, I shall teach you."

In the low buildings which house considerable stabling and a noisy and foul-smelling kennel, Longshawe and Fletcher find their friend and ours, William Pike. Pike is busy oiling various items of leather tack. He looks up and sees the familiar faces.

"James! Guy! Well met, gentlemen, well met! I had not realised your party had arrived."

"It hasn't, yet. We're here in advance to check the preparations."

"Is the king really coming? We were not sure whether-"

"He comes, Will. But you might not get the chance to show him how good a shot you are with that gun of yours. I don't think he will ride out."

"What about the prince?" Pike asks.

"Edward is with the party. Perhaps the king intends to let him off the leash a bit. He's barely been outdoors in the last couple of years. Hertford is coming as well, you know."

"Has the king spoken on Edward's minority?"

"You mean who is to rule in his stead? Not directly, but it does not take a great deal of wit to fathom it."

"So Norfolk and Surrey are no longer in attendance?"

"They've hidden themselves away at Kenning Hall, after Surrey made one false move too many."

"Really?" Pike raises an eyebrow.

"Have you not heard? Surrey has been up to all manner of schemes. He tried to convince Mary to marry him, despite his already being married... Then he told the prince that Norfolk would be named protector." Pike lets out a snort of amusement. Longshawe shakes his head, then carries on. "That's not the end of it. He went again to the prince, seeking to gain influence over him. From what de Winter said, he threatened Mary with violence."

"Ah. And having done so, fled to his estate?"

"Indeed. It's a wonder that he has not been arraigned yet. I suspect that the Seymours need only a little more to persuade the king to make it so."

"Enough of politics," Pike says, decisively, tossing the saddle he has been working on into a corner. "I see that Master Fletcher has his own sword now."

Guy Fletcher beams with pride. "I do. I know how to use it, as well."

"We must test that claim, Guy!" Pike cries, with great enthusiasm. "En Garde!" He reaches over and picks up his own sword, plainly sheathed but of good quality. Let us leave them to their sparring, and be assured that Guy has learned well from Longshawe, and can look after himself.

Lady Elizabeth rides a near-white palfrey, flanked on her right by William Grindal and on her left by Edward Strelley. Neatly sidesaddle, she leans over her left shoulder to address a comment to Strelley.

"I understand my father the king has assigned your friend Longshawe the important duty of preceding our arrival at Hampton Court. An unusual role for a Yeoman of the Guard..." Elizabeth raises her eyebrow as she speaks.

"I did not know that My Lady followed the fortunes of such as Longshawe and myself." Strelley offers her a disarming smile, and pushes his hair back off his forehead.

"Only a select few," she replies, laughing. "Master Grindal!" She turns herself. "What do you think of the hunt, Sir? We have not discussed it in our lessons."

"No, Madam, we have not," Grindal says decisively. "It is not of great significance to your learning. Though a young prince may spend his time at sport, it does not so much become the wife of the said prince."

"Interesting, Sir. I take it that you yourself do not hunt, if the choice is presented to you."

Grindal anticipates the next line with a sigh. Elizabeth continues. "No? Does that make you more of a man, or more of a wife?"

"My Lady, as ever your reasoning is impeccable, but perhaps you pursue an easy target, knowing you will score a victory." Grindal waves his hand. Elizabeth turns back to Strelley.

"Do you hunt, Sir?" she asks.

"I have, but it is not to my tastes."

"Really? I had thought you to be a man of action in your

previous life."

"As My Lady is well aware, my soldiering days are thankfully long in the past. Killing animals does not appeal to me as sport, though."

"You do not see any thrill in the chase and the kill?" Elizabeth's eyes glint as she imagines.

"May I ask you a question, Madam?" Strelley says, deflecting her. She nods. "How often does the hart or the boar win?"

"Does God not ordain that the animals are there for man's use?" she counters. Strelley puffs out his cheeks.

"Indeed he does. But what sport is there in it, if the outcome is so certain?"

"Bah!" Elizabeth cries. "You two shall be no fun at all. I shall have to find companions with more lust for the pursuit!" She spurs on her horse, which leaps forward at a canter, chasing a knot of riders a furlong or so in front. Strelley and Grindal exchange a glance before quickening their pace slightly.

Later that day, the royal procession arrives at Hampton Court. The king's daughters take their rooms, and Prince Edward is housed in the most magnificent suite. Henry himself, struggling to conceal the pain that his leg causes him, takes rooms that are warm and comfortable, rather than grandiose. Edward Seymour has cleverly arranged matters so that he has easy access to both King Henry and Prince Edward. There is a fine meal served in the late afternoon, which allows some of the various households to spend their time at leisure as the palace staff take the burden of the duties.

Longshawe and Strelley, temporarily relieved of their duties, go to find Pike with Guy Fletcher. De Winter is still engaged in service of Lady Mary, but Andrew Shepherd, brought along with de Winter, makes his way along.

Pike takes them around the grounds, showing them the formal gardens and the boundaries of the park about. As they walk, Longshawe and Strelley tell him all that has happened to them since last they met. Guy Fletcher and Andrew Shepherd, some distance behind, likewise share their tales of recent happenings. It is much later when they return to the servants' quarters and discover de Winter, who has finally found himself at leisure.

"It sounds as though the king will not ride tomorrow," de Winter says, rising from his seat as the others enter into a sort of mess-room where he has been waiting. "The prince will lead with the Earl of Hertford."

"Hertford seems to have entered into his role of Lord Protector already," Longshawe adds.

De Winter nods. "Surrey is in disgrace and Bishop Latimer is hardly welcome at court either. It seems that we Catholics have little to hope for at the succession."

Strelley sniffs, chewing his lip. "Why don't you try to bend a little before the wind, rather than this needing to stand up all the time? You know that it is the tallest poppies that lose their heads? Your devotion to your religion will be the end of you."

"Let us not start this again," Longshawe says.

"Ah, but we shall, James." De Winter holds up his hand. "Once Henry is gone, I shall have to choose between my faith – my conscience – and my king. You-" he points at Longshawe "-who share Edward's evangelism, or you, Strelley, if you're willing to alter your opinion to suit the times, you have no such choice to make."

Pike takes off his gloves, of a fine leather but plain in colour, and puts them on a table. He scratches his clean-shaven chin thoughtfully. "Strelley is right, though, isn't he? God does not expect each of us to endure trial by fire to show him the strength of our conviction. That is an invention of men and men alone."

At the mention of the fire, Longshawe, Strelley and de Winter all pull faces of disgust. Guy Fletcher looks from one to the other before speaking in a quiet voice. "I should not wish to die by the fire, however strong my beliefs."

"Indeed not," de Winter says, decisively. "Perhaps my mistress shall move abroad to somewhere that still practises the traditional ways."

"That's probably treason, George," Pike laughs.

The following morning, the hunting party assembles early. The king, as de Winter has said, is not present. The Master of the Hunt approaches Prince Edward, but the questions he asks are impenetrable to the boy, who has no experience of this sort of pursuit. Hertford steps in, guiding him in each choice. Edward is delighted with his uncle's advice, and eagerly states his desire that they should ride together at the van. With this most illustrious pair ride a few of the huntsmen, along with Longshawe, wearing his guard's uniform and a wide, satisfied smile.

Elizabeth and Mary follow close behind, each with their small retinue. De Winter and Strelley have positioned themselves close together, snatching a few words of conversation before the hunt begins. By the clever work of each, both Guy Fletcher and Andrew Shepherd find themselves part of the group. Grindal is absent, despite Strelley's presence.

"Now you *shall* enjoy this, Master Strelley," Elizabeth says, half-turned to face the two young men behind her. "I command it. It is not always that a tutor's servant rides with the royal hunt."

"No, madam, I did not expect to, um, be invited to join this expedition," Strelley replies, "but I am grateful."

"You must thank My Lord Hertford. He seemed very pleased with me that I could identify your friend. He was more than willing to grant my request that you join me."

De Winter's ears prick at the mention of Strelley's friend. He leans over and asks, "what does she mean?"

"Hertford asked if she knew who the guard was who had lifted her father with him. Elizabeth knew straight away that it was James."

De Winter raises his eyebrows. "So Longshawe gets to ride with the prince and his protector?"

"Think about what you're saying, George. He is not protector yet."

Elizabeth turns in her saddle, catching the conversation. "Sister," she says to Mary, who is absently watching the prince take instruction from Hertford and the Master of the Hunt, "I believe that our servants are discussing matters concerning our brother."

Strelley has the presence of mind not to reply immediately. De Winter, unfamiliar with Elizabeth's cantankerousness, returns her look. Mary watches him, an amused half-smile on her face.

"Madam is mistaken," de Winter ventures. Elizabeth affects a hurt expression, so de Winter explains further. "We were discussing the good fortunes of our friend."

"Ah yes." Elizabeth relaxes herself, not pursuing her tease. "He is in good company indeed. The earl asked me if I knew him, so I pointed him out."

"Lucky James," de Winter mutters. At that moment, a piercing call from a hunting horn sounds, and the party sets out at a gallop, preventing further conversation.

After a ride of some half hour or so into the grounds, the party gradually reassembles at a meeting point. During the brief pause, Pike has chance to show off his marksmanship, bringing down a bird at a range of as far as a hundred paces with his long-barrelled gun. Even Hertford and Prince Edward themselves are drawn to applaud. Strelley goes over to him as he cleans out the barrel.

"I shall ask my merchant friend in London if he can provide you with a powder that doesn't foul the barrel so."

"It would be a great boon to the huntsman, though I dread to think what it could lead to in war," Pike replies.

As they exchange these words, they both realise that Hertford has led the prince over to speak to Pike. Edward Tudor addresses Pike in his high voice. "I am most impressed with your shooting, Sir. I should like you to instruct me in the manner of handling such a weapon some day."

Pike bows, but retains his composure enough not to blush. The prince nods to Strelley. "Good day to you, Sir. I see my sister has seen fit to bring you along."

"I have thanked the lady for her consideration, Your Highness."

"I should not like Master Cheke to join me in the hunt. He reminds me of my lessons." Prince Edward pulls a face, showing his distaste. "Now we are here, outside, at sport, I should not wish to have to think of my Latin verbs or my rhetoric. Though I am pleased to see you here."

Strelley smiles back at him, bows a little, but does not reply.

"Ah well," the prince continues, "My Lord Hertford is certainly a more exciting instructor than my tutor." The prince's words are stifled by a commotion a few yards away.

Lady Mary's is mounted on a horse that is skittishly circling around, throwing vicious kicks at those who approach. Longshawe moves cautiously forward, but retreats as the animal threatens to rear. He begins to loosen the pistol at his belt, but stops when de Winter puts his hand across him. Seymour and Prince Edward step forward, but this seems to enervate Mary's horse further. After a moment during which the party exchange worried looks, de Winter steps around into the horse's sight.

Slowly, tentatively, he lifts his hand, laying it gently on the irritated steed's muzzle. It snorts, but the nervous movements slow to a halt. Mary looks down at de Winter, her grey eyes showing white all around. He offers his hand, and assists her in her dismount. She almost falls away, but de Winter and Longshawe, coming close as the horse settles, catch her and right her.

"Would it be possible," Mary breathes, "that I continue the chase on another mount?"

Several of the courtiers gathered around laugh quietly. Hertford nods at de Winter, who continues to stroke his hand down the nose of the now riderless horse, then at Longshawe.

Later that day, the party falls upon a great stag, chasing it through several miles of the forest country west of Hampton Court. Prince Edward has grown in confidence, and shows almost filial affection for Edward Seymour, who has relaxed his guiding hand, but stays close to the prince. Hertford pushes the chase, encouraging the Master to allow the prince to feel that he is leading, making the running. The beaters channel the deer, keeping its course within the wooded park. After a half an hour, it is brought to bay in a clearing, surrounded by dogs. The exhausted animal collapses, its chest heaving with the exertion. It barely manages to keep the dogs away until they are pulled clear by their masters.

Seymour charges his horse forward, dismounts in a single smooth action and positions himself next to the prince, helping him down from his saddle. He hands Edward a huge knife to deliver the coup de grace. The stag barely kicks as warm blood covers the prince's hands as it expires. The gathered crowd applaud him, and he raises himself to stand over the body, looking triumphant. He glances to Edward Seymour, who smiles his approval.

"I wish that my father was here to see this," the prince says, looking down at his victim. "Perhaps my sisters would speak of it to him. I should not like to appear boastful." Hertford goes over to him, clasping a hand over his shoulder. Mary and Elizabeth dismount and congratulate him. Elizabeth ignores the blood on Edward's hands, but Mary pulls away, not eager to stain her clothes. A hubbub of conversation strikes up, as the various hunters exchange their praises, all greatly in favour of the prince's kill. Servants step forward to mount the carcase on poles, preparing to carry it back to the palace to be prepared for a grand supper. Hertford helps the prince back on to his horse, and they lead the party back towards Hampton Court, their chase done for the day.

In the early evening, Elizabeth is arguing with her chamber-lady, Katherine Campernon. Campernon is exasperatedly trying to dress the young lady.

"I shall wear my red and gold dress, Mistress Kat," Elizabeth says decisively, "and I do not appreciate your direction in these matters. I am old enough and wise enough to choose for myself."

"But My Lady must appreciate the need for-"

"Have I not just told you that I do not need your direction in these matters? I should prefer that you follow my instructions," Elizabeth huffs. Campernon's cheeks colour.

"My Lady," she says, and holds up an admonitory hand to silence her young charge, "My Lady, you must dress according to the form. You must not wear your cloth of gold if that is what the Prince Edward intends to wear."

At that moment, the door of the chamber resounds with a knock from outside. Campernon goes to the door and opens it a fraction, not allowing the visitor inside as the lady is yet not dressed to receive. A short intercourse follows, during which Campernon twice looks round to Elizabeth.

After a moment, she closes the door. "My Lady, it appears that the prince has chosen a different outfit and you may thus wear what you choose." Campernon's face wears a look of relieved triumph.

"Mistress Campernon, am I to understand that you have arranged matters thus?"

"Madam should dress herself." Katherine Campernon nods as she speaks. Elizabeth smiles in return.

"I thank you," she says, picking up her red-and-gold dress and smoothing the skirts. She cocks her head to one side as she looks at her governess. "I detect a change in you, Mistress Katherine."

Campernon colours again, flustered by Elizabeth's observation. "I don't know what you mean, My Lady," she replies.

"I note that you are more tolerant of my behaviour. I imagine that this softening of your attitude is not due to anything good that I have done." Elizabeth inspects her fingers carefully.

"My Lady should not concern herself with the affairs of her inferiors." Campernon hides her face by positioning herself in a corner, trying to look busy.

"Ah, but you know already that I do!" Elizabeth laughs, and begins the long process of undressing by removing her jewellery.

The great banquet features Prince Edward's first victim as its centrepiece. Elizabeth appears in her finest red-and-gold dress. Her sister Mary is equally resplendent in a truly regal gown of blue velvet. Edward wears an embroidered doublet in a silver cloth, which has the unfortunate effect of making him seem both younger and paler than he in fact is. He is flush with excitement, proud of his earlier achievement. King Henry has not yet arrived, and in his absence the various courtiers are speaking to each other in quiet whispers, remarking this fact.

Hertford directs the prince to a high seat at a table raised on a dais, and sits down next to him, on his right. The king's own seat, to Edward's left, is grandly decorated, with gilt on the arms and an elaborately carved back. There is some commotion as a pair of guards, one of which is our friend James Longshawe, step through a gap in the tapestries that cover the walls. The guards strike the paved floor with the butts of their halberds, and the king shuffles in, limping on his bad leg. He raises a hand in a gesture of greeting, and, flanked by his guards, sits on his chair, which creaks piteously as he lowers his weight on to it. Further along the table, Mary and Elizabeth watch their father as he begins the feast.

At the back of the hall, Strelley, de Winter and Pike have positioned themselves side-by-side so as to be able to see the top table. They watch, standing still and upright in the same pose of attention as Longshawe behind the king, trying to catch his eye. Strelley leans slightly over, and says to the other two, "look at the king! He's barely able to walk."

De Winter doesn't move his head, but whispers back, "you'll hang for treason if you're heard." After a moment of contemplation, he continues, more relaxed and less quiet. "Our mistresses seem to be getting on well." Mary has just told Elizabeth something that has made her laugh, throwing her head back and showing off her long, pale neck. Mary does not have that same pale complexion, having more of her mother in her, with darker hair and eyes. The three young men watch the king's daughters as they eat, occasionally turning their attention to the king, the prince, and the current favourite, the Earl of Hertford. Hertford is explaining the prince's kill in great, gruesome detail. The king is listening with enthusiasm, although there is the merest hint in his demeanour of jealousy, of resignation to his descent into decrepitude. Longshawe maintains his concentrated focus, eyes straight ahead. Once or twice, Strelley pulls a face at him, testing his composure, which is unflappable.

As the food is cleared away, the musicians begin a jolly tune. King Henry, whose smile is part genuine, part forced, cries out for a dance, which request is met with the scraping of chairs as various of the nobility rise to indulge. Hertford requests the hand of Lady Mary for the first dance, and Prince Edward dances with the younger of his two sisters. After the first dance, Hertford releases Mary and sits down next to the king. Mary dances with some other Lord. Strelley and Pike go over to where Elizabeth sits, leaving de Winter to watch his mistress as some courtier or other tries to impress her.

Strelley bows as he approaches Elizabeth. "My Lady, may I introduce my friend Master Pike? He was on campaign with us in Scotland, and is an old acquaintance of mine from before..." He falters. Elizabeth offers her hand, which Pike takes and kisses, bowing more deeply than Strelley.

"Master Pike," she says, flicking her eyes from him to Strelley and back, "I hope I can get a little more from you about your experiences of war than I have from Master Strelley. One would barely believe he had been present at a battle, the way he tells it."

"My Lady," Pike replies, "I must defend Edward. He is as brave and worthy a companion and soldier as you would wish to meet."

Strelley snorts. "Just a little reluctant?"

Pike's expression shows his surprise at Strelley's impropriety. Elizabeth notices, and explains. "Master Strelley is encouraged to be familiar with me, Sir, else he should not prove so useful in my education. It is to his credit that he takes me, and those with responsibility for me, at their word."

Pike glances at Strelley, then back at Elizabeth. She laughs, but Pike is too nervous to join in. The two young men withdraw, finding a corner from which to watch the dancing.

"Elizabeth allows you this sort of liberty?" Pike asks.

"I-" Strelley begins, then checks himself. "Yes. Despite her rank, she gives me licence. She is similar with her governess, but refuses to be so with Grindal. It is not pernicious."

"Grindal allows it?"

"Elizabeth forces him. I imagine that she threatens him in my absence!"

"She could be queen one day. Imagine that... you, addressing a future queen of England as though you were a close friend."

"I think I'm the closest thing to a friend that she has."

Pike's eyes narrow. "That does not speak well of her situation."

"Indeed not. She is a young girl, desperate to share her experiences of the world with people like her, not these fusty nobles and, for all his intelligence, Grindal. Kat Campernon is the most down-to-earth, but Elizabeth seems to spend all her time winding her up."

"Do you enjoy teaching her?"

"I don't do much that could be called teaching. I do a lot of checking of her work, preparing materials for Grindal, and a fair bit of writing as we go. But it's an easy life for me, because I can do all of that without exercising myself."

As Strelley says this, de Winter saunters over, keeping one eye on his dancing mistress. He has a cup of wine in his hand, from which he drinks as turns away from the dancing.

"Evening!" he says in greeting. "Did you see James with Lady Mary earlier on? I wouldn't put it past him to make a pass at her, you know."

Strelley laughs. "Perhaps he would. But not now that she's in your care."

"So he has a little respect for me now, does he? Anyway, that's not what I wanted to tell you. I heard a discussion earlier, that when this hunting party returns to Greenwich or Whitehall, Hertford and his men are going after Norfolk and Surrey."

Pike and Strelley both look serious in response to this. Pike says quietly, "what do you mean, 'going after' him?"

"I mean, I think, that they intend to arrest them both and arraign them for treason."

"On what charge?" Strelley rubs his chin. "Surrey had that ludicrous notion about marrying Mary, but that seems to have passed. He never even got started on Elizabeth."

"I think Hertford has it that Surrey is after the throne for himself," de Winter replies. "Whether that's true or not, he's seeing what he can do now that he's definitely destined to be protector to Edward when he is king. Henry can't have long left, we can all see that." Furtively, the three of them look across the room to where the king sits, torpid in his elaborate chair. De Winter suppresses a shudder as he goes on. "Hertford is one of your Evangelicals." He nods at Strelley.

"I don't think I could claim to be a Protestant, George." He allows himself a wry smile as he replies. "I'm not sure they'd have me."

"But don't you see what this means?" De Winter is agitated now. "It means that everything we Catholics have fought for, every barrier to the king's reforms, every bit of steering that Winchester and all those that went before him have offered to keep the king on the path of righteousness..." He tails off. "All wasted." He adds in an undertone, "if Edward has his way, Mary will be forced to convert." The three of them pull faces, admitting that none has an answer to this.

"Shall we get another drink?" Strelley asks after a quarter-minute, and they head off in search. They find Longshawe, finally relieved of his duty, and Strelley tells him of that which they've discussed. Longshawe is not surprised.

"No," he says, "some of the guardsmen seem to have picked up on Hertford's plans as well. No doubt Surrey will be warned by the time he's arrested."

De Winter shakes his head. "Even if he is, My Lord Surrey is proud enough not to take pains to hide any pretension he has to the throne. He will be his own downfall." The four of them nod in agreement. Let us leave them now to their drinking as their conversation turns to lighter matters.

29: The Trap is Sprung

Early the following morning, Strelley is surprised to find himself awoken by Longshawe, already dressed in his guard's uniform. "Edward!" Longshawe is hissing. "Wake up!"

Strelley shakes himself awake. "What?" he asks, irritable.

"We're on our way – now – to arrest Norfolk and Surrey."

"What?" Strelley's eyes blink open and closed as he adjusts to the light.

"Hertford has arranged for a party to go to Kenning Hall and take them both. He seems to think there is some evidence of their treason. I'm going with them, and I need to go, now. Tell de Winter and Pike. But I need you to do something else."

"What?" Strelley is sitting up on his pallet now, rubbing his eyes.

"Get the message to the earl. He needs to know."

"Shrewsbury?"

"How many other earls do we know? Yes, Shrewsbury. He's our sponsor, our Guardian Angel. Without him... I don't have time, but you do. Don't use anyone we can't trust... Guy! Send Guy. Goodbye." A moment later, Longshawe is gone. Strelley realises that Longshawe was carrying his full complement of weapons, sword, pistol, and the distinct wooden noise of him taking up the halberd propped outside the door of Strelley's small room.

Throughout the hours before Grindal and Elizabeth are awake, Strelley is busy. He first finds Andrew Shepherd, lounging about outside the buttery trying to find breakfast for himself and de Winter. He sends him with the news to find de Winter, and entrusts him with passing the same message to Pike.

As he makes his way round the palace trying to find where Guy Fletcher was sleeping, Strelley notes an unusual level of activity for the early morning. Several pages and retainers are flying about this way and that. The stables are practically empty, and he sees Pike already up about his tasks. He walks over, trying and failing to seem calm.

"Have you-" he begins, but Pike cuts him off.

"They rode out a few minutes ago. Hertford is with them. If you're looking for Guy, he's in the hayloft."

Strelley makes his way into the stables, looking for the ladder up to the hayloft. For a moment, he considers the possible impropriety of disturbing Guy at his sleep, but dismisses the thought with a shake of the head. He finds Guy alone, sprawled comfortably among the hay.

"I did wonder..." Strelley says. "But James hasn't taught you everything just yet, has he?"

Guy looks at him without understanding.

"I have a job for you," Strelley says. "This is important, and it needs someone discreet."

"Name it," Guy replies, resolute.

"Go to Sheffield Castle. Find the Earl of Shrewsbury and pass him this letter." He hands him a scrap of paper, folded and sealed with wax. "If you are taken, Guy, please, do not give this letter away. If things do not go well... Suffice it to say that if we haven't backed the winning side, we might all be guilty of treason."

Guy nods his assent and understanding. "I shall be swift and vigilant."

Strelley smoothes Guy Fletcher's shoulder. "We have chosen the right side, Guy, I'm sure of it. You must urge the earl to travel to London as soon as possible. It will benefit us all if he is able to establish his loyalties..." He trails off. "Go as soon as you can." Guy Fletcher begins to gather his meagre possessions, including the sword that Longshawe bought for him. Strelley descends the ladder to find Pike waiting outside the stable door.

"Does he need a mount?" Pike asks, inspecting his fingernails, one foot raised so the sole lies flat on the wall. Strelley is momentarily nonplussed by his nonchalance, then confirms with a gesture.

"The fastest that's still in the stable."

"Already prepared. Good horse, actually, thought she was lame but turns out she's not. Five day's rations in the saddlebags."

Strelley looks at him askance. "How did you know?"

"It makes sense, doesn't it? Hertford's going after Surrey, isn't he? And his father. Longshawe was with them, so our friend the Earl of Shrewsbury needs to be told." Pike surveys the parkland around them, eyes narrowed by the low sun of the winter morning. Slowly, he continues. "Shrewsbury will need to act carefully now, won't he? One cannot simply be loyal to king and country anymore... Even an earl needs to select his patron with the greatest prudence."

"Shrewsbury isn't naturally aligned with the likes of Hertford. He doesn't share the Seymours' preference for the new religion."

"No. But then, it seems we shall all be sharing that preference sooner or later, whether conscience dictates or not."

"All of us will have to act according to policy, to pragmatism, rather than our deep beliefs. We can only hope that Edward proves to be easier to read than Henry."

For the briefest moment, Pike's eyes flash. "Don't you believe in anything, Edward?" he whispers. "Don't you see how men could cleave to all that matters to them even to death?"

"I cannot see that God would reject a man for whether he believes that wine really is blood or not."

"Then I shall pray for you, if there is no cause for which you would die." Pike's voice has settled into calm again, and he smiles slightly as Strelley stares at him. Each spends a moment trying to penetrate the thoughts of the other. Pike takes a breath, blows it out noisily, then says with an air of finality, "you are right, of course. There will be much to lose for those whose religion is a matter of true belief rather than of what brings the greatest safety."

"Are you honestly so firm in your convictions?" Strelley asks, one eye closing as he looks into the sun.

"No. Except for one belief that you and I share. Whatever man interprets into the word of God, that does not change God Himself."

"Your father was – is – a Catholic, and so you are a Catholic. That's how most of us come to our beliefs, isn't it? Longshawe's father is a Lutheran, so Longshawe is the same. If you had been born in the East, you would be a Mohammedan."

"And I thank God that I have had the fortune to be born into the true religion."

Strelley shakes his head in frustration at Pike's intransigence, but doesn't speak further. A moment later, there is a clatter as Guy Fletcher descends the ladder from the hayloft, clothed and armed for his long ride. Pike leads him away into the stables, as Strelley stands outside. Guy emerges leading a small but well-made horse, and Strelley rushes to help him mount while Pike holds the rein. Guy calls out his farewell, and is off at a gallop towards the road north.

Strelley turns to Pike. "I do not wish to argue further."

"Nor do I. We shall all need each other before the end of this, I think." Strelley nods and pats his friend on the shoulder.

At Kenning Hall, two days' fast ride later, the party of royal guards and various nobility accompanying Hertford heaves into view.

The mass of mounted soldiers does not kick up dust, as the ground is wet in midwinter, but it makes for a fine sight, steel glinting in the low early morning sun. As the band approaches, there is movement in the window embrasures. Footmen can be seen moving about the grounds, their urgency obvious. Hertford rides out in front, ensuring that he has the pleasure of announcing the purpose of the raid.

"My Lords!" Hertford calls, some distance short of the main gate, "I come bearing grim tidings." One of the Howard retainers stands framed in the gateway, making an obscene gesture towards Hertford, who looks down, sees him, and carries on his harangue with a gleeful smile on his face.

"His Grace the Duke of Norfolk and his son, the Earl of Surrey, are to be arrested on charges of treason!" Hertford does not manage to stifle his laugh at the end of the sentence. The retainer repeats his gesture, turns his back on Hertford's party and walks casually away into the grounds. The mounted soldiers follow, fanning out as they pass through the gate, occupying the sward within, arms presented.

A few moments pass as Hertford scans around. He makes a sign with two fingers, at which one of his party comes forward. "You know where to find it?" Hertford asks. The man nods in response. Hertford takes a deep breath, before calling out once again. "Thomas Howard, you are arrested in the king's name! Henry Howard, you too are arrested in the king's name!"

A major-domo comes out from a within the keep. "His Grace the Duke of Norfolk *is* willing to receive you, Master Seymour," the servant deliberately emphasises the incorrect address, "if you would only stop shouting..." Hertford looks down on him, eyes narrow, chest rising and falling with hot anger at the insult.

"I shall see to it, *Sir*, that you join your masters on the block," Hertford spits, then leaps from his horse. He puts his hand to the hilt of his sword. "Perhaps I should see to your fate myself?" The servant, rattled, turns and makes his way inside. Hertford signals again, and a small group of men, led by the one who came forward a moment ago, dismount and enter the castle.

There is a lull, during which the horses stomp and snort. A few minutes pass, and the party of men emerges, one of them carrying a painting. Hertford gasps in delight. It depicts Surrey standing over a broken pedestal, surrounded by cherubs. "And the arms? He displays the arms?"

"All over the castle, My Lord. The Confessor's sign is everywhere."

"Then we have them," Hertford says, smiling.

Another five minutes pass, after which a small body of men emerges, heavily armed, from the castle. They are led by Henry Howard, Earl of Surrey, himself fully armed and sumptuously dressed.

"Good morning!" Howard snarls. "I heard my servant running round saying something about you being here, but I did not credit that you would dare to come without an invitation."

"Ah, well," Hertford replies, glancing behind him, weighing up the sizes of the two bodies of men. "I have a warrant for your arrest, signed by the king, as my invitation. And as I know how loyal you are to His Majesty, I did not hesitate to present it to you." Howard bristles, but does not move. Hertford unrolls a parchment, and looks from it to Howard and back again. "It seems I am mistaken. *This* warrant is for the arrest of your father," he laughs, and rolls the parchment up again, putting it into a saddlebag, and withdrawing another. "This is the one! I would address you as 'My Lord', Henry, but I can't imagine you will be that for more than a week or two."

Surrey stares at Hertford, who watches him, smiling. "Have you nothing to say?" Seymour taunts. "An unusual state of affairs for you! Well, Henry, the die is cast and it seems that it has fallen in my favour. You might have prevented my brother marrying your sister, but that was your last move."

Hertford waits for Surrey to respond. Several of Hertford's men have dismounted, and are beginning to crowd round Surrey, blades bright in the sun.

"How did you know-" Surrey begins, but stops himself. "A traitor...? What sad times are these when *you* command such loyalty. Or perhaps it was your thirty pieces of silver? I shall go to my grave ready to face God, but I pity those among us who will not." He looks around behind himself, a wry smile across his face, before settling his gaze again on Seymour. "I pity the poor soul who has you for his protector."

Surrey draws his sword with a flourish, and breaks it across his knee, spitting furiously in Seymour's direction as he does so. The armed men, among whom is James Longshawe, move forward and surround the Earl of Surrey. Surrey continues to stare malevolently at Hertford as the men push him around. Longshawe approaches close, and as he catches Henry Howard's eye his face breaks into an expression of sympathy. Howard smiles as Longshawe rearranges his features.

Hertford presents himself to the king at Whitehall, coming into the royal presence with a rolled-up canvas under his arm. Henry is red in the face, hacking and coughing, moving himself gingerly to find comfort in his throne. Hertford steps forward, bowing slightly.

"Your Majesty," he says, obsequious. "I have proof of the treachery that pervades the house of Howard."

"Proof? I would not have thought the Howards so careless as to allow it." Henry's voice is cracked and uneven.

"Nor did I, Sire, but it seems their villainy is yet more brazen than we could have anticipated. Not only do they display the Confessor's arms openly throughout their house, but I found this..." He unrolls the canvas with a dramatic flourish, displaying the painting which shows the Earl of Surrey standing over a broken pedestal. "There can be no doubt, Your Majesty, that the pillar is the House of Tudor. Surrey – Howard, I should say – intends to usurp the throne from your son."

"I had hoped that Norfolk would exercise some control over him." The king's disappointment is audible in his voice.

"Norfolk is just as guilty as his son, Sire. He must share the punishment."

"Very well. I understand you were not able to arrest the father. See to it."

"I shall, Your Majesty. You should also see the letter Surrey wrote to the Duchess of Richmond on the subject of marriage to my brother."

"I have no doubt that the men of the law shall take into account what they must."

"Sire, it is imperative that you read... It touches Your Majesty's personal dignity. Besides, the duchess is willing to testify personally. She believes that her father and brother are guilty."

"I do not follow you, My Lord."

"The Duchess was refused permission to marry my brother by Surrey, or Norfolk. I know not which. In either case, she had conceived a great desire for the match, and was sorely disappointed to be denied it. I think the Howards found it not to their liking. A marriage alliance would make their plans to take the throne-"

The king holds up his hand. "Enough, Edward. I grow weary.

See to the trial. You and Master Wriothesley can handle it."

"I have Your Majesty's permission to go ahead?"

"Indeed you do. Now leave me to my repose."

"Before I do, Sire, there is another matter, that of your will."

"I do not wish to be reminded of my mortality today, Edward." Henry waves his hand in dismissal. "Go, please."

Hertford bows deeply, retreats to the rear of the room, turns and is let out by a guardsman, whom the reader will once again recognise immediately as our friend James Longshawe. Once Hertford has gone, the king summons Longshawe to approach.

"It seems I have need of you, Sir." Longshawe bows his head, ready to listen. "I trust to your discretion. You must not allow Hertford to take the throne when I am gone. I shall write to my son, a letter to be opened only after my death. I shall counsel him to seek your help – and that of your friends – should he fear to lose his throne, even to his uncle." Longshawe raises his gaze to the king's face, and sees that he is crying.

"Sire-"

"Ignore my weakness. God, how I wish the prince was ten years older! I despair of his future in this realm, Master Longshawe. Promise me that you will do all you can to keep him safe." Longshawe nods. "I hope you will enlist all of your friends to my son's cause, even if that makes you marked men."

"I shall serve your son the prince before all others, Sire."

30: Trial

The Guild Hall is packed with people watching the trial of Henry Howard, still correctly titled 'Earl of Surrey', despite Seymour's taunting. Among the jurors sits Thomas Wriothesley, wearing a huge satisfied grin to go with his rich cloth of silver and lord's ermine furs. Edward Seymour, Earl of Hertford, stands beside him, reading a packet of papers in front of him on a long trestle table, equally finely attired. A moment passes during which Seymour looks about the room, surveying the crowd of assembled nobles and gentlemen. He too allows a smile to pass across his face, before arranging his features in a more studied expression of dignified seriousness. He raises his hands in a gesture that silences the many conversations going on throughout the hall.

"Let us begin our examination of the defendant!" Seymour cries. The tension is palpable. Each pair of eyes focuses on the door through which Surrey is to be led in to defend himself. He is preceded by a Yeoman of the Guard, pristine in his red uniform. Surrey has dressed sombrely, whether through choice or coercion, lacking the ostentatious golds and furs of those who surround him in the room. Indeed, he could have been the lackey of the guard who leads him. Behind follow another two guards, armed with swords rather than halberds. One of these is our friend James Longshawe, who watches Surrey's back as he walks, not allowing himself to look out at the assembled crowd.

A few rows back, Edward Strelley watches the scene as it develops. Between him and William Grindal sits a small figure, disguised in swathes of enveloping cloak. One might, as Gilbert joked, mistake the figure for a leper were it not for the close proximity of its near neighbours, but the reader will surely have guessed already that it is Lady Elizabeth Tudor, once again prevailing upon her tutor and his servant to escort her to watch events that will shape history.

Surrey stands erect at a lectern, hands clasped behind his back. He does not show the swaggering confidence that he previously has, his mood and demeanour matching the dourness of his clothing. He scratches his face, mouths a few words to himself and looks about the room. His lips curl into a wry smile, accompanied by a sigh that indicates his resignation. He does not see a friendly face throughout the crowd, only those who are bent on his family's destruction, and those who are at best indifferent to it, here to see the spectacle of the formerly great brought low.

Elizabeth leans towards Strelley slightly, and speaks in a very low voice. "He does not have the look of a man who sees himself as heir to the throne."

Strelley continues to watch the proceedings in front of him, but inclines his head slightly as he replies. "Even in his own mind, he never has been heir to the throne. At most, he sees his father as the next in line after your brother. But the king's various statutes have seen to that. His pursuit of your sister..." Strelley finishes whispering as Hertford begins to speak. Elizabeth nods, remembering her sister's and her own elevation to the line of succession.

"Henry Howard, Earl of Surrey, you are charged with the crime of High Treason against His Majesty the king, in the respect of quartering your heraldic arms with those of Edward the Confessor, an act which is only appropriate for an heir to the throne. You have designs on becoming king yourself. You are also charged with several counts of treason by act or omission, including many actions prejudicial to the succession of His Majesty's rightful heir, Prince Edward. We have heard varied testimony to that effect, from several trustworthy persons. Do you intend to offer a defence for your actions?" Hertford affects to look out from under his raised eyebrows solicitously. Surrey returns his gaze, impassive for a moment, considering his response. The few words that he mouthed to himself moments ago return, this time voiced for all to hear.

"My Lords, Your Graces, I shall not demean the honour of my family and my name by stooping to defend myself against these slanderous charges. Any for whom the weal of this nation is at their heart will see in me its stoutest defender. No amount of calumny and lies will tar that name, nor that honour, which cannot be bought with such fawning servility." There is a crackle around the assembled mass. A few of them exchange the briefest comment. Two jurors lean in to discuss the import of this statement. Surrey waits for the surge to pass, before beginning again, strident in the immenseness of the silence. "I shall not give you the pleasure, *My Lord*," he sneers at Hertford, "of hearing me prove my innocence only to be then found guilty by such judges as you have seen fit to assemble. I shall limit myself to remarking that loyalty-" he fixes his gaze on Wriothesley at this point, "seems to be a lost virtue among the great of this nation. I submit myself to your guilty verdict, ordained such as it is."

There is a gasp from a few mouths about the hall. Surrey

continues to looks from Hertford to Wriothesley. Hertford is flustered, unsure how to continue, expecting to have had to question Surrey at this point. Wriothesley intertwines his fingers, displaying shining gold rings in the light from the low winter sun outside, but says nothing.

"Have you nothing to say, My Lord Hertford?" Surrey laughs. "You told me a moment ago that you had all manner of evidence against me. You do not wish to present it to me to counter?"

Hertford licks his lips, coughs, and breathes in. "This court has already heard all it needs to condemn you twice over, Sir, but your confession-" Surrey raises a hand. Hertford is shocked into silence, the condemned man commanding both his accusers and the crowd with his gesture.

"I made and I shall make no confession, My Lord Hertford, which the court would have noted were it inclined to listen to what was said before it." Surrey jabs a finger in the direction of the panel of judges.

"Your contempt of this court will not stand you well when it comes to your sentence." It is Wriothesley who replies, calm, even. "I would remind you, My Lord, that it is within our power to condemn you to death for your crimes."

"And I would remind you, Master Wriothesley, that I am fully aware that this court has already sentenced me to death."

Wriothesley straightens his back but remains seated. Hertford has turned to him, licensing him to continue. "Then you accept our verdict?"

"No. I recognise that it is made, and that no word of mine could alter that decision. I also see that this lèse-majesté of which I am accused is no more than your scheme to clear the path for your own tilt at the crown." The crowd erupts into noise at this. Hertford's palpable discountenance is the antithesis of Surrey's sang-froid, his colour risen to the brightest scarlet, his brow covered with sweat despite the December cold in the air. It is a full five minutes before order is restored.

During that time, Elizabeth turns to Strelley, no longer concealing her girl's voice with her hoarse whispering. "Is Hertford so inclined?"

"No one can know that until your father dies. It has always seemed that there would be a council, not a single protector. To allow Hertford to elevate himself... No, it could not happen. There are too many left among the nobility who are loyal to the House of Tudor, to the king."

"It gladdens me that you have such faith in my father's subjects. I am not sure it is well-placed."

"That is why your father seeks such men as Longshawe and myself. We are unimportant, as far as the nobility goes, but our proximity to you and to your brother gives us some value."

"In that you can guide and protect him?"

"I suspect so. The king wants men like us to make sure that your brother is not led astray or ignored by Hertford, or whoever else it may be."

Grindal leans over to them as they converse. "Please do not speak further. I do not wish to have to explain our presence here to the king," he whispers, putting a stop to their exchange.

Strelley surveys the room as it begins to quieten. He notices Viscount Lisle nodding his head enthusiastically in conversation with some unrecognised noble. He also sees de Winter, although he is not accompanied by a clandestine, shrouded figure. De Winter watches Surrey with great interest, eyes not straying for a moment to the jury bench.

The room eventually falls to silence. Hertford deliberately studies the bundle of papers before him, although he is not reading. He smoothes his beard, coughs, and slowly raises his gaze once again to the Earl of Surrey.

"My Lord, as you do not present any further defence, it is the jury's duty now to consider the case against you. As you have heard, there is much evidence against you, and very little other than from partisan witnesses in your favour. Your portrait and those items at Kenning Hall bearing the arms of the Confessor quartered with your own are enough to see you condemned. I ask you again, before I proceed, is there aught you wish to say?"

"And I say again that I will not give you the pleasure of ignoring my testimony and finding against me in spite of my proved innocence. So proceed with your verdict, and with your sentence."

Once again, the crowd bursts into tumultuous noise as Surrey wins the exchange. Hertford this time remains calm, as he looks down the jury bench and catches the eye of each member as he does. Each by a gesture or a nod of the head gives Hertford his notice that the verdict shall be 'guilty'. It is a mere formality, once the crowd has quieted again, that each pronounces this verdict. Wriothesley takes a little time over his turn, although his expression is inscrutable. Whether he feels remorse for his betrayal of his erstwhile ally or pleasure at his avoidance of his fate does not show.

It falls last to Hertford to make his judgement. "You are guilty, Henry Howard, of the crime of High Treason, and this court sentences you to be hanged, drawn and quartered at Tyburn. Your offence against the Crown and the nation is of the most heinous kind, that of using the power and influence of your position to damage the king and his heirs. Your continued adherence to the bishop of Rome is yet further confirmation of your refusal to be an obedient subject. Your late plot to have your rightful marriage annulled in favour of a match with Lady Mary proves your guilt. I have no doubt that your father will, when he faces trial, equally be found guilty and condemned to a traitor's death." He raises his a hand to quiet the growing murmurings from the crowd. "I shall end by reminding all here present that this same fate awaits all who betray the king and his trust."

Surrey continues to look at him, the same wry smile as before passing across his face, but does not speak. The room is filled with a hiss of whispering as those present predict what will happen next. In fact, Surrey is led away by his guardsmen, and no more words are exchanged by the jury. Wriothesley shakes Hertford's hand, and the two men converse quietly, reliving those moments just past. Lisle has risen from his seat and joins them, adding his voice to their discourse.

Grindal turns to Strelley and Elizabeth. "We should leave before we are noticed," he says, and with a waving motion of his hands indicates to them to rise and exit. Strelley cranes round for a last look at his friend, but Longshawe is long since disappeared, escorting Surrey back to his prison to await the grim fate of the traitor.

Later that day, Longshawe, Strelley and de Winter are gathered in the garret loft that is Strelley's lodging. They share a handful of dainties that have been brought by de Winter from Lady Mary's table, and each drinks dark beer from an earthenware cup.

"I did not realise that Hertford would accuse Surrey of being a follower of the Pope," de Winter says, taking a sip of his beer. "Or that it stood as a crime equal to that of treason."

"It does not pay," Longshawe replies, "to follow the bishop of Rome in this kingdom. The king sees Papistry as a type of treason, doesn't he? If you reject Henry as spiritual leader, you are denying some part of his power. In any case, the wind blows ill for the Catholic, and well for the Lutheran."

"Indeed," de Winter nods. "It seems that those of us who retain the old ways will soon be fighting more than severance from the Church of Rome. It had been tolerable, I suppose, that the king had his feud with the Pope. Though now it presents those of my faith with a dilemma: we cannot accept the king as Supreme Head of the Church, but better that and keep the Mass than lose it all if Cranmer and his ilk get their way. Perhaps I shall leave for France."

Strelley clucks his tongue. "I don't think Surrey is a papist. It's just that he couldn't prove that he isn't, and that is enough for Hertford and the king. So yes, there is much cause for despair among the Catholics. The king was right, you know. The boy and Elizabeth are both being taught Lutheran ways, and the queen is the one who has seen to it. She seems to have escaped lightly. Perhaps Henry did not have the heart for another of his queens to be dispatched."

De Winter takes a deep draught of beer, and wipes his lips with the back of his hand. "Mary is not safe, is she? If she persists – as she will – in her loyalty to Rome, Seymour will see to it that she is persecuted."

"Both Seymour and Prince Edward," Strelley confirms. "It is no secret to any but the king himself that Seymour is of a reformist bent."

"But Mary stands next in line to the throne!" de Winter sighs. "Should Edward die without issue... It is hardly a remote chance, is it, given our present king's troubles?" Longshawe and Strelley nod in agreement. "And what then? Can *he* remove her from the succession?"

Strelley runs his tongue across his teeth, considering. "If Henry can remove his two daughters... There are many who would have rejected that as illegal. I reckon that if Edward were to have died before Mary and Elizabeth were restored, Mary would have been queen, Catholic or not."

"The people of this nation," de Winter says, "do not have much time for the king's fine distinctions on matters of religion. Nor, I think, does it matter to many other than those who wield the power of government whether we answer to the Pope or to Henry as head of the church."

Longshawe replies, "it may be that the people aren't bothered, but that only adds to the weight of responsibility on our leaders, doesn't it?"

"Shrewsbury still practises the old religion," says Strelley, "though perhaps our counsel will see him doing so less openly in the future. I think he is pragmatic rather than dogmatic."

"Indeed so," de Winter says. "Though men like him ought to bear responsibility to their conscience rather than their well-being."

Longshawe spits out the beer he was drinking as de Winter spoke. "You think that the earl should stand up in defiance of the king?"

"I think he should have shown more courage in defending his faith with this king. And that if Edward Seymour leads the country further away from the true faith, that he ought to stand against him."

Longshawe stares at him for a few seconds. Strelley's eyes flick from the one to the other, his jaw tightens, but he does not speak. Longshawe shakes his head. "Truly? You think that the earl should commit treason against the king to defend his church?"

"The king's laws are not valid if they are conceived in disregard of a higher authority." De Winter sits back, unconcerned. "And nothing you say can change that. You are loyal to your sovereign, are you? I am loyal to my conscience, as Shrewsbury should be. When you stand at Peter's gate, will you say 'I obeyed my king'? Or would you want to say 'I did what was right'?"

Longshawe shakes his head. "Your zealousness is frightening, George."

"I shall be proved right, in time. God will not allow this nation to fall yet further from his grace."

Strelley thinks about saying something, but stops himself. Instead, he rises, picks up a book together with a manuscript, and sits back down. "A little something to entertain us, gentlemen? A taste of the mysterious East?"

Longshawe looks at the paper. "Is this more of your Mohammedan chaff?"

"This is good, I promise you," Strelley replies.

31: Fall

Surrey sits in his cell at the Tower, composing. He scratches his quill pen across a sheet of vellum already partly covered with writing, now and again looking across to his bible, open at Psalm 55. He finishes writing the words 'God shall not suffer the righteous to be moved.' Then he sits back in his chair, moving his oil lamp so as to see the earlier part of his work, reading back. His lips move as he assesses the sound of his poesy.

He raises his eyes from his piece as he hears the distinctive noise of the lock being turned. A Tower Guardsman opens the door and holds it open, half-turned so his face does not show. A heavily cloaked figure passes through, and then the guard pulls the door closed. The figure throws back his hood to reveal himself. It is the Duke of Norfolk.

"Father," Surrey says, quietly. "I did not think I would see you."

"Be thankful that you have," Norfolk replies. His weariness shows in his demeanour. That he has recently wept is clear from his red face.

"You too are condemned, then?" Surrey asks.

"I am. It seems that our family's lot is to die for the king."

"I am sorry. For my faults as a son."

"Your faults as a son are my failures, Henry, as your father. I shall pray for you."

"Pray instead for the king. He shall answer for Hertford's sins, and soon."

"You still have such anger, my son. Do not take it to the grave with you. Hertford is not the only one guilty of pursuing his own ends."

"You would forgive him? When I shall die tomorrow for his pride? Any man of honour would challenge him and kill him, though I don't doubt that he would avoid the fight."

"Rest your scheming, Henry. It is over for us. I too, with all my years of service, loyal service, shall go to the block and die a traitor's death." Surrey sits silent, staring at his father. Norfolk continues, voice shaking. "Not only do I forgive Hertford and his followers... I forgive you."

Surrey laughs. "You forgive me? For standing proud for this family? For every strain and wound of war that I received making glory for our name?"

Norfolk shakes his head. "Two generations shall go to the block for your folly!" he shouts. "Your lack of policy has been the end of us."

Surrey speaks calmly, quietly. "You disappoint me, father. I had hoped that we shared a desire to make our name as great as it ought to be, and now you censure me with this pathetic cowardice in the face of death. Have you no courage?"

"I am a braver man than you. You shall lose only your own life, but I am condemned to watch my own son die for no reason other than his own ambition."

"Leave me, father. I have no wish to prolong this further." Surrey turns away from his father, returning to his work. Norfolk watches him for a moment, before turning, knocking hard twice against the door, and being let out by the same guard as before. After he is gone and his footsteps have faded, Surrey picks up his inkwell and throws it violently against the wall, splashing black across the cold stones.

The following morning, a substantial crowd has gathered on Tower Hill. The scaffold is prepared, looming in the low sun of the new year. It casts dismal shadows over the gathered mass of people. A loud hubbub of conversation gives the gathering the incongruous atmosphere of the festival. Many of the throng are smiling in anticipation of the gruesome spectacle to come. Some distance away from the grim scaffold, where the crowd is more rarefied, stand four young men in a circle of conversation. One is dressed in a familiar black riding cloak, stroking his moustache with kid-gloved hand. One wears the jacket of a gamekeeper, hat low over his eyes in the morning light. One wears a fine Yeoman's uniform, but is not armed for duty. The other is wrapped in a furred cloak. The reader will have recognised our four heroes, de Winter, Pike, Longshawe and Strelley.

"So what were the charges?" Pike asks the others.

De Winter answers him, "high treason, amongst other things. On account of his escutcheon bearing the arms of Edward the Confessor. The king's mind was made up before the trial, though. Edward Seymour had persuaded him that the Howards would usurp the crown after his death, and that his mockery of a trial was the only way out."

Strelley continues the story. "We were there at the trial. The jury was loaded against Surrey. But then, the king was right: he was a threat to the succession."

De Winter's face creases in challenge. "You truly believe that it was in Surrey's power to affect the succession?"

Strelley nods in reply. "Yes. But whether I believe it or not, Seymour managed to persuade the king that he was dangerous for his son. Henry's mind is not as clear as it has been, and his fear of death has left him haunted with terror for the future. It was easy for Hertford, I think, to prey on that terror."

Longshawe joins in. "And Hertford being Prince Edward's uncle, the king can hardly doubt that he has his best interests at heart, can he?"

De Winter answers, "we shall see. Hertford is himself as much of a danger to the stability of this nation as Surrey ever was. He is over-mighty, convinced of his own significance. It shall be a time of great strife when the prince reaches his majority. I do not see Hertford surrendering power easily."

Strelley shakes his head. "From what I have heard at the palace, the king has seen to it in his will that there will be a Council of Regency, but no Lord Protector."

"From whom?" de Winter asks.

"A secretary to Lord Chancellor Wriothesley. He seemed to think that the Council will exist with Hertford a part of it but not the head."

De Winter snorts. "And you don't think that Wriothesley and Hertford will have laid plans to secure their spoils after the king's death? I thought you were shrewd, Edward!"

"The idea had occurred to me, George. Wriothesley is a slippery bastard, with little sense of loyalty beyond what he can get for himself."

"In any case," Longshawe says, "couldn't the Council simply nominate Hertford as its head after the king has died?"

"It depends how strong the earl's grip is on the prince. Once the boy is King Edward... It may be that in his minority, Hertford will find some way to persuade the boy to personally name him protector," Strelley theorises, running his tongue over his front teeth. "Or perhaps the earl will just take power by force. Do not underestimate his desire."

"You are certain that Hertford wishes to rule?" Longshawe asks.

"No, I'm not. But he has shown ambition. Why?" Strelley replies.

"*I* have promised the king that I shall act in the prince's interests when Henry has died, and I do not take that promise lightly. I do not yet know whether the boy's interests lie in Hertford's designs succeeding or failing."

De Winter laughs again. "We ought to think of the nation's interests! The prince shall soon be king, and he needs to kept free of the influence of reformist heresy so that he can make the decisions that God wills. The people require guidance, and they have not had it from this King Henry. Nor shall they get it from the next one if Hertford has his way."

Longshawe and Strelley share a glance, each with his eyebrows slightly raised. Strelley is the one who speaks next. "I have told you before, George. Prince Edward has been educated as a reformist. He thinks he is ordained by God to take England away from the old ways and he will allow no gainsaying. Even were the Lord Jesus Christ himself to appear before him and tell him otherwise, Edward would remain unpersuaded that the Pope is His voice on Earth. He is indoctrinated. Whether Hertford holds the reins or not is irrelevant to that matter."

De Winter draws breath slowly before making his answer. "Then we ought rather to consider the matter of whether Hertford will make a good king, for king he shall be if he is not stopped."

At that moment, there is a beating of drums. The crowd gathered to witness the death of Henry Howard falls into an expectant silence as the prisoner is led out from within the Tower. His last few yards are greeted with shouts of encouragement. The trained bands who hold back the crowd look for the individuals who have shouted, but it is futile in the morass.

Pike leans in to his companions. "The earl still has some support, it seems." He smiles at them. "Much good that it will do him now."

The guards around the Earl of Surrey push and pull him forward, treating him as though he were a common prisoner. He is dressed in a fine white shirt, but wears no doublet outside it. His fine beard is combed and oiled, and his face is impassive. He gives the impression of disdain, indifference. Occasionally he casts his eyes around the crowd. His gaze lingers particularly on the ostentatiously clad pair of Hertford and Wriothesley, who are conversing earnestly, their good humour unhidden. There is a moment when Wriothesley looks up and sees Howard staring at him. The battle is fought and won in a moment, as Wriothesley lowers his eyes, before going back to his conversation with Hertford. Howard's words, muttered to himself, are inaudible.

Again the guards move him forward, ever closer to the scaffold, where the executioner and confessor await. The noise falls again to quiet as he reaches the bottom of the ladder which leads to the platform. He mounts it slowly, deliberately, taking the time to look again at the Earl of Hertford, who has now lapsed into silence and is watching carefully.

The man of the cloth approaches Howard, but is dismissed with a gesture. Howard looks out across the crowd, fixing on no face in particular as he delivers his final address.

"My Lords, Ladies, Gentlemen and all of you who have gathered here to witness the execution of my death sentence! Hear me now. I appear before you, condemned by the law of this great land, and shall forthwith die for my crimes. I pray that God shall forgive me for my trespasses, and I thank the king's Majesty that he has commuted my sentence. I hope that he will in time come to recognise in me nothing else than the humble and dedicated servant I am and have always been, just as my father the duke has.

"I have been accused, convicted indeed, of treason. Let it be known now that I have never had design on the throne. Posterity, do not remember me as a man condemned for his crime against the majesty of the throne, but rather as one who fought through all of my life to prevent such abuses, to defend the land from its enemies. At the end I shall go to God with a clear conscience, and I shall stand before Saint Peter, confident that as he enumerates my failings, my sins, I have atoned for them in prayer and by the effort of my body and soul in the service of this nation." He holds out his hands, palm-up, in a supplicatory gesture. "Let my legacy be an end to the needless strife that grips this land, caused by those who seek their own aggrandisement-" at this, Hertford makes a chopping motion with his hand. The guards who surround Henry Howard on the scaffold converge on him, forcing him towards the block. For a moment, he thinks about struggling and making the last of his speech, but he is beaten by the aggressive shouting of the men around him. He bends over the block, but raises his face to look once more on the crowd, raucous with anticipation.

The executioner kneels beside him, whispering the customary plea for forgiveness. Howard's eyes close briefly, but his lips mouth the words "I forgive." The crowd once again quietens, and Howard uses the opportunity to speak once more. "God will remember!" he shouts. "God will recognise his own, and he will cast out those who revel in treachery and intrigue!"

His exhortations are cut short as a guardsman steps forward and stuffs a rag into his mouth as others hold his limbs. The confessor leans over him. "My Lord Surrey, face your death like the great man you are!" he hisses. Surrey, held by the guards, goes limp. The executioner looms over him, casting a long shadow in the January morning. Guards step away, the confessor likewise withdraws to the edge of the platform. The axe rises, then falls. The crowd erupts as the executioner raises Surrey's bloodied head. The mood is mixed, some cheering, some agitating. The militia struggle to contain the surges and eddies of bodies, some breaking through to the base of the scaffold and soaking handkerchiefs and other items of clothing in the dripping blood. Surrey's body lies still, blood draining from the neck onto the wood, replenishing the puddle that Surrey's supporters seek.

Longshawe speaks without looking away from the scene in front of him. "So passes Surrey. I wonder if Norfolk shall have as much to say?"

Strelley turns to him, but Longshawe still doesn't move. "One has to admire the artfulness of his words. A true poet indeed. Not once did he actually admit to any kind of treachery. But he will not be remembered as having met his end with dignity."

Pike says, "Wriothesley will have the records altered to show that Surrey surrendered meekly. Or else he is not such a worthy ally to Hertford..."

Strelley sighs. "Wriothesley is no one's ally but his own, I think. If the country is in his hands in a month, we had all better consider our futures. Mercenary soldiering abroad begins to look more attractive."

De Winter nods in agreement. "I for one shall be joining you. I cannot countenance living so far estranged from my mother church," he jokes.

"But you will stay for Lady Mary, George," Pike reminds him. "Just as Edward will stay for Lady Elizabeth, and James for the prince."

The four of them share an honest laugh at Pike's words. "I do not jest, though," he says. "We are bound by our loyalty to those who act as our patrons, and though we shall be but little accounted by history, it is men like us that shape us, is it not?"

11314932R00159

Printed in Great Britain
by Amazon.co.uk, Ltd.,
Marston Gate.